SUPERIOR

ALAN W. PORTER

First IngramSpark Edition

ISBN: 979-8-218-61819-3

Published independently by Alan W. Porter Minneapolis, MN, United States of America

Cover design by Hofmeister Design

Printed in United States of America

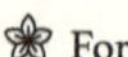 Formatted with Vellum

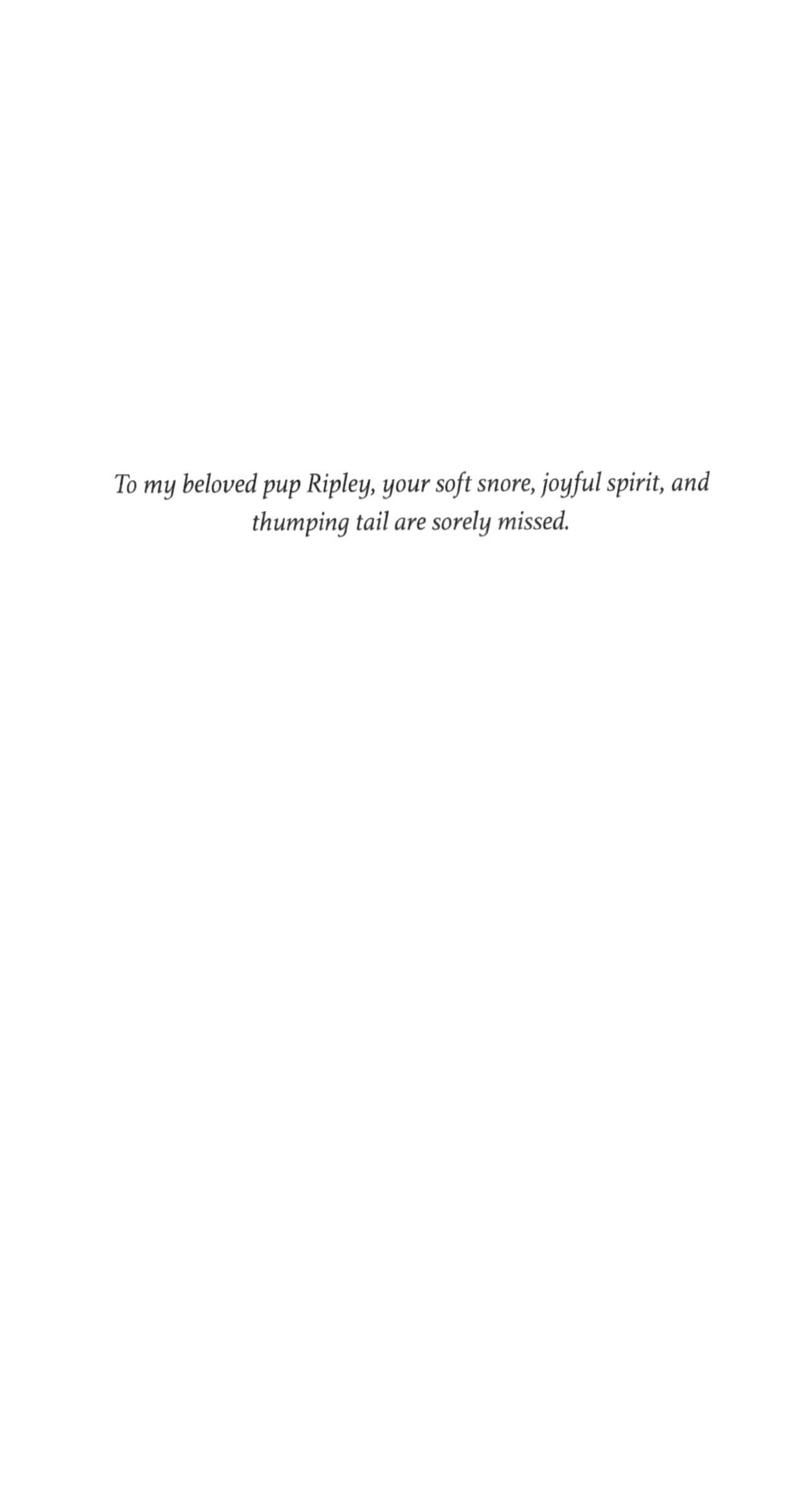

To my beloved pup Ripley, your soft snore, joyful spirit, and thumping tail are sorely missed.

To Whiskers, after ten years of indifference thank you for offering affection and companionship during a difficult time.

To Jameson, who somehow inherited the best parts of my nature while avoiding my worst. Every day with you is filled with laughter and love.

To Mom, the poetess—none of this would have been possible had you not instilled in me a love of storytelling.

And finally, to Susan, my wife and friend—the heart and soul of our family. Thank you for giving me the courage to share my stories. You are my rock and my light.

ACKNOWLEDGMENTS

To my amazing beta readers:

Phil—thanks for bringing your keen intellect, sharp eyes, and spot on analysis to bear on this project!

Susan M. and Shari—thank you for a decade of support and encouragement. This book doesn't happen without you.

Kirsten and Joe—I don't know why you read a five-hundred page manuscript from a guy you barely knew, but thanks!

Sam—I hope I've done justice to your experiences and conveyed the deep respect I hold for all who serve.

PROLOGUE

Lake Superior's gray-blue surface stretched to the horizon without visible end, protected by both dense forests that hugged its shoreline like a jealous lover and fearsome rock formations determined to stand against all but the most intrepid explorers. "Gitchi-Gami," or "Great Sea" as the lake is known to the Ojibwe people, needed no such guardians. More predator than prey, Superior, with its unpredictable winds, frigid waters, and vast maw, lay in perpetual wait, eager to swallow ships great and small, with equal indifference.

1

The sky above Lake Superior was clear and bright, as only a cold winter sky can be. A multitude of stars shone down from the blackness of the void, providing Carson Ten Bears ample light as he shuffled through knee-deep snow toward a small cabin.

A hunched and frail Native man with eight decades under his belt, Carson moved steadily, eager to escape the cold but not foolish enough to move too quickly. One didn't reach his age hurrying along a slippery path, especially on a night when the air temperature registered twenty-five degrees below zero, cold enough to freeze falling water in mid-air.

It was mid-February, and the grounds of Roaring Shores Resort, at which he'd been caretaker for the past forty years, were empty, the last of the interlopers from the south having packed up their palatial tents, high-tech camping gear, and designer outdoor wear months ago.

The resort's owners ritually migrated south at the first sign of snow, uninterested in the headaches associated with maintaining the property for the few guests willing to brave the elements for a weekend of cross-country skiing or snow-shoeing. Their departure left Carson the only person around for miles. Were he to fall, death would surely come for him. "On the other hand," he reasoned, "the cabin was close enough to crawl to if necessary." Still, no sense busting a hip. His prized boxed set of *Sex and the City* VHS cassettes wasn't going anywhere.

Carson reached the cabin's front door and leaned against it. Over the years, it had become more difficult for Carson to catch his breath, reminding him he had only so many left and should savor each one. Heeding that prompt, Carson looked skyward with surprisingly youthful black-brown eyes. The gray-white hair framing his weathered face blew in the breeze as he scanned the heavens for the band of undulating green and red flares known as the Northern Lights.

"No Waawaate tonight," he sighed and pulled a jingling clump of keys from his pocket. Carson's fingers, wrinkled and curved with age and numbed by the cold, fumbled over a dozen keys until they found the right one. He inserted the key into the ancient lock and twisted. The lock didn't turn, no doubt fused by moisture that had frozen inside the mechanism.

Carson chided himself for not spraying the lock with emollient as he'd planned. As he set his feet to twist with both hands, he felt a presence, a slight tickle at the base of his neck, and whirled to see an orange ball of light streaking downward toward the lake. "Anang-bangishin," Carson exclaimed reverently, eyes wide with wonder as the curve of a smile threatened to crack his frozen face and lips.

Despite having seen hundreds of Anang-bangishin, Carson sensed this was no ordinary shooting star. Most made no sound whatsoever, and those few that did produced little more than a high-pitched sizzle. This Anang-bangishin let out a banshee scream that soured his stomach. He tried to shake off his discomfort, hoping to enjoy the fireworks before retiring for the evening. But his body refused to comply, and Carson watched the descending meteor with growing unease. The flaming projectile appeared to be *slowing down*.

CARSON STUMBLED INTO THE CABIN, slammed the door shut, and fell against it, his breath escaping in rapid puffs as he tried to calm himself. The sound he'd heard was like nothing he'd ever encountered. Only heaven and earth made such sounds: waves crashing against the shore, thunder in a lightning-filled sky, or the rumble of the ground shifting during a quake.

He guessed the Anang-bangishin had slammed into Superior at high speed, displacing thousands of gallons of water. He also surmised the Anang-bangishin's arrival was an omen of something both miraculous and deadly.

WAVES RUSHED from the Anang-bangishin's point of entry in every direction, gliding across the lake's surface in a perfect circle, only to be swallowed by Superior's voracious pull. Where the circle of water made landfall, it found a willing medium in the snow and pushed its new ally ahead in a tumultuous front that engulfed everything in its path. As it gathered momentum, the surge became a wall of kinetic energy, demanding genuflection from every tree it encountered, sapling and ancient alike. Those that would not bend, it toppled without mercy.

2

Jackson Bennett, a black man in his early fifties, aimed his Toyota Tundra pickup down a back road, his ebony hands firmly gripping the steering wheel at ten and two. His dark brown eyes scanned ahead, giving the impression he was tentative, fearful even. He wasn't. If there were one word to describe Jackson, it would be *attentive*. Jackson believed the universe gave plenty of advanced warning if you looked for it.

This philosophy had served him well over the years, from his time as a college football player to the twenty-two years he'd spent as an officer with the Chicago Police Department. Unfortunately, the philosophy had its limits. It didn't help him foresee the minefield of potholes and slick spots that caused his pickup to shimmy, rattling his teeth along with those of his passenger.

"You have driven on snow, right?" Kirk Campbell asked from the passenger seat. Dressed in travel-rumpled fatigues, Kirk looked the part of a military man. Despite also having eclipsed fifty, he had retained the requisite square jaw and hardened physique of a soldier, although his temples, striped gray amidst an otherwise full head of close-cropped blond hair, hinted at an advanced age. One of Kirk's strong, calloused hands gripped the dashboard as his arm locked at the elbow to steady him against the pickup's herky-jerky motions.

"I spent two years in this area, remember?" Jackson adjusted his grip on the steering wheel.

"Yeah, but you didn't have a car then. You hoofed it everywhere."

"It's not like we don't have snow in Chicago."

"Coulda fooled me. I've been on roads in Mazar that didn't scare me half as much as your little shortcut. And those roads had more IEDs than potholes."

"Roads? I thought the great Kirk Campbell only traveled on the backs of angels."

Kirk offered Jackson his middle finger. "Just get me there in one piece, Jack. I didn't come all this way to buy it in a ditch five miles from home."

Jackson smiled. Only a handful of people called him "Jack." And most of them were no longer speaking to him.

JACKSON'S PICKUP pulled into the driveway of an unremarkable brown and tan split-level. Kirk stepped out of the vehicle and stared at the house. "Good to be home." He wiped his eyes with the back of his hand, even though any tears were already frozen on his face.

Jackson climbed out of the pickup, grabbed a military-issue duffel bag from the bed, and tossed it to Kirk. "Well, I'll let you and the house get reacquainted." He offered Kirk his hand, and the two men shook. "Give me a call when you get settled." Jackson pounded on the side of the truck and headed for the open driver's side door.

Kirk frowned. "You're not staying?"

Jackson shook his head. "We had a deal. I did my part. We're square." Jackson pretended to wash his hands. "Besides, I have an early day tomorrow."

Kirk looked at the dark house again. "I can't believe they aren't here."

Jackson nodded his sympathy. "They wanted to be, but they've been driving back and forth to visit Marnie's mom. Rochester's a long drive."

"I know, but..." Kirk's voice trailed off as he saw Jackson smirking. "What's so funny?"

"Never thought I'd see a big tough guy like you pouting like a four-year-old."

Kirk glowered. "You'd pout too if you hadn't seen your wife in eighteen months." Jackson's smirk melted away, and Kirk shook his head regretfully. "Shit, man, I'm sorry."

Jackson bit the inside of his cheek against the ache shooting through his chest, then quickly changed the subject. "Explain to me again why it took you so long to get home after Kabul?"

"Oh, it was a real *Planes, Trains, and Automobiles* situation." Kirk adjusted his duffel bag on his shoulder. "Me and a group of Afghan interpreters loyal to the U.S. made our way to Karshi-Khanabad Air Base, which would have taken half a day by car, with potty breaks.

"Potty breaks?"

"I don't want to talk about it. Anyway, we laid low in Mazar-i-Sharif, then snuck across the border to Tezmek. On foot. The whole 98 kilometers. I damn near died of dehydration.

Jackson could only shake his head at his friend's story.

"Once I was on my feet, I flew to Al Udeid Air Base for debriefing, which took another six weeks because everything was such a shit show after Kabul. After things got 'straightened out,' I got routed to Syria for two weeks, which was *not* awesome. After that, I did a five-week stint in Slovenia before the scheduling geniuses realized I wasn't *Kurt* Campbell, an AWOL eighteen-year-old black kid from Georgia. Finally, after a thirteen-hour flight to St. Paul, I spent another week at JFHQ convincing them I wasn't a deserter."

Jackson ignored Kirk's use of JFHQ instead of Joint Forces Headquarters and put a hand on his friend's shoulder. "I've changed my mind. How about I take you up on that beer?" Jackson ushered Kirk up the front walk. "Maybe it'll wash those annoying acronyms out of your mouth."

FINGERNAILS SCRATCHED against drywall in the darkness for several seconds before Kirk's agitated voice broke the stillness. "Son of a bitch. Where's the goddamned light switch?" There was an audible "click" but no light.

"Bulb must be out," Jackson offered as they waited in the darkness.

"Yeah, I got that, Captain Obvious. I asked you to stay with Marnie and the kids so there'd be a man around the house. What the heck did you do while you were here?"

"I've been working on a little something..."

Snickers and muted laughs were followed by a burst of light that revealed a minefield of discarded shoes and boots in the cramped foyer. Kirk puzzled at the mound of footwear, then did a double-take, eyes widening as he spied a dozen smiling people huddled in the adjacent living room.

Before he could react, they screamed, "Welcome home, Major!"

Marnie, a middle-aged woman with hazel- green eyes and gray-blonde hair cut just above her shoulders, burst from the crowd and wrapped herself around Kirk. A lanky boy of sixteen and a wiry girl of fourteen, both the spitting image of Kirk, attached themselves to him, threatening to knock him off his feet. Kirk tried to maintain his cool, but his trembling lower lip and glistening eyes betrayed the stoic man.

Amidst clapping and cheering, Jackson grabbed Kirk in a bear hug. "Welcome home, man. Glad you made it back in one piece."

KIRK AND JACKSON stood on a wooden deck attached to the side of the house, hands at their waists. Vapor rose, accompanied by the sound of liquid hitting snow as the drunk men urinated. Kirk hoisted a beer in his free hand. "I appreciate you looking after Marnie and the kids while I was gone," he said.

Jackson waved him off yet again.

"Don't wave me off, Jack. I love my family, but they can be a handful."

"Handful?" Jackson arched his eyebrows. "They're monsters." Kirk laughed as Jackson continued. "And don't get me started on Marnie. What's up with that thing she has about socks?"

Kirk threw up his free hand, spilling most of his beer. "Right? I mean, what the hell? Socks are made for your feet. Where else do they belong if not on the damn floor?"

Jackson laughed. "Seriously. It was fine. It was nice seeing familiar faces every day."

Kirk gave Jackson a sideways glance. "That better be all you were looking at."

"Dear Penthouse Forum," Jackson whispered lasciviously. "I never thought I'd be writing to you, but my husband is deployed in the Middle East, and his best friend, the very epitome of virility and manhood, is sleeping downstairs. I find my nights growing long and the hunger in my loins growing more unbearable every day..."

Kirk laughed. "You just can't get over the fact she chose me over you."

"She didn't choose you over me. You slithered in and asked her out first."

"Slithered?" Kirk feigned incredulity.

"Slithered. You know damn well, I only got in the dessert line so I could introduce myself. I turned to grab an ice cream bar, and next thing I know, you're laying the moves on her."

"You snooze; you lose." Kirk checked Jackson with his shoulder and looked toward the driveway. Jackson's truck was the only vehicle in sight.

"Where the hell'd everybody park?" he asked.

"On the main road, which I cleverly avoided by taking that very 'dangerous' shortcut."

"Sneaky son of a bitch." Kirk took a half-assed swing at his friend. Jackson dodged the punch, causing Kirk to lose his balance and fall. He lay splayed out on the deck.

"Careful, Dorothy, you're not in the desert anymore. You're gonna have to get reacquainted with ice," Jackson teased.

"Ain't the ice; it's the beer," Campbell growled.

Jackson zipped up and helped Kirk to his feet. Once steadied, the inebriated soldier brushed himself off, none the worse for wear. "Speaking of which. You up for another round?"

"No can do...unless you want to talk."

"Talk about what?" Kirk's eyes narrowed.

"Did you seriously think Marnie wouldn't tell me?"

Kirk's lower lip quivered.

"Sorry, if it's too soon. We can do it some other time." Jackson looked away, allowing his friend to reconsider without pressure, but when Kirk remained silent, Jackson wiped his hands in the snow.

Kirk snapped to attention as if returning from a state of contemplation. "Nah. I'm good. I was just thinking it would have been nice if you'd cleaned your hands *before* helping me up."

FIERCE WAVES CRASHED against the lakeshore, carrying a whitish-gray foam that coated the randomly strewn sedimentary boulders jutting from the sand. Something else rode the waves ashore. Long, thin, and dark, it might have been inert, like a tree branch or old semi-tire, but instead of sprawling on the shore like so much flotsam, it moved.

With unmistakable intent and intelligence, a shadowy figure righted itself, swaying unsteadily on four limbs like a newborn fawn, then expelled a torrent of water from its lungs in a raspy gurgle. Rivulets of water cascaded down its body as the faceless wraith straightened at the hips and rose into the air. Once steady, it took several tortured steps toward the water before releasing a defiant bellow, as if issuing a challenge to Lake Superior itself.

JACKSON AND KIRK sat across from one another at the dining room table, surrounded by a mess of paper plates, plastic utensils, and party decorations. The rest of the house was quiet and dark, and the pair, hunched over from intoxication, spoke in the careful, low tones of men trying unsuccessfully to keep their voices down.

"Bullshit," Jackson slurred. "You didn't win every practice. Just most of them."

"Name one time I lost." Kirk's eyes shone with the self-assurance of a man confident of his recollection.

"Summer practice."

"That was almost thirty years ago. Can you be more specific?"

"My freshman year, your junior year. Coach Summers lined us up on the five-yard line after practice and said, 'Four tries. Offense scores, they hit the showers while defense takes three laps around the track. Defense holds, they hit the showers, and offense takes two laps around the track.' " Jackson mimicked the coach, his voice gravelly, part drill sergeant, part evangelical preacher. "When Oakerson asked why the offense only had to do two laps, Coach said—"

"Because offense is for pansies!" Kirk did his own impersonation of Coach Summers.

"So, you do remember?" Jackson grinned.

"How could I forget? It was ninety and humid. Felt like one hundred-ten degrees." A wry smile stretched across Kirk's face. "And you were offsides."

"Like hell I was. I took you down fair and square."

Kirk shook his head as if trying to rid himself of a painful recollection.

Jackson studied his friend's face and saw a storm brewing. He knew better than anyone that Kirk would argue the point until one or both of them passed out. That wouldn't be a good way to celebrate his friend's homecoming.

"Tell me about Afghanistan."

Kirk blinked, then raised the shot glass, eyes fixed on something in the distance. "I was in Kabul when the evacuation began. I was helping load the office staff and other civilians into a C-17 when the bad guys showed up. We took heavy fire. Automatic weapons, side arms, rocks, arrows, you name it."

He studied his raised glass before downing its amber contents. "Our guys returned fire but were outnumbered. Still, they held them off until we got the civilians squared away, then climbed on themselves. That flight crew had brass balls. Kept that plane on the ground until the last possible second."

"Well, not the *last* possible second."

Kirk shook his head. "No. It was my fault. I came in hot and got one foot on the ramp. The other one caught the edge, and I face-planted on the tarmac."

Jackson gawked. "So, they just left you?"

Kirk looked as if he'd been insulted. "Not just me. Hundreds of people, many of them women and children. They didn't have a choice."

Jackson's brow furrowed. "If you didn't make it on that plane, how are you here?"

"I hid." Kirk gripped his glass. "While the insurgents were trying to bring down the transport, I humped it for the nearest cover and hid under a pile of construction materials. By the time they got bored and left, night had fallen. I made my way in the opposite direction."

"How long before anyone picked you up?"

Kirk set his shot glass on the table. "Three weeks."

"You lasted three weeks in Kabul with no food, no weapon, and no water?" Jackson smacked the table with an open palm. "I'm calling bullshit."

Kirk chuckled. "You're half right. I was *outside* Kabul. And I didn't last three weeks. I got caught. Third day out, I tripped coming down a hill and smacked my head on a rock. While I was lying there in the sun, dying of thirst, bleeding out from the gash on my head, I saw a patrol heading my way. I knew even if they didn't kill me, they'd take whatever gear I had, so I hid my most important possession."

"Your radio?" Jackson waited impatiently as Kirk refilled his glass.

"The compass at the end of my survival knife."

Jackson frowned. "Hid it where?"

"The only safe place I had."

Jackson squirmed in obvious discomfort, and Kirk laughed.

"Could've been worse. All they took were my shoes, belt, and dignity. I'm just lucky they left me my shirt and pants. Without them, I might have died of exposure."

"Why'd they leave you your uniform?"

Kirk flashed a smile. "Had a little accident when I banged my head. I didn't smell great."

"Lovely. How long before you saw that compass again?"

"Not sure exactly. A few hours, maybe," Kirk posited. "I waited until I was sure they weren't coming back, but I was afraid once they got back to their village, the news would spread, and Al Qaeda would come looking for me. So, I stuck my fingers down my throat. No dice. I'd waited too long. The compass had already left the stomach and headed into my intestines."

Jackson's mouth screwed into a line.

"I stumbled around looking for water, any water. All I found was a stagnant pool of yellowish-brown muck that smelled like a New York sewer. I dropped to my knees and took a drink. A long drink."

"And then you threw up?"

Kirk shook his head. "I had dry heaves like you wouldn't believe, but nothing came up except the yellowish-brown muck."

Jackson smiled knowingly. "You weren't trying to make yourself throw up..."

"That would have been too easy." He looked at the ceiling. "I spent hours waiting for that compass. Lying there in the heat and the sun and the dust, wishing I would throw up, wishing I'd made it on that transport, wishing the patrol had shot me instead of leaving me there to die. I thought nothing could be worse than what I was going through. I was wrong. When it happened, it happened fast. A torrent of shit ran down my legs onto my ankles and feet and dried on like papier mâché. Flies and bugs were crawling all over me."

"You gave yourself the squirts."

"Not just the squirts." Kirk raised his shot glass again. "Dysentery."

Jackson stared with utter respect as Kirk threw back the contents of his shot glass, stretched, and got up from the table. "Well, time to get reacquainted with the missus."

"After half a six-pack and three shots of Macallan?" Jackson flashed a devious grin. "Marnie's in for a disappointing reunion."

Kirk flipped off his friend and stumbled to the door.

3

The old boar smelled the interloper long before he saw it. However, its scent struck him as foreign, so he hadn't recognized it as a threat. He knew the tall, skinny creatures, with their loud noises and strong smells, and decided whatever approached wasn't one of them.

The tall, skinny creatures were dangerous. They carried long sticks that shattered the quiet of the woods and sprayed rocks that stung when they struck his dense coat. He'd always survived, but others had died from the wounds, so he avoided the stick bearers at all costs. Fortunately, it wasn't difficult. The old boar's keen olfactory sense usually enabled him to recognize danger from great distances.

Although the interloper's approach was stealthy, the boar had heard it and assumed he had time to finish his meal and saunter away. The flaw in this thinking was believing that because he'd never encountered the interloper's scent, it posed no threat. The assumption, while incorrect, was not unreasonable.

At five years of age, old for a feral hog, the boar had few

predators. Odds were good that the trespasser was smaller than he or slower. Despite his bulk, the boar was swift enough to escape both the tall, skinny creatures and the large furry ones with their massive paws and sharp claws. Fortunately, the latter disappeared during the colder times and wouldn't be a problem until warmth returned, signaling the furry ones' emergence from their dens with young ones in tow.

As the mystery creature's smell grew stronger, the boar thought he recognized it after all. Most of the boar's diet consisted of plants and bugs, but he was an opportunistic eater. He wasn't above eating any small animal he encountered, including birds, bees, mice, and the slithering snakes sometimes found coiled underneath a log.

The boar hesitated, torn between continuing his meal and remaining on the lookout. Whatever approached smelled like a snake, but he wasn't certain. There was something more pungent about the approaching creature. That difference unsettled him. Nonetheless, he declined to face the oncoming intruder. A surprise attack was unlikely, given his three-hundred-ten-degree field of vision. Unlikely, but not impossible.

A dark shape rushed from the swaying brush, moving faster than the boar had expected, faster than he could run. While the boar's first instinct was to flee, exposing his rear to the creature would allow it to attack from within his tiny blind spot. He fought instinct and turned to face his attacker, confident his bulk and sharp tusks would protect him.

The interloper struck with surprising force, lifting the boar's front legs off the snow and knocking him backward. Before he realized what happened, the boar found himself on his back. Powerful claws, long and tipped with sharp nails, dug into his belly, tracing a path from his throat to his testicles. Thinking he'd only suffered a scratch, the boar squirmed away, scrambled to his feet, and set himself to charge.

Then he felt a tingling sensation and wetness in his belly. He shook it off and tried to take a step. His body refused to obey, and he dropped to the snow. Confused, he rolled onto his side, trying to survey his underside, but his neck was too thick and his chest too broad.

Had he been able to see his belly, he would have been surprised to see the contents of the peritoneum that once held his internal organs, spilling out in a steaming heap.

4

M orning light peered through the curtains, revealing a cramped and messy room strewn with clothes. Jackson lay face down on a single bed, his face buried in a pillow adorned with baseballs, footballs, and basketballs. Still dressed in his uniform from the night before, he was cadaver-still, knees bent and boot-clad feet one on top of the other; likely in the same position he'd taken when he collapsed onto the rainbow-colored duvet the night before.

A faint creak caused Jackson to stir. He remained face down but opened one bloodshot eye as the door to the room slid open and Kirk's daughter Sarah tiptoed in. Rather than approach, Sarah peered at Jackson from a distance, like a kid at the zoo staring through glass at a slumbering panda.

"What?" Jackson's head pounded. His mouth felt like he'd been chewing handfuls of cotton.

"You're in my bed." Sarah continued to eye Jackson. "I had to bunk with Scottie."

Jackson groaned as he lifted one hand and let it fall to the bed. "So?"

"He's a sixteen-year-old boy. His room is disgusting."

"This room isn't exactly sterile."

Sarah's eyes narrowed. "My room is messy, not dirty. There's a difference."

Jackson would have laughed at Sarah's response, but feared it would hurt. She was a good kid, more spirited than sassy, and he usually enjoyed their interactions, but he was hungover and still half asleep; he lacked the energy to humor her. "What can I do for you, Sarah?" He sounded like a tired cashier forced to wait on a last-minute customer.

"Mom said you were hungover." Sarah frowned. "It's not as interesting as I'd hoped."

Jackson laughed and immediately regretted it as a sharp pain shot through his head. "Sorry to disappoint you, kiddo."

"No worries." Sarah spun on her heel and left the room.

Jackson closed his eye, hoping the return to darkness would squelch the pain in his head. No sooner had he returned to a fitful sleep than his cell phone rang, its earnest plea like a jackhammer to his skull until he rolled over and jammed a pillow over his head. The phone offered four more persistent rings until he finally relented and answered. "Jackson here..." He rubbed his face as he tried to negotiate a minimal state of wakefulness. "Hey, Lex. What's up?" He listened with one ear and half of his brain when his eyes flipped wide open. "I'll be there in twenty minutes." Jackson wobbled and collapsed onto the bed. "Make it forty."

JACKSON THRUST his hands into his jacket pockets against the cold as he made his way along a barely defined path through the woods. Without the use of his outstretched hands to balance, he carefully navigated the slick terrain, threatening to fall with each step, until he emerged from the canopy of trees into a clearing where a small cabin nestled. On his way to the cabin, he passed a vintage AMC Eagle and a filthy, salt and mud-covered Dodge Ram 1500 Diesel with a magnetic Department of Natural Resources decal on the side that matched the one on Jackson's Tundra. He shook his head at the Ram's condition and looked toward the cabin where Lexy Richards, a striking blonde woman in her mid-twenties, waited on the porch.

Her legs and feet swung over the edge of the porch in leisurely fashion as she sipped from a thermos and watched with undisguised amusement as Jackson navigated the slippery path. "Going shave and shower-optional today, are we?"

Jackson gave Lexy a look that said, "Too early," and regarded her thermos. "You bring one of those for me?"

"Sorry, I only have the one," Lexy responded, although her tone indicated she was not the least bit sorry.

"Ever heard of a Styrofoam cup?" Jackson tiptoed up the ice-covered stairs to the porch.

"Ever heard of an iron?" Lexy climbed to her feet. At six feet, two inches, she towered over Jackson. The pair locked eyes for almost fifteen seconds until Lexy looked away.

"Guess I'm still in charge," Jackson crowed.

"Whatever, Boomer." Lexy smoothed the wrinkles from her trousers. The gesture was entirely unnecessary. Although Lexy and Jackson wore the same DNR uniform, Lexy's looked pressed while Jackson's looked like he'd rescued it from the bottom of a hamper.

"Gen-X."

"Like it matters. You'll all be dead long before your

Styrofoam cups biodegrade." Lexy stepped through the already open door into the cabin.

Jackson paused to look at the heavy, weathered front door, which hung stubbornly from one hinge. After a quick study of the other two twisted hinges, he followed Lexy in.

JACKSON SURVEYED THE DIMINUTIVE CABIN. It looked as if a tornado had touched down. "You got me out of bed for this?"

"Do you not see this mess?"

Jackson shrugged. "If keeping a messy house or car were a crime, you'd be doing forty to life on Rikers Island."

"This isn't messy." Lexy gestured around the cabin. "It's been ransacked."

Jackson zeroed in on a bookshelf across the room where volumes by Zane Grey, Larry McMurtry, and William Johnstone sat alongside titles by Stephen King, Harper Lee, and Euripides. The shelves appeared to be the only part of the cabin left untouched. Jackson picked his way through the rubble, moving books aside and pulling them off the shelves at random. "Interesting."

"Ruh row, Shaggy. Has Scooby found a clue?" Lexy teased.

Jackson ignored the joke and stared at her expectantly. "What do you see?"

"I take it playtime is over?" Lexy's eyebrows arched.

Jackson nodded, and Lexy slowly perused every inch of the room. It seemed not a single cabinet, closet, or drawer had escaped unscathed. Utensils, boxes, and blankets littered the cabin. Spilled food covered the kitchen floor. The refrigerator gaped like an open maw, its door hanging from its hinges, its metal shelves rent from their slots.

"Looks like B and E, boss," Lexy announced.

"Obviously, breaking and entering. But for what purpose?"

Lexy made a second scan of the cabin. "They were looking for something."

"You sure it wasn't vandalism?" Jackson asked. "Just a couple of kids having fun?"

Lexy nodded confidently. "Certain."

"How can you be sure?"

Lexy's gaze returned to the bookshelf. "The decision to vandalize is often premeditated, but the act itself is indiscriminate." She pointed at the bookshelf. "Vandals thrive on chaos. A shelf of carefully curated books represents a sense of order. Order is anathema to vandals."

"Meaning?"

"Order is to a vandal what garlic is to a vampire."

"I know what anathema means, smart ass." Jackson's eyes narrowed, but a smile caressed his lips. "What's your conclusion?"

"I stand by my original conclusion. These weren't vandals. There's no way vandals could resist destroying that bookshelf."

"Nice." Jackson nodded. "Anything else?"

"The door."

"What about it?" Jackson spoke softly, coaxing a response rather than demanding.

"It was yanked outward, off its hinges." Lexy moved to the door.

"Agreed. And what does that tell us about..."

"I'm not done yet." Lexy pointed upward. Above the door, a sleek black shotgun rested on hooks. With its angled pistol grip jutting from underneath the trigger and anodized black finish, the gun was as sexy as it was lethal. "Second. This thing is still here."

Jackson whistled in admiration. "Benelli M4. Pretty weapon. Expensive too."

Lexy inspected the shotgun but left it on its perch. "Exactly my point. If you're going to break into a cabin to steal stuff, you're not going to leave something like that behind."

"So, you're ruling out burglary?"

"What teenager in his right mind could resist a shotgun?" Lexy regarded the shotgun again. "I'm no gun groupie, but that thing makes my nipples hard."

Jackson laughed, then glanced into the kitchen. His brow furrowed as the wheels in his head started turning. "Maybe it was an animal."

"People are animals." Lexy offered.

"I meant like a raccoon."

"I suppose." She surveyed the discarded food on the kitchen floor. "Although that would have to be one seriously roided-up raccoon."

Jackson tiptoed around the kitchen, careful to disturb the discarded food wrappers and utensils as little as possible. He paused mid-step as if engaged in a game of red light, green light. "Does Nordgren have any enemies? Anybody who might have a grudge against him?"

"Beats me. He's out back. Why don't you ask him?"

"Why didn't you say so?" Jackson didn't hide his exasperation. "And don't say 'because you didn't ask.' "

Lexy held up her hands. "I wasn't going to."

"Yes, you were." Jackson picked his way to a second door. Lexy followed, grinning.

"Okay, yeah. I was."

. . .

Jackson stepped onto a ten-by-ten, snow-cleared concrete patio where Remy Nordgren, a man in his late sixties, sat on a bench, hands held over a small fire corralled by a rusted steel ring. Remy gazed at the fire, oblivious to Jackson's arrival. Despite the temperature, he seemed comfortable in a fleece pullover, faded and stained jeans, and a black Carhartt stocking cap that failed to contain his mop of salt-and-pepper hair. Black snowmobile boots, half plastic, half leather, covered his legs and feet up to his knees. Dressed as he was, he would have looked just as comfortable inside the cramped confines of a fish house on a frozen lake.

"Mr. Nordgren?" Jackson approached the man and pulled out his badge, careful to keep his distance but trying to get as close as possible to the warming fire. Remy looked up, his light gray eyes blank. "I'm Officer Bennett with the Department of Natural Resources. Would you mind if I asked you a few questions?"

"You work for the Valkyrie?" Remy asked, his voice rough, his accent an odd mixture of choppy French Canadian and Minnesotan, complete with the stereotypical extended enunciation of long "ohs."

"Actually, I'm Officer Richards' supervisor."

Remy shifted his gaze to Lexy. "And you can vouch for him?"

Lexy smiled. "Just this once."

Remy's craggy face lit up. "Well, in dat case," he turned to Jackson, "I believe I can have a word wit' you, sir."

Jackson nodded toward the bench. "Mind if I sit?"

"Not at all," Remy responded, running the words "not at all" into a single word.

Jackson sat next to Remy on the bench. "I'm very sorry this happened to you, Mr. Nord–"

"Remy." Remy continued staring at the fire.

"Pardon?"

"Call me Remy."

Jackson extended his hand, and the men shook. "Thank you... Remy. Like I said, I'm sorry this happened to you."

"Ain't so much happened to me as it did my place." A lost expression crossed Remy's face. "On the other hand, I guess I did felt a bit violated. I mean, I lived here thirty years, nobody ever mess with me or my tings."

Jackson nodded. "I'm sure it's tough to figure out from the looks of things, but is anything missing?"

Remy turned to Jackson. "Missing?"

"Did they take any valuables, any property? Electronics, money, weapons?"

Remy puzzled. "What would a bear want with any of that stuff?"

Jackson and Lexy exchanged a surprised glance. "What makes you think it was a bear?"

It was Remy's turn to look surprised. "The door, for one. Other than the front door and the fridge, none of dem was broken. Lower cabinet doors, refrigerator, pantry. Dem was all gone through, but all dem got latches or handles. Be near impossible for most animals, but a bear might could manage. That's why I call you instead of the police."

"Hold on." Jackson leaned in. "All of them were gone through, but nothing was missing?"

"Nope. Well, except food." Remy pulled at his beard. "And then, only food he take is da meat."

Jackson stifled a chuckle. "Well, Mr. Nordgren, bears *are* carnivores."

Remy glanced at the gold DNR patch on the left breast pocket of Jackson's jacket, then at Lexy, raising a single eyebrow in silent judgment.

"Actually, boss, they're omnivores," Lexy whispered.

"She right. Bear ain't picky 'bout what they eat. They eat pretty much anything, especially when they starving. This one should still be asleep dis time of year. He probably skinny as a rail and looking to put on some fat. Cookies, cake, anything with carbs or sugar. Didn't touch any of dat stuff though. He only go for da meat. Nothing else, just dat meat."

～

JACKSON STOMPED for a clump of trees beyond the clearing. Lexy was right behind, struggling to keep up. "Hey!" she yelled after him. "Are you okay?" Lexy was smiling, but her eyes hinted at concern. When Jackson didn't respond, Lexy's smile disappeared, replaced by a look of disbelief. "Are you mad about the omnivore thing?"

Jackson whirled. "I'm mad that you corrected me in front of Mr. Nordgren."

"I whispered. How was I supposed to know he had ears like a moth?"

Jackson shook his head. "Did you say 'ears like a moth'?"

"Yes. Moths have excellent hearing. It helps them avoid bats, who, *not* coincidentally, also have excellent hearing."

Jackson deflated. "No shit?"

"No shit."

On the one hand, Lexy's correction of him stung. It had been hard for him to earn the respect of the locals, and he feared that if word of his gaffe and Lexy's subsequent correction got around, his already weak credibility would further diminish. On the other hand, he had a great deal to learn about the job and couldn't have a better tutor than Lexy.

"Well, you could have waited until we were alone." Jackson's tone held enough sharpness to make his displeasure apparent, but was gentle enough to indicate the incident was only a speed bump in their relationship.

"You really think it was a bear?" Lexy's previous truculence vanished. She'd transformed from surly employee into uncertain mentee.

"I don't know." Jackson smiled, acknowledging Lexy had been the bigger, more mature person. "Like you said. Coulda been a raccoon."

Lexy wrapped her arms around herself, suddenly aware of the subzero air. "I'd hate to meet the raccoon that can rip a solid oak door off its hinges."

"Maybe there was more than one. Probably had matching jackets and Jordans."

Lexy giggled, and relief washed over Jackson. Hearing the childlike sound emanating from the tall, formidable woman, he couldn't help but laugh as well.

"See you back at the office?" Lexy asked.

"Negative. I'm going to head to Frieda's for a cup of coffee first."

"Might want to get some food too, boss. Hungover and hungry is not a good look."

"Careful," Jackson warned. "You're starting to sound like my ex-wife."

Lexy made a "blah, blah, blah" motion with one hand and climbed into the Dodge.

Jackson chuckled to himself as Lexy drove away. Some at the DNR complained she took nothing seriously, but Jackson knew better. Lexy was smart. Whip-smart. He imagined being intelligent had some disadvantages, just like being as good-looking as she was.

In his experience, people always found a reason to dislike someone. Lexy gave them two, neither of which was within her control. Short of not wearing makeup, which had little effect on her natural beauty, there wasn't much she could do about her looks. Intelligence, however, was easily hidden. But she didn't dumb herself down. Instead, she acted as if the world were a joke.

He was making his way back to his truck when he heard footsteps behind him. Eyes wide, he spun to see Remy approaching. "Mr. Nordgren. What can I do for you?"

Remy shoved his hands in his coat pocket and hunched his shoulders. "Sorry, I don't mention this earlier, but I just remember."

"Remembered what?" Jackson kept his voice low and soothing. Despite his efforts, the man's shoulders remained hunched, his eyes averted.

"You ask if anything other than food gone missing. I was so throw'd off by your bear comment, I forgot 'bout my old hunting knife. I check everywhere, but it never turnt up."

Jackson ignored Remy's slight jab. "Is there something special about the knife? I mean, it's a miracle the Benelli is still there. I'd say you got pretty lucky."

"Won the Benelli at a raffle. Didn't cost nothing but a ticket. That knife though..." Remy's eyes turned wistful. "She's not worth much, but she's strong and sharp. Can't figure why anybody would take her and leave the Benelli."

Jackson nodded his sympathy. Clearly the knife meant a great deal to Remy, but the odds of him seeing it again weren't good, and he didn't have the heart to tell the quiet French Canadian that whoever had taken the knife had likely done so because, unlike the Benelli, the knife required no ammo to be lethal. "Tell you what. I'll keep an eye out and see if we can't get your knife back to you."

The crow's feet around Remy's eyes deepened as he smiled.

From the outside, Frieda's Coffee and Whatnot wasn't much to look at. Consisting of tan cinderblock and an arched tin roof, and plopped in a parking lot that was more dust than gravel, the coffee shop resembled an abandoned bank. Between the Formica tables, mismatched chairs, and a counter built from reclaimed untreated lumber, the inside of Frieda's was no better.

Tim Frieda, the shop's proprietor and namesake, suffered no delusions that Frieda's might make anybody's "Best of" list or even the back page of a magazine's "hidden gems" section. Still, he had more than enough business to keep the lights on. Tim told anyone who asked that his success was due to the quality of his pies and his fair prices, but locals and tourists would have insisted that Tim, who stood six feet seven inches tall, was the main attraction.

An outdoorsy man of sixty, Tim was both jovial and erudite, the sort of person who could carry on a conversation about anything with anyone. On the rare occasion he lacked knowledge of a topic, he asked questions. From horticulture to homebrewed beer, if Tim didn't know about it, he could name someone who did and could spit out details like he'd seen or experienced them firsthand. Tim wouldn't take credit, he was far too honest for that, but he could make the listener believe he'd taken part.

Tim and Jackson weren't well-acquainted. Jackson had been coming to his shop for almost two years and while he was certainly amiable enough, he'd seemed to have had something happen in his life that were either still too raw or too personal to disclose across the counter, at least at this stage of their friendship.

Nonetheless, Tim considered Jackson a friend and liked

to think Jackson considered him one as well. It was probably the budding connection between the two men, similar in age and situation, that enabled Tim to spot Jackson's haggard look when he plopped himself down on a barstool at the counter.

"You look like fresh hell." Tim's nose wrinkled. "And you reek."

Jackson forced a chuckle and picked up one of the laminated menus Tim kept in front of every stool. "In that case, maybe I'll take my business elsewhere."

Tim responded with a dismissive flick of his wrist. "Don't be such a baby. The way you slid in after the breakfast rush and before the lunch crowd, I'd swear you timed it that way."

"I know how I smell."

Tim shook his head. "I'm not sure you do. There's a hose and a floor drain in the storage room. You might want to step in there and spray yourself down."

Jackson put down the menu with an exaggerated sigh. "Is there anybody in this town who doesn't think I need a goddamned nanny?"

Tim grinned, showing healthy teeth for a man who made his living peddling sugar-filled pie. "City boy moves to the North Shore, we gotta take care of him. It's our way."

Jackson picked up the menu again. "Fine. Next time you make it down to Chicago, I'll see to it you get mugged and have your car stolen. That's our way."

Tim scoffed. That was how the men communicated, through snide comments, with an occasional snort or chuckle thrown in for good measure. "Please, I've been to Chicago. Bunch of skirt-wearing pansies if you ask me. I'll put my money on me and my hunting rifle over a bunch of mob pricks and gang bangers any day of the week and twice on Sunday."

Jackson looked up from the menu. "Let me guess? *Next of Kin* was on last night? Should have known by the way you're strutting around here with your jeans hiked over your ass crack."

"Liam played one tough hillbilly S.O.B., didn't he?" Tim beamed.

"When are you going to get over your crush on Liam Neeson?"

"Never." Tim fluttered his eyelashes. "The heart wants what the heart wants."

Tim liked that Jackson was comfortable with him speaking openly about his sexuality. Not that he hid it, but he didn't flaunt it either. As a small business owner in a small town, one never knew who might take offense at the slightest deviation from the "middle," whether politics, sports team affiliation, sexual orientation, or a preference for iPhone over Android.

Tim didn't care what people thought of his lifestyle. His private life was just that, but he also wasn't looking to lose customers over something that wasn't anybody else's business.

"You've been coming in here for a while now." Tim crossed his arms. "When are you going to realize the ten pies on the menu have been the same since W was President? What the hell makes you think I'm going to change them now?"

"Optimism."

Tim snatched the menu away and flipped Jackson the finger. "Whatta you want, smartass?"

"Just coffee for now." Jackson rubbed his face.

"Coming right up." Tim grabbed a white ceramic cup off

a towering stack of identical cups and shoved it under the spigot of a shiny chrome coffee machine. As the cup filled with rich brown liquid, he looked back over his shoulder at Jackson, who rested his head on the counter. "So, what's this I hear about a break-in at Remy Nordgren's place?"

Jackson raised his head. "You heard about that already?"

"No tourist gossip to keep us occupied this time of year." Tim returned with the cup of coffee and set it in front of Jackson.

Jackson nodded his thanks and sipped. After a moment, he looked at Tim. "What do you know about bears?"

"They're typically asleep this time of year."

"Do they ever wake up early from hibernation?"

"Sometimes. You think that's what broke into Remy's cabin?"

"Not sure. But I can't have a bear breaking into cabins, hungry or not." Jackson raised his cup to take another sip.

"You're gonna want to get yourself a tracker."

"A what?" Jackson's coffee cup hung in the air.

Tim pulled a stool up to the counter. "A tracker." He grunted as he sat down on the stool. "Unless you're planning on tracking the bear on your own."

Jackson gave Tim's suggestion some thought before the two men broke into laughter. Tim laughed longer and louder than Jackson, and it wasn't until Jackson cleared his throat that the tall man stopped. "I know a good tracker. Charlie Battice. If there's a rogue bear wandering around out there, Charlie will find it."

Jackson pulled his cell phone from his pocket. "This Charlie got a phone number?"

"Charlie's particular when it comes to clientele. Invitation only." Jackson's eyes narrowed, and Tim grinned. "But I'd be happy to put in a good word for you."

Jackson got up from his stool. "Appreciate it." He took one last swig of coffee, dug into his pocket, and threw a couple of wrinkled dollar bills onto the counter, drawing a scowl from Tim.

"How many times do we have to go through this? Badges and Vets don't pay for coffee."

Jackson left the money on the counter. "Consider it a tip for putting up with the stench."

"Fair enough." Tim pocketed the money and watched Jackson head for the door. "Now that you've stunk up my shop, answer me this before you go?"

Jackson rested one hand on the door. "Here we go…"

Tim's face was serious. "How the hell did you end up with the DNR, anyway? You may have been a badass on the mean streets of Chicago, but you don't know the first thing about the outdoors, and I'm pretty sure you can't tell a brown bear from a koala bear."

Jackson mimicked Tim's serious expression. "Friends in high places."

5

Massasauga River wound its way twenty-four miles from its inception at Kingston Lake to Superior, cutting through soil, trees, and a formidable layer of bedrock. Although the river's waters were colored a muddy brown by erosion from the river's bed, it painted a beautiful picture as it sped through narrow gorges and over majestic falls. During winter, the river's brown hue contrasted with the ice and snow that covered all but the occasional patch of open water.

Evergreens silently looked down on Scottie Campbell, pale, blond, sapling thin, and small for sixteen, and his sister Sarah, whose surplus of freckles disappeared on a face turned deep red by biting wind and temperatures below freezing.

Scottie and Sarah clamored over the snow-covered terrain, slipping and sliding as they moved with the practiced ease of veteran explorers; Sarah more so than Scottie. Sarah took point, making her way between rocks and through crevasses like a feral cat picking its way through a back alley. Scottie followed, content to let his younger sister lead the way.

While he'd rather have been hanging out on the computer or in the local convenience store, Scottie didn't mind spending time with Sarah. She was smart, funny, adventurous, and unlike almost everyone else, including the loose consortium of losers, outcasts, and dorks he called friends, Sarah didn't treat him like the awkward teen that he was. "Sarha," as he'd called her since she was two years old, treated him with respect. On those occasions when she agitated him, it was a result of them being very different people, rather than a conscious attempt to get under his skin. As little sisters went, she was a keeper.

At that moment, however, Sarah inched into "annoying kid sister" territory as she increased the distance between them. Scottie's big brother instinct, which had blossomed when their father deployed to Iraq eighteen months earlier, escalated from DEFCON 5 to DEFCON 4 due to the speed at which Sarah navigated the slick and jagged rocks of the gorge.

Since Sarah was nimble and knew the area, Scottie wasn't overly concerned. The most that was likely to happen was a twisted ankle or a minor cut on her hands or knees. Worst-case scenario, he washed a bloody hand in the river or wrapped a sprained foot in his scarf, and it took them longer to get back to the bicycles they'd chained to a road sign along the highway.

"Hey, wait up!" Scottie yelled as Sarah continued to pull away. He increased his speed, hoping to close the distance, but the increased speed, coupled with his annoyance at Sarah's cavalier behavior, resulted in the normally cautious Scottie taking several steps without looking. Scottie's foot slipped on a slanted rock covered in a thin layer of ice, and he tumbled to the ground in an ungainly fashion, his friends would have found hilarious.

He lay, splayed on a bed of rocks, lichens, and snow, and took stock of his extremities as the warm sensation of oozing blood spread along his left side. To his great surprise, he was fine, aside from a dull throb in his hip. Maybe he was just numb from the cold and would feel the extent of his injuries once he thawed out. Didn't matter at the moment. Scottie laughed at his good fortune. "Nice one, shithead," he said aloud, half expecting Sarah to chime in with a triumphant and mocking "Nice fall, Dumbass!" Scottie climbed to his feet, only then realizing Sarah was nowhere to be seen.

Scottie kept his composure, remembering one of his father's favorite sayings, "Don't freak out until you're certain what there is to freak out about." Observe, assess, and plan, and if, after doing those three things, the situation appears worthy, feel free to freak out.

Scottie went through the list in his head: observe. He'd already done that in every direction except up. He craned his neck and looked skyward, scanning both sides of the gorge. No Sarah. Assess. Sarah was out of sight. He'd already called her name and gotten no response, so she was either out of earshot or injured and unable to respond. Both possibilities caused Scottie to break into a cold sweat, and he tightened his hands into fists, forcing himself to remain calm. Through sheer force of will, he moved on to Plan. "Get help," he mumbled to himself.

Scottie unzipped his coat and reached inside. He dug around the inside pocket, growing more concerned by the second, and then, relieved, he retrieved his cell phone and held it in front of his face. Triumph turned to distress as he saw the spiderweb of cracks crisscrossing the phone's glossy face. The fall on the slippery rock had sent Scottie down on his side, where his phone had been nestled "safely" inside his coat. While the phone might have saved him a bruised hip, it had absorbed the brunt of the fall and appeared to be a lost cause. Scottie brushed at the screen as if he could smooth away the cracks in the battered device.

He screamed for Sarah, not because he expected her to respond, but because he didn't know what else to do. She had to know he'd be losing it right now. He screamed in every direction, cupping his mouth and adding even more reverberation to his voice than the gorge walls already provided. After several desperate attempts, his voice grew hoarse, and he sank to the ground, pulling his knees to his chin.

What would he tell his parents? They had put him in charge, and he failed to keep track of his sister. Bile climbed in his throat, rising at the same rate as the panic that had taken a vice-grip hold on his heart and lungs, causing him to hyperventilate.

"Scottie!"

Scottie snapped to attention.

"Scottie! Come quick!" Scottie's head swiveled left and right as his ears and brain tried to triangulate the direction from which Sarah's voice had come.

"Hurry up! Come now!"

Scottie scrambled to his feet. "Sarah?"

"Scottie! Hurry!"

Scottie's face brightened as his ears and brain obtained a lock on Sarah's general location. He lumbered across the frozen river, slipping, sliding, and almost losing his balance again, but stayed on his feet despite the uneven and slippery terrain and the ache in his side.

As he rounded a jog in the river, Scottie stopped. He was confident Sarah's voice had come from this direction, but there was no one there. No Sarah. Just ice, snow, patches of open water, and a frozen waterfall a few yards away. Scottie broke out in a sweat again. He didn't want to think about Sarah having fallen through the ice, but forced himself to sprint for the nearest hole.

His feet sent chunks of ice into the air with each step, and Scottie was aware the ice could give way at any moment, but he didn't care. It had been at least a minute since Sarah's last call. If she'd gone under, every second counted. As he approached the open water, all he could think was, *At least the water is cold. Sarah could survive longer than if she'd gone under during summer.* Scottie flopped stomach-first onto the ice and looked into the hole, but found the water murky. He plunged his arm into the hole up to the shoulder and felt around. The freezing water had already leeched most of the feeling from his arm, but he didn't care.

"What are you doing with your arm in that hole? Noodling is illegal."

Scottie couldn't believe his ears. He looked up, and there was Sarah. Fifteen yards away, standing at the base of the frozen waterfall, hands on her hips and staring at him like he'd just passed gas at the dinner table. He yanked his arm from the river and stood up. Any anger he'd felt before evaporated. "I thought you were—"

"Follow me. I found something." Sarah disappeared into thin air, and it took a moment for Scottie's eyes and brain to register what had happened.

Sarah had gone behind the waterfall.

~

THE SUN'S RAYS, filtered by the wall of ice, lost some intensity behind the waterfall but had taken on an ethereal look. Ordinarily bright colors were muted as if covered by a thin layer of gauze, while previously subtle colors gained a syrupy quality as if mixed with mercury. The effect was a pleasant one, but Scottie scarcely noticed. He had lost Sarah once again and struggled to keep dread at bay. "Sarah?" He was startled by the echo inside the cave.

"What?" Sarah's response came from closer than Scottie had expected. He squinted as Sarah came into view, only a few feet away. This time, at least, she had not intended to elude him. And now that he'd found her, he had no intention of letting her out of sight. His fraternal instincts receded, replaced by anger. "Why didn't you answer me? You scared me half to death."

Sarah giggled. "God, you're such a worrywart. It's just a hidey-hole."

"I don't care what it is. We're going home." He lunged for Sarah, but she sidestepped him. This came as no surprise. Despite being two years Scottie's junior, Sarah ran faster, climbed higher, and swam deeper. If Sarah didn't want Scottie to catch her, he wouldn't.

He gave up the chase. It was pointless. He had to resort to other methods when she got into one of her "impish moods," as their mother described them. He elected to go with pity. "Look, Sarha," he emphasized the whine in his voice. "I'm tired, my arm is frozen, my side hurts, and I think I broke my phone. Can we please just go home?" He stood there in the low light, looking as pathetic as possible. A bedraggled puppy couldn't have looked worse.

"Okay, Scottie, we can go—" Scottie's hand shot out like a cobra striking at a mongoose. He grasped Sarah's wrist in a vice-like grip and yanked her toward the mouth of the cave. Sarah screamed, "Let me go!" But Scottie was determined and dragged her toward the sunlight.

"Lemme alone, you shithead!" Sarah's voice cracked with fury. She dug in as best she could, feet sliding along the cave floor in a desperate search for purchase amidst the mixture of rocks, snow, and ice. Sarah had always been strong for her size and age, but Scottie was still amazed by her strength. His grip loosened, and in a last-ditch effort to hold on, he yanked Sarah toward him while moving in her direction. The sudden change of direction threw Sarah off balance, and Scottie grabbed her in a headlock.

"Let me go!" Sarah screamed again as she thrashed, kicking with both feet and punching with her free hand, which she had balled into a fist.

Scottie knew he had only a short time to calm his sister down before she went ballistic and hurt herself or him. He considered granting her wish and letting her go, but in her current state, she was likely to attack him. Instead, he soothed her. "It's okay, I'm gonna let you go, but you have to calm down first."

His words had an immediate effect, and she thrashed less. "Are you ready to calm down?" He knew she wasn't, but this was part of the process. It was the only way he knew of to calm down Hurricane Sarah. He loosened his grip and pulled her close until her head rested against his chest.

"Okay, nice job." He stroked her hair. She flinched at first, but he was persistent, and after several caresses, she ceased struggling. The only evidence of her fit was her elevated breathing, which had slowed. Scottie released Sarah's wrist but kept his arm around her. "I'm going to let you go now, okay?" He didn't wait for a response before removing his arm and stepping away. It wasn't far enough.

Sarah attacked. She closed the distance between them in one step, then, balanced on one foot, pulled the other back like the hammer on a .357 Magnum. Once cocked, Sarah's foot swung forward on a pendulum powered by taut tendons and the centrifugal force created by the heavy hiking boot that covered her foot. Her steel-toed boot struck Scottie square on his shin with a sickening *thwack*, and he collapsed to the ground with a howl rivaling that of the most deep-chested Basset Hound.

As Scottie rolled about in the throes of agony, Sarah stood over him, nostrils flared, eyes narrowed with malice, and a triumphant grin on her face. "That's what you get, asshole!"

Her moment of victory was short-lived, however, and as Scottie moaned and writhed while holding his injured shin, Sarah's expression of triumph morphed into one of concern.

"Scottie?" Sarah moved closer. "Are you okay?" A low whimper replaced Scottie's moans, and he no longer writhed, having replaced his spastic contortions with a soothing rocking back-and-forth motion.

"Scottie? Please answer me. Say something." Sarah kneeled next to her brother, and he opened his eyes, which he'd squeezed shut to block out the pain, but continued to rock back and forth. Sarah placed a hand on his knee. "I'm sorry. I didn't mean to kick you so hard. I was just so mad. Please say some—"

A throaty roar reverberated from the bowels of the cave. Scottie turned toward Sarah with wide eyes. "What was that?"

She raised a finger to her mouth.

A wet and airy hiss, closer than the preceding roar, echoed toward them.

Sarah's eyes also widened with fear, but unlike her brother, she sprang into action. "We gotta go." She climbed to her feet and held out her hand to Scottie.

Another roar echoed loud enough to make the hairs on

the back of Scottie's neck stand at attention. "Jesus, Sarah, what is that?" He searched Sarah's face.

"Who cares?" She bore his weight and steered him forward, half carrying and half dragging him out of the cave as if they were engaged in the most important two-legged race of their lives.

Outside the cave, the pair picked up speed and hobbled across the frozen river, Scottie huffing and chuffing, Sarah, eyes locked on a point in the distance as she timed her footfall with that of her brother. In seconds, they settled on an imperfect but workable tempo and distanced themselves from the cave.

As the full spectrum of the afternoon sun's rays fell on Scottie's skin, his fear level dropped from petrified to merely frightened. Optimism, a feeling he'd forgotten existed, rose in his chest. The muscles in his legs relaxed just enough to disrupt the tenuous cadence negotiated with Sarah.

"Scottie, no!" Sarah warned, feeling the balance of their shared gait shift, but it was too late. Scottie pulled away, causing Sarah to lose her grip on his neck and shoulder. Sarah possessed agility and balance and might have corrected for Scottie's movement, but she had not accounted for the hole in the ice.

In the brief time they'd explored the cave, a crust of ice had formed over the hole, making it invisible against the rest of the frozen river but too thin to bear a human's weight. Most of Scottie's foot cleared the hole and rested on stable ice, but his center of gravity shifted, putting too much weight on his sore hip, and he collapsed.

Sarah twisted in a desperate attempt to avoid falling, but her fate was tied to her brother's. No amount of athleticism could overcome the weight disparity between the siblings, and he fell to the ice, dragging her down with him. Sarah anticipated the fall and curled into a ball on the way down, suffering little more than a glancing blow to her back.

Scottie wasn't so lucky. As he fell, he instinctively spun around to protect his face. The move had the desired effect. Scottie hit the ice butt-first, but his head whiplashed to the ice with a resounding *thwack* that he neither heard nor remembered.

6

Jackson swayed back and forth under a hot stream of water, lost in a blissful state of thinking about nothing. His ex-wife, Tanya, often lost her temper when he told her he was thinking about nothing, but he wasn't being evasive when he said it. It was true. He enjoyed thinking about nothing. It was like sleeping while awake. Peaceful and relaxing. The sensation was one of exquisite serenity.

Tanya either would not or could not accept that he, or any man, could think about nothing. In Jackson's mind, this utter lack of empathy for anyone other than herself had contributed to the end of their marriage—that and the months they'd spent dealing with what happened in Chicago.

As he ran a threadbare washcloth over his skin, he took stock of his body. He had the obstinate paunch of a fifty-something-year-old man, along with an ever-increasing number of white hairs in his hair, beard, and other places he was loath to mention, but he wasn't yet at the "dad bod" stage despite a steady diet of meat and liquid carbs.

Even after almost three years without morning calisthenics and a daily run along the Chicago River, Jackson felt he was in good shape. His muscles still had definition underneath his unflattering uniform, and he looked like he worked out every day, even though it was more like every three or four days. The only noticeable sign of wear and tear (other than those pesky white hairs) was the menagerie of scars that adorned his body.

His eyes studied the wounds, from the off-white, pinstripe-thin disfigurements on his arms and hands to the relief-map-textured keloids on his chest and abdomen, three shades darker than the rest of his skin. He smiled at his keepsakes. He'd earned them through years of high school and college football, and his years on the force. The scars told a story of commitment, pain, failure, and resilience, and he bore them with pride.

The ringer on Jackson's cell phone blared, ending his self-assessment. He stepped out of the shower, grabbed a frayed towel off a nearby hook, sniffed it, and found it just shy of moldy. He knew he should replace it with a fresh one, but figured he could get at least two more uses out of it before discarding it in favor of one of the other members of his mismatched collection.

Jackson wrapped the towel around his waist and picked up the phone from its perch on the back of the toilet tank. "This is Jackson." He held the phone away from his head as a muffled voice boomed from the handset. Turning on the speaker, he returned the phone to the back of the toilet, unwrapped the towel, and dried himself.

"Jackson?" A woman's voice inquired. "Are you there?"

Jackson winced as he dried his graying hair. "I'm here, Doris. What's up?"

"We got a problem over in Massasauga Park."

Years of smoking and drinking had taken their toll on Doris' voice, giving it a rougher quality than the voice of someone her age had any right to have. Not that Doris was young, but her voice sounded much older, and her tendency to yell when she knew the person on the other end of the line was on a cell phone only exacerbated the problem. Jackson grabbed the phone and turned the volume down. "Can Lexy handle it?"

"She's checking out a boar carcass over in Babbitt."

"An escaped pig?"

"What? No. I said a *boar*." Doris's tone indicated she found Jackson's clarification both unnecessary and stupid.

Jackson rubbed his face. "So, this problem in Massasauga Park…"

Jackson wasn't claustrophobic, but the confines of the cave made him nervous. It wasn't the small size or the low ceiling that caused him discomfort. It was the fact that the cave formed via a combination of dripping water and the river's frozen surface. As beautiful as the translucent stalactites and mirror-like ice floor were, they gave him a sense of fragility that no amount of reasoning could shake.

He knew the cave floor was likely six to nine inches thick, more than thick enough to hold his weight, and that the six-foot-long, javelin-like, light-refracting icicles wouldn't come close to melting for another two months, but he remained on edge. The impermanence of the ice castle in which he now walked unnerved him in the same way that prop planes and helicopter rides at the state fair made him uneasy. The word "flimsy" came to mind.

As he looked around the cave, still safely within a few

feet of the arched opening, he saw a hulking figure moving toward him. He backpedaled so quickly that he banged his head on a low spot hard enough to draw stars. Still smarting from the impact, he fumbled for his Glock but gave up when he heard a familiar deep voice boom inside the cave and his skull.

"About damn time!"

Sheriff Jesse Wyatt was a large man who filled a space as much with his personality as he did with his girth. With his white hair and handlebar mustache, he would have been a ridiculous caricature of a man if it weren't for the fact that he fit the part so well. One glimpse of Sheriff Wyatt and the only thought that came to mind was "Wyatt Earp."

Sheriff Wyatt was a cowboy in every sense of the word. Not of the "Old West" variety, but the cattle rancher variety. He just looked like a guy better suited for life raising sheep in Wyoming than chasing down criminals on the shores of Lake Superior. He reminded Jackson of both the Marlboro Man ads he'd seen on the back of old magazines stacked in his grandparents' attic as well as Dennis Weaver, the actor who played the lead in the seventies television show *McCloud*. Of course, at sixty-four, Sheriff Wyatt was older than the Marlboro Man and Dennis Weaver had been during their respective heydays, but he was universally respected and, in some circles, feared, despite his advanced age.

At the moment, however, he looked every bit as unnerved as Jackson felt. Maybe more so, based on the way he clutched his enormous Smith & Wesson .357 caliber handgun in one bear paw of a hand. "Whoa, Dirty Harry," Jackson held up his hands, "same team." The sheriff holstered the menacing weapon and replaced it with a tactical flashlight, which he shined into Jackson's face.

"Did I catch you on a spa day?" Sheriff Wyatt croaked. Jackson lowered his hands and approached him. The big man offered his hand, which enveloped Jackson's.

"I was just getting out of the shower when I got the call," Jackson offered, more in explanation than apology.

The sheriff looked him up and down. "Kinda late in the day for a shower. You and that intern of yours been up to some sort of afternoon delight?"

"Lexy's not an intern. She's been with the DNR longer than I have. And you know damn well there's a policy against interdepartmental fraternization."

"Maybe you ought to consider a transfer."

"What would be the point? She's half my age. I'd be dead within a week." Jackson humored the sheriff, even though he knew he shouldn't. "Assuming she would even be inter-ested in a broken-down old man who graduated from college before she entered kindergarten."

The sheriff nodded his approval. "A man who doesn't think with his pecker. You're a bit of a unicorn." Jackson was about to point out that his race, rather than his self-control, made him a unicorn when the man continued. "Although I gotta say, in this case, it must suck to be you. That Lexy is a real looker."

Jackson smirked, telling himself it was a polite way to end the conversation and the best course of action given the circumstances. Still, he felt a flush of embarrassment. Lexy was an employee, mentee, and friend, and comments about her appearance or his relationship with her made him uncomfortable.

"What's the scoop?" Jackson looked around the cave.

Wyatt gestured haphazardly. "Couple of kids were in here exploring when they heard a noise."

"What kids?"

"How the hell should I know?"

"What kind of noise?"

The big man shrugged. "Some kinda animal. Something big from the sound of it."

Jackson huffed. Trying to get information out of the taciturn lawman was like trying to get information from a four-year-old. "A bear, maybe?"

"Looks like it." Wyatt pointed his flashlight at the cave floor, and the blue-white glow illuminated a pile of leaves, sticks, pinecones, and tufts of fur. Jackson knelt to inspect the pile, but was careful not to disrupt its contents.

"So, where's our guest?"

"Beats me." Wyatt scratched his head. "Maybe after the kids woke him up, he went for a stroll."

Jackson stood. He was no expert on the hibernation habits of bears, but the cave didn't seem like a good place to crash for the winter. The entrance was tall enough for Jackson to walk through without bending, and light, although diffused by the icy walls and weakened by the low angle of the sun, was still bright enough to be an irritant to even the most determined sleeper. "This place doesn't look big enough for a bear."

"It's plenty big." The sheriff aimed his flashlight at a nearby rock wall, revealing a dark recess. "This is just the foyer. There's an indentation in the rock that runs back pretty far. I suspect things get even more interesting the farther in you go."

Jackson peered into the dark hole.

"Wonderful."

"Tell me about it." Wyatt cut off his flashlight, plunging the recess into darkness again.

Jackson heard the man's footsteps as he headed for the mouth of the cave. "Where are you going?" The sudden darkening of the recess was jarring, even with the soft glow of the day's dying light keeping the cave just bright enough to see.

"Anywhere but here. Bears are your jurisdiction, not mine. Good luck."

Jackson turned on his flashlight and quickly checked the recess before turning toward the departing man. "What happened to interagency cooperation?" He aimed the beam of light from his military-grade flashlight at Wyatt. The man had stopped at the cave entrance and was looking back at Jackson. He wore the worried expression of a man who'd consumed a meal of burritos and beer, only to discover there was no more toilet paper in the bathroom stall.

"Nothing personal, but I don't plan to be here when that bear comes back."

Jackson nodded toward the bulge under Sheriff Wyatt's jacket. "Well, could you at least leave me that oversized pea shooter of yours?"

He patted the holstered .357. "Not on your life. Agnes and me go back a long way. You'd have to pry her from my cold, dead hands. Now, if you'll excuse me, I'm going to head home and drink until the heebie-jeebies go away." He offered a curt wave and ducked out.

Jackson peered into the darkness and took a step forward. Although he'd been unnerved by the filtered light flowing into the cave, he preferred it to the inky black stillness that stared back at him from the depths of the recess. He took a deep breath, removed his Glock from its holster, and resumed his trek into the impression. A few steps in, he had to stoop to walk as the cave walls and ceiling closed in. As he trained the flashlight on the walls, he marveled at the deep striations, ragged and uneven, as if the dripping water that had carved its way through feet of bedrock had done so in a great hurry.

His nerves calmed, and his breathing returned to normal as he inched along, one hand on the abrasive wall; at least until a sharp *crack* echoed from behind him. He spun, flashlight aimed at the source of the sound, but saw nothing. He was the cave's only inhabitant and convinced himself the sound was that of a stalagmite falling from the ceiling or possibly a stalactite. Ten minutes ago, he'd known the difference, but now the fear that had gnawed at his courage since he'd stepped foot in the cave clouded his memory.

He turned his back on the unidentified sound and the only means of escape and inched deeper into the cave. The flashlight's spotlight turned ovoid as walls, and a descending ceiling closed around him. He couldn't be sure the cave was growing smaller, but sensed it was. He felt the opposite of a frog in a pot of water that didn't realize the temperature was rising toward boiling. He was very much aware of his predicament. As if in support of that analogy, something wet ran down his forehead.

The cave was below freezing. He shouldn't be sweating, especially to the extent that it ran down his forehead. "Fuck this." Jackson wiped his forehead with one gloved hand. As he turned to leave, the flashlight beam played over his free hand, and something caught his eye. Closer examination revealed a dark smear. He sniffed his glove and recoiled at the coppery odor. He trained the flashlight on the cave walls, ceiling, and floor.

Red splotches decorated every surface.

THE TWO HARBORS office building of the Minnesota Department of Natural Resources was a study in bland design and uninspired architecture. Wide and flat, the building squatted amidst a smattering of skinny birch trees, barely protected from the persistent icy winds that bent the adolescent trees at the waist. Purposely made as dull as possible, the half-tan, half-brown bungalow sported a dark brown roof with matching doors and shutters.

Jackson's Tundra eased into the parking lot, deliberately and with exaggerated care. He stepped out of the truck and shoved the door closed. As he crossed the parking lot, he passed Lexy's mud-covered Dodge Ram, which had taken up residence in the coveted parking space nearest the front door. Jackson rarely claimed that spot, as it often fell to the first person to arrive at the office in the morning.

He shook his head, impressed by Lexy's dedication yet annoyed by the notion her early arrival made him appear lazy by comparison. Never mind, he'd spent most of his morning hunched over in a cave with an ill-mannered sheriff. His face twisted into a scowl as he offered his security badge to the scanner next to the door, then waited for the cricket-like chirp. The scanner complied, and Jackson pushed open the door when a battered pickup truck with a tortoiseshell pattern of black paint and orange-brown rust banged into the parking lot, pulling a tarp-covered flatbed trailer behind.

Jackson sighed as the pickup truck skidded to a stop, taking up three spaces. Ordinarily, a vehicle taking up multiple parking spaces would have caused Jackson's eye to twitch, but he watched calmly as Clem Butler, a man in his mid-seventies with a face further etched by decades in the summer sun and winter wind, climbed out.

Butler, sporting the Carhartt coat, work boots, and camo

hat uniform of a North Shore farmer, one of the few who remained this far north, ambled to the flatbed trailer without a word to Jackson and worked the bungee cords that held the tarp down. "Afternoon, Mr. Butler, what is it today? Coyotes? Foxes? Democrats?"

The old farmer didn't acknowledge Jackson's presence until he unhooked the last bungee cord. "What are you going to do about this?" He said stiffly as he yanked back the tarp, revealing a mangled carcass.

Jackson gawked at what looked like a pile of ripped-up meat. "What is it?"

"What's it look like?"

Jackson had yet to grow accustomed to Minnesota stoicism and, like many non-Minnesotans, interpreted such impassiveness as standoffish or even rude. For this reason, he elected to avoid the passive-aggressive exchange that was sure to follow, opting for a direct approach. "Just answer the question, Clem."

If Butler was disappointed by Jackson's approach, he didn't let his feelings bubble to the surface. "Found it on my farm this morning."

Jackson took another peek at the carcass. "Something attack one of your cows?"

"Ain't a cow."

"Is it an elk?"

Butler shook his head, and Jackson let out a long sigh, trying hard not to lose his temper. "I'm running out of options, Clem. Is it a moose?"

Butler gawked as if Jackson had grown a third eye. "You see any hooves?"

Jackson inspected the animal more closely. It had been stripped clean of fur and skin, leaving the muscles, tendons, and bones visible. He followed the length of one long leg to an enormous foot tipped by deadly claws, then frowned. "Is it a...bear?"

Butler turned his head and spit, careful to do so with the wind, and away from himself and Jackson. "Looks like it."

"What the hell could have done this to a bear?"

"You're the game warden. I was hoping you could tell me." Butler caught and held Jackson's eye.

Jackson knew that look. He'd seen it in the eyes of men, women, and children caught up in disputes between unreasonable, unyielding, and often armed men. Butler's clear blue eyes watered, but not from the constant assault by the wind. This man, who had withstood attempts, both legal and illegal, by powerful men to turn land that had been in his family for generations into condos and casinos, appeared unsettled by what lay on the flatbed.

JACKSON ENTERED the lobby to see Lexy hanging out by the water cooler. She looked up from her study of the transparent tank.

"What was that all about?"

"What was what all about?" Jackson played along.

"Nice try. I saw you talking to Clem Butler."

"Oh, that." Jackson was tired after his ordeal in the cave, but had enough energy to continue the charade. "Nothing major. Clem thought something got at his herd."

Lexy's eyebrows went up. "You think it was our bear?"

"Probably not," Jackson offered, more cryptic than he'd intended. Lexy strode over to him.

"Spill it." Lexy challenged him with an impish smirk. He tried to hold her gaze, but her proximity made him uncomfortable, and this time he took a step back.

"How about I just show you?" Jackson headed for the far side of the office. She hurried after him, a happy grin lighting up her face.

JACKSON FLIPPED A SWITCH, and overhead lights flickered to life, casting blue/white light and gray shadows around a three-stall garage. Lexy shivered. Despite the shelter afforded by the garage, her breath was visible in the cold air.

"Okay, so what's with the Area 51 routine?" Lexy asked as she looked around.

Jackson moved to the rear of the garage, where Clem Butler's tarp covered the floor. He nodded toward the tarp, intending to focus Lexy's attention on the lump that bulged underneath. "Grab a corner." Lexy looped her finger into one of the four metal rings embedded in each corner of the tarp and waited for Jackson to do the same. Together, they pulled the tarp away.

Lexy's brows knit as the carcass underneath was revealed. "You dragged me in here for roadkill?"

"Take a closer look," Jackson said, smirking.

Lexy peered closer. After a moment her eyes widened. "What in the fuckety fuck...?" She turned to Jackson, her expression a mixture of revulsion and excitement. "Is this a freaking bear?"

Jackson nodded, embarrassed by how easily Lexy identified the animal when he couldn't.

Lexy turned back to the carcass. "What could do that to a bear?"

"I have no idea." Jackson shrugged. "I'd like to have someone identify the cause of death, but there's no one around here with the right setup."

Lexy peered at the carcass, leaning over for a better view. "You need a forensic lab."

Jackson threw the end of the tarp back over the carcass and motioned for Lexy to do the same. "Unless we got one yesterday, I'd have to send the carcass and my samples to St. Paul."

"What samples?"

Jackson reached into the front pocket of his jacket and pulled out the plastic top of an ink pen, along with the transparent barrel.

"From the cave."

"You used a pen to gather samples?"

"It's all I had."

"Well, you don't have much time. The courier's gonna be here any minute. You know he hates waiting."

Jackson stared at the carcass. "Yeah, but this won't keep forever, even inside this garage."

Lexy's face brightened. "Instead of sending the samples by courier, you could drive them down."

"Why would I do that?"

"So, you can take our friend here along for the ride." Lexy nudged the tarp with her foot.

"I'm not driving to St. Paul with a carcass in the back of my truck."

"Come on. You can keep him covered with the tarp. It's plenty cold out today. He'll keep until you get to the forensics lab. It gets the carcass out of the garage and gets you the results of your blood samples sooner."

Vapor rose from Jackson's nostrils as he huffed quietly. Lexy had a point. The sooner he got the samples analyzed, the better. And, if one or both of the samples belonged to the dead bear, it might shed some light on the situation. "Actually, that's not a bad idea."

Lexy pumped the air with a clenched fist. "Road trip! I'll bring the tunes."

Jackson laughed. "I said it wasn't a bad idea. I didn't say it was the only idea. We're not going to St. Paul."

"You said you wanted the results ASAP."

"I do."

Lexy threw up her hands. "Then, what's the problem?"

Jackson wanted to know who or what their mystery attacker was, but suspected his junior officer was more excited by the prospect of a road trip, room service, and per diem. "We don't have the budget for gas to and from St. Paul, let alone two hotel rooms."

Lexy deflated like a punctured pool float. "You're no fun."

Jackson strode the long hallway from the garage to the front office, head down, hands behind his back, fingers entwined. He could feel Lexy's eyes on him, but paid no attention.

"What's going on in that head of yours?" Lexy asked finally.

"Huh?"

"I assume you're thinking about the cave. What's the plan?"

"For now, it's back to chasing down litterbugs and drunk anglers. If the St. Paul office comes back with something interesting, we'll change tack."

Lexy looked at him hopefully. "Do you think it really could be something interesting? Something unusual?"

"Probably not."

Lexy's face fell, and Jackson, noting her disappointment,

put on his best "supervisor" smile. "But if it does turn out to be a rogue bear, I'm all in. Even if it means dipping into petty cash and the Christmas party fund."

A SMIRKING Doris greeted Jackson and Lexy as they entered the front office area. Jackson ignored the woman and placed the pen pieces on the desk. "Can you have these couriered to the lab in St. Paul? I need them to go out today."

"Sure thing." Doris set the pieces aside as if a pen barrel filled with blood was the most normal thing she'd seen all day. As Jackson and Lexy walked away, she called after them. "Where did the two of you get off to?"

Jackson looked back over his shoulder. "Grow up, Doris."

Doris looked at Lexy with wide eyes.

Lexy forced an uncomfortable, unconvincing smile. "Got anything for me?"

"Let me check the call sheet." The older woman picked up the sheet with shaking hands and scanned it. "Not much, just the usual. A call came in last night about a couple of stolen cars. They're sitting on the shoulder of Highway 16. I figure the owners left them running, and some teenagers took 'em for a joyride."

"Got it." Lexy nodded in the direction Jackson had gone. "Don't take it personally, Doris. He hasn't had his coffee this morning and is in a mood. He asked me to go to the garage so no one could hear him yelling at me over some paper-work error."

"That must have been fun."

"You have no idea," Lexy offered a quick wave and a sympathetic smile before disappearing down the hallway.

Jackson's office would have baffled the most skilled psychiatrist. Small, gray, and sporting minimal decoration, it provided no clue as to Jackson's personality and no real signs of occupation other than a DNR coffee mug, corresponding coffee rings on the desk, a coat hanging from a hook on the back of the door, and the outdated computer and monitor at which Jackson stared. Except for his eyes, which darted back and forth, Jackson was motionless until the knock at the door. Even then, he only sat back in his chair, content to ignore the knock.

Lexy poked her head in. He motioned for her to enter, but she declined, choosing to lean against the doorjamb instead. "It's probably safer out here."

He looked up from his desk, a pained expression on his face. "Did I overdo it?"

"A bit." Lexy waggled one hand. "Poor Doris damn near shit herself."

Jackson pinched the bridge of his nose. He'd lost his temper, and even though Doris deserved it, he shouldn't have. "I'll make it up to her later."

"You sure you're okay?"

He faced Lexy, shoulders slumped. "Don't you ever get tired of the snide comments? The constant innuendo?" Jackson searched Lexy's face, looking not for an answer but solidarity.

She waved him off. "It's a small town. We're outsiders. She didn't mean anything by it."

"Yeah? And what would she have said if we'd taken an overnight trip to St. Paul?"

"Is that why you said we didn't have the budget?"

When Jackson didn't answer, realization spread across

Lexy's face like a storm cloud over a doubleheader. "Look, I know you were just sticking up for me, but I can take care of myself."

"Is that so?"

"Damn right it is. I've got a gun and a badge, same as you."

"If you say so." He tried to sound gruff, but his voice was playful.

"I know so." She patted the doorframe. "I'm headed to Highway 16 to check out some derelict cars. Be back in a couple of hours."

As Lexy turned to leave, Jackson lifted his head. "Be careful."

"Sure thing, boss."

7

Lexy stepped out of her truck and approached an Econoline van and a tired Dodge pickup on the side of the road. The windshields of both vehicles were dusted with snow and opaque with a thin layer of frost, but were free of the orange and white state-sponsored graffiti that MNDOT used to indicate the abandoned vehicles were slated for towing.

She popped the retention strap holding her sidearm in place. Keeping one ear tuned to the highway for cars, she inched toward the abandoned vehicles. She checked the white Econoline van first, pleased it was a passenger version and had windows the length of the van, giving her a clear view inside without having to open the doors and risk ambush.

She moved to the burgundy pickup and stood on tiptoe to peer inside. She recoiled, disgusted but also impressed by the ankle-deep mound of beer cans, condom wrappers, and rolling papers that filled the truck's footwells. A quick walk around the vehicles revealed nothing more than rusted fenders and salt spatter indicative of years of Minnesota winters. She buttoned the retention strap and leaned into her shoulder-mounted radio.

"Doris?" Lexy systematically searched her surroundings until Doris' voice crackled through the radio.

"Go ahead, sweetheart."

"Just finished up on Highway 16. Two vehicles matching the description of the two stolen from the ValueAmerica last night. No major damage, just a couple of scratches that might have already been there and a shit ton of garbage in the pickup. Whoever they were, they partied pretty freaking hard. Based on the number of bottles and rolling papers, they were lucky not to have wrapped themselves around a pole." Lexy started toward her squad car. "I'm going to hang out here until MNDOT shows up, then head back to the station."

"Negative," came Doris' voice, chipper to the point of annoyance. "We just got a report of an attack over in Denmark Falls. Jackson wants you to check it out."

"What kind of attack?" Other than the occasional bar fight, attacks were a rarity this time of year. No matter how angry or drunk people got, it was too cold to bother with fisticuffs when frostbite could set in within minutes.

"Some kind of animal broke into a hobby farm and chewed up one of the horses." The cheeriness had left her voice.

Lexy cringed at the description, especially the phrase *chewed up*. Also, the thought of a horse suffering made her angry. The oddest part of Doris's call, however, was the location. "Denmark Falls? That's more than two hours from here." She enjoyed driving, but trekking to the once dying town kept afloat by a sugar beet processing plant and an influx of Mexican migrant workers was out of her way.

"I understand, Hon, but that puts it at more than three

hours from here. Wouldn't make sense for Jackson to go when you're closer. His words, not mine."

Lexy kicked one booted foot in a mini-tantrum. "Isn't that Blake Hansen's jurisdiction?" She already knew the answer.

"Chief Hansen's on the scene, but wants someone from DNR to check out the horse. I guess it's pretty gnarly."

Lexy stiffened. "Okay, I'm on my way."

"Copy that, Lex. I'll let Grumpy Grumperson know."

Lexy laughed as she let go of her handset and headed for her truck. Usually, she walked the yellow demarcation between highway and shoulder with her eyes on the road, on the lookout for approaching vehicles, but something prompted her to glance at the berm. She had an overwhelming sense that something or someone was watching her from the winter foliage.

Stopping as her body tensed into a mass of coiled muscles, her jaw grew taut as she peered into the tangle of winter-dead cattails. Except for a blink of her eyes and a careful swallow that sent a ripple down the length of her throat, she remained motionless despite every instinct screaming at her to run. She scanned the berm for any sign of movement but saw nothing.

And then, there they were, barely visible amidst the overgrowth, a pair of wide-set eyes. Lexy knew they belonged to an animal. Most likely, a dangerous one. The eyes were large, forward-facing, and far apart, their greenish-yellow tint unlike anything she'd seen on anything human—the eyes of a large predator. The eyes were locked on her, blinking in the tranquil manner of a hunter confident of its superiority. It was that stare that unnerved her most. It was as if whatever watched her was unconcerned with her presence and unconvinced of her ability to defend herself.

She decided to test the animal's resolve. As she reached for her sidearm, she avoided locking eyes, for fear the animal might perceive it as a challenge. There was also a chance that the sound and motion of unsnapping her holster's strap and removing her weapon might provoke an attack. Her stalker had waited this long; no reason to prompt it to strike now.

Lexy wanted to say "nice doggie" but wasn't sure the thing lurking in the weeds was a wolf. It could have been a mountain lion or even Jackson's insomniac bear. It didn't matter. She just wanted to get to her truck in one piece.

She recited the rule aloud. "Get big, make noise, and never turn your back." Of course, this might have been more easily achieved had thousands of years of fight-or-flight instinct not been telling her to run. Determined to survive the encounter, she forced herself to remain calm.

At only twenty-six years old, Lexy had things she wanted to do before she left this earth. Being killed by wildlife on the side of the road didn't fit into her life plan. With that thought in mind, she unsnapped her sidearm and eased her Glock from its holster. "Please go away," she whispered. "I don't want to hurt you."

The eyes blinked with contemptuous disinterest, and Lexy sighed. "Fine. I didn't want to do this, but if you're going to be stubborn..." Lexy raised her Glock level with the eyes and released the safety. She raised her arm until the weapon rose past level and pointed to the sky. She let out a soft breath and pulled the trigger. The air exploded.

A guttural growl, ominous and threatening, raised the hairs on the back of Lexy's neck. She experienced the growl as much as she heard it. The frequency was so low it registered just within the range of human hearing. Lexy gasped as fear gripped her bowels and bladder, threatening to squeeze them both empty in an act of protest. She set her jaw and lowered the Glock until it was level with the eyes, which had taken on a baleful glare.

"Okay. Have it your way," Lexy said. She squeezed the trigger, but before the Glock's firing pin engaged the 9 mm cartridge, the yellow-green eyes vanished, barely shaking the clump of cattails as their owner disappeared.

Lexy returned her Glock to its holster and hurried to her truck. She never turned her back and stopped only when her butt touched the front of the vehicle. With one last glance toward the berm, she sprinted to the driver's side door and jumped into the idling truck. Once inside, she locked the doors, shivering as she sat silent for what seemed like forever.

"Fuck!"

Night had fallen by the time Lexy turned off Highway 61 and onto County Road 2, yet her thoughts remained on her encounter on Highway 16 and the scene in Denmark Falls. Mostly on Denmark Falls. While the incident on Highway 16 had frightened her, the fact that she never saw her hidden observer made it difficult for her to dwell on it.

The hobby farm was a different story. The marks on the mutilated horse carcass didn't match the lupine modus operandi. Jackson would have gagged at her use of the Latin term, but no other option made sense. Wolves, cougars, and bears all attacked in identifiable fashion. Cougars killed by attacking the neck and throat, wolves by attacking the hindquarters, and bears by biting the head and spine.

Even the way they consumed their prey differed. Cougars and wolves often ate the internal organs first, while bears preferred to start with their victims' stomach contents. Lacerations caused by the killer's teeth and claws showed characteristics of all three animals, with wolves being the most likely because they were more prevalent than cougars in Minnesota.

Although she and Jackson were likely dealing with a bear, the odds of a second bear waking from hibernation and running amok were slim. Within one hundred forty miles of the first? That would be a statistical anomaly.

Lexy shuddered as she recalled the remains of the poor horse, a beautiful Morgan named Moses. Moses had been shredded in his stall, unable to run or defend himself. The thought of the proud animal dying in pain and fear brought tears to Lexy's eyes.

The stable doors hung on their hinges, as if wrenched open by force. Such an entry suggested that wolves were not responsible, yet, when Hansen pressed for her opinion, Lexy lied, conceding it was most likely wolves, even though she questioned what the evidence suggested.

Chief Hansen had theorized the wolves didn't kill and consume the horse, opining that the animal had died overnight, perhaps from exposure to the cold. That, in Lexy's opinion, was wishful thinking. There was blood on the ground, mixed in with the bedding, as well as evidence of hemorrhaging from the tissue, which wouldn't have occurred had a wolf or some other animal been scavenging an already deceased animal.

Lexy didn't press the issue. Although she thought Hansen, like Sheriff Wyatt, was an old-school cop with antiquated ideas about law enforcement, she respected his dedication to his job and the tiny town of Denmark Falls. Today, however, he struck her as out of sorts. The entire time Lexy inspected Moses' wounds, Chief Hansen had been fidgety, glancing at the stable doors as if he had somewhere to be.

When Lexy jokingly asked him if he had a "hot lunch date," the man snapped at her, chastising her to "keep her mind on her investigation." Usually, she would have snapped back, but something in Chief Hansen's eyes made her bite her tongue, and when he glanced at the stable door for a second time, Lexy saw that he wore the restless expression of a man expecting someone or something.

Lexy hadn't known who or what and wasn't inclined to ask, but Hansen's disquiet was contagious, and she'd wrapped up her work and gotten out of the stable as quickly as possible. However, as soon as she'd returned to her truck, she called Connie Morales, Chief Hansen's sole deputy.

Lexy and Deputy Morales weren't friends, but they were friendly. They'd met two years ago at a week-long seminar in Minneapolis for women and people of color in law enforcement and developed a kinship. Connie was witty, funny, and self-deprecating, referring to herself as a "three-fer" due to her status as a Latinx woman and a member of the LGBTQ community. The two of them had hung out every evening, seizing the opportunity to avail themselves of the area's restaurants and nightlife. Lexy grinned as she recalled Connie's kid in a candy store reaction to the queer pop-up events and gay/lesbian bars that Denmark Falls lacked.

Connie picked up right away, answering the phone with a sigh. "What'd he do now?" When Lexy explained that Chief Hansen had been gruff during their investigation of the incident at the hobby farm, Connie laughed. "Have you not met him?"

Lexy laughed too, clarifying that Hansen had been weird

the whole time, checking the door to the stables and looking over his shoulder. Connie fell silent momentarily, responding only after Lexy asked if she was still on the line. When she finally spoke, it was in hushed tones and a seriousness unusual for the outgoing officer.

Connie explained hunters had found a feral hog north of Denmark Falls the day before. Lexy thought she understood Chief Hansen's concerns. The animals, a hybrid of feral hogs and domesticated pigs, bred at an alarming rate and were a scourge to farmers and environmentalists alike, causing damage to crops and eliminating native plants and animals with their voracious appetites and destructive feeding habits. Their steady trek southward from Canada kept conservation officers awake at night.

Connie explained that while the hunters only found a single hog, the attacker had partially consumed the large, mature animal. Nausea rose in Lexy's throat as Connie described the hog remains, noting with apprehension the similarities between the dead hog and the mutilated hobby horse she'd spent her afternoon examining.

Although the hog had turned up almost ninety miles from the hobby farm, she couldn't ignore the similarities. Given Chief Hansen's considerable experience, he no doubt suspected a serial predator, one sadistic enough to mutilate a good-sized domesticated horse and a large and powerful boar capable of mounting a formidable defense. No wonder Hansen was on edge. Whatever had attacked the horse and feral hog was dangerous *and* could cover a lot of ground.

Lexy thanked Connie for the insight and promised to meet up once the weather warmed, but her mind wasn't on social engagements. Three hours later, still trying to make sense of the disparate evidence, she missed her turn into the DNR driveway.

"Shit!" Lexy slammed on the brakes. She threw the truck into reverse, but in her agitated state, failed to check her rearview mirror before stomping on the gas, and had to hit the brakes again to avoid a truck exiting the DNR parking lot at warp speed.

"Son of a bitch!" Lexy gripped the steering wheel, frustrated by her lack of attentiveness. "Where's the fire?" She bellowed after the departing truck. Although meant rhetorically, Lexy's exclamation blossomed into actual curiosity when she recognized the vehicle as Jackson's truck. It sped away without so much as a backward glance from the driver.

8

Sarah found the cramped recovery room mind-numbingly dull, with its bland paint job and minimalist décor, consisting of photographs of flowers and the hospital's exterior, which shared the drab color scheme. She sighed to herself as she looked up from her tablet and glanced at Scottie's bed. While he'd seemed okay following the morning's events, the fact that he hit his head scrambling from the cave caused great concern to Sarah's parents and the physicians at Choice Care in nearby Duluth. Because of Scottie's lingering nausea, dizziness, and headaches, the on-call physician, Dr. Anders, a pleasant man with a round face, thinning hair, and kind eyes, had insisted on a CT scan, which showed nothing likely to result in long-term physical issues.

Mental issues, however, were another story. Scottie suffered repeated nightmares during the short naps he took that evening, but he had always been susceptible to horror movies and tragic stories on the news, and the onset of nightmares after such a traumatic event came as no surprise. Sarah's parents had been understandably relieved by the positive diagnosis and, in Sarah's mind, had chosen to ignore Scottie's nightmares, choosing instead to focus on the fact that Scottie and Sarah had escaped with only a few scrapes and bruises.

Although Sarah shared their relief, she struggled not to resent their willingness to disregard Scottie's recurring dreams. After all, they hadn't heard what she and Scottie had. Something primal yet supernatural. As she sat in the uncomfortable visitor's chair, she searched countless WAV files for any sound that resembled what she'd heard at the river. While neither she nor Scottie had seen the ice cave's occupant, what they'd heard had scared Scottie to the point of paralysis. Sarah had hurried Scottie from the cave only to keep her brother safe, and now, in the safe confines of the hospital, she wondered what creature made a noise so horrible that their hasty exit caused Scottie to fall and hit his head.

Sarah turned toward the door, drawn by the sound of her mother's voice from the hallway. She couldn't make out Marnie's words but could tell that her mother was on the phone and, judging by the pointed tone, meting out a severe tongue-lashing to her father.

Sarah couldn't help but sympathize with her father. After she'd used Scottie's phone, which, while cracked, had still functioned, to call 911 and then their parents, Kirk had raced to meet them at the hospital, but when the results of the CT scan showed Scottie suffered only minor contusions, he returned home to retrieve Scottie's e-reader and Nintendo Switch to keep him occupied during his extended stay for observation. However, that had been several hours ago, and Kirk's delayed return had not gone over well with Marnie, as evidenced by the rising volume and pitch of her voice.

Sarah returned her gaze to Scottie. As she watched her brother sleep, a smile crossed her face. Scottie was a dork and a nerd, and every other word she could think of for a brother who would have made a great character in the show *Stranger Things*, but he was kind and protective, which was why she didn't mind that Scottie abhorred almost everything she loved, especially sports and outdoor activities such as hiking and camping.

The fact that the siblings were virtually nothing alike was why they were so close. They were yin to each other's yang. Sarah was strong in those areas where Scottie flailed and vice versa. Scottie was quiet and introverted, whereas Sarah was loud and extroverted. Between them, they had the whole world covered.

The one thing they had in common was computers. Scottie was more into the technical side and loved to build gaming computers in his messy room that reeked of stale socks and body odor, while Sarah enjoyed using them. She was adept at navigating the internet and its myriad apps to her advantage. She was no hacker, but she could find anything she wanted on the web and was as savvy as any teenager at hiding her age and identity online.

Unbeknownst to her parents, Sarah could tap into the world of online services, which allowed her to secure food, music, transportation, and other services from the comfort of her home with a stroke of the keyboard or tap of the screen. At her age, Sarah had little use for the vast array of online products and services but was very much aware of their availability.

The hiss of the pneumatic door interrupted Sarah's thoughts as her mother entered wearing a deep scowl. Although Marnie's expression was all the answer Sarah needed, she asked anyway. "Is Dad coming back?" Marnie's scowl disappeared, replaced by a reassuring smile and a strained response. "Maybe later."

"Why don't you go home, Mom?" Sarah put down her tablet. "Scottie isn't doing anything but sleeping. I can hang out."

"That's sweet of you to offer, but this isn't your responsibility."

Sarah hung her head. "If he hadn't been chasing me, this never would have happened."

Marnie grabbed Sarah in a crushing hug. "Don't you dare blame yourself! This isn't your fault. None of it." Marnie kissed Sarah's forehead, stroking her hair between kisses. "I don't ever want to hear you say that again." Marnie took Sarah by the shoulders. "Do you understand?"

Sarah nodded and fixed her gaze on the floor until she heard her mother drop into the visitor's chair across the room. She glanced up to see Marnie checking email on her phone. *If I could go back in time, I never would have gone into that stupid cave.*

JACKSON LINGERED in front of recovery room 316. He'd never been a fan of hospitals, having visited them frequently, both during his days as a college football player and his time on the force. He associated the bright lighting and tile-covered floors and walls with pain and suffering, and the sterile chrome and steel medical equipment with torture. "Don't be such a baby," he chastised, but steeled himself against what he feared he might encounter behind the door. As he grasped the doorknob, he realized his associations weren't entirely accurate. Children were born in hospitals. He had visited both Scottie and Sarah in a hospital not far from here just hours after their respective births. The memories brought a smile and, clinging to that positive recollection, he twisted the doorknob and pushed the door open.

MET by an austere cube of a room and the sight of Scottie lying motionless in a utilitarian bed, Jackson pushed down the lump rising in his throat. A hot flush of anger made its way across his face, neck, and chest, but he pushed that down too. During his twenty years with the Chicago Police Department, he'd learned that anger clouded judgment and clouded judgment got people killed. Scottie's condition didn't present a life-and-death situation in the same way as an armed perp and pissed-off cops, but it triggered Jackson's fight-or-flight instinct. However, the absence of the tangle of tubes and wires typically associated with patients in a life-threatening state along with the steady rise and fall of Scottie's chest relieved him of the panic he'd felt moments earlier.

"Jackson!"

He whirled to see Sarah racing toward him. Before he could respond, the teen wrapped herself around him in a hug strong enough to draw a grunt. "How's it going, kiddo? I heard you had quite the exciting day."

Sarah loosened her grasp enough to respond with a lopsided shrug. Jackson marveled at the girl's reaction. She was her father's daughter. Tough as nails, and impossible to rattle. He rustled her hair and took the opportunity to gently extricate himself from her grip. Once free, he scanned the room for Scottie and Sarah's parents but saw only Marnie, slumped in a chair in a strategically chosen corner of the room that provided a view of Scottie's bed, the recovery room door, and Sarah's now vacant chair.

Marnie rose shakily from her chair. Jackson moved to meet her where she sat, but she waved him off and gave him a fierce hug, followed by a peck on the cheek.

"How's he doing?" He instantly regretted the question as a tear slid down Marnie's cheek.

"Good. At least good enough that they were comfortable letting him sleep."

"Where's Kirk?" Jackson asked, again searching the room, as if Kirk might be hiding somewhere within the tight confines.

"He's on his way, I guess." Marnie's lips tightened to a thin line.

"He left?"

"Got caught up with study hall, or church, or... something." Marnie sank into her chair.

"When are they letting him out of here?" He tilted his head toward Scottie.

"The doctor said tomorrow afternoon."

"That's good, right?"

Marnie's shoulders sagged, and her legs splayed out in front of her. The woman looked spent. "If you and Sarah want to head home, I can sit with Scottie."

"I couldn't ask you to do that."

"I'd be happy to. I could use a few minutes of quiet time."

Marnie hesitated. It was clear a battle raged inside her. Finally, she spoke. "You sure you'll be okay?"

Jackson leaned against a corner of Scottie's bed. "I'll be fine. Got my phone to keep me company, and there's a row of vending machines down the hall if I get hungry."

"I can stay too," Sarah chimed in.

"No. You have school tomorrow, and I'm sure you have homework."

Sarah huffed and heaved herself out of her chair.

"I'll save you some Sour Patch Kids," Jackson promised. "What kind do you like?"

The offer drew a smile from Sarah. "Watermelon."

"Watermelon, it is."

Marnie grabbed her purse and herded Sarah out of the room, but not before the girl gave Jackson a lazy wave. He moved to Marnie's vacated chair and plopped down next to the sleeping Scottie. As he watched the teenager sleep, his brow furrowed.

"What the hell did you see in that cave, kid?"

"Nothing."

Jackson nearly soiled himself. "How long have you been awake?"

Scottie opened his eyes and smiled. "Since you got here."

"Why didn't you say anything?"

Scottie struggled to a sitting position. "I didn't want Sarah and Mom fussing over me."

"That's what mothers do."

"Yeah, but Sarah gets this mopey expression when she looks at me." He frowned. "I think she thinks she's responsible for what happened."

"Why would you think that?"

"Because she said, 'I think I'm responsible for what happened.' "

Jackson laughed. "Very funny, smart ass."

Scottie grinned, but the expression quickly faded. "Is my dad coming?"

Jackson winced inwardly. "Your mom said he had something going on at church."

Scottie's lips trembled.

"Hey, I'm sure he wanted to be here."

"Yeah. Right."

Jackson locked eyes with the boy. "What's that supposed to mean?"

"I don't think he thinks I'm hurt."

"That's not true."

Tears streamed down the boy's face. "I'm not like him. Short of a broken limb, nothing ever kept him from a game, work, or church."

Jackson scoffed. "I know for a fact that isn't true."

Scottie's eyes narrowed. "Really?"

"Really." Jackson flashed a conspiratorial smile. "Junior year, he missed two games with a groin injury that he got trying to jump a park bench on a five-dollar bet. Don't let it get to you. Your dad is amazing, but he wasn't the Superman he thinks he was."

Scottie offered a faint smile and toyed with a frayed corner of his tan blanket.

"But that's not really what's bothering you. Is it?"

Scottie's eyes darted back and forth. "He'd be here if it were Sarah."

"Also, not true."

"Yes, it is." Anger flashed across Scottie's face. "Sarah's adventurous, brave, and into sports. She's the son he always wanted."

Jackson knew the boy was deeply hurt, but ignored the self-effacing comment. He knew firsthand that once self-pity took root, no amount of positive reinforcement could break its hold. The only path forward was redirection.

"I never heard exactly what happened in the cave. How about you get me up to speed?"

Scottie eyed Jackson suspiciously. "You didn't ask Sarah?"

"Not in front of your mother. She's freaked out enough already."

Scottie let out a long sigh. "I don't remember most of it."

"That's okay." Jackson smiled. "Tell me the parts you remember." He shifted in his chair, settling in. "Start from the beginning."

Scottie resumed his attack on the blanket, this time extracting a long beige thread, which he wrapped around his finger. "We were exploring the river. Just messing around. Sarah ran ahead like she always does, and I lost track of her. I shouted for her, but she didn't answer. I figured she was just being a jerk, but then I saw a hole in the ice…"

Jackson leaned forward in his chair.

"Tell me about the cave. And the noise. You don't think it was a bear?"

"Didn't sound like a bear. It sounded almost human."

"Human?" Jackson's head tilted to one side. "Did it speak?"

Scottie's smirk indicated he found Jackson's question ridiculous. "No. But it sounded grumpy. And it didn't just make a sound. It was longer, almost like a sentence, as if it were talking. Like an old man yelling at us to get off his lawn."

Jackson sat up.

"Exactly what kind of sound did it make?"

"Air. A whoosh of air. I didn't know what it was, I just knew we needed to get out of there." Scottie lay back in the bed, spent. He closed his eyes. Within seconds, his chest rose and fell in a steady cadence, and a soft snore rose from his nose.

"Sarah isn't the only brave one," Jackson whispered, then closed his eyes as well.

~

Sheriff Wyatt wiped his eyes on the sleeve of his jacket, momentarily losing sight of the road. In that moment, he turned the steering wheel to the left, sending his Ford F-150 across the yellow centerline. Thankfully, there had been no one on the opposite side of the highway, and he yanked it back without incident.

That was fortunate because Sheriff Wyatt, "Big Jess" to his friends, was toasted. Not to the extent he was an immediate danger to himself or others (the momentary blindness was unrelated to his state of intoxication) because drinking wasn't an issue for a man of his size. He held his liquor better than most. He hadn't been sleeping well, however, and had a cold, both of which sapped his strength and contributed to him being more inebriated than he realized.

The aged sheriff wiped his eyes again. The damn cold was making his eyes water, and the wind whipping in his window only made things worse. He'd lowered the window a smidge to keep himself awake on the drive home, and the sliver of a breeze was hitting him square in the peepers. He'd tried to adjust the window, but it didn't help. He couldn't find a happy medium. Any farther down and there was too much air, any less, and the heater negated the cold night air's sobering effect. Given the choice between two evils, Wyatt chose cold air in the face, figuring it was easier to contend with watering eyes if he wanted to stay awake.

As he stared into the night, Wyatt gripped the steering wheel, frustrated. He'd told Conservation Officer Bennett he was headed home to drink until the shakes went away, but he'd told a half-truth. He'd drunk until the shakes went away, but not at home. He'd stopped by the Blue Turkey Tap for a quick beer and ended up yakking it up with Joanie, the pretty redhead bartender, and drinking for free most of the night. All because he didn't want to be alone after leaving that cave. It had given him the willies.

Ironically, Jackson's presence in the cave had freaked Wyatt out more than being alone. He had struggled with claustrophobia since childhood, and his size only made him more sensitive to small spaces. Sure, the cave's cramped quarters bothered him more than he liked to admit, but the DNR officer sharing the space only added to his discomfort. The clincher, though, had been the idea that a bear could have shown up at any moment.

Not that he was scared of a bear. He wasn't. He feared the bear's bulk. Another body in that tight space would have been more than Wyatt could have tolerated. The mere thought of the three of them together had caused him to sweat, and he'd had to get out. Another minute in that cave, and Wyatt might have turned Agnes on himself.

Wyatt forced all thoughts of the cave to the recesses of his mind and wiped at his eyes yet again. His watery vision cleared just long enough for him to spot a shape on the opposite side of the highway. At the speed he was traveling, the shape zipped through his field of vision in an instant, but he was sure he'd seen something or someone in the ditch.

He laid his foot on the brake, but the Big Ford would require another one thousand feet before slowing enough for Wyatt to turn around. That gave him time to reconsider, which he did. "Screw it." He lifted his foot off the brake pedal. "Probably just a poacher." He was a hunter himself and appreciated the service hunters provided by thinning the herds, especially given that chronic wasting disease infected a large portion of the deer population.

"Why go through the trouble of giving the guy a hard time, especially given my condition? The man was just trying to score a few venison steaks and some deer jerky." Convinced he'd made the right call, Wyatt aimed his truck straight ahead, not giving the poacher or his purloined deer a second thought.

KIRK REGARDED the coffee vending machine with disdain. Unlike the coffee maker at home, this one was complicated, and he found the number of blends, roasts, and creamer options overwhelming. Flustered and frustrated, he punched a button and watched as a paper cup descended and quickly filled with steaming brown liquid. He moved the clear plastic door aside to retrieve the cup when he heard footsteps behind him.

"Nice of you to show up."

Kirk whirled at the sound of Jackson's voice. His friend stood before him, rumpled and unshaven. "You look like you just rolled out of bed."

"That's because I just rolled out of bed. If you want to call a hard plastic chair a bed."

"Yeah, sorry." Kirk shifted the scalding cup of coffee from one hand to the other. "I got tied up. Thanks for filling in."

Jackson's eyelashes fluttered indignantly.

Kirk recognized this as a sign he'd offended the weary man. "Welcome to the family," he said with a laugh and a boyish grin, hoping to defuse the situation. "Sleepless nights are par for the course in the Campbell household."

"That's all you have to say?" Jackson's question dripped with disapproval.

Kirk flinched. Since Jackson's first year on campus at UW-Superior, Kirk had been the one to express disapproval.

He had taken Jackson under his wing, helping him navigate college life and cope with being away from home for the first time. Even now, thirty years later, despite Jackson's age, Kirk continued to look out for the younger man. Hell, without his help, Jackson would probably still be unemployed. The lack of gratitude triggered him. "What the hell is up your ass?" Kirk snapped.

Jackson jabbed a thumb toward Scottie's room. "Your son is in there hurting, and you're out here getting coffee like nothing's happened."

"The doctor said he's going to be fine. It was just a concussion."

Jackson scoffed. "Maybe so, but Scottie isn't a soldier, Kirk. You can't expect him to gut it out. He heard something in that cave that scared the hell out of him, and instead of recovering from his injuries or the emotional trauma, he's in there beating himself up because he thinks he can't measure up to the great Kirk Campbell."

Kirk craned his neck toward Jackson in a display of aggression. "Hold on. I appreciate you watching out for Marnie and the kids while I was gone, but this is a family matter."

"A few seconds ago, you said I was family."

Kirk clamped his mouth shut. When his friend was right, he was right. There was no point in making excuses; Jackson would see right through them like he always did.

"I can't go in there."

"Why not?"

Kirk let the question hang, hoping Jackson might let him off the hook. No such luck. He squirmed as Jackson looked into his eyes, into his soul, demanding an answer.

"Seeing him in that bed like that...," Kirk squeezed his

hands into fists. "It makes me feel like I failed him. Like I let Scottie down."

"I understand. You're feeling—"

"Do you, Jack? Because last I checked, that isn't your child in there!"

He saw hurt register on Jackson's face and instantly regretted his words. He wanted to apologize, knew he should, but a contrite shrug was the best he could muster.

Jackson offered a tight smile. That smile, and thirty years of friendship informed Kirk that the slight might be forgiven but not forgotten, at least not anytime soon.

"This isn't about how *you* feel," Jackson said evenly. "It's about Scottie."

Kirk closed his eyes against the onset of tears and felt his oldest and dearest friend's hand on his shoulder. He was surprised at how reassuring the simple gesture felt.

"Go talk to your son, Kirk."

9

Jackson trudged past Doris, who looked up from her desk with the wary expression of an explosive ordinance specialist deciding whether to cut the blue or red wire. "Morning." Despite recent events, Doris's tone was warm with sympathy.

Jackson smiled. "Good morning, Doris." He continued toward his office, then stopped.

Lexy's cube was empty. "Is Lexy here?"

"Since seven a.m., just like every day."

Jackson glanced around but saw no sign of the junior officer. "Where is she?"

Doris slouched.

He returned to Doris' desk. "Doris..." She was a good woman and den mother to everyone in the office, including Jackson, but she had the sort of open-faced demeanor that made it impossible for her to hide her feelings.

"She's in a meeting." The woman refused to meet Jackson's eyes.

He placed both hands flat on Doris's desk and leaned in. Despite lingering guilt at having dressed her down the day before, he had no reservations about taking advantage of Doris's inability to withhold information. "Who is she meeting with?"

"I really shouldn't say."

"Never mind." Jackson turned away from the desk and started down the hallway. He took his time, knowing without looking that Doris was already beginning to fret and fidget as the information threatened to burst from her mouth. Jackson got only a few steps away before he heard a breathless whisper from behind.

"She's in your office."

Jackson whirled. "What?"

"With some scientist. I didn't catch his name." Doris's eyes fell. She looked guilty as hell, but Jackson believed her. She was a gossip, but she was no liar.

"Scientist?" Jackson's brow furrowed. "Did he say what he wanted?"

A constricted gurgle formed in Doris's throat as her eyes pleaded with Jackson not to force her to reveal even more information.

"It's alright, Doris. I'll ask her myself."

JACKSON OPENED the door of his office and saw Lexy sitting in the guest chair. Behind the desk was a short, rotund, bearded man with graying brown hair, in black-rimmed glasses. Neither acknowledged Jackson as he stepped inside. "So, is this VIP only, or can anybody come in?" He asked in a jovial tone, but his expression left no doubt as to his displeasure.

The short man rose from Jackson's chair. "You must be Officer Bennett. Alexandra has nothing but good things to say about you!" The man smiled broadly as he extended his hand.

Jackson found the man's effort as phony as his smile, but shook the outstretched hand nonetheless. "And you are?"

"This is Dr. Harlan Farley," Lexy gushed. "My old academic advisor from college. He works in the St. Paul DNR office."

"I certainly hope I don't appear as old as Alexandra makes me out to be," Harlan said, his voice saccharine sweet with false modesty.

"When you're Alexandra's age, everyone must seem old," Jackson mused.

"Was that some sort of Gen Z crack?" Lexy crossed her arms.

Jackson maintained eye contact with Harlan, who stood behind Jackson's desk as if he belonged there. "How can I help you, Dr. Farley?"

"Lexy tells me you need help with a case."

The condescension in the man's voice made the palms of Jackson's hands itch. He glared at Lexy, who offered a crooked grin in apology.

Harlan puffed out his chest, which had little effect given the considerable overhang of his belly. "I hope you aren't feeling threatened, Officer Bennett. Before I joined the DNR, I spent years teaching molecular biology at the University of Minnesota."

"Well, thank goodness, the cavalry has arrived." Jackson walked around the desk, past Harlan, who stood between the desk and the chair. "Pardon me." He sat down, rearranged the desk, and reclined in the chair, flashing a smile that put both his upper and lower teeth on display. "So, what brings you all the way from St. Paul, Dr. Farley?"

"Hold on." Lexy hurried to close the door and leaned against it.

Harlan, apparently unaware he'd just witnessed a primal territorial display, pushed his glasses back on his nose. His face flushed with excitement. "I have some thoughts about your blood samples."

"Let me guess, it wasn't a bear."

"Jackson..." Lexy shot her boss a warning glance.

Harlan continued, undaunted. "Oh, it was a bear. Regular old *Ursus americanus*. No doubt about that. Well, at least very little doubt." Harlan danced from foot to foot like a child on the verge of soiling himself. "Brown bear awakens from hibernation for battle to the death," he thundered, sounding P.T. Barnum under the big top. "Remarkable!"

"Harlan, you're going to give me a seizure," Lexy complained. "How much pop did you have on the way up here?"

"Just the one. But it was a twenty-ouncer."

Jackson rapped on the desk. "Is someone going to tell me what's going on, or am I going to have to break out the taser?"

Harlan laughed. "All in good time, Officer Bennett, but before we continue, could you do me the favor of answering a few questions?"

"Harlan, I don't think—"

"It's okay, Lex. I've waited this long; I can wait a few more minutes." Jackson sounded calm even as his jaw tightened. "Go ahead, Dr. Farley."

"Where exactly did you find the samples?"

"In a bear cave."

"You mean a den," Harlan corrected.

"Pardon?"

"Bears don't hibernate in caves. Caves are spacious and

cold. Dens are small and cozy. They conserve heat and offer protection from attack. A bear would just as soon hole up in US Bank Stadium as seek shelter in a cave. You may have been thinking of bats."

"What is it with you people and bats?" Jackson muttered.

"To the naked eye, both samples would have appeared identical," Harlan continued, ignoring Jackson's comment. "I must say, given the long odds of two bears being active in the same area in the middle of winter, the fact that a conservation officer would think to collect two separate samples is nothing short of remarkable."

Jackson forced another insincere smile. Although Harlan had phrased his comment like a compliment, Jackson recognized it as a thinly veiled insult. Regardless, the former professor had driven a long way and was doing him a favor. At the very least, he could try to be cordial.

"Experience."

Harlan raised an eyebrow.

"The blood pattern," Jackson continued. "Splotches and drips. I've seen it before." Harlan's lips parted, but Jackson cut him off. "I've seen fights. Lots of them. Knife fights, fist fights, gun battles. In those situations, both sides take their licks, as opposed to a murder scene, where one side is the aggressor, and the other is the victim. In a fight, both sides bleed. That's how it was in the cave. One side bled profusely, leaving puddles of blood. The other bled in drips and dribbles, like they were injured, but not fatally. One of them lived to fight another day."

"That's a great deal of presupposition, Officer Bennett."

"There was a great deal of blood. That's why I reached out. I was hoping your spectrograph might sort things out."

Harlan gasped. "My department does not use spectrographs. We employ a DNA sequencer."

Jackson shrugged. "Spectrograph. Sequencer. What's the difference?"

The scientist's nose wrinkled with disdain. "A vibrational spectroscope uses infrared light to identify and analyze chemicals in the blood sample using a series of specific algorithms. Such analysis can quickly reveal what sort of animal the blood might belong to."

"Might?"

Harlan nodded. "A good vibrational spectroscope can determine the source of the blood, animal versus human, cat versus dog, cow versus...bear. What it cannot determine is species—tiger versus lion, garter snake versus rattlesnake. You need a sequencer to make that sort of precise determination. For example, to distinguish *Ursus americanus* from *Ursus arctos horribilis*, one needs to get down to the genetic—"

"Did you identify the animals or not?"

Harlan cleared his throat. "As I was saying, analysis of DNA involves a significant amount of data, enough information, in fact, to determine whether another *Ursus* attacked your carcass."

"Can't we just show him what's in the garage?" Lexy whined.

"What's the point?"

Lexy threw up her hands. "Isn't that why we sent the samples to St. Paul? To get someone else's opinion?"

"I doubt he'd be interested in anything other than the sound of his own voice."

Harlan let out an indignant snort. "Alexandra, it's been wonderful seeing you, but this was obviously a waste of time." He retrieved his jacket from the coat hook and opened the door.

Lexy slammed her hands on Jackson's desk and leaned in until they were nose to nose.

"Show him the goddamned bear."

LEXY AND HARLAN smirked at each other as Jackson struggled with the straps holding the tarp in place over the bed of his truck. Harlan shivered, blowing into his hands to keep them warm. "I hope this won't take long. I don't do well with the cold."

"I told you to bring gloves," Lexy chided.

"Got it!" Jackson yelled triumphantly as the last stubborn strap gave way, and he yanked the tarp from the truck bed. The bear carcass looked, in all its skeletal and sinewy splendor, like the world's angriest side of beef.

Harlan's hands dropped from his mouth. His eyes bugged as he gawked at the remains. "What in the fuckety fuck?" He peered at the carcass. "Is that *Ursus americanus*?"

"If by *Ursus americanus*, you mean 'big ass dead bear,' then, yes."

Lexy laughed as Harlan walked around the pickup. "What happened to it?"

Jackson perked up, happy to provide an answer. "Based on its condition—the lack of fur or flesh, I thought it might be hunters or poachers. But then we saw this..." Jackson grabbed the bear by the snout with both gloved hands and tugged, lifting the front quarter of the bear off the truck bed and revealing a massive gash down the bear's neck and shoulder. Raw flesh, ragged and torn, shrank away from the bone.

Harlan nearly leaped into the truck bed at the sight of the mutilated bear. After an extended inspection of the carcass in which his nose and mouth almost touched the dead animal, he looked at Jackson and Lexy. His eyes were bright with awe. "This animal appears to have been mauled, partially consumed, and field-dressed by its attacker. This is highly unusual."

"That's what I've been trying to tell you."

Lexy peered over Harlan's shoulder. "You think it was another black bear?"

Harlan offered an open-handed gesture, indicating he didn't know.

"What about *Ursus arctos horribilis*?"

Harlan dismissed the notion with another wave of his hand. "Other than zoos, there probably hasn't been a grizzly in Minnesota in fifty thousand years. It could have been *Canis Lupus*, but they don't typically take on mature bears, especially ones the size of this specimen."

"What about a mountain lion?" Jackson asked.

"A cougar?" Harlan shook his head. "Also, unlikely. Like *Canis Lupus*, *Puma Concolor* is more likely to attack the very young or the very old; cubs or sick or elderly animals, not a mature boar with no obvious signs of infirmity."

Jackson puzzled. "What do pigs have to do with this?"

Harlan and Lexy giggled like a pair of grade school kids. "You see, Officer Bennett, 'Boar' is the term applied to male bears," the scientist lectured. "Just as 'sow' is the term applied to female bears."

Jackson rubbed his face. He was no longer puzzled; he was just agitated. "Dr. Farley, did the sequencer offer a match or not?"

"Not in any useable fashion."

"But did it offer a match?"

"I just told you—"

"Match or not? It's a 'yes' or 'no' question."

Harlan's face clouded. "The results were anomalous, in a fashion that made the sample unidentifiable."

"So, it didn't offer a match?"

"No...I mean, yes. But it made no sense." Harlan glanced at Lexy, but she offered neither support nor assistance.

"Why not?"

The scientist pushed his glasses back on his face even though they hadn't moved. "Because the answer was... impossible."

"Impossible like a dinosaur? Or impossible like a unicorn?"

Lexy gave Jackson a stern look. He responded with a devilish grin.

"Perhaps."

"Perhaps?" Jackson was pouring it on now. He knew he was being petty, but the little man had gotten under his skin. Deep under. And he was in no mood to go easy on him.

"Yes. Although improbable might have been more appropriate."

"Okay. So, we agree the sequencer offered a match, albeit an improbable one?"

"That is correct."

"And what match did the sequencer offer?"

Harlan pulled at his jacket collar. "Actually, it offered several: the Opah, Great White Shark, Komodo Dragon, and the Argentinian Black and White Tegu." His forehead glistened with sweat. "However, the percentage matches were minuscule, less than one percent in the best case. Given the Opah and Great White are native to oceans, I assumed it was an error."

"You made a mistake?" Jackson's eyes shone with mischief.

"No!" Harlan sputtered. "The *sequencer* made a mistake.

Rather than defaulting to 'unidentifiable' or 'match not found,' it produced an inaccurate reading."

Jackson crossed his arms. "We've already established the sequencer's response was improbable rather than impossible. Are you now saying the sequencer's response was wrong?"

"If I remember correctly, the blood arrived in a pen cap and cylinder. Hardly ideal for collecting untainted samples."

"I would have thought your precious sequencer could screen out a little bit of dirt."

The biologist scowled as if personally attacked. "The sequencer accounted for trace amounts of environmental contaminants."

"Then what did it come back with?"

Harlan hesitated. "Are you familiar with the Argentinian Black and White Tegu?"

"He's not a biologist, Harlan," Lexy interjected. "I think we can assume he is not familiar with the Argentinian Black and White Tegu."

Harlan addressed Jackson directly. "The Argentinian Black and White Tegu, also known as *Salvator Merianae*, is, as the common name suggests, a black and white lizard indigenous to South America."

Jackson shook his head. "Sheriff Wyatt and I found no evidence of a lizard."

"There is absolutely no reason you would. While Tegus are an invasive species in parts of the continental United States, the odds against encountering a live Tegu in Minnesota outside of a zoo, especially this time of year, are astronomical."

Jackson glanced over his shoulder toward the door separating the garage from the office. The last thing he needed was Doris peering in and seeing the three of them huddled around the grotesque carcass. "So, what's our next step?"

"I'd like to visit the site."

"Why? I already examined the cave—den."

"And I'm sure you did a wonderful job..." Sarcasm dripped from Harlan's words. "But I'd prefer to see for myself."

JACKSON, Lexy, and Harlan stooped inside the cramped cave. Jackson's return trip was better than the first for two reasons. For one, the body heat from the three of them and their high-powered flashlights made for a more comfortable environment. Second, Lexy brought another weapon to the fight in case an inhabitant, bear, or otherwise, returned to the cave.

These additional comforts allowed Jackson to concentrate on the task at hand, a luxury his discomfort at being alone in the cave hadn't allowed the first time around. Of course, the fact that it was Harlan rather than Jackson crawling around on the cave floor, his face mere inches from the ground, made for an easier trip as well.

Harlan looked up from the dirt and mud floor. "There should be more of a mess in here." Concern creased his forehead.

Lexy trained her flashlight on the cave walls, revealing lingering blood stains and deep gashes. "Looks plenty messy to me."

"Compared to a human dwelling, yes, but for a cave where a carnivore fed, slept, and fought, there should be more evidence of habitation. Where are the bones from the Tegu? The scat?"

"Then we're going with Tegu?" Jackson quipped.

"I hope not. I had my heart set on calling our mystery creature Fred."

Harlan cleared his throat. "Could we get down to business, please?"

Jackson and Lexy straightened like chastised schoolchildren, each stifling a smirk. In the near dark, faces illuminated from below like villains in a black-and-white film, their already exaggerated expressions were further distorted into ghoulish caricatures. Their funhouse mirror visages caused Lexy to burst into laughter.

Harlan climbed to his feet, haughtily brushed the front of his pants, and held his flashlight under his face, creating his own funhouse mirror appearance that sent Lexy and Jackson into hysterics. Harlan huffed and waited for the two law enforcement officers to stop giggling. When they finally gathered themselves, he took a deep breath and continued. "Where are the remains?"

"What are you talking about? You inspected the remains yourself."

Harlan shook his head. "Yes, you provided skeletal remains, but even assuming the bear you showed me was the same one engaged in battle here, what happened to the rest? The entrails, the ligaments, the skin, and the fur? Did you dispose of them?"

"No. All I found was the blood."

"Harlan shined his flashlight at the cave floor and sighed. "Just as I feared. I came here hoping for answers, but all I've found are more questions."

Lexy laid a hand on Harlan's shoulder. "Sorry, we got distracted. We want to figure this out as much as you do."

Harlan's lower lip jutted out in a pout, but when his former student held his gaze, he turned to Jackson, who responded with a solemn nod. Apparently placated, Harlan pushed his glasses back on his nose. "Whatever it is, we have to find it."

"And how do you propose we do that?"

"I have no idea. I spend my days in temperature-controlled environments. We need someone who knows more about animals than their Latin names."

"You mean a real man," Lexy teased, suppressing a smile. Jackson scowled, but Harlan only nodded.

"Yes," he agreed. "Do you know any?"

FRIEDA'S COFFEE and Whatnot was empty except for Lexy, Jackson, Harlan, Tim, the gregarious proprietor, and a smattering of customers. Lexy, Jackson, and Harlan sat at the counter while Tim hovered on the other side, a pot of coffee at the ready. "I already told you I had a tracker. You never listen."

"In Jackson's defense, you do talk a lot." Lexy quipped.

Tim's face bunched up like that of a wounded puppy. "Gee, Lexy, that wasn't at all hurtful."

"She's not wrong, Tim," Jackson chimed in. "You're a walking infomercial."

Tim topped off Jackson's cup of coffee. "Nice way to treat the guy who just did you a favor. I could have set you up with some weekend warrior, but I sent you to Charlie."

Jackson stiffened. "You *sent* us to Charlie?"

Tim nodded. "I told you. Charlie doesn't work with just anybody."

Jackson checked his watch. "You sure this guy is the ace you say he is? Because he's getting off to a rocky start."

"I bet Charlie would say the same about you."

Jackson frowned. "What's that supposed to mean?"

A Native woman in her forties approached the counter. She acknowledged Lexy with a nod and ignored the rest of the group as she laid down a ten-dollar bill. "Great pie, Tim. Best on the North Shore." She smiled warmly.

"Keep your money." Tim pushed the ten dollars across the counter.

"Okay, but I don't know how you make any money giving pie away for free."

"I charge tourists double," he whispered.

The woman laughed and left the counter, giving Jackson a disinterested glance as she headed for the door. Jackson and Harlan stared after her as she pulled a camo-colored stocking cap from her coat pocket and pulled it over her long black hair. As she pushed the door open, Tim called after her, "See you around, Charlie."

Jackson gawked. Tim crossed his arms and nodded toward the departing woman. "Better hurry. Like I said, she's in high demand."

JACKSON BURST from the shop to see Charlie climbing into a Jeep Grand Cherokee. "Hey!" Jackson called after her. "Hold up!" Charlie waited, half in and half out of the vehicle, as Jackson approached. He leaned against the Jeep and took a moment to catch his breath, then, noticing Charlie's raised eyebrow, removed his elbow from the Jeep's roof. "We had a bit of a mix-up back there. We were supposed to discuss a job."

Charlie mustered an insincere smile. "I've decided to pass. Thanks anyway." She pulled on the driver's side door.

"What? Why?" Jackson was baffled by the woman's aloofness and direct nature.

"You're not my type."

Jackson laughed. "This isn't a date. I need help locating a dangerous animal."

"Then you *really* aren't my type. I don't track animals down to be killed just because someone finds their presence inconvenient."

"Then why track them at all?"

"For study, conservation efforts." Charlie's tone was heavy with righteous indignation.

"I never said I was going to kill it. Maybe we'll relocate it to a more hospitable location."

Horror crossed Charlie's face. "Relocation? You may as well just kill the animal."

Jackson huffed. "Look. I have an animal control problem. No one has been hurt, but we are dealing with a large, powerful, aggressive animal."

"Has it attacked a human?"

"Not that I know of," Jackson admitted. "But I'd like to find the creature before it does."

"Creature?"

"It's another word for animal." He fought back a grin.

She stepped away from the Jeep. "Why did you use that word?"

"No reason," Jackson shrugged, suddenly feeling self-conscious as the woman eyed him with a gaze so intense he found it difficult to meet her eyes.

"You don't know what it is."

"Of course we do," Jackson objected. "It's a bear. Probably."

Charlie's face brightened with an expression approaching joy.

"No. You don't. If you did, you would have scrounged up some yahoo with a 12-gauge and a twelve-pack and hunted it down already."

"Then you'll do it?"

Charlie considered, tapping one booted foot. "You got a recent location?"

"No, but—" Charlie turned for her vehicle. "Hold on. Gimme thirty seconds." He pulled out his cell phone. "Please."

Charlie waited as Jackson dialed the phone and held it to his ear. "Doris? Any chatter on dead or missing animals? Pets? Livestock? Anything?" Jackson held up one finger. His eyebrows arched. "Really? Schroeder? You got a name and address? Perfect. Give the guy a call. Tell him we'll be stopping by tomorrow." He gave Charlie a thumbs-up. "Thanks, Doris, you're a peach." Jackson ended the call, beaming.

Charlie sighed. "As long as you promise we're not going out there to kill it." Jackson nodded. "Fine." She sighed again. "See you at 0400 hours."

"0400 hours tomorrow?" He whined.

"Large predators can easily travel twenty miles a day. Every second counts." She climbed into the Jeep and started the engine.

"Hey," Jackson called, tapping on the window as if he'd just remembered something.

Charlie rolled the window down, and Jackson leaned in. "Why did you walk out without even talking to me?"

"It was a test."

He blinked stupidly.

"I was in Frieda's the whole time. Never once did you consider I might be the tracker."

Jackson gawked. "Wait. You left because you thought I was being sexist?"

"Weren't you?"

Jackson crossed his arms. "So, you knew who I was the minute I walked in, but didn't introduce yourself."

"Maybe. At worst, that makes me rude."

"Except that you purposely neglected to introduce yourself. You set a trap. In which case, I'm not so sure I'm the asshole here."

Charlie's eyes narrowed. "I never said you were an asshole."

"No. But you implied as much."

Charlie's face clouded. She strummed the steering wheel with her fingers. After what seemed like forever, her face cleared, and she thrust her hand through the window with an urgency that made Jackson take a step back. "Charlotte Battice. You may call me Charlie."

Jackson gave Charlie's hand a firm shake. "Jackson Bennett, DNR Conservation Officer, and occasional unintentional asshole."

Charlie rolled up her window and backed out of her parking spot.

Jackson watched, chuckling as the Jeep pulled onto the highway. Once Charlie was out of sight, he shook his head. "0400 hours."

"IN THE MORNING?" Harlan exclaimed, wearing a pained expression. "That's crazy. I won't be able to get to St. Paul and back before then. Even if I could, I'd have to drive all night."

"Then I guess you can't go. Sorry." Although Harlan seemed friendlier since they'd met, Jackson had yet to forgive the man for going out of his way to condescend in his office. As far as he was concerned, Harlan could return to St. Paul and his beloved DNA sequencer, leaving the real work to Jackson.

"You can crash at my place." Both men looked at Lexy. "On the couch," she clarified.

"But I have work tomorrow," Harlan whined. "Besides, I'm not equipped for a walkabout."

"He has a point. Between the weather and the terrain, it could be a tough couple of days for him without proper clothing or gear."

"What about you?" Lexy looked Jackson up and down. "You don't have proper 'gear' either. You think you'll survive out there in your DNR issue jacket and orthopedic inserts?" She looked at Harlan. "And you. You're the head of the forensic studies department. Take a freaking vacation day. Take two. Hell, take a week. What else are you going to do with them, fly to Bermuda with Rachel?"

Jackson shot Lexy a questioning glance.

"Rachel's great!" Lexy exclaimed. "Smart, funny, beautiful. Did I mention she's a cat?"

Jackson burst into laughter as Harlan's mouth pursed into a line.

HARLAN STEPPED into a small apartment that bordered on claustrophobic. Although minuscule, it was modern and stylish, with white cabinets capped with chrome knobs; granite countertops, shiny new appliances, hi-tech window dressings, and electrical outlets outfitted with USB charging stations. It was a handsome apartment, but it was also a mess, mostly due to the clothes strewn over chairs, the couch, and even the dining room table.

"This is a lovely space, or at least it could be." Harlan dropped a half dozen shopping bags on the floor. "How can you afford it on a DNR salary?"

Lexy set an oversized cup of soda on the kitchenette counter. "It's a first-floor studio apartment with a sliding glass door. I get a break on rent because of the high possibility of someone breaking in and killing me in my sleep."

"I wouldn't worry about that. They'd have to find you under the piles of clothes first." Harlan looked around. "On the other hand, hiding your body would be a simple matter."

"I wasn't expecting company."

"I imagine not." He brushed aside a bra and sat down on the couch. "Still single, I assume?" His comment drew a huff from Lexy. "I'm not prying. I'm just concerned."

"Yeah, well, don't be." Lexy perched atop a barstool next to the kitchen counter.

Harlan sighed. "I'll admit you seem happy, but is this all you want out of life?"

"It's not like there are a lot of options in a town this size."

"I'm not talking about your dating life, Alexandra." His voice took on a parental tone. "I'm talking about your career. You have a sharp and inquisitive mind. How can you possibly be satisfied reporting to a man like Bennett? I can't imagine he challenges you intellectually."

"You don't know anything about him."

"I know men like him. My father was a man like him. Myopic, thin-skinned, threatened by anyone who exhibited an interest in things outside his sphere of knowledge."

"Are you any different?" Lexy asked. "You're the smartest person I've ever met, Harlan, but you don't know who won the Super Bowl last year, or the Oscar for Best Picture, or who replaced Matt Lauer on the Today Show."

Harlan scoffed. "That's because those things aren't important."

"They aren't important to *you*, so in your mind, they don't matter. That is the very definition of myopic. And this hostility you have toward Jackson? That's based on what? The fact that he doesn't know the Latin name for a mountain lion?"

Harlan fell silent but eventually met Lexy's gaze. "You care about him."

"Of course I do!" She threw up her hands. "Jackson is my friend. Just like you're my friend. In a few hours, I'm supposed to go on an expedition with the two people I respect most, but I don't want to do that; I *won't* do that if you're going to be at each other's throats."

A smile crossed Harlan's face. Lexy puzzled at his expression. "What?"

"You used some form of 'I' four times in a single sentence. I never realized how much of a narcissist you are."

Exasperation crossed Lexy's face. "Duh? It's like we've never met."

Harlan nodded toward the pile of shopping bags. "Thank you for helping me prepare for the expedition. It was a great expression of selfless behavior."

Lexy shrugged. "I got to go shopping, and it didn't cost me a penny. Besides, I don't want you to freeze to death out there. Who would take care of Rachel?"

Harlan's eyes widened. "Speaking of which..." He grabbed his cell phone and dialed. He placed the phone against his ear and turned his back to Lexy. "Hi, Laura? It's Harlan. Listen, I'm out of town for work the next couple of days and was hoping you could swing by my place and make sure Rachel has fresh food and water."

He listened as the voice on the other end of the line

responded, then said, "Of course, you can spend the night. I'm sure Rachel would enjoy the company." The voice chimed in again, and Harlan replied, "I'll miss you, too," and hung up to see Lexy staring at him.

"I guess I'm not as pathetic as you'd like to believe."

Jackson, dressed in sweats, a ratty T-shirt, and a pair of hiking socks that doubled as slippers, hummed as he retrieved a bottle of ginger ale from the fridge and made the short walk from the kitchen to the dining room where he grabbed a Styrofoam food container and plopped down on the living room couch with a contented sigh.

His rented house consisted of one bedroom and a partially finished basement, but it was cozy and clean. The kitchen fixtures, flooring, windows, and woodwork were new. Sure, he could see the back door from the front, and the living room, dining room, and kitchen combined were smaller than the living room in the house he and Tanya had shared, but the rent was cheap and leasing rather than buying had given him options if the job at the DNR hadn't worked out.

Jackson picked up a television remote and aimed it at the 42-inch television on the wall. "Alright, let's do this." The on-screen menu appeared on the screen, and the cursor moved from one channel listing to the next, eschewing local stations and a smattering of national cable news providers before stopping on a sports channel.

Jackson smiled as the green seats of a basketball arena bathed the living room in an emerald glow. An excited announcer's voice blared from the television. "The crowd is getting restless here in Ferrell Center! While Baylor has cut the lead to twelve, time is running out for the tenth-ranked Bears to prove they deserve their ranking..."

He opened the Styrofoam container, revealing a slab of ribs sticky with BBQ sauce, a side of steaming collard greens, and a yellow-gold mountain of macaroni and cheese. He wrenched the cap on the ginger ale, releasing a "hiss" of carbonated air, and lifted it to his mouth. He gulped half the bottle and let out a throaty belch devoid of self-consciousness. As he waved away the eructation, the announcer's voice continued to blare from the television.

"...out of the time out, the Bears push the ball up the court, and Baker's three is good from the corner. It looks like the comeback is on!"

Jackson rested his feet on a ratty ottoman and reveled in his solitary bachelor existence, but only briefly. The house, which usually felt cramped despite him being the only resident, suddenly felt cavernous. No, not cavernous. Empty. No roommate, teammates, partner, wife, or adopted family in the Campbells. For only the second time in months, he was alone. The solitude that had brought joy only moments ago now brought only emptiness.

And memories of Tanya.

Tanya and Jackson met at a City of Chicago gala, where Tanya, still the shiny new toy in the Chicago Police Department's public relations toy box, had been trotted out to present the Police Chief an award for efforts to clean up the city. Jackson had also been ordered to attend the event by his superior, but did so under protest, fully aware it was a PR moment for the department.

While standing at the bar during an intermission from

music and dancing, Tanya approached Jackson and asked if he was part of the dog and pony show. Jackson understood precisely what she'd meant and, conscious of the many ears in attendance, commented only that he was there to "make sure the photographs matched the brochure." When Tanya gave him a quizzical look, he explained that department brochures often showed a level of diversity wildly out of proportion with actual department statistics.

Tanya had laughed heartily, but soon after, the smile faded as she leaned in. "I don't care why they trotted us out. If it helps me reach my goals, I'll do this six days a week and twice on Sundays." Jackson scanned Tanya's face to see if she was serious and noticed that while the smile had returned, the joy had not.

After noting the delicate bone structure, clear milk chocolate skin, high-wattage smile, and amber eyes, he asked what Tanya's goals were. He was shocked and delighted to discover she shared his belief that one way to address the growing distrust between black communities and the officers who policed them was to hire people familiar with the communities they served.

Jackson knew that an officer didn't need to live within the city limits or be of a particular ethnicity to be effective. Still, he felt that if he wasn't willing to join the officers who interacted with the black community daily, he had no standing to complain about the tenuous relationship.

As the night progressed, Jackson and Tanya eschewed the festivities, remaining in their assigned seats long enough for Tanya to present the Police Chief's award and pose for the customary photo ops before retreating to the most secluded corner of the Four Seasons' Lakeview Ballroom to continue their discussion.

Despite a ten-year age gap and differing backgrounds—

Jackson was the first in his family to earn a college degree while Tanya was the product of two high school teachers—the pair found common ground. Both knew that by joining law enforcement, they were subjecting themselves to scorn from both the black and law enforcement communities. They would find their blackness challenged at every turn, along with their allegiance to their police families.

After one too many complimentary drinks, Jackson admitted to Tanya that after twelve years on the force, the tug-of-war between the two worlds had taken a toll. But as their conversation stretched into the night, he found himself reinvigorated by the intelligent, determined, and good-looking young officer.

Tanya, it turns out, was the quintessential high achiever. At thirty years of age at the time they met, she had already been a cop for eight years. After graduating from Hampton College, she attended the Virginia State Police Academy and joined the State Police, where she served for four years. Following the widely publicized shooting of an unarmed woman in Chicago, Tanya applied to the Chicago Police Department as part of the department's efforts to implement changes to the department's policies and practices.

She quickly established herself as a rising star who climbed the ranks to become a detective in a fraction of the time it had taken Jackson. In his defense, Jackson was already thirty by the time he joined the CPD, having spent years working on a Master's degree in Criminology while attending the University of Illinois-Chicago, but Jackson didn't mind. He immediately recognized that Tanya was right for him and, after only six months of dating, asked her to marry him. Their partnership had been a successful and solid one. Right up until the day it wasn't.

He aimed the remote at the television and was about to kill the image when he realized two new teams had replaced the two he'd been watching. He glanced at the bottom of the screen where the graphic showed less than two minutes remaining in the first half. He'd spent nearly an hour reminiscing about Tanya, but it had felt like only minutes.

Jackson turned off the television and surveyed the couch. A wasteland of take-out containers and empty soft drink bottles spread out before him. He considered straightening up the mess but decided against it. 0400 hours would come quickly and he feared the effort of picking up the living room would take him from his drowsy state to wide awake, making it impossible for him to get any sleep before heading out the following morning. He stretched out and yanked the dangling metal chain hanging from the lamp next to the couch. The living room went dark except for the slow fading afterglow of the lamp's lightbulb and the Cylon-like single point of red light emanating from the bottom of the television.

10

Jackson sat in his idling pickup, sipping coffee out of a thermos and tapping his fingers on the steering wheel. It was early or late, depending on one's perspective, but regardless, it was pitch black. The sun had yet to even consider breaking the horizon, and here Jackson was fully dressed and preparing to head into the wilderness with a woman he didn't know, his capable but inexperienced employee, and an arrogant academic who looked like his only means of exercise was walking to and from a vending machine.

The worst part of it was that Jackson hated the cold. Absolutely, hated it. The numb fingers and toes, the cold car seats, the frozen nose hairs and eyelashes. No matter how many undershirts, wool socks, and pairs of thermal underwear he wore, he could never stay warm. He'd hated it in college, and he hated it now. "And yet," he thought ruefully, "here I am, back in the Northwoods, freezing my ass off." If it weren't for the incident in Chicago that left him black-listed in every law enforcement agency in the country, he would not have asked Kirk to put in a good word for him at the DNR.

"What a waste of money," he thought as he looked at his red parka with its faux fur-lined hood, insulated black ski pants, and Wheat Nubuck Timberland boots, all of which still had their price tags less than four hours ago. "Oh well, maybe I can return some of it," he thought. "How dirty could it get on a one-day excursion?"

He glanced at the dashboard clock. 3:45. Plenty of time for breakfast. He reached into a white paper bag and pulled out a cake donut. He had no sooner lifted the donut to his mouth when Charlie's Jeep pulled into the parking lot. Upon seeing the vehicle, Jackson looked down at his stomach and, after a moment's hesitation, put the donut back in the bag and stepped out of the truck.

Charlie alighted from her Jeep looking like she'd had a full eight hours of sleep, even though that was impossible given the early hour. As Jackson approached, she greeted him with barely a nod, but enough of a smile to be cordial. Before he could respond, the passenger door opened. Jackson frowned. Charlie had made no mention of anyone else joining the trip, and the presence of another person took him by surprise.

He wondered how he would explain the additional expense to Doris as a man in his twenties stepped out of the Jeep. The man reminded Jackson of an Abercrombie and Fitch model, with his perfectly groomed stubble and frat boy features, and blue eyes that were both striking and kind. The man saw Jackson staring, and a smile spread across his face, revealing perfectly straight, perfectly white teeth. The man removed one of his thick gloves and offered his bare hand. "You must be Officer Bennett."

Jackson shook the man's hand. "And you are?"

The man glanced at Charlie, wearing an accusatory frown.

"That's my brother Mattie. Matthew, when he's done something to piss me off. Sorry, I didn't mention him yesterday. He was supposed to be on a ski trip to Aspen, but it fell through at the last minute. I didn't want him playing video games on my couch for the next twenty-four hours, so I invited him along."

"Nice to meet you, Mattie," Jackson noted Charlie's dark hair, brown eyes, and toasted wheat complexion, comparing them to Mattie's Scandinavian features. Like the two sets of blood samples in the cave, they were not a match.

Charlie opened the Jeep's rear hatch and peered inside, eyes scanning a mound of backpacks, tents, and camping equipment. "What are you doing?" Jackson asked.

"Taking stock of our gear. Once we leave this parking lot, there's no turning back."

Jackson puzzled. "Didn't you do that before you left home?"

"Of course, but things get overlooked." She turned to Jackson, expression even, but her eyes hinted at amusement. "For instance, I noticed you don't seem to have brought tents. Where were you planning on sleeping?"

"I thought this was more of a day trip."

Charlie scoffed. "It's as long a trip as our quarry determines it is. Good thing for you; my crew brought three tents that sleep at least two people each." She turned back to the gear and resumed taking inventory.

Jackson turned to Mattie. "Is she always this intense?"

"She's a little groggy this morning. She's normally way worse."

Jackson chuckled, then, hearing yet another door open, moved to the far side of the Jeep. He peered around the vehicle to see a slim, bearded man with long reddish-blonde hair and a ruddy complexion step out of the rear passenger-side door. The man grinned upon seeing Jackson.

Jackson recognized that grin. It wasn't a friendly grin but a predatory one, the grin of someone scanning an opponent for weaknesses. The man spat a string of brown spittle onto the ground.

"You must be Ranger Rick."

Jackson blinked, genuinely confused. "Excuse me?" The man continued grinning, and Jackson noticed bits of chewing tobacco in his teeth.

"From Yogi the Bear. You're the park ranger, right?"

A wave of earthy menthol washed over Jackson; the stench of chewing tobacco was rank enough to make his empty stomach flip-flop.

"Quit being a dick, Jasper," Charlie said, in a tone that suggested being a dick was Jasper's default setting. "I realize it's second nature, but can you not do the dog-marking-his-territory thing just this once?" Jasper waved Charlie away and kept his eyes on Jackson.

"He knows I'm just kidding, don't you, Ranger Rick?"

Jackson eyed the man, assessing his height, weight, and build. He wanted an idea of what to expect if things got heated. The younger man was thin and wiry, like a coyote, and like a coyote, he was probably quick, strong, and more intelligent than he looked. "That's Ranger Bennett to you," Jackson said, forcing a smile that falsely hinted at goodwill.

"Suit yourself." The younger man's eyes narrowed. "But understand, we're the professionals." He gestured at Charlie, Mattie, and himself. "Things will go smoothly as long as you do what you're told."

Jackson's eyes met Jasper's. The mutual dislike was instantaneous. Jackson opened his mouth to respond but closed it again when he saw a pair of headlights tracking across the still-dark pavement. After one final assessment of Jasper, he turned to meet the approaching vehicle.

Harlan stepped out of Lexy's pickup, looking like a model from a Columbia outerwear catalog. His beige coat was long and cumbersome, with a seemingly endless number of pockets and a ring of faux fur around the edge of a sturdy hood. The coat would have looked fine on a trimmer man, but with Harlan's prairie dog physique, he looked like an empanada turned on end. Rounding out the ensemble were baggy, neon-yellow ski pants that clashed with his coat and sleek black boots better suited for a Park City film festival than the woods of Minnesota.

"Did you dress in the dark?" Jackson asked playfully.

Harlan looked down at his attire. "No. Why?"

Jasper shook his head and spat out another string of brown spittle. "Guess we know who the Red-shirt is." He snickered at Jackson as he headed back to Charlie's Jeep. "I was kinda hoping that would be you, Ranger Rick."

Jackson looked to Harlan for an explanation, but Mattie chimed in. "It's a Star Trek reference. The guys in red shirts usually die." Mattie glanced in the departed Jasper's direction. "I'm surprised Jasper even knows what that means."

"I'd be surprised if your guy Jasper can even spell Star Trek," Jackson quipped.

Mattie's face took on a pained, apologetic expression. "He's not my guy. He's my sister's ex. And in case you haven't noticed, he can be kind of a jerk."

"Oh, I noticed." Jackson moved toward Lexy's truck.

Lexy unloaded gear from the back of her pickup, making neat piles on the ground. She was dressed similarly to Harlan, but on her, everything looked perfect. From the cut to the colors, her coat, snow pants, and boots, although not color coordinated, were selected with care.

"Nice outfit, when's the photo shoot?"

Lexy fixed her gaze on Jackson. "Remember when you asked me to point out when you're being a sexist jerk? Well..."

"What? You look like a model in a ski magazine."

"Did you comment on Harlan's outfit?"

"Of course, I did." Jackson nodded toward Harlan. "Why would you let him go out in public looking like that?"

Lexy resumed unloading the pickup. "I went to the food court to get a soft pretzel, and by the time I got back, he'd already bought and paid for all of that. It's like he didn't even try it on."

Jackson laughed, but his amusement quickly disappeared as Jasper appeared like an unwelcome apparition. The man looked Lexy up and down unabashedly.

"I don't believe we've met." Jasper turned to Jackson. "Aren't you going to introduce us?"

Jackson looked as if he'd swallowed a teaspoon of castor oil. "Lexy, this is Jasper. Jasper, this is Conservation Officer Richards."

"So, you're with Ranger Rick?"

Lexy angled her head to one side. "No. He's with—"

"Great. You can ride with us!"

"Actually..."

She looked to Jackson, who smirked but offered no assistance. She opened her mouth to respond but abandoned the effort when Charlie barked from across the parking lot.

"Jasper, I don't see the flare gun. Did you pack it?"

"It's in the cubby!"

"I already looked there," Charlie yelled, this time, her voice tinged with annoyance.

Jasper huffed. "Hold on, I'm coming. I got everything in there just the way I like it." He turned to Lexy. "See you on the trail."

Jasper sauntered off.

"Is that guy for real?" Lexy said as soon as Jasper was out of sight. "I didn't think they made that model anymore."

Jackson chuckled as Charlie appeared. "You about ready?"

"As soon as Jasper finds the flare gun." Charlie offered Lexy her hand. "We haven't met. I'm Charlie."

"Lexy." She shook Charlie's outstretched hand.

"Are you with the DNR?"

"Don't let the tailored hiking gear fool you," Jackson said. "Lexy is—"

"I was talking to Lexy." Charlie shot Jackson an icy look that left the man open-mouthed.

"Yes, I am." Lexy stifled a grin.

"Guess we're following you." Charlie started toward her Jeep. Jackson watched her go. Lexy followed his line of sight and elbowed him in the ribs.

"Well, that had to be embarrassing for you."

～

Jackson glanced at Lexy, who snored softly as she leaned against the passenger side door, her head cocked at an uncomfortable angle. He smiled. She probably would have been horrified to learn he'd heard her snore, but he wouldn't hold it against her. With her face smashed against the window, it was a wonder she could breathe at all.

He resisted the urge to aim for a pothole, resulting in Lexy's face bouncing off the window and waking her from her slumber. Chuckling at the thought, he knew she'd have done the same had their positions been reversed. He took one last glance and returned his eyes to the road.

Lexy was a pain in the butt, but she was a good person, an excellent officer, and an even better friend. She kept him in line, ensuring he didn't eat or drink too much or let his temper and mouth get him in trouble. She especially excelled at ensuring he evolved with the times. She frequently urged him to listen to the latest music, see the newest movies, and stay up to date with the latest slang terms. Lexy refused to let him descend into curmudgeonly old age, and he appreciated her efforts.

He glanced at the rearview mirror, expecting to see Charlie's Jeep. The mirror, however, displayed a reflection of Harlan, his head down, chin to his chest, eyes closed, and mouth open. Shuddering at the image, he adjusted the mirror until his line of sight settled on Charlie's Jeep.

The Jeep's tinted windshield made it difficult to make out much more than a silhouette behind the wheel, but Jackson couldn't take his eyes off the dark image. It wasn't until his truck's wheels tracked the angle of an upcoming curve that Jackson returned his attention to the road. He yanked sharply on the steering wheel, and the truck's tires screeched as they aligned themselves with the highway.

Lexy stirred but didn't wake, and Jackson cleared his throat, embarrassed he'd risked his life and those of his passengers to steal a peek at a woman he barely knew and could scarcely see. He shook off the moment and placed both hands firmly on the wheel, taking his eyes off the road only long enough to read a road sign. *Welterton Township 4 miles.*

"Hey," Lexy said, voice gravelly from her nap.

Jackson glanced over.

"Just checking to see if you're okay."

"Why wouldn't I be?"

Lexy peered through the windshield at the passing snow-kissed trees. "I'm sorry about how Professor Farley and I acted." When Jackson didn't respond, Lexy angled toward him.

"I feel like I ditched you at a bar and left with some other guy. Harlan and I are old friends, and I really thought he could help."

"First of all, that's a truly disturbing analogy. Second, your relationship with Harlan is none of my business."

"Still..."

"Still nothing. I'm your boss, not your parole officer. Who you choose to associate with is none of my business."

Lexy eyed Jackson, but when he didn't elaborate, she resumed staring out of the window.

"Although, you guys were kinda assholes, with your *Canis Lupus*, *Puma Concolor*, and *Ursus Horribleness* or whatever the hell it's called."

"Oh, and was that not you who said, 'I've seen fights. Lots of them'?" Lexy teased, doing a spot-on impression of Jackson. "I thought you were going to whip it out and ask for a ruler."

Jackson winced. "Did your parents not hug you enough growing up?"

"WHEN DID this truck become a time machine?" Lexy groused as they bounced and slid along. "I feel like we went back to a time before the invention of cement or salt."

Jackson ignored her as he struggled to slow the vehicle. He committed the cardinal sin of steering and braking simultaneously until the antilock brakes kicked in, causing the truck to shimmy violently.

Lexy braced herself against the dashboard with one hand and held onto the grab handle above her head with the other. Harlan had no such handles and settled for bracing his feet against the back seat rails while grasping Lexy and Jackson's headrests. Still, he swayed side to side, his head jostling like a Bobblehead toy.

"Do I get hazard pay for this?" Lexy asked once the truck straightened.

"Forget hazard pay. I believe my spleen came loose." Harlan complained from the back seat.

THE PICKUP CAME to rest just shy of a meticulously plowed driveway. Not a speck of ice or snow remained on the thirty-foot cement slab despite three feet of snow piled on either side.

A flagpole towered over the driveway, bearing a large American flag and a blue flag with the state seal of Minnesota in the center, both of which flapped in the breeze.

At the end of the driveway sat a handsome rambler, blue with white trim and a gray roof. Although the house appeared at least sixty years old, it had been well-maintained. The paint was perfect, the windows clean, and the sidewalk leading from the driveway was immaculate.

Jackson eased the pickup into the driveway until all four tires were safely off the road. That was as far as he went, though, as to go further would have been a serious faux pas.

As it was, pulling into the driveway was poor form, but given the state of the road, Jackson wasn't entirely sure he would have been able to get the truck moving again had he parked in the street.

"We're here." Jackson put the truck in park and cut the engine.

Neither of his passengers moved. Jackson opened the door and stepped out. "You guys coming?"

Lexy shrugged. "I'm good right here."

"Me too." Harlan settled into the back seat.

"If you think I'm walking up to that house by myself, out of uniform, you're crazy."

Lexy scoffed. "He knows we're coming. It's not like you're showing up unannounced."

Jackson glanced toward the house. "He knows someone's coming, but he doesn't know *I'm* coming." He stalled, but when it was clear neither Harlan nor Lexy intended to accompany him, he closed the door. As he took several steps toward the house, footsteps crunched behind him, and he turned to see Charlie hurrying to catch up.

"Figured you might like some company."

"This isn't my first time responding to a call."

The edges of Charlie's mouth rose. "I'm sure it isn't, but don't you find *some* people respond better to a stranger knocking on their door when that stranger is female?"

Jackson stepped aside with a flourish, allowing Charlie to lead the way.

Charlie approached the front door, taking a moment to appreciate the brass door handle and matching knocker. Like the rest of the house, they were in pristine condition. "What do you want to bet he's ex-military?" Charlie said as she thumped the knocker against the door.

A deadbolt clicked, and Charlie stepped back. The door opened, and a tall, thin man of about eighty, with unnaturally black hair combed neatly to one side and black horn-rimmed glasses, peered out. He looked first at Charlie and then Jackson. "May I help you?"

"Mr. Nelson?" Charlie asked. The man nodded, and Charlie gestured to Jackson. "Mr. Nelson, we're with the Department of Natural Resources. We're here to speak to you about a report of a mutilated moose carcass."

Mr. Nelson looked from Charlie to Jackson again. "May I see some sort of identification?" Charlie balked at the request, but Jackson stepped forward, reaching into his coat pocket to retrieve his badge. He held the badge to the man's face and let him inspect the gold shield. The man nodded his satisfaction and looked expectantly at Charlie.

"My name is Charlie Battice. I'm a contractor with the DNR." She eased her hand into her coat. "I can show you my driver's license if that would make you more comfortable." Jackson saw Charlie's reflection in the door's transom window. She'd added a 100-watt smile, but neither Nelson's expression nor demeanor changed.

"In what capacity?" Nelson inquired.

"I'm sorry?" Charlie asked.

"In what capacity are you working with the DNR?"

Charlie cleared her throat. "I'm a professional tracker. We're hoping to identify the animal that killed the moose and determine its whereabouts."

"Well, you never know who's at your door these days. Let me get my coat." Mr. Nelson closed the door, leaving Charlie and Jackson alone. Before either could say a word, the door opened again, and Mr. Nelson stepped out, wearing a light jacket and holding an AR-15. Jackson and Charlie blinked at the sleek, black rifle.

"Do you really think that's necessary?"

Mr. Nelson shut the door behind him. "Once you see that moose, you'll understand."

A CLEARING half the size of a basketball court carved out of a dense clump of towering conifers provided cover from the elements as the search party congregated around a neatly laid-out tarp, weighted down at the corners by large brick pavers.

"That's a pretty tidy job of covering up you did there," Harlan commented, "especially given you had to haul the pavers all the way out here."

Mr. Nelson shrugged. "Thought it best to consider this a crime scene until I learned otherwise. Didn't want anyone or anything coming along and disturbing it before your people had a chance to take a look."

Charlie gazed at Mr. Nelson's handiwork. "You wouldn't happen to have a military background, would you?"

Mr. Nelson's mouth tightened. "Matter of fact, I do."

"Thought so. You don't see that kind of precision every day. Your home, the way you laid out this tarp. One usually only sees that sort of attention to detail from ex-military."

"Or someone with a stick up his ass," Jasper quipped.

Mr. Nelson fixed his gaze on Jasper for an instant, then faced Charlie. "What branch were you in?"

"Oh, I didn't serve."

Mr. Nelson's eyebrows arched. "Coulda fooled me. You've got a way about you."

Charlie's eyes and voice dropped. "Thank you."

"She was raised by nuns," Mattie interjected. "After her birth mother died, and before she came to live with our mom and dad, I mean." Charlie looked daggers at Mattie, and he went back to inspecting the tarp, leaving Charlie and Mr. Nelson to resume their awkward exchange.

"Catholic, huh?"

"Yes, sir."

"Was raised Catholic myself." The old man smiled for the first time. "Some of those nuns were tougher than any drill sergeant." Mr. Nelson gave Charlie a quick wink.

"Should we get started?" Jackson asked. Receiving nods all around, he kneeled in the snow and removed a paver from a corner of the tarp. Mattie did the same at the opposite corner.

"One, two, three..." Jackson and Mattie tugged at the corners of the tarp. They struggled to maintain control of their respective ends of the tarp as it billowed in the strong wind, and while they heard gasps and even a threatened retch from the rest of the team, it wasn't until Jackson and Mattie corralled the wayward tarp that they saw what the uproar was about.

The remains of a moose lay in the snow; rear legs splayed at angles that defied logic and physics. The animal's front legs were missing at the shoulders. In their place were bloody lengths of tendon and muscle that spread out like the frayed edges of a pair of cutoff jeans. The enormous rib cage—white bones streaked red with blood and bits of flesh—bloomed outward like petals of a flower. More striking, even than the missing limbs and unnaturally spread rib cage, were the thick neck twisted like a length of rope, and the missing head.

"What the fuck?" Jasper murmured, his usual insolent grin replaced by a grimace.

"I'll second that." Harlan acknowledged. "Where do we even start?" No one said a word. They couldn't. Gloves covered their mouths and noses. Only Mr. Nelson eschewed the makeshift masks, but his hands quivered inside his jacket pockets.

"How about the fact somebody tauntauned him?" Mattie said, his voice muffled.

Jackson looked away from the mutilated animal. "They did what?"

"Tauntaun. Somebody scooped out his insides."

"Like in *Star Wars*," Harlan added.

"*The Empire Strikes Back*," Mattie corrected. Harlan nodded humbly, and Mattie grinned.

Jasper groaned. "Great, now there's two of them."

"I can't believe this happened so close to a populated area." Charlie looked back at Mr. Nelson's house. "It can't be more than one hundred yards."

Mr. Nelson patted the AR-15. "Now you know why I've been holding onto this."

"How did you even know it was out here?" Charlie asked.

Mr. Nelson gestured upward. "Birds. Crows in the trees and buzzards in the sky. Assumed it was a dead coyote or deer. Wasn't until I came out that I saw it was a bull moose. And a big one at that."

"Where's the rest of him?" Jasper looked around. "There should at least be innards."

Although surprised Jasper had something helpful to contribute for once, Jackson agreed with him. "Could coyotes have made off with the entrails?" He looked at Charlie for confirmation.

Charlie hovered in a squatting position, gazing intently at the ground.

Mattie stepped in. "No coyote tracks."

"What about wolverines?" Jackson asked. "They eat carrion, right?"

Harlan shook his head. "They do," he also spoke through the gloves covering his mouth and nose, "but there aren't any wolverines this far south or this far west."

"What about the birds?" Lexy inquired.

Mattie gazed at the dead animal. "This guy had to be upwards of twelve hundred pounds. Half that weight would have been innards. There's no way birds made off with that much meat." Mattie edged closer to the carcass, his head practically in the exposed cavity.

Harlan edged closer and peered over Mattie's shoulder. "What are you looking for?"

"Bear hairs. Do you see any?"

When Harlan didn't answer, Mattie turned to see the scientist sprinting away, coughing and gagging. The group watched as Harlan dropped to his knees and spewed his breakfast, or last night's dinner. Afterwards, he wiped his mouth on his sleeve, washed his mouth with a handful of clean snow, and returned to the group as if nothing had happened. "Lots of bear fur," he said thickly, "I mean, lots. Like the thing was shedding."

"So, we're sure it was a bear?" Jackson asked, his voice hopeful.

"Mostly." Charlie circled the carcass, employing a duck walk as she continued her examination.

"Care to elaborate?"

Charlie inspected what appeared to be a shoulder. "For one, the legs were pulled off."

"So?"

"A bear would have used its teeth and claws." The tracker surveyed the ground around the carcass. "At a minimum, it would have used its teeth to start the process. These were pulled off, like somebody pulling a drumstick off a Thanksgiving turkey. It's a different kind of force resulting in a different trauma to the flesh."

"Maybe it was one pissed-off bear." Jackson looked at Lexy, smiling. Lexy returned his smile, but her eyes conveyed concern.

Charlie stood with a soft grunt and brushed off her knees. "We should get our gear and get going." She turned to Mr. Nelson. "Do you have someplace to stay for the next few days?"

Mr. Nelson frowned. "Why?"

"The bear is probably miles away from here by now, but he might circle back. Based on what I've seen, I think it would be better if you weren't around if he does."

Mr. Nelson eyed Charlie, but when she held his gaze, the old man relented. "I'm sure I can work something out."

"Thank you." Charlie patted Mr. Nelson's arm, and the man smiled again.

Jackson nudged Charlie and gestured at the ground where she stood. "Get any clean tracks?"

"Got everything I need," Charlie reassured him. "At least enough to get us started."

Jackson took a quick accounting of his companions and spied Harlan on his knees next to the moose carcass. "We're going to hit the trail. You ready to go?"

Harlan flinched, as if startled, then looked at Jackson with a sheepish grin. "Yes. Just give me a moment." The scientist shifted his weight as if preparing to rise, but when Jackson turned away, he surreptitiously continued his review.

JACKSON HELPED Lexy and Harlan unload gear from his pickup while Charlie, Jasper, and Mattie did the same with Charlie's Jeep. He'd moved the pickup from the driveway to the street after Mr. Nelson agreed to vacate the house, recalling how long it had taken Charlie to mobilize her team back in Tim Freida's parking lot.

His assumption proved correct. As Jackson removed a sleeping bag and roll from the back of the pickup, a mechanical clatter arose from inside Mr. Nelson's garage. The garage door rose, and a mint-condition 1989 Oldsmobile 98 Regency backed out. The white wall tires of the long, blocky "luxury" car crunched on wet concrete as Mr. Nelson guided the pristine vehicle along the driveway like a commander guiding a battleship out of dry dock. Given the condition of Mr. Nelson's house and car, it came as no surprise that the garage was also immaculate. Every tool hung neatly on the wall. A red tool locker rested in one corner; a snow blower in the other. Both appeared meticulously maintained.

Jackson watched the car back at a glacial pace and come to rest next to him. The driver's side window rolled down, and Mr. Nelson peered out. The old man nodded toward the pickup and Jeep. "You're welcome to park your vehicles in the driveway while I'm gone."

"Thank you, but that won't be necessary. Besides, I wouldn't want to leak oil on this beautiful driveway."

Nelson scoffed. "You'd be doing me a favor. It'll make it look like somebody's home."

"Seems like a quiet neighborhood. Do you have a problem with crime out here?"

Nelson's face screwed into a scowl. "Crime isn't just in the cities anymore. Between meth and the economy, people are always scrambling to feed their families or habits."

Jackson agreed. He'd seen far too many cabins and fish houses ravaged by meth heads and laid-off factory workers to dispute Mr. Nelson's assertion. "In that case, we'd be happy to use your driveway. It's the least we can do."

Mr. Nelson nodded his appreciation and beckoned Jackson closer. "Noticed you didn't bring any firearms."

"It was a condition of Miss Battice leading the expedition."

"No disrespect to the lady, but that moose had to be over fifteen hundred pounds." The old man leaned in. When he spoke again, it was in a low voice. "He didn't go down easy. Whatever ripped it apart was strong in a way I've never seen."

Mr. Nelson's stoic manner and no-nonsense approach had grown on Jackson since the man had answered the door, but Jackson sensed it was time to forego the niceties. "If you're trying to tell me something, Mr. Nelson, how about you quit dancing and get to it?"

Mr. Nelson smiled for the third time since the team's arrival. "You strike me as a man with a good head on his shoulders. But let's be honest, you wouldn't know a deer tick from a water bug." Nelson pointed at Charlie, who was busy pulling sleeping bags from the Jeep. "The state might be footing her bill, but you work for her. Not the other way around."

"I don't understand."

"These woods are beautiful, but dangerous, especially in winter. Everybody knows the cold can suck the life out of you, but it's the trees that do you in. Too easy to get disoriented. You could freeze to death ten feet from civilization without even knowing. If you want to have a chance in hell of bringing everybody back from this trip," he pointed at Charlie again, this time with one shaking finger, "that young lady has to find that thing before it finds you. She can't do that if she's busy babysitting your team."

Nelson reached into the passenger's side footwell of the Oldsmobile, retrieved the AR-15, and offered it to Jackson. "Take this. Got a box of .22 mm cartridges too."

"Thanks, but we won't need it." Jackson backed away.

Mr. Nelson struggled to keep the weapon horizontal, but when Jackson further resisted, he grunted his disapproval and rested the butt of the rifle on the window's edge.

"When Miss Doris told me you'd be stopping by, I looked you up on the internets."

Jackson blinked, caught off guard by the octogenarian's use of technology to run a rudimentary background check.

"I don't know the details of what happened to you down in Chicago, and frankly, I don't care to. But I figure whatever got you run out of there; you did it knowing all hell would rain down on your head. And you did it anyway. You do the same for Miss Battice, and you might just come out of this in one piece."

Jackson felt a lump form in his throat. "I appreciate the vote of confidence, Mr. Nelson."

"Save the humility for the reporters," Mr. Nelson snapped, then offered the AR-15 to Jackson once again.

"I gave Charlie my word."

"I can respect that. But there's such a thing as not letting honor get in the way of common sense." The old man returned the rifle to the footwell, put the car in gear, and rode the brake.

"Where you headed?" Jackson asked.

"To stay with my son in Willmar. He's the one who gave me the fancy pea shooter. Thought it'd be good fending off coyotes." Mr. Nelson's bushy eyebrows bunched. "You be careful, Officer Bennett. Whatever's out there ain't no coyote." He drove off, the Oldsmobile's tires splashing snow and muck up the sides of the previously spotless vehicle.

"What was he doing with the rifle?" Charlie approached.

"He wanted me to take it. I told him we didn't need it."

"Thank you." Charlie watched the Oldsmobile depart. Despite her words, her expression suggested she would have preferred that the weapon remain.

11

attie, Harlan, and Lexy trudged through the dim arboreal canopy with Charlie in the lead and Jackson and Jasper bringing up the rear. Although the hoods of their coats obscured their identities, the differences in the age of their gear differentiated seasoned hikers from novices, with Jackson, Lexy, and Harlan sporting clean new backpacks while Charlie, Mattie, and Jasper made do with their old, tattered versions.

Charlie moved briskly, scanning the ground intently for several seconds before looking up to regard her surroundings. The pattern repeated except when she occasionally stopped to inspect a broken branch or snow-covered bush, but otherwise kept her eyes to the ground. Mattie followed six feet behind Charlie, stepping in his sister's footprints. Lexy and Harlan eschewed the single-file approach and walked side by side, allowing them to converse while Jasper followed, his attention on Lexy's rear.

Jackson maintained a ten-foot cushion between himself and Jasper. The position afforded him a clear view of the team, including Charlie, yet allowed him to walk at a leisurely pace. With a slight turn of his head in either direction, he could check the dense tree cover ahead for any signs of danger.

He'd been jumpy at first, but after a couple of miles, he settled into his role as protector and let his mind wander. He found himself enjoying the sounds of the woods, the three-note twitter of the boreal chickadee, the inquisitive peep and sharp chirp of the Canadian Jay, the wind blowing through the trees, and the occasional creak and crack of branches giving way under the weight of heavy snow. He was lost in the moment when he noticed Jasper falling back. He slowed his pace to maintain the cushion between himself and Jasper, but the man stopped suddenly, almost causing Jackson to collide with him and his ratty backpack.

"You're falling behind," Jackson growled.

"Not falling behind, just slowing down."

"Why?"

"I have a question."

Jackson knew the subject without asking. Despite drawing even with Jackson, Jasper had scarcely taken his eyes off Lexy.

"What about her?"

"Are the two of you a...thing?"

Jackson stared at the younger man. "Are you asking if I'm sleeping with my subordinate?"

"Figured it was only polite to ask." Jasper grinned. "Didn't want to start this expedition pissing on somebody else's fire hydrant."

Jackson returned his attention to the path ahead, but Jasper continued to walk in stride, his head moving back and forth as if contemplating another question. Finally, he turned to Jackson with a pensive expression. "You think I got a shot?" He tilted his head in Harlan's direction. "Or does she only go for eggheads?"

Jackson increased his speed, intending to pull ahead, but curiosity got the better of him, and he glanced back to see Jasper disappear into a cluster of deeply fissured White Pines. "Hey, where are you going?"

"Gotta hit the head. Don't wait up."

Jackson hurried to catch Lexy and Harlan, who were several yards ahead, still engaged in a quiet but intense conversation. The pair grew silent as he came within earshot, and Lexy tendered a cautious smile. She and Harlan looked like a couple of teenagers caught smoking in the bathroom.

"What's up, boss?"

"Just passing through." Jackson's brow furrowed. "Why?"

"You had a strange look on your face."

"I had a chat with Jasper. It was enlightening."

Lexy searched the path behind them but saw no sign of Jasper. "Where is he?"

"Using the bathroom."

"Shouldn't we wait?" Lexy stopped walking, and Harlan followed suit.

"He said not to," Jackson replied, as he continued toward Mattie. He pulled even and timed his pace to match that of the younger man. "How's it going?"

Mattie kept his head down, and Jackson tapped him on the shoulder. Mattie nearly leaped out of his skin. He faced Jackson, eyes so wide that Jackson feared he might attack.

"Easy. Just checking on you."

"Everything okay?" Mattie yelled as he removed a set of earbuds from his ears. His loud voice adjusted mid-sentence.

Jackson held up his hands. "Yep. All good. On my way to check in with Charlie."

"Sorry, got caught up in a podcast."

"What are you listening to?"

"A podcast about horror movies."

Jackson's eyebrows knitted. "You might want to try something less terrifying while we're out here."

Mattie smiled and stuck his earbuds back in.

Jackson pressed ahead, closing the distance between himself and Charlie, who trudged along a few feet ahead. Jackson reached out to touch her shoulder, then hesitated, recalling Lexy's admonishment that there was rarely any reason for a man to touch a woman he didn't know without her knowledge and consent. He needn't have worried. Charlie whirled, eyebrows raised as if she'd caught him stealing a pie from her windowsill.

"How's it going back there?"

"Good. Got bored watching Jasper stare at Lexy, so I thought I'd check in."

Charlie huffed. "He's like a pubescent teenager. I hoped he'd age out of it, but I guess it's true some men never grow up."

"He does that to you, too?"

"Not anymore," Charlie said with a laugh. "First time I noticed him checking me out on the trail, I dropped an aluminum trowel on the path. He was so busy staring at my ass that he tripped over the trowel and fell face-first into a tree stump. It cost him a chunk of skin over the right side of his mouth. That's why he wears the mustache."

"Glad to know it wasn't a fashion choice." They walked in silence, the crunch of their boots breaking the ice-encrusted snow the only sound. Jackson grew uncomfortable with the quiet and glanced over his shoulder.

Still no Jasper. He felt a twinge of concern but quickly shook it off. The man was experienced, young, and in decent shape. He could take care of himself. Jackson returned his attention to Charlie. "You're from Wisconsin, right?"

"Yeah?" Charlie tensed, as if steeling herself against further inquiry.

"How do you know where we're going?" He surveyed the surrounding woods. "Have you been here before?"

"No. But it doesn't matter. I'm not searching the forest, I'm following tracks."

"What tracks? I don't see anything."

"Helps to know what you're looking for."

"Touché," Jackson laughed good-naturedly, then scanned the sky. The sun had climbed higher since they left Nelson's place, providing an angle at which its rays more easily penetrated the forest canopy. Jackson appreciated the additional sunlight. Although it offered only nominal warmth, the psychological impact was immeasurable. He'd almost forgotten the fact he'd been awake since four a.m.

"How long ago do you think it passed this way?"

"Ten hours. Maybe more."

"Ten hours? Shouldn't the tracks have melted by now?"

Charlie shook her head. "It's below zero. Between the thick tree cover and lack of direct sunlight, tracks stay viable longer than they might otherwise."

"Otherwise?"

"The ground is frozen solid. Without snow, there wouldn't be much to follow."

Jackson followed Charlie's line of sight but still saw little other than what appeared to be random shapes in the snow. "Guess we got lucky."

"That, and this animal seems to be on a mission."

"What kind of mission?"

Charlie looked away from the trail and into the distance.

"Most times, an animal takes its time traveling. It has no temporal constraints. No tee times, no nine-to-five job, or happy hour to get to. Unless it's in search of food or sex, it has no incentive to move with urgency."

"And our bear?"

"He hasn't stopped much. Not even a potty break."

Jackson giggled.

Charlie's mouth curved into a slight grin. "He fed recently. I'm surprised he hasn't stopped to relieve himself." She puzzled at the trail ahead. "Unless he hasn't ejected his fecal plug."

Jackson's nose wrinkled, and the tracker laughed.

"Yes, it's exactly what you think. Most hibernating animals don't defecate while they sleep. Some, because they don't eat during hibernation, and others because a mass of undigested food, vegetation, body cells, and even rocks, forms a plug in their colon."

"Could it have left the trail to do its business?"

Charlie laughed, but when Jackson didn't join in, she stopped. "You were serious?"

"Is that not a thing?"

Charlie pinched the bridge of her nose.

"What?"

"Don't tell me you've never noticed how dogs look uncomfortable while they squat?"

"Of course. But we're talking about bears, not dogs."

"What's the difference?"

"When a dog looks uncomfortable squatting, it's because it knows it's vulnerable. It's a survival instinct."

"Why wouldn't that apply to bears?" Jackson challenged.

"I doubt anything powerful enough to take down a full-grown bull moose has many natural predators," Charlie smirked. "If it left the trail, it was for some other reason."

"So, you're saying I'm anthropomorphizing."

Charlie's eyes bugged. "Wow. How long have you been holding on to that one?"

"Since about the seventh grade."

Charlie let out a coquettish giggle that caught Jackson off guard. Unsure how to respond, he turned to the hikers trailing behind him. "Speaking of animals with human traits, where's Jasper?"

As if on cue, Jasper burst through a clump of trees and fell in line behind Harlan and Lexy.

Jackson took a deep breath and let it escape. The relief he felt at the younger man's return came as a surprise, but he was more surprised to feel a hand on his arm. When he checked to make sure he wasn't imagining the sensation, Charlie quickly removed her hand.

"Thanks for the nature lesson," Jackson muttered, before hurrying away.

"Thanks for the vocabulary lesson."

Jackson looked over his shoulder, expecting to see Charlie mocking him. Instead, she gave him a lingering, bashful look before resuming her journey up the trail.

He collected himself and ambled to the back of the line, first passing Mattie with a slight nod, then Lexy and Harlan, who paused their conversation just long enough to acknowledge him.

Jasper, however, grinned a Cheshire Cat grin. "Chatting up the boss, I see."

"Just seeing what's what," Jackson said breezily. He hadn't intended to stop for further conversation, but Jasper reached out a hand and blocked his path.

"You sure that's all you were up to?"

Jackson eyed Jasper, brow furrowed and mouth downturned.

The younger man quickly lowered his hand.

"Charlie and me got a history. I figured I could save you the trouble of trying to figure her out on your own." Jasper grinned. "Of course, I expect the same courtesy." His gaze strayed in Lexy's direction.

"I wouldn't hold my breath."

Jackson resumed his position at the end of the procession.

12

Carson Ten Bears awoke to find himself bleeding from the forehead and mouth. While he recalled seeing the Anang-bangishin descend from the sky, he did not wait around to see it plunge into *Gitchi-Gami*, sending the white wave of ice, snow, and water across the icy lake surface. Nor did he see it reach landfall, where it continued its destructive path toward the tiny cabin. He didn't even recall hearing the sound of impact when the wave hit, leaving him to surmise he'd been flung across the room, bounced off the couch pillows, and hit his head on the hardwood floor. He smiled, considering it a stroke of luck that the window at the back of the cabin had given way without breaking. Left hanging from one stubborn hinge, it had provided an exit for the angry wind that had blown open his front door, leaving two-inch-high snowdrifts from the door to the couch.

As he checked himself for further injuries, Carson again marveled at the lack of damage to himself or the cabin. He could sweep the snow out the front door, reseal the window with plastic and duct tape, and patch up what he correctly assumed was a good-sized gash in his forehead with antiseptic and bandages. "I got off easy," he mused.

And then he remembered the rabbits.

THE RABBIT HUTCH WAS ENORMOUS, standing six feet high, not counting its angled roof. It housed three French Lop rabbits, a large, fluffy breed that Carson initially bred for meat and fur but came to love because of their affable nature. The "girls," as he called them, had long since ceased to be "meat and fiber" animals. They were companions.

As Carson plodded through the snow to the hutch, his earlier apprehension eased. Like the rabbits it housed, the hutch was sturdy and well-fortified against winter weather. The angled roof kept snow from building on top, and the canvas flaps, already deployed, kept out the frigid winter air. Although snow covered the entire hutch, Carson hoped the flaps, heated water dishes, and hay-filled nesting boxes had provided respite from the tsunami of snow.

With shaking hands, Carson brushed away the snow accumulated around the hutch. It was far less than Carson had expected, and he was relieved the tough little cabin had taken the brunt of the arctic blast, deflecting the force away from the hutch. Still, the rabbits' safety concerned him. Even if they'd avoided any physical harm, it wasn't uncommon for rabbits to suffer cardiac arrest when subjected to severe stress.

Wincing with anticipation, he lifted the nearest canvas flap. To his delight, all three rabbits looked up at him with wide eyes and twitching noses. Mary and Florence, both of the darker gray variety of French Lop, and Diana, who was of the broken heather and fawn variety, scooted toward him in search of a reassuring scratch behind the ears. Carson's first instinct was to carry them into the cabin where they would be free to move about in relative warmth. But between his weariness and the aches and pains from being flung the length of the cabin, he elected to wait until morning. He peered into the hutch to ensure the heated water dish remained upright and still contained water, then gently lowered the canvas flap back into place.

"Goodnight, ladies," he whispered before turning toward the cabin.

Carson woke the next morning with his "mink" blanket pulled to his chin. The blanket, which wasn't actual mink but an acrylic/polyester blend embossed with a Korean Hangul character he didn't understand, kept him warm even though he'd lacked the energy to seal the rear-facing window the night before. Instead, he'd shoved it into place on its remaining hinge before climbing into bed fully clothed.

He glanced at the old-fashioned round thermometer beside the fireplace and saw the red needle hovering at forty-eight degrees. He shook his head. He considered the heavy burgundy bedspread a technological marvel. Even on the coldest nights, he was cozy under its weight, yet comfortably slept under the blanket well into June despite outside temperatures soaring into the sixties and above. Carson was glad for the creature comfort the mink blanket provided.

He slid out from under the blanket and shuffled to the stove, where he gazed through the window at a large white capsule-shaped propane tank that provided the fuel necessary to run the cabin's stove, water heater, and fireplace. He also had a wood-burning stove that he used for backup heat when propane prices skyrocketed, but it was dangerous to use at night due to the risk of carbon monoxide build-up while he slept.

A generator that ran on propane and gasoline, along with a series of solar panels on the roof, rounded out his energy sources. Carson thought about the solar panels. After last night, the odds of them working were slim. They had been a splurge purchase funded partly by grants from the county and state and a twenty-year loan from the local energy cooperative.

"Joke's on them." Carson chuckled. "What kind of idiots offer a twenty-year loan to an eighty-year-old man who lives in the woods by himself half the year?"

Carson set about making his usual breakfast of oatmeal, orange juice, and instant coffee. After breakfast and his morning constitutional, Carson washed the dishes and straightened his bed. When one lived in a space the size of the average living room, one had to keep things tidy to keep one's sanity, especially this time of year when the great outdoors wasn't always so great and escaping into the woods wasn't a viable or wise option, at least for him.

As he smoothed the mink blanket across his bed, Carson smiled at the prospect of bringing the girls inside. French Lops didn't do well when caged for extended periods, indoors or out. So, in the warmer months, he fenced off an area of his property for them to move about as they pleased. The woods being what they were, though, he couldn't let the girls "graze" unattended as the slow-moving rabbits lacked the survival skills of their wild cousins and would likely have become a meal for the many predators.

Unfortunately, the rabbits, particularly Diana, didn't care for being cooped up during the winter either, which meant Carson had to move them indoors during the coldest months. While he enjoyed having the girls close at hand for a month or two, the litter boxes he kept in the cabin during their stay grew ripe with the scent of urine and feces, and their natural leporine odor was cloying enough that he had to open a window. Still, he was eager to bring the girls inside and quickly placed three separate litter boxes in three different corners, then filled them with litter from an industrial-sized bag. Task complete, he put on his gear to head outside.

CARSON STEPPED OUTSIDE and squinted into a sun still low in a clear blue sky. The air was crisp, and the wind was calm. Coupled with the blue sky, it was bitterly cold, likely near zero or lower. The tears caused by the direct sun froze almost immediately on his eyelashes, shutting one eye and forcing him to view the world through a prism of colors filtered through ice. But he made his way to the rabbit hutch with the assured gait of a man who'd lived on the same plot of land over half his life.

Sensing the hutch was close by, Carson wiped his eyes, clearing his lashes of ice, then picked up speed, hoping to reach the hutch before the warm puffs of breath from his nose and mouth froze his eyelashes again. He smiled as he squinted to focus on the nearby hutch, but as he approached, the smile wavered before disappearing altogether.

The rabbit hutch was gone. In its place was a pile of splintered wood, mangled chicken wire, and shredded canvas surrounded by uneven snow decorated in a red and white piebald pattern.

13

The sky had gone from gray to dark gray while the tracking party made its way through the forest. The sun had yet to dip below the horizon, but the canopy created by the combination of densely packed conifers and thick-trunked leafless deciduous trees dimmed the forest to the point it resembled nightfall.

Slow and deliberate footsteps echoed off naked tree trunks, filling the otherwise silent woods with arrhythmic crunching as Jackson lurched forward, shoulders hunched. He couldn't recall experiencing such fatigue, not even during two-a-days, when his high school football team endured practice in the sweltering summer heat twice a day for an entire week. This was much worse. On top of the physical exertion, the unrelenting cold sapped whatever energy his body had left, leaving none for heating his weary frame. As far as he could tell, the rest of the procession wasn't fairing much better.

He assessed his companions with tired eyes. Lexy and Harlan walked in silence, too exhausted to engage in conversation. Lexy moved slowly but at least looked steady on her feet, whereas the scientist's feet barely cleared the snow, creating a muddy sludge where his boots broke through the packed snow and dug into the dirt. With each step, his breath puffed into the air, escaping in a wheezy rasp that hinted at a sedentary lifestyle and a diet devoid of fruits and vegetables.

Mattie's earbuds hung from their wires around his neck. Young legs continued to lift his boots above the snow, but his hands clutched the straps of his pack, his thumbs tucked into his palms to prevent his arms from dropping to his sides. Like Harlan, Mattie breathed audibly, but steam issued from his nose with a soft whistle rather than a rattling gasp.

Jasper continued his usual gait, knees still approaching full horizontal with each step, arms swinging in a wide arc, lips parted just enough to supplement the supply of air to his lungs through his nose. Jackson had to admit he found Jasper's stamina impressive, but took pleasure from the fact that the younger man, whether due to fatigue or frustration, had lost interest in Lexy's rear end and focused his gaze on the path ahead.

Up front, Charlie's footfall remained crisp, each step taken with the same precision she'd exhibited when the team had undertaken the expedition hours earlier. Impossibly, her breath was still even and measured. The woman moved with the efficiency of a long-distance runner.

Jackson filled his lungs with icy air and leaned into the slight breeze that buffeted his body, allowing gravity to pull him along. He gritted his teeth and stepped off the path worn into the snow by his fellow travelers. He found the deviation more difficult than anticipated as he sank into virgin snow up to his knees. Undaunted, he willed himself forward, increasing his speed enough to pass Jasper,

Harlan, Lexy, and Mattie on his way to the front of the procession.

The effort nearly killed him. By the time he reached Charlie, his lungs and throat burned, his legs ached, and breath escaped him in a phlegmy death rattle that made Harlan's wheezing sound like a cat's purr by comparison. Between his wheezing and the crunching of ice and snow underfoot, Jackson made a tremendous racket.

Charlie whirled, her expression one of obvious annoyance.

Jackson held his hands together in a placating gesture. "Mind if we call it quits?" He indicated the trailing procession. "I can't speak for your team, but the DNR folks are bushed."

Charlie looked to the trail.

"If you don't want to," Jackson offered. "That's fine, I just thought—"

"No, no," Charlie said quickly. "Actually, this is a perfect place to set up camp. We're in a clearing but protected from the wind. Besides, it's getting too dark to see the trail, and if he's holed up for the night, we might end up walking right into him."

Jackson's jaw dropped.

"I wouldn't worry." She struggled to keep from laughing. "If he was anywhere near here, we scared him off with as much noise as we're making." Jackson peered ahead at the trail with a look of concern. "He had a pretty good head start. I doubt we caught up to him in one day."

Jackson faced the procession and held up a hand. "That's it for today."

"Thank God." Harlan plopped down where he was and lay back. Resting on his backpack, arms and legs splayed, the scientist looked like a turtle stranded on its back.

Lexy stepped over her colleague without so much as a glance and sat on a downed tree. She bent over, untied one boot, and pulled it off. She wiggled her toes inside her white sock and winced. The wince disappeared almost immediately, but didn't escape Mattie's attention.

"You okay?"

Lexy looked up as she rubbed her foot through her sock. "I think I chose the wrong boots. I guess I'm not used to such long hikes."

"Wrong feet is more like it." Mattie swung off his backpack, found another downed tree, and sat down. "I'll bet you have pedicured feet."

Lexy's eyes narrowed.

"What you need are a few callouses. They're like an insurance policy against blisters."

The officer's eyebrows rose as she considered Mattie's theory. "Thanks for the tip."

Mattie saluted and reached into his pocket. After a bit of digging, he pulled out a stubby gold packet, which he ripped open, revealing a power bar. He bit the bar in half, chewing absently as he fished a water bottle from his backpack. He looked up at the sky where the waning sun peeked through the trees, turning the forest a pinkish-orange hue. He gulped his water, letting out a long burp, after which he grinned sheepishly.

"Mind if I sit?" Mattie scooted aside as Jackson settled next to him and let out a groan worthy of a man twenty years his senior.

Jasper stood off to one side, shaking his head disdainfully. "What a bunch of pussies."

Lexy caught Jackson's eye and mouthed, "What an asshole."

Jackson acknowledged the comment with a wink and

took a quick headcount. Four bodies, including his own. He leaned forward to untie his boots, then suddenly sat upright again. With panic growing in his chest, he scanned the camp again, eyes darting wildly.

Charlie stood at the edge of camp, staring into the forest like a caged animal desperately seeking a glimpse of freedom.

Jackson cupped his hands to his mouth, too tired to consider getting up from his seat. "Everything okay?" His voice carried across the clearing.

Charlie tore her attention from the forest. "Just wondering if we should have put in another mile or two."

"No takebacks. Harlan's nearly dead, and Lexy already took her boots off." Jackson gazed fondly at his exhausted crew. "They might mutiny if you make them walk another step."

Charlie reluctantly swung her pack off her back.

NIGHT SURROUNDED THE CLEARING, held at bay by a crackling orange fire, the piercing white light of four LED battery-powered lanterns, and two strategically placed Coleman liquid-fuel lanterns that not only produced a surprising amount of light but also kicked out waves of glorious heat, making the frigid night air tolerable. Between the light, ample heat, mesh camping chairs, and the protection of three tents—two two-person tents the size of a Honda Civic and one six-person tent the size of a backyard shed—strategically positioned to protect against the slight wind that blew through the clearing, they managed to sit comfortably.

Charlie, Jasper, and Mattie sat on one side while Jackson, Lexy, and Harlan occupied the other. They hadn't drawn sides on purpose. It had merely been a matter of familiarity, but Jackson liked the configuration as it allowed him to gaze across the fire at Charlie without turning his head. It wasn't as if he stared. He mostly looked directly into the flames, but whenever Charlie spoke, he gave her his full attention.

At the moment, however, no one uttered a word. They were too tired or simply content to listen to the crackling and popping of the fire, the occasional howls of coyotes, or the deep and throaty hoot of great horned owls.

Jasper broke the peace. "This is boring." He was like a petulant teenager at a family reunion.

Charlie shot him a withering glare. "You're welcome to turn in for the night."

"And miss all this lively conversation?"

"Anybody got a deck of cards?" Mattie broke in. When no one responded, he grinned. "What else is there to do? Tell campfire stories and sing Kumbaya?" Jasper ignored Mattie's attempt at levity, got up from the campfire, and hobbled toward the largest tent.

"Where do you think you're going?" Charlie climbed to her feet.

"To bed."

"Not in that tent, you're not."

Jasper huffed. "Where am I supposed to sleep?"

Charlie looked at Jasper as if he were crazy. "With Mattie."

"Why me? He snores *and* farts," Mattie complained. When Jasper grinned without remorse, Mattie scanned the camp, brightening when he saw Harlan. "What if I bunk with the Professor?"

Harlan's face lit up. "Works for me."

Jasper surveyed the remaining candidates and lit up

when he saw Lexy trying to escape his gaze. "How about I double up with Backwoods Barbie?"

"Jasper…" Charlie scolded.

"Come on, I wasn't serious." Jasper didn't bother to hide his disappointment as he turned to Jackson. "Guess that leaves you and me, Ranger Rick."

Jackson shrugged. "Can't be any worse than that moose carcass."

Lexy hadn't said a word during the exchange, but her audible exhalation revealed her relief. Charlie smiled across the fire at Lexy. "Great, then it's just us girls."

Lexy let out a girlish squeal that had everyone, including Charlie, staring at her. She cowered sheepishly. "I swear, I really am a ranger. I have a badge and everything."

JACKSON STARED past the dying embers of the once glorious fire into the forest, which was as deep a black as he'd seen in his life. He glanced upward, peering through the treetops at a sky streaked by the occasional ribbon of light that peeked through thick clouds. As he returned his gaze to the surrounding forest, his brow furrowed. He wondered if he'd ever enjoyed such peace.

Sure, the day had been grueling, and the thought of a dangerous animal roaming the woods unnerved him. But the stillness filled him with an uncommon calm. He regretted never having tried camping in the two years he'd been paid to protect the very forest in which he now sat.

"You look miserable." Charlie's voice came from nowhere like a question from the heavens, and Jackson whirled to see Charlie crossing the campsite. She looked down at him, genuine concern on her face.

"That's because I *am* miserable." Jackson lied. "It's ten below."

Charlie laughed. "Some people like that."

"Not my people. We don't like the cold or the snow."

"What about Matthew Henson?" Charlie challenged. "He didn't seem to mind."

Jackson was familiar with Matthew Henson, the African-American explorer and guide who had accompanied explorer Robert Peary to the Arctic. Henson had joined Peary on several other expeditions, including Nicaragua. Jackson suspected the man preferred the warmth of Central America to the body-numbing sixty-five-degree below zero temperatures he experienced in the Arctic, but, like Jackson, had returned North because that's where work took him. "Yeah, well, one guy doesn't exactly count as a pattern of behavior for the entire race."

"Hey, you're the one who generalized. I'm just pointing out the facts."

Jackson nodded in concession, and Charlie plopped into the chair next to him.

"Is Lexy asleep?" Jackson indicated the large tent that the two women shared.

"Yep. We chatted for a couple of minutes, then she crashed mid-sentence."

Jackson laughed. "Guess she was literally one tired camper."

"It's sweet the way you look out for her."

"She doesn't need looking after. She's capable and way tougher than she looks."

"Oh, I agree. It's still sweet."

"Please, stop saying that." Jackson squirmed. "It makes me sound like a creepy old man."

"There's nothing creepy about it. Not many men express

affection without an agenda. I think it's…" Jackson's eyes narrowed, but Charlie ignored the warning. "Sweet."

He peered into the forest again, and they listened to the soft rustling of pine needles and the occasional protesting creak of trees reluctant to bend in deference to the wind. Jackson glanced over at Charlie and saw her face, previously home to a child-like grin, had taken on a worried expression. Her body language was tense and coiled.

"What's wrong?"

Charlie shook her head. "Nothing."

"Come on. I was married for fifteen years. I recognize tension when I see it."

Charlie's chair creaked as she straightened. "There's a storm coming. A big one."

Jackson shrugged. "It's Minnesota. There's always a storm coming. Then again, you'd know more about the weather."

Charlie's eyebrows arched. "Why? Because you think I have some special power to divine the will of the weather gods?"

Jackson's mouth opened, but nothing came out except the strangled gurgle of a man choking on his own words. "I didn't—"

Charlie burst into laughter. Jackson watched, confused, as she clamped her hand to her mouth in an unsuccessful attempt to stifle the sound. Once she finally stopped laughing, she wiped tears from her eyes. "Man, that was easy."

She pulled out a small black phone and waggled it before Jackson. "Satellite phone. I checked in with the office. They said a big storm is on the way." Jackson gawked stupidly, and Charlie started laughing again.

Jackson found the joy she got from his discomfort amusing. When she continued to chuckle with no signs of stopping, he flashed a devious grin. "So, you and Jasper used to be an item?"

Charlie stopped laughing. "Wow. Okay, I see how you are."

"What? He's an *interesting* individual."

Charlie leaned back in her chair. "Yeah. He's a lot, but he grows on you."

"Kinda like a foot fungus?"

"He has some good qualities. He's dependable when things go south, he's loyal, and he's nothing if not consistent."

"Consistently annoying."

"I never said his good qualities outweighed his bad ones. But underneath that annoying exterior, he's a good guy."

Jackson remained unconvinced. "Is that why the two of you are no longer together?"

The edges of Charlie's mouth turned upward. "You've got a bit of a mean streak."

"Is that good or bad?"

"I'm not sure yet." Charlie got up from her chair. "Get some sleep. Tomorrow's going to be a long day."

"We've been up since 0400. How much longer could it be?"

Charlie flashed a mischievous smile and headed for the large tent. He watched unabashedly as she strode across the camp and disappeared into the tent without a word.

He figured she knew he was watching, but he didn't care.

Jackson unzipped the half-moon door flap of the two-person tent and lowered his head to clear the tent's ceiling, which was less than four feet high. He entered and immediately grimaced. The tent reeked of boiled eggs and burned coffee. "Jesus. Smells like sulfur and regret in here."

"Sorry." Jasper shifted in his sleeping bag.

"You should be." Jackson waved his hand in front of his face as he fumbled with the zipper on the tent door. "I should write you up for air pollution."

Jasper laughed as dim light permeated the tent. A small, battery-powered lamp glowed between their sleeping bags. Jasper gazed at Jackson, a curious look on his face. "You have a good talk with Charlie?"

Jackson sat on his sleeping bag and loosened the strings on his boots. "I did." He unlaced the top two eyelets of the boots, ignoring Jasper, who stared at him expectantly. He pulled off his boots and set them aside before taking off his coat.

"What'd you talk about?"

Jackson climbed into his sleeping bag and took his time zipping it. Once inside, he scooted and squirmed, purposely taking far longer than necessary to make himself comfortable. He slid his arms behind his head, lacing his fingers together.

"Oh, this and that. The weather, the news, our hopes and dreams. Turn-ons and turnoffs never came up."

"Did I come up?" Jasper propped himself on one elbow like a teenager at a slumber party. His smirk was visible, even in the low light.

"Of course." Jackson rolled over in his sleeping bag, facing away from Jasper.

"Figured I might. Charlie's never really gotten over me."

"Yeah, kinda like herpes. It leaves, but it's never really gone."

Jasper chuckled. "Oh, so you're a comedian *and* a park ranger?"

"Nah, but if I see something that strikes me as humorous, I'll make a comment or two."

Jasper sat upright. "You think I'm a joke?"

"More of a mystery." Jackson didn't bother to face Jasper. "An enigma."

"How's that?"

"You're difficult to figure out."

"I know what *enigma* means. *How* am I an enigma?"

Jackson sat up, partly for comfort and partly to ready himself in the event of an attack. He made a point of facing Jasper. "I can't figure out why Charlie would ever give a guy like you the time of day."

"You walk behind me for a couple of hours and think you know me?"

"I've got a pretty good sense of who you are."

"Yeah? And who am I?" Jasper pushed his sleeping bag below his hips.

"A guy looking to rile people up."

"So, it worked."

"Yep." Jackson's voice remained placid. "But probably not the way you were hoping it would." Jasper remained silent, and Jackson continued. "At first, I thought you were just your average, run-of-the-mill dipshit, but that didn't make sense. Why would Charlie have dated you? That's when I realized you're not an idiot; you're just a guy who wants to see the world burn—an anarchist. Personally, I'd prefer an idiot. At least then I'd feel sorry for you."

Jasper sat up, and the dim light illuminated his face like a villain in a sci-fi movie. "You got me all wrong-. I'm no anarchist. I'm a goddamned klaxon. A wake-up call. People these days are too afraid of hurting each other's feelings. It's not natural. You know what is natural? Conflict."

He shifted within his sleeping bag. "The universe thrives

on it. Hell, even the tiniest particles and molecules have opposing actions and reactions. It's part of the natural order. But not with people. Not anymore. We've beaten the conflict out of one another. I'm just trying to wake people up before it's too late." Jasper turned off the lamp and lay down. It might have been his version of a mic drop.

"Sounds noble when you put it that way." Despite the darkness, Jackson's sarcasm came through loud and clear.

If Jasper had a comeback, he kept it to himself.

14

Carson Ten Bears moved slowly, even for a man his age. But he was in no hurry. This would be his last errand, the final act in an eighty-year performance. So, he walked, head down against the wind and snow, confident in the inevitability of a showdown.

With the loss of his precious rabbits, Diana, Mary, and Florence, there was nothing to tether Carson to the world. As a child, he'd been forced to accept a culture and religion that weren't his own. As a young man, he'd traveled far from home to fight a war not of his own making and returned to find his contributions absent from history and the consciousness of all but a few. Now, as an old man, he was often ignored, discarded, and forgotten.

Nonetheless, he'd found solace. Solace in the company of gentle creatures who offered companionship in exchange for protection and kindness. And now they were gone, along with Carson's will to live. But before he exhaled his last breath, he would track down the killer, this murderer of innocents, and he, Carson Ten Bears, would destroy it.

Carson's adversary didn't appear to move particularly well in the snow. He found its tracks blurred and haphazard, tentative even, as if walking in snow was a novel experience. Carson, however, was accustomed to traveling in rugged, inimical terrain in inclement weather. The slow pace was easy on his old bones. Even in deep snow, he maintained a speed as predictable and steady as the ticking of a grandfather clock. The logging axe slung across his back kept time almost as well, its wooden handle jostling against his metal canteen with every step, making a dull *thunking* sound as he walked.

Carson nearly missed the tracks. Longer than they were wide, as if made by a large man's boot, they resembled nothing he'd ever seen before. But there were toes. Five of them, long, with four knuckles on each toe, and what appeared to be claws at the end of each. The prints were also unusually far apart, so far apart that Carson initially thought them an anomaly— a trick of the ice and snow, created by uneven melting that produced an impossible imprint.

That was until he spotted a second print almost four feet away. Carson had puzzled at the distance. A large man's stride typically measured between thirty and thirty-three inches. Such men tended to be between six and six-and-a-half feet tall. A seven-footer might have a stretch of thirty-six inches.

Starting at the heel of one print and walking off the distance to the heel of the next, Carson calculated the creature's stretch at forty-three inches, which put the murderer at more than eight feet tall. Carson's breath caught in his chest. His quarry towered over all but the tallest of men ever to walk the earth.

For an instant, Carson questioned the wisdom of

confronting a creature of that size, even with his trusty double-bit axe. But the desire for revenge burned white hot, not to be extinguished by fear, logic, age, or infirmity.

As Carson walked, he pondered what he was following. He was sure it wasn't human, but he was aware of only three bipedal animals of such enormity: the Kodiak bear, the Grizzly Bear, also known as the brown bear, and the polar bear. None of those were native to Minnesota, and none walked on their hind legs for an extended distance. Even had such a bear escaped a zoo, to his knowledge, there was nothing with a footprint the size or shape of what he'd seen. Carson was tracking something very different.

But what? No creature he'd ever encountered or even read about matched the information he'd gathered. It was as if the creature wasn't real at all, like it was some mythological creation conjured by his grief and imagination.

Carson paused. *Imagination.* That was why the answer had eluded him. He'd only been thinking of animals he'd seen or experienced. He'd never considered those he'd heard as a child, from his aunties, grandparents, and great-grandparents. He hadn't considered the obvious. The size, the enormous prints made by bootless feet, the inhuman manner in which it had consumed his rabbits. Only one creature came to mind, one so foul and unholy he dared not think its name. He should have realized who'd done this as soon as he'd seen the tracks, sinking deep into the snow under the weight of immense evil—a creature whose sole purpose was to break the hearts, minds, and wills of men.

CARSON TRAVELED LIGHTER than one might have expected, given that he didn't know how long he might need to track the beast. He carried only his axe and aluminum canteen, a large box of matches, a high-tech survival knife that was light but strong and ridiculously sharp, a three-pack of flares, three packages of blueberry toasted pastries, a king-sized resealable package of teriyaki beef jerky, two rolls of toilet paper, a resealable bag of instant coffee premixed with powdered creamer and sugar, a tin cup, a camping shovel, a nylon hammock, a can of spray lubricant, and an extra fleece in case the one he was wearing became wet with sweat.

Although the inventory sounded excessive, it wasn't. Everything except the axe and canteen fit nicely into Carson's old canvas backpack. He had even forgone bringing along his rifle or shotgun. Now that he knew the nature of his quarry, the omission appeared almost prescient. Bullets and buckshot were useless against a malevolent supernatural spirit. Only by incinerating the beast in a cleansing flame could he defeat it.

As he continued his carefully measured steps, Carson thought about the stories he'd heard as a child. His grandparents originally hailed from Alberta, Canada, and had told stories of their experiences. Of all the stories, those that stuck in his head most were those about the Flesh-Eater, the fearsome demonic creature that fed on humans.

According to his grandparents, the Flesh-Eater was one of many spirits that inhabited the forest, but unlike other spirits, it was a creature of winter. The Flesh-Eater thrived during the most treacherous parts of winter when Carson's people were most vulnerable. When temperatures were lethally cold and food at its most scarce, the Flesh-Eater would appear. Sometimes, as a human host who had fallen prey to the Flesh-Eater's power and savageness. Other times in its natural form, which was, according to some descriptions, a towering, emaciated being with long arms, lethal claws, and an elk's skull for a head.

During the warmer months, First Nation families often lived in large groups, hunting, fishing, and gathering food, leading a life of peace and relative prosperity provided by the forest's bounty. With the onset of winter, the days shortened and temperatures fell. Families went their separate ways as the abundance of the spring and summer dwindled to an amount no longer able to support the multitude of mouths gathered in a single location.

Despite separating into family-sized groups, starvation and isolation threatened their survival. As morale and resolve waned, the Flesh-Eater struck, usually overtaking the mother or father. According to legend, possession occurred slowly, evidenced by a gradual change in the victim's behavior. The transformation was slow enough that the victim knew they were under spiritual attack and would sometimes plead with their loved ones to kill them before it was too late. In those communities where more than one family remained to brave the winter, the men and women of the unafflicted family would take matters into their own hands and either burn the afflicted soul or chop off their heads with an axe.

In those instances where a single family hunkered down to wait out the winter in the close quarters of a single dwelling, the family often lacked the will or strength to overpower and subdue the possessed family member. Instead, they watched helplessly as a change in behavior accompanied a change in physical appearance and the onset of a growing, all-consuming hunger for human flesh.

Those were Carson's least favorite tales. Ones where children perished violently, consumed by their parents, one by one, until only the afflicted family member remained, having fully transformed into a tortured, soulless being bearing little resemblance to their original self.

Carson shook himself out of his contemplation. He could never face the Flesh-Eater if he let fear overtake him. He had to locate the creature. Such an act of savagery couldn't go unpunished.

15

Jackson woke the following day to find Jasper awake but still in his sleeping bag. To Jackson's surprise, Jasper clutched a tattered hardcover book. "Is it Saturday already?"

"Look outside."

"Why? What's outside?"

"Just look." Jasper kept his nose buried in his book.

Jackson shimmied out of his sleeping bag. He unzipped the tent and drew aside the flap. Wind, snow, and cold smacked into him with the force of a heavy door. Through eyelashes fused by ice droplets, Jackson barely made out a wall of snow that rose to a height of three feet, covering the forest floor in a blanket of sparkling fresh powder.

"This should be fun."

"Not going to be anything. Cause we ain't going out in that." Jasper spoke matter-of-factly, shrugging his shoulders mildly for emphasis.

"Why not?"

Jasper closed his book and carefully slipped it into a zipper storage bag. "Because we won't make much headway in snow that deep, and the wind would make it impossible to see your hand in front of your face, let alone animal tracks. Not to mention, it's fifteen below out there, not including the wind chill. At least one of us would die. I'm putting my money on the old fat guy."

Jackson surveyed the tent. The translucent nylon walls and fiberglass posts shook with every gust of wind. "Are we going to be warm enough in here?" He ran one finger along the curved wall of the tent. It came away glistening with condensation.

"Probably not."

"Did you bring tent heaters?"

"For what?" Jasper licked his finger and flipped a page. "We walk all day. We're only in the tents long enough to sleep. Heaters aren't worth the extra weight."

"Well, we're not walking now. How are we supposed to keep warm?" Jackson's tone bordered on a whine.

Jasper stretched like a tomcat napping in the sun. "Don't worry. Charlie's got it covered."

JACKSON, Jasper, Harlan, Mattie, Lexy, and Charlie huddled in Charlie's tent. Despite housing six adults, the shelter wasn't cramped as Charlie's tent was considerably larger than Jasper's, and appeared more spacious inside than its outward dimensions suggested.

"Why is this tent so big?" Harlan marveled at the palatial accommodations.

"I spend a lot of time in the woods. I like to think of this tent as a home away from home."

"Home is right. This thing's almost as big as my apartment." Lexy joked.

"The only thing missing is a pile of clothes on the floor," Harlan quipped.

"Are we going to be warm enough in here?" Jackson zipped his coat up to the chin and pulled his hat down over his ears, but wouldn't have objected to an additional source of warmth.

"We'll be fine," Charlie said. "Six bodies will keep us warm until the weather breaks."

"And when will that be?" While pleased to have someone other than Jasper for company, the crowded tent brought back memories of Jackson's time in the cave with Sheriff Wyatt.

"Once the sun goes down," Charlie responded. "If we're lucky."

A chorus of groans and grumbles rose within the tent.

"What are we supposed to do, cooped up in here all day?" Jasper demanded.

"Let's play a game," Mattie chirped.

Harlan smiled at that. "What kind of game?"

Mattie considered for a moment, but before he could answer, Jasper chimed in. "How about Worse Day Ever?"

"No." Charlie's voice and expression were stern.

"Come on," Jasper pleaded. When Charlie stared at him, he glanced at Jackson. "It'll separate the men from the boys."

Charlie huffed. "Didn't we just talk about not being an asshole for one day?"

"What's 'Worse Day Ever'?" Lexy looked at Mattie.

Charlie gave Lexy a look that said, *You don't want to do this.*

Jasper saw the exchange and gave Charlie a wink. "Who's in?"

Harlan puzzled. "I'm not familiar with that game. How does it work?"

"It's simple," Jasper began. "We go around the circle, and everybody tells the single worst thing that ever happened to them. The grossest, weirdest, scariest, or most fucked up thing you can think of. The one with the best story wins."

"And what does the winner get?" Harlan rubbed his hands together. He hadn't shown much interest in anything since the sequencer's ambiguous results.

Jasper locked eyes with Charlie. "The winner gets to share Charlie's tent."

"Fuck off, Jasper," Charlie spat.

"And what if Charlie wins?" Harlan asked.

"Doesn't matter. I'm not playing. Besides, I already have a roomie." Charlie leaned over and extended a clenched fist toward Lexy.

"I'm out too." Lexy fist-bumped Charlie.

"Come on," Jasper whined. "It'll be fun. Better than sitting in here smelling each other's farts all day." He turned to Jackson. "How about you, Ranger Rick? You in?"

"I'll pass." Jackson yawned languidly.

"Anybody else in?" Jasper asked, undeterred. "Mattie?"

Mattie shook his head. "Nothing interesting ever happens to me."

Jasper sighed. "Looks like it's just me and the Doc." He looked at the old scientist. "Since Charlie's tent is off-limits, what's the prize?"

A mischievous grin spread across Jackson's face. "How about your book?"

Jasper glanced at the book tucked under his arm as if he'd forgotten it was there. "It's just an old book. It's not worth anything."

Harlan straightened. "It's dog-eared. I'm guessing you've

read it several times." He leaned forward and squinted at the book's spine. "Tom Wolfe's *Radical Chic & Mau-Mauing the Flak Catchers*. Based on your careful handling, I'm guessing it's a signed copy."

Jasper clutched the book against his chest like a little boy reluctant to give up his favorite teddy bear. Wide-eyed, Jasper looked frantically around the tent and was met with unsympathetic smirks at every turn, except Lexy. She wasn't looking at Jasper. She glared at Harlan, a deep scowl on her face.

"Harlan..." Lexy chided. "Leave him alone."

Lexy's tone triggered something in Jasper. He held the tattered book out to Harlan as if it meant nothing to him. "What are you putting up, Doc?" The bravado had returned to his voice, but the slight shaking of his hand betrayed that the anthology was of substantial value to him.

"Two hundred fifty dollars." Harlan delivered his counter with the nonchalance of a high-stakes gambler.

Jasper swallowed hard and forced a confident smile. "Fine." He returned the book to the safety of his armpit. "You go first."

Harlan rubbed his hands together. "Remember when the Space Shuttle exploded?"

Charlie and Jackson nodded.

"Which one?" Mattie asked. "I wasn't alive for the first one, but I remember the second."

"The first one. Challenger."

Mattie grimaced. "Jeez, I'm bummed already."

Harlan winked at Mattie. "Don't be. It ain't that kind of story." Jackson and Lexy exchanged an amused glance at Harlan's atypical use of colloquialism.

The scientist's expression turned serious. When he spoke, it was in a storyteller's voice, low and expressive.

"When I was fifteen, my grandfather died in a car crash. Grandpop was the best friend a kid could ever hope for. He was more of a father to me than my father. He was an intelligent, thoughtful, and kind man, unlike my father, who was a fifties sitcom dad in public, but a boorish, drunken anti-intellectual behind closed doors."

Harlan glanced around the full tent. "I was a constant disappointment to him, and he to me. When my grandfather passed, I was inconsolable and angry. I needed someone or something to blame other than the wet road that caused the crash. So, I blamed God. More than that, I decided there was no way a god who claimed to love humanity would allow a man so wonderful as my grandfather to be taken from this world."

Mattie shifted, and the scientist rubbed his hands together before continuing.

"The more I thought about it, the more it made sense. Death, plague, famine, all the ills of the world visited upon the innocent. A caring God wouldn't allow such things. Going forward, I poured myself into my studies, particularly science. As cliché as it sounds, science became my religion. It required no faith and passed no judgment. I embraced only what could be qualified or quantified and found comfort in the certainty."

Charlie flinched but said nothing.

"Then, on January 28, 1986, the Space Shuttle Challenger exploded. I was a senior in high school." Harlan looked at Lexy and Mattie. "History books cannot even begin to convey the extent of the horror, especially for people like me who had deified NASA and its astronauts. In addition to the loss of life, there was, at least to me, a loss of confidence, the confidence that if you worked hard, did the math, double-checked the math, and then triple-checked it, nothing would go wrong. I felt like I'd lost my grandfather all over again."

Harlan wiped his eyes on the sleeve of his parka. "Fortunately, I didn't have long to wait before the universe reached out and placed a reassuring hand on my shoulder, metaphorically, of course." He offered a thin smile. "February Third, the Monday after the accident, I was in AP English, morose, shellshocked, and numb. We were studying Hamlet that day, but I grasped none of it. It was as irrelevant to me as tennis shoes to a mermaid."

The man's chest heaved as if he were having a heart attack. No one said a word, but everyone was on edge, torn between interrupting an emotional moment and providing whatever emergency aid Harlan might need.

Charlie leaned forward. "Harlan? Are you okay?"

He stared into space, mouth slightly agape, eyes fixed in an almost catatonic fashion.

"Harlan?" Lexy asked quietly.

When he didn't answer, she reached for him. Her fingers were inches from Harlan's shoulder when he finally spoke. "And then it happened."

Lexy's hand hovered in the air. "What happened?"

"Boom. Boom."

Everyone turned to Lexy for an explanation. "Don't look at me. I have no idea what he's talking about."

"The space shuttle," Harlan explained, "creates a pair of sonic booms shortly after reentry, one at the nose and one at the tail, just like any other aircraft moving at supersonic speed. That double sonic boom sounds like a single report with most aircraft because the second boom occurs almost immediately after the first. The space shuttle, however, is so long that its sonic booms are separate and distinct."

He let his words hang in the air, allowing the group to

grasp their significance, but met with blank stares. "The shuttle mission was scheduled to last six days. The Challenger was scheduled to return on Monday, February 3rd, at 9:12 a.m. Pacific time, but exploded shortly after launch. On February third, at nine-thirty-two a.m., there was a sonic boom above my high school. A double sonic boom from a spacecraft that no longer existed."

Silence lingered for a beat before Jasper's face contorted with confusion. "That doesn't make any sense. How could there have been sonic booms if the shuttle blew up?"

"There couldn't." Harlan sat back in his chair. "And yet..."

"Are you sure you didn't imagine it?" Jasper prodded. "I mean, you were in a pretty bad place. Maybe you heard what your mind wanted to hear."

Harlan conceded with a slight nod. "There were twenty-seven people in that classroom. Twenty-six students and our teacher, Mrs. Brooks. We all heard it. We all knew it was impossible. And not one of us doubted what we heard. The shuttle and its crew were twenty minutes late, but they were there. Maybe not in body, but certainly in spirit."

Jasper squirmed. "How come we've never heard about this? Somebody in that classroom would have told someone else. It would have gotten out."

"You'd think so." Harlan shrugged. "I can't speak for anyone else. Maybe some wrote it off as an aural mirage or group hallucination. Maybe some were scared to say anything for fear they'd meet with skepticism." He glanced at Jasper, who sank contritely into his sleeping bag.

"Maybe some took comfort in their belief God snatched the souls of those seven brave astronauts from the sky and took them directly to heaven, and, maybe some," his face grew solemn, "decided the small miracle was a personal matter between them and their God, and chose not to speak of it again until now."

The tent fell silent, except for the owls, coyotes, and foxes, who resumed their hoots, howls, and yips. It was as if they'd temporarily muted their cries out of respect for the professor's story.

Harlan saw Charlie's eyes welling with tears and acknowledged her with a silent nod.

"Don't worry, Jasper," Mattie said, finally breaking the quiet. "I'll order you a new copy of your book next time we're in town." Harlan laughed, as did everyone else, even Jasper, who held up his hands to signal the contest wasn't yet won.

"Hold on, Nerd Boy. I ain't gone yet. Get ready to be dazzled."

Jasper stretched his legs and then returned to a cross-legged position. As Harlan had done before him, he leaned in. "Back in my twenties, I sorta drifted from place to place. The hippie types would have called it 'trying to find myself,' but I was waiting for something to find me. I mostly stayed in the Midwest, bouncing around construction jobs in towns like Cedar Rapids, Appleton, Rochester, and Lincoln.

"One day, I got a call from a buddy that he had a good gig building cookie-cutter houses in suburban Chicago. I didn't have anything going on, so I headed down. The work wasn't hard, and the pay was decent. After we called it quits for the day, we mostly hung out at strip mall bars, drinking overpriced beers and hitting on bored housewives."

"Is this going to get interesting at some point?" Lexy sighed.

"Hold your horses, Big Bird. I'm doing what they call a setup."

Lexy stuck out her tongue, and Jasper reset. "One night,

this corporate dude comes in with some of his buddies, and we get to talking about the state of things, the country, the world, the price of tea in China. I just nod and smile. The guy is throwing around his credit card like a Frisbee, and I'm enjoying the free beer, so I let him keep talking.

Charlie rolled her eyes but remained silent. "By the end of the night, the guy's got his arm around me like we'd been buddies for years, and I'm about to take off because I gotta be up early for work when he asks us if we like sports. Personally, I don't give a shit about a bunch of rich guys playing a kid's game, but my buddy goes 'Sure, what'd you have in mind?' The rich dude says he has tickets to the White Sox game tomorrow night, but can't go and asks if we want them. I shrug it off, but my buddy was one of those guys who called them 'the ChiSox' like he was from Chicago, which he wasn't. Anyway, he hopped on the tickets."

An exaggerated snore rose inside the tent. Jasper scanned the group and saw Mattie grinning from ear to ear.

"Sorry, I must have fallen asleep."

Jasper gave Mattie the stink eye and picked up where he left off. "So, we go to the game, and it was pretty boring. When it ended, we filed out of the stadium and headed back to our car, but the traffic was for shit and we were stuck there for an hour. Finally, my buddy had enough and starts cutting down alleys and driving over curbs to avoid the crowds. I woulda drove, but I had never driven in Chicago and figured my buddy buzzed was still better than me sober, so I sat in the passenger seat and kept my mouth shut. After an hour of dipping and dodging, I realize we're not in Kansas anymore."

"Why didn't you just pull up Google Maps?" Lexy squinted in amazement.

Jasper sneered. "I was living paycheck to paycheck. I wasn't exactly in the market for an iPhone back then, Veruca Salt."

Jackson and Charlie burst into laughter while Harlan and Mattie looked at one another. Harlan leaned and whispered to Mattie. "Who is Veruca Salt?"

Lexy shot him a wicked glare, then motioned for Jasper to continue. "Anyway, I looked around, and even though there wasn't a ton of people on the streets, I figured it wasn't a good idea to ask the locals for directions."

"Why not?" Mattie asked.

"Let's just say we were in hostile territory. We figured it was best to hightail it out of there, so we headed for the nearest main street. As we go screaming through the neighborhood at seventy miles an hour, we heard what sounded like a gunshot up ahead. So, my buddy—"

"Does this buddy of yours have a name?" Charlie asked.

"His name was Ray, but we always called him Buddy. Happy?"

Charlie giggled, and Jasper continued. "Anyway, *Ray* got spooked and took his eye off the road. Right then, this guy comes running out of an alley and right in front of the truck. Ray slammed on the brakes but clipped the dude pretty good, and we lost control. Ended up hitting a telephone pole. Ray jumped out of the truck and he's screaming his head off about the broken headlight and the dented fender."

Lexy covered her mouth with her hand.

"I'm trying to calm him down when the guy on the ground starts begging for help. He's got blood coming out of his mouth, ears, and forehead, and he's holding his gut. I got down on one knee and see this guy's bleeding from the stomach. Gunshot wound, stab wound. I couldn't tell. I yell for Ray to call an ambulance, and he starts freaking out about how he's going to go to jail. I told him if we don't call an ambulance, we're definitely going to jail. He says 'fuck that' and is about to take off on foot when we hear more gunshots."

"We jump into the truck, but it won't start. We're about to bail on foot when these guys come out of the alley and start kicking the crap out of the guy on the ground. It was savage. One dude even pulls out a Deagle and unloads into the guy's chest."

Jasper had everyone's attention, even Jackson's. Mattie, however, broke the silence. "What's a 'Deagle'?"

"I believe it's a portmanteau of the words 'Desert' and 'Eagle'," Harlan whispered.

Mattie pondered. "What's a portmanteau?"

"*Anyway*," Jasper said in a voice that drew further giggles from Charlie and Jackson. "Ray gives the truck another try, and it started. I'm yelling, 'Go! Go! Go!' and he slams it into gear and stomps on the gas. We had no idea where were going, and we didn't care. All we knew was if we stayed there, we were as good as dead, so we go tearing ass down the alley and pop out onto a major street. Just when we were thinking we're home free, we hear a car hauling ass up the alley, no lights, no nothing, just "boom, boom, boom" and the muzzle flash from the Deagle. We've got bullets bouncing off the pavement, and a couple punch through the truck. We start screaming like a couple of schoolgirls on a roller coaster."

Almost every face in the tent took on the same anxious expression. Jackson, however, simply crossed his arms, sat back in his chair, and waited for Jasper to continue.

"I see a sign that says the freeway is up ahead, and Ray guns the motor. The rear end comes around, and we're bouncing off parked cars like a fat dude in a mosh pit. Ray can't get the truck under control. The front suspension's trashed, and he can't get it to track in a straight line, and he hits another telephone pole. The truck stalls out.

"We're sitting there, shocked we were both alive when this Impala pulls up next to us. Four guys step out. One of them is holding the Deagle. We're fucked. There was no way he was gonna miss at that distance. Turns out we didn't have to worry about that because another guy pulled out a machete. They were going to gut us instead. We were just waiting to die when we heard sirens up the block. The guys looked at each other, then one of them yells, 'You motherfuckers got lucky tonight,' and they hopped into the Impala and drove off."

Harlan let out an audible sigh of relief.

"As the sirens got louder, we started laughing. We'd made it. After all that shit, we were still alive. The cops pulled up and ordered us out of the truck. We climb out, hands in the air, and there's this wetness in my pants. I look down, thinking I pissed myself, and see my shirt and pants are covered in blood. Turns out one of those rounds got me in the stomach."

"Bullshit," Lexy said.

"Hand to God." Jasper raised one hand and placed the other over his heart.

"Let's see the scar."

Jasper climbed to his feet. Unlike his tent, Charlie's tent afforded considerable headroom, and he was able to stand without hunching. Without a word, he lifted his coat, sweatshirt, and T-shirt to reveal a three-inch scar running horizontally along the right side of his abdomen. Lexy stared, mouth agape, as Jasper sat back down.

"I think we have a winner," Harlan exclaimed. "Unless Jackson's changed his mind."

Lexy locked eyes with Jackson and cocked her head slightly to one side, but he responded with a simple shake of his head.

Mattie hobbled over to the door flap and unzipped it. He poked his head outside and looked around before pulling his head in like a turtle ducking into its shell. "Storm's over."

"Thank God." Jasper scrambled to his feet. "I've had to pee like a racehorse for hours." He zipped the door all the way and squeezed past Mattie.

"Me too!" Harlan hurried after Jasper, leaving Mattie in the doorway. He grinned sheepishly. "I need to pull up a tree, myself."

He slipped out, and Jackson watched as the door seemed to zip itself shut.

"What about you? Do you have to *make* too?

Jackson turned and saw Charlie smiling. "I'm good. So, when do we hit the trail?"

"We don't."

"But the storm stopped."

"Yes." Charlie checked her watch. "But we lost a lot of time today. By the time you factor in teardown now, and setup after we hike, we won't make much progress before dark."

"What about the bear? You said he could cover as much as twenty miles a day."

Charlie glanced at the tent door. "We have to hope he doesn't make much progress either."

Jackson stared. Was this the same woman who'd wanted to continue their march for another ninety minutes just yesterday?

Charlie sighed as if she'd read his mind. "Look, it's not ideal, but the winds are still churning up a lot of snow. I can't risk someone getting lost or falling into a crevasse."

Jackson acknowledged Charlie's point with a reluctant nod. He'd heard what sounded like genuine disappointment in her voice and saw no reason to force the issue. "So, what do we do for the rest of the day?"

"I loaded half a dozen books on my eReader. I thought I'd plow through one of those." She gestured at an open spot on the floor. "You're welcome to pull up some floor."

Jackson hesitated. He hadn't anticipated an extended trip and brought along nothing to read, figuring tracking a rogue bear would be entertainment enough.

"You could always take a nap."

"I don't know…"

"Come on, boss," Lexy urged. She had already removed her coat and boots and climbed into her sleeping bag. "When's the last time you slept between two hot women?"

Jackson couldn't suppress a smile. "That does sound better than spending the day with Jasper and his beef jerky farts." He gave Lexy a stern look. "But don't tell Doris or Wyatt. I'll never hear the end of it."

LEXY CAREFULLY ROLLED up her coat and snow pants and laid them on top of the rest of her gear. Usually, she would have left them on the floor where she'd discarded them, but she didn't want Charlie to give her grief about her messiness. Not that she cared about a ribbing. She found the woman's tracking skills and business acumen impressive, and didn't want to come off as some sort of flaky lightweight. She climbed into her sleeping bag and tried to zip it, but the teeth remained unzipped no matter how far she moved the pull tab. She puzzled over the mechanism, then let out a snort as she remembered that it had two pull tabs, one right after the other, and the second opened the bag an instant after the first closed it.

Lexy noticed Charlie smirking at her. *So much for not coming off as a flaky lightweight.*

"You do much camping?"

"Some. Summer camp, resorts on the lake. Not *real* camping." Lexy gave an apologetic shrug. "Nothing like this."

"Nothing to be ashamed of. Roughing it isn't everybody's thing."

Lexy laughed. "We're in a six-person tent with two-hundred-dollar sleeping bags, LED lanterns, and sleeping pads that are more comfortable than my mattress at home. I wouldn't exactly call this roughing it."

Charlie laughed too. She slid out of her snow pants and into a pair of flannel pajama pants, but kept her thermal underwear on underneath. She saw Lexy watching and flashed a smile. "I can't stand the sound of ski pants when I'm in the sleeping bag. It makes me feel like an individually wrapped hot dog."

"Omigod!" Lexy exclaimed, her face lighting up. "That's exactly what it's like! I wish I'd brought pajamas." She put on a sad face and climbed into her sleeping bag.

"I should have mentioned this yesterday, but I have an extra pair if you want them."

Lexy considered, then shook her head. "No offense, but your pajamas wouldn't even cover my shins."

"Yeah. Must be tough dealing with those long model legs of yours."

"Absolute nightmare." Lexy broke into a grin. "Unless I need to get something off the top shelf of my cupboard."

Charlie reached for the lantern and then paused. When

Lexy nodded, Charlie killed the light. The tent went black, and the two women lay quiet in the darkness.

"Tired?" Came Charlie's voice.

"Beat. The first day took it out of me," Lexy responded. "You?"

"Not really. But I'm used to long hikes."

There was a swishing of polyester as Lexy sat up in her sleeping bag. "I can stay up for a bit if you want to chat. I can't promise an all-nighter, but I'm game for a little convo."

More swishing, as Charlie also sat up. "You sure?"

"Sure. So, do you want to talk about boys?" Lexy asked playfully.

"I most certainly do not." Charlie delivered her answer with conviction, and the tent went silent again. "Why? Do you?"

"No. But I do have a question."

Charlie sighed in the dark. "About Jasper…"

"Eww. No. About Mattie. What's his deal?"

"What do you mean?"

"I mean, he seems nice." More swishing as Lexy adjusted in her sleeping bag. "Kind, polite, funny…and good-looking."

"Seems almost too good to be true, doesn't he?"

"I didn't mean to—"

"It's okay. Mattie's great, but he's a dreamer. He doesn't care about politics, sports, or romance." Charlie pointed upward. "He's more interested in what's going on up there."

Lexy nodded and sighed, drawing a laugh from Charlie.

"So. Any more questions about my baby brother?"

"I've been dying to ask how the two of you could have come from the same…litter."

"What? You don't see the family resemblance?"

"It sounds terrible, but if one of you isn't adopted, I

understood the genetics unit in biology class a lot less than I thought."

Charlie laughed again. "We get that all the time."

"You don't have to talk about it."

"I don't mind, but it's a long story."

Lexy placed her hands in her lap. "Fire away. If I get bored, I'll snore until you stop talking."

"I grew up on a reservation in Wisconsin," Charlie began. "It was me, my mother, and my older sister, Janine. When I was twelve and Janine was fourteen, we were on a bus from Ashland to Duluth. It was only a two-hour trip, but it was the farthest I'd ever traveled at that point. It was the most incredible adventure of my life. We saw things we'd never seen on the reservation. To us, it was like traveling the entire world."

Lexy rocked in her sleeping bag, creating a swishing sound as she pulled her legs into a sitting position that caused the bag to bulge.

"Janine had been collecting pop bottles and stealing change from unlocked cars for weeks to save up for the bus tickets. They weren't expensive, but to us it was a fortune. We had enough for the tickets but nothing else, so we squirreled away food by hiding parts of our dinner in napkins in the back of the freezer for days before the trip."

Charlie laughed to herself. "We must have looked like hobos climbing on the bus with our plastic shopping bags. To this day, I'm shocked nobody thought to call our mother." Charlie's voice hitched. "Then again, we were obviously from the res, so people probably just chalked it up as two little Indian girls whose parents didn't care where they were."

"What was in Duluth?" Lexy asked.

"Freedom." Charlie's voice sounded far away. "The area

around the ports was mostly office buildings and factories then. The hotels, restaurants, and shops didn't appear until later, but it was still pretty cool. The lift bridge was already there, and gigantic ships from all over the world came and went. We used to fantasize about their exotic cargo." Charlie's voice thickened. "We had no idea what was on those ships."

Charlie took a moment to reset. "On the bus, we were just two kids enjoying the view from the window. It was a wonderful respite from our daily lives. Once we got to the city, we sat on the rocks, watching people, families, factory workers, whoever happened by. It was a perfect day, with a light breeze, sunshine, and the clang of the lift bridge bell as ships passed. It was like a scene from a movie..." She trailed off. When she spoke again, her voice had taken on a nasal quality, as if she'd been crying. "I went to the bathroom. It was just across the street, nestled between two buildings. I wanted to go alone, but Janine insisted on walking me over."

A high-pitched yip broke the stillness, followed by several more in rapid succession that caused both women to flinch, but as the yips melted into a forlorn howl, they exchanged a knowing glance.

"*Canis latrans*?" Lexy whispered.

"Yep. Wolf howls don't faze me, but I've never quite gotten used to coyote howls. Little bastards get me every time."

The tent remained quiet until cotton rustled against nylon as Charlie resettled.

"It was one of those enclosed open-air bathrooms where the outer walls were open but covered by chicken wire, and the stall doors started a foot above the floor and ended four feet from the ceiling. I sat there, feet swinging above the concrete floor, listening to the world outside, exposed and safe at the same time. I heard every car that went up or down South Lake Street and every conversation."

"I finished, washed my hands, and hurried out, eager to get back to our picnic. Janine wasn't there. I looked up and down the street, but she wasn't anywhere. I'd seen enough after-school specials to know that if I went looking for Janine, we would never find each other, so I waited.

"After three hours, I gave up and ran to the closest office building and told the receptionist what happened. She was a sweet older white lady and very kind, but the look on her face when I told her my fourteen-year-old sister was missing..." Charlie's voice took on the nasal quality again. "That was the last time I ever saw her."

Lexy was torn between the need for clarification and her desire to respect Charlie's feelings, but she had to ask. "Did anyone search for her?"

"Mom came down. We called the police. That's when I learned native women used to disappear all the time."

"They still do," Lexy offered grimly. "You were lucky to get away."

"I was small for my age, scrawny, undeveloped." Charlie shrugged. "I barely looked ten, let alone twelve. Janine looked like a woman, *was* a woman, even at fourteen. She was round and curvy. She'd been attracting stares from men for a couple of years. We couldn't go anywhere or do anything without comments from men and women. They acted like Janine was looking for attention. She wasn't. She hated it, but she was cursed."

"I'd tell you I'm sorry, and that it wasn't your fault. But I know it won't help." Lexy's voice was even and calm, like that of a grief counselor. "And it won't take away the guilt."

Lexy reached into the darkness and placed a hand on Charlie's leg. She'd debated whether to do so, concerned the woman might misread her gesture, but as she worked her hand up Charlie's leg, she was relieved to feel Charlie clasp it in a tight grip.

"Mom and I went back to the reservation and tried to get on with our lives," Charlie continued, "but Mom never got over losing Janine." Her voice hitched again. "Janine was always her favorite."

"I find that hard to believe."

"Believe it." Charlie managed a chuckle. "I was the worst at that age. Lippy, devious, you name it. Janine was the good one. Kind, responsible. She was like a second mother to me. Not that my mother was a bad mom. She worked hard and spent as much time with us as she could, but after Janine, the pain was too much." She sighed again. "Within a year, Child Services shipped me off to live with a nice white couple in Milwaukee."

"And that's when you met Mattie," Lexy said, completing Charlie's thought.

"Mattie was a miracle baby." Charlie's tone lifted. "He came along when I was fifteen, two years after I was adopted. Arlene, my adopted mom, was the age I am now, and Roger, my dad, was about Jackson's age. They didn't have the energy to chase a toddler, and, by the time Mattie was a teenager, they couldn't keep up with him anymore. So, I filled in." Charlie squeezed Lexy's hand. "As you can imagine, I'm protective of Mattie."

"No need to imagine. It's pretty obvious." Lexy slipped her hand out of Charlie's and snuggled deep into her sleeping bag. The tent fell silent when Charlie cleared her throat.

"Not so fast. This has been a one-sided conversation so far."

Lexy propped herself up on one arm. "What do you want to know?"

"What are you doing out here?" Charlie's words were accusatory yet jovial.

"Looking for a rogue bear. Same as you."

"No. That's what *Jackson* is doing out here. What are *you* doing here? You're smart and capable. If you'd walked into Frieda's shop without that uniform, I would have pegged you for a doctor, lawyer, or accountant. Heck, I would have believed you if you said you were the fashion editor of Vogue. Anything but a DNR officer."

Lexy bowed her head.

"Tell me something about yourself."

"Like what?"

"Anything. Something interesting. But don't lie. I'll know."

"Is that so?"

Charlie let out a long breath. "I've been stomping through forests and jungles all over the world for years. Spent more time around men than most men. I know a lie when I hear one."

Lexy laughed but kept her head down.

"Come on." Charlie's insistence was gentle but firm. "I'll bet you've been dying for a conversation that didn't revolve around sports, guns, or trucks. Besides, this excursion will be over soon. Then you'll never see me again. Why not take advantage of a sympathetic ear?"

Lexy lifted her head.

Jackson sat in his camping chair, huddled beside a sad excuse for a campfire. Haphazardly stacked kindling burned on one side but barely sputtered on the other. He didn't care. It provided sufficient warmth, and he liked the smell. He stared at the clouds, watching them float lazily across the dark sky.

"Good Lord, who taught you how to make a fire?"

Jackson whirled to see Charlie approaching with her camping chair in hand. He grinned as she set her chair next to his and plopped herself into it.

"I'm not great at this whole camping thing."

"Yeah, I noticed. That fire looks like a drunk Cub Scout made it." Jackson was about to protest when Charlie followed up. "This space is cute, though. Very cozy and nicely laid out."

"Cute and cozy is exactly what I was going for."

Charlie scooted her chair closer to the fire. "What brings you out in this cold with your sketchy fire-building skills?"

"Self-preservation. Jasper ate an entire can of baked beans before he turned in."

"Ugh. He can be such an asshole."

"That's the impression I got, but I'm trying to keep an open mind." He stoked the fire half-heartedly. "How about you? What brings you out at this time of night, despite the big comfortable tent and a roommate that doesn't spew noxious fumes?"

"Lexy and I enjoyed some girl talk, then she fell asleep. I wasn't tired, so I figured I'd see who else was still up."

Jackson resumed looking at the sky, and the pair was content to watch the clouds morph into a menagerie of shapes. Meanwhile, the fire flickered, bobbed, and weaved, intertwining with the smoke in an occasional swirling tango whenever a light breeze passed through the camp.

Charlie leaned forward, elbows on her knees, like an ice fisherman hovering over a hole. "So, a Chicago cop, huh?"

"Yup."

"That must have been quite the experience. Compared to what you do now, I mean."

Jackson grunted but offered nothing more.

Charlie tapped her foot. "Is it something you'd rather not talk about?"

"Not much to it. I caught my partner torturing a suspect and told him to stop. He refused, so I shot him. Lost my job, my wife, and my friends. You know. Same old story."

"Have you spoken to anyone about it? Professionally?"

"I don't need therapy."

"Of course, you don't. You went through an intense mental and emotional experience, followed by the end of two significant relationships. Why pursue treatment that might keep you from shooting up a mall?"

Jackson blinked. "You don't pull any punches, do you?"

Charlie wore a sly grin. "Life's too short to tiptoe."

He heaved himself out of his chair. His tendons and bones popped and cracked like he'd stepped on a bag of pretzels, and he wondered if Charlie had heard. Her hearty laugh told him she had. Jackson smiled. The woman's laugh was loud and completely lacking self-consciousness. It was the laugh of someone comfortable in their skin. "Turning in soon?"

"In a few." Charlie scanned the dark forest around them. The fire was bright enough to reveal the tips of the nearest tree branches, which bowed under the snow that clung to the needle-covered branches in puffy clumps like bits of cotton blooming on a stem. "Now that the wind has quieted down, the forest will come back to life. I think I'll listen in for a bit."

Jackson reconsidered, but the bite of the night air

knifing through his clothes made him think better of it. "Well, good night."

JACKSON ENTERED the tent to find Jasper propped up on one arm, reading under the light of a battery-powered lantern. He unzipped his coat and climbed into his sleeping bag.

"How come you didn't tell a story?"

Jackson burrowed into his sleeping bag up to his neck and had just gotten himself zipped in when he heard the soft rustle of Jasper closing his book. He looked up to see Jasper watching him. He had laid down the book but remained propped up on one elbow.

"Didn't want to steal your thunder."

"Please. My story had it all. Guns, violence, gangs, car crashes, *and* sports. Somebody ought to turn it into a movie."

"I'm pretty sure somebody already did."

"What are you talking about?"

Jackson rolled onto his side. "Came out in the early nineties, about a bunch of guys who were chased through a rough part of town by a drug lord and his cronies."

"Never seen it."

"Really? I think Charlie Sheen was in it."

"I got no idea what you're talking about." Jasper pulled his sleeping bag up around his neck.

"You sure? It had a killer soundtrack." When Jasper didn't answer, Jackson shrugged. "Might have been before your time." He lay down again and zipped the sleeping bag up to his chin. "Good night."

Jasper reached for the lantern. With a click, the tent momentarily descended into darkness and silence.

"How come you didn't tell anyone?" Came Jasper's voice. "That I made it up."

"What would I gain from that?"

"Two hundred-fifty bucks."

"Your bet was with Harlan, not me. Like I said, what do I gain by making you look like an ass in front of the team?"

Jasper scoffed. "I don't need help making an ass of myself."

"You'll get no argument from me there." Jackson fluffed his pillow and snuggled in. He sensed Jasper staring daggers at him in the dark but didn't care.

16

Carson Ten Bears spent most of his early life close to the wilderness. Not *in* the wilderness but wilderness-adjacent. Between reservations, encampments, and working multiple jobs, Carson had never spent much time in the forests but longed to do so. However, his parents thought it best he received an education, and he'd abided by their wishes until no longer required to do so.

After graduating from high school in 1958, he moved to Duluth and got a job in the steel mills. The work was hard and dangerous, but he'd made more money than he'd ever seen. He'd stayed on in Duluth until the local economy declined in 1963, then headed up the lake toward the Canadian border, where he bounced from resort to resort, doing odd jobs for lodging and a nominal paycheck.

Fifteen years later, Carson's skill and expertise made him an indispensable employee. While he still didn't make much, between his income from the resorts from May to October and working odd jobs during the off-season, he saved enough for a down payment on a tiny roadside resort near Grand Portage. Unfortunately, not a single bank would finance the purchase. The banks' blatantly racist treatment might have crushed most people, but Carson refused to wallow in bitterness and continued to split his time between the various resort cities that hugged the coastline of Superior.

Now, Carson found himself fully immersed in the wild. It seemed fitting that his final act would take place in the great woods. He wished he had time to enjoy the quiet and solitude, but he was on a mission. Yes, anger fueled his desire to destroy the Flesh-Eater, but he couldn't allow that anger to make him careless. He couldn't afford an injury, not before he located the beast. Even if he escaped the encounter unscathed, he doubted he'd survive the return trip to his cabin. He didn't care. He didn't find the prospect of life without his beloved rabbits particularly appealing.

From up ahead came a snort like that of an agitated horse. Carson cocked his head and waited, swaying on numb feet. "Hello?" His voice was hoarse from disuse and exposure to frigid air. Receiving no response, he shook his head, embarrassed he'd called out to something so obviously not human.

He resumed his march, convinced whatever he'd heard had either moved on or never existed, but when a long, wet hiss came from ahead, he staggered backward. Although he managed to stay upright, the effort caused his metal cup and tin canteen to clatter, and he grasped at the offending gear, trying in vain to silence them, but only succeeded in losing his balance again. This time he fell, hitting the ground with a thump. Ignoring his bruised dignity, he hoisted himself to his knees, but before he could coax his aged body to rise further, he heard sounds of effort and exertion behind him.

Although petrified, Carson fought the urge to run.

Whatever was behind him might not appreciate the sudden movement. But his body had other ideas. Flooded with fear and adrenaline, it demanded he act. *Our life depends on it.* Survival instinct overcame logic and pride, and Carson prepared to flee, but the "evolved" part of his brain sought confirmation, and he glanced back, expecting to see a groggy bear or agitated moose. He saw neither.

A dark figure rose high into the air, its immense height magnified by Carson's position on his knees. Matted fur covered the creature, although the shadows of the forest canopy made it hard to determine its exact color. Its elongated head reflected the moon's light like a polished motorcycle helmet, emitting enough luminosity to make its appendages visible.

Long arms curved away from a broad chest and hung almost to its knees. Its legs, defined by bulging muscles and taut tendons, somehow both long and thick, were the circumference of telephone poles at the hips and a baseball bat at the ankles. With its lanky limbs and lethal appendages evolved solely for dealing death, the creature reminded Carson of a praying mantis.

Strangely, Carson no longer felt the compulsion to flee. His brain was too busy rationalizing the horrific vision before him, leaving his body in neutral, awaiting instructions on what to do next. Long dormant neurons fired, urging him to articulate the word his brain had refused to utter until his tongue and lips, chapped and withered by the cold, spoke a single word: "Wendigo."

The creature reacted with a hiss. Carson swung the pack off his shoulders and, with shaking hands, dumped the contents on the ground. Ignoring the fear that racked his body, he sifted through the pile until he found a lighter and a can of lubricant, then clambered to his feet.

As he staggered toward the creature, it tilted its head in apparent curiosity. It wasn't afraid of him. Then again, why would it be? The thing was neither human nor animal. It was an evil spirit with no reason to fear a man brandishing a tin can. Carson continued forward, aware he'd already placed himself within the long-limbed creature's reach.

No matter. His plan was a good one, a clever one. With a vengeful cry, he depressed the can's spray nozzle. Lubricant spewed forth in a frothy stream that covered the creature's face in a milky sheen. But something was wrong. The lubricant should have been a mist. Instead, it was liquid.

Regardless of form, the creature didn't care for the emollient. It raised its baseball glove-sized hands to its muzzle, trying to rid itself of the sticky residue, but only succeeded in smearing the oily white glaze into its eyes. The creature roared and batted at its smooth white face. The sticky wetness seemed to infuriate the beast, and it howled indignantly, ignoring Carson as it spun like a dog chasing its tail before plunging its face into the snow.

Carson watched, open-mouthed. Why hadn't his plan worked? Why hadn't the substance come out in a suffocating cloud? He checked the can, noting its red and black color, and winced. He'd bought a knock-off brand, half the price of his normal product. Ignoring the creature's enraged shrieks, he turned the can over and peered at the small print.

His heart sank. Unlike the name-brand lubricant, which had a minimum operating temperature of -40 degrees, the knock-off brand had an operating temperature of -15 degrees. The temperature outside was at least twenty degrees below zero. *I'm going to die because I saved a couple of pennies at the hardware store.*

Carson looked at the creature. It had stopped howling

but was still wiping at its face, using handfuls of snow to flush the lubricant from its eyes. He still had time, but he had to act quickly. Carson raised his lighter and flicked the flint wheel. It didn't budge. He tried again and again, but the flint wheel refused to spin. Furious, he clenched his fist, determined to smash the lighter into pieces, but his thick gloves prevented him from applying enough pressure.

The gloves! Carson yanked the glove from his hand with his teeth and transferred the lighter to his bare hand. He rubbed his thumb across the flint wheel and heard the gritty "snick" of metal against flint as blue and orange flame plumed from the lighter. Carson held the can over the two-inch flame and turned it like the tumbler in a dryer, moving the can back and forth with each turn. He felt the can grow warmer with each revolution. Soon, the contents would return to their pressurized liquid state. He would have his weapon. He would destroy—

The creature's breath washed over him. The acrid, pungent, ammonia-like tang of rotting meat overpowered the strong citrus-butterscotch aroma of the lubricant. The beast was only a few feet away. It would be on him in seconds.

Carson shook the can as hard as he could, prompting a staccato growl from the beast. The growl became a snarl as Carson rested his thumb on the can's nozzle. He hoped he'd shaken long enough. "For the girls," he whispered, pressing the nozzle for the second time.

Mist sputtered from the spray can's nozzle and intersected the lighter's flame. A tongue of fire arced through the night, striking the creature.

Residual lubricant from Carson's first attempt changed from solid to liquid, from liquid to gas, before igniting in a fireball that enveloped the creature in an orange blaze.

Carson raised his arms against the heat as the beast bellowed and gyrated. It dropped to the ground again, this time writhing and batting at the flames with its hands, but the fire refused to die. As Carson watched the creature burn, he thought of his *Nookomis* and *Nimishoomis*. His grandparents. They had been right. The Wendigo was real. It thrashed before him, burning underneath its fiery cloak.

He should have been delighted. He should have taken pleasure in the creature's demise. But he didn't. It pained him to watch any beast, even this incarnation of evil, suffer.

Carson turned away. What would he do now? He had not expected to survive the confrontation. He had not planned for life after revenge.

A snort came from behind him. The same horse-like exhalation as before. Carson turned slowly to see the creature rise to its feet and brush the snow off its body as if brushing lint from a sports coat. Carson blinked in amazement. The scent of burning hair filled his nostrils, but there was no hint of charred flesh. Other than the singed fur around its shoulders and neck, the creature appeared unaffected by the flames, except for its disposition. The Wendigo was angry.

Carson's reaction was remarkably measured. He reached behind his back, eased the axe from his shoulder strap, and raised the tool over his head. "If I cannot melt your icy heart, I will cut it from your chest." As Carson charged the forest demon, his thoughts returned to his girls, Diana, Mary, and Florence, and the fear and pain they'd suffered at the hideous creature's hands. The Wendigo would pay for what it had done, what it had taken from him. It would pay for—

A single foil, sharp as a razor, whistled through the air in a half arc. Carson felt a slight pressure in his neck and slumped to the ground. Although disoriented at first, he regained his bearings and saw a skewed view of his surroundings. The view didn't last long.

Darkness invaded from the periphery, quickly shrinking his vision to a single point. As he died, Carson's final thought wasn't of the cabin, his life, or his beloved rabbits, but the curious image of his headless body lying in the snow mere feet away.

17

Charlie crossed her hands over her midsection and stared at the tent ceiling. She had a pit in her stomach, and while the weight and heat of her hands on her belly eased the pain, it could not erase the unfamiliar feeling. The feeling of failure. She'd lost trails before, but that had been over two decades ago, before clients paid her handsomely to track animals.

Yesterday had been different. There were no last-minute clues to spot, no twigs bent the wrong way, no errant clumps of fur stuck to a tree, or frozen yellow puddles giving off the faint ammonia scent of urine, hinting at her quarry's whereabouts. To make matters worse, she'd forced the team to trek through the snowy forest longer than she should have. Had it just been Mattie and Jasper, she might have gone another ninety minutes, but the DNR people were novices. Lexy had complained of soreness, and she was the most fit of the DNR crew. It was a minor miracle the professor hadn't keeled over. Worse yet, they were *customers*. She was billing almost twice her normal rate to lead the expedition, and she'd put them at risk.

And then there was the weather. The previous day's heavy snowfall made for a treacherous hike, and the high winds only exacerbated the issue. Not only was travel difficult, but the snow covered almost all evidence of life, and what evidence might have been available had been rearranged or erased, leaving no sign of the thing's passage through the forest.

Charlie winced at her use of the term *thing* but couldn't conjure a more suitable word. She knew whatever had eviscerated and consumed part of the bull moose was neither vegetable nor mineral, but it was anyone's guess what sort of animal it was. The prints, when visible, matched nothing she'd ever stalked. The wide track and long stride hinted at a bipedal animal, but she'd followed the prints for miles, and no non-human could walk on two legs for such a distance. Unnerving as the details were, at this point, they were moot. She'd lost the trail and had little confidence she could find it again.

Charlie glanced at the sleeping Lexy. *Ignorance is most definitely bliss.* But that bliss would be short-lived. Even though Charlie had lost the trail and likely forfeited her fee, the fact that an unidentified dangerous animal shared the woods with them wasn't something she felt comfortable hiding any longer.

Lexy rolled over, and Charlie held her breath. Despite the pangs of conscience, she wasn't ready to break the news just yet, and when Lexy didn't wake, she exhaled a sigh of relief. As she snuck out of her sleeping bag, Charlie marveled at the young woman's ability to sleep so late. Mattie possessed the same talent, as did Jasper, to a lesser extent. Sleeping in, she decided, was a talent, and a curse, of the young.

Charlie pulled on her coat and unzipped the door flap.

She'd slept in her boots, as she'd done the previous night. Not knowing much about her quarry, she thought it best to leave her boots on in case she had to be on her feet in a hurry. As she stooped to exit, Lexy stirred.

"Is it seriously nine o'clock?" Lexy croaked, sounding like she'd spent the night in a smoky bar. "We should have been on the trail by now."

"We're fine." Charlie forced a smile.

Lexy sat up quickly. "What's wrong?"

Charlie grimaced. She should have known the beautiful young woman could spot bullshit from a mile away. People probably lied to Lexy every day.

"Nothing you're going to want to hear on an empty stomach. Come outside and I'll fill you in."

THE GROUP HUDDLED around Jasper's tent, half-asleep and shivering in the morning cold. Charlie waited for them to settle, then took a deep breath.

"I need to apologize." Her voice was contrite yet confident. "I thought this would be just another job, a couple of days in the woods searching for a hungry bear, and then back to Milwaukee in time to watch my Badgers. I was wrong."

She scanned the team and was met with quizzical looks. "I underestimated how much the weather would affect my ability to track the...animal. We got more snow than forecasted, and the high winds weren't helpful, but I overestimated how much the forest cover would preserve the tracks. Long and short, I have no idea where this thing is."

No one uttered a word until Jasper stepped forward.

"You're telling me we wasted an entire day dicking around in your tent, and you have no clue where it is?"

Charlie ignored Jasper and turned to Jackson. "Of course, I'll be waiving my fee." Jackson opened his mouth to speak, but Jasper exploded before he could respond.

"Hold on. I've been out here freezing my ass off and we're not even getting paid?"

"Calm down," Jackson commanded.

"Don't tell me to calm down," Jasper spat.

"Okay, okay. How about everybody just relax?" Charlie said. "We have a bigger problem. Potentially much bigger."

"What kind of problem?" Harlan's voice quivered. His skin, already pasty, seemed to have grown more pale.

Charlie addressed the whole team but looked at Jackson in particular. "Truth is, we aren't tracking a bear."

Jasper reacted as if struck. "Then what the hell are we tracking?"

"Come on, Jasper. You saw that moose. When have you ever come across a bear kill like that? A one-ton moose pulled apart at the seams, ribs splayed open like a birthday present?" Jasper's eyes dropped. "And what about the missing head? It wasn't just ripped off; something *twisted* it off. What bear has the manual dexterity to do something like that?"

"Coulda been wolves." Jasper's retort came off as half-hearted at best.

Charlie shook her head. "Wolves would have stretched the neck tissues as they pulled. Whatever took that moose's head wrenched it off like it was pulling off a chunk of taffy."

Jasper laughed. "Jesus, Charlie, it's just an animal. Crocs and gators twist off chunks of their prey all the time. It's called a death roll."

When Charlie refused to budge from her position, Jasper looked to Harlan. "Tell her, Doc. This isn't some monster. It's a bear that woke up early to take a piss and realized it was hungry."

Harlan offered a sympathetic shrug. "I'd have to agree with Charlie. Whatever took apart that moose exhibited primate-level intelligence and brutality." He glanced at Lexy, who confirmed his position with a nod. "Based on observation, I'd say the killer placed a foot on the carcass for leverage, then used two hands to exert the torque necessary to remove the head."

Jasper's eyes grew wide. "Hands?"

"Clawed hands perhaps, but hands capable of complex and intricate manipulation."

Jasper turned on Mattie, fury reddening his face. "Did you know about this?"

Mattie initially shrank away, then, as if suddenly remembering he had a spine, squared his shoulders. "You saw those tracks, Jasper. How could you look at them and think 'bear'?"

"I'm not paid to look at tracks." Spittle flew from Jasper's mouth. "I'm paid to make sure none of you gets trampled by a moose or shot by some drunk idiot with a gun."

He looked from one face to the next. "I hardly looked at the goddamned moose or the tracks. Why would I? Charlie's the fucking expert!" He noticed Jackson standing with his hands in his pockets and stepped toward the older man. "What about you? Did you know?"

"I did not." Jackson shot Charlie a withering glance. "Guess this village has two idiots." He calmly hiked his pack on his shoulder and disappeared into a wall of trees.

The group looked at each other in stunned silence.

"Where's he going?" Charlie said finally, whirling toward Lexy.

"He'll be fine," Lexy assured her. "He just needs to cool off."

"Cool off? He could get lost out there and freeze to death." Charlie stared after Jackson. "If he's gone more than ten minutes, I'm going after him."

"He won't go far. I guarantee he'll be back in twenty minutes like nothing happened." Lexy's voice was authoritative. Her expression was anything but.

THE DEEP SNOW should have been an impediment to stomping off, but Jackson was too furious to let it stop him. Lexy and Harlan had known something was amiss and kept it from him. He'd considered the possibility their omission had been unintentional, but quickly dismissed it. Their shared arrogance had been apparent the moment he'd found them huddled in his office. This was just a continuation of the theme. In this case, they felt they were tracking something so unusual and historic that he couldn't possibly have appreciated the magnitude of their discovery.

He couldn't shake the idea that they thought of him as a cop who saw the world through a black-and-white lens. Jackson stopped in his tracks. Lexy and Harlan had "Mean Girled" him not once but twice in the last few days. Instead of excluding Jackson because he wasn't pretty or popular, they'd assumed he lacked the intelligence to comprehend the gravity of the situation. He shook his head. *Appreciate* and *comprehend* were code for "he's not one of the smart kids."

Jackson stopped stewing long enough to check his surroundings. He didn't know where he was or where he was headed. He wasn't even sure why he'd stormed out of camp, but the answer came as he shivered in the cold. It was why he'd left Chicago to play football at UW Superior when he'd had offers from schools closer to home. It was why he'd left Chicago again when his marriage and career fell apart. He found it easier to run than to confront his feelings.

He hated confrontation of any sort. Tears, crying, yelling, screaming. Jackson preferred to avoid theatrics whenever possible. In this case, it had been foolish of him to leave the safety of the group, especially knowing they weren't tracking a bear but something far more dangerous. The thought sent a shiver down his spine. Angry or not, he'd have to swallow his pride and head back to camp. He took a deep breath in preparation for the return trip and encountered a stench so pungent it stung his nostrils and made his eyes water.

THE MOOD around the camp was dour. The team conducted tear-down in a slow, sullen fashion. No one spoke as they rolled bags, buried leftover food, and painstakingly deconstructed tents to ensure each piece returned to the appropriate carrying bag.

Lexy was the only one not engaged in the tear-down. She'd already stowed her gear and neatly stacked for departure. Although not part of the effort, she was hardly idle. She was busy pacing back and forth at the edge of camp and glancing anxiously at her watch.

Harlan looked up from his sleeping bag, which he struggled to roll small enough to fit back into its built-in carrying pouch. "I'm sure he's fine. We would have heard a weapon discharge if he'd met with any trouble."

Charlie was nearby, and her head snapped up at Harlan's mention of a weapon. She said nothing, however, as she saw no reason to inform the scientist that neither Jackson nor Lexy carried weapons at her insistence.

She finished loading the backpack and zipped it shut. It pained her to see Lexy fret over the DNR officer, and with a sigh, she grabbed her backpack and walked over to the woman. "All that pacing is driving me crazy." Charlie unzipped the backpack and retrieved a medical kit as Lexy looked at her curiously.

"What is that for?" Lexy's utterance was as much an accusation as a question.

"Better to have it and not need it." Charlie pointed Lexy in the direction Jackson had exited. With a maternal pat on the back, she urged Lexy forward. "Let's go find him."

At that exact moment, Jackson ambled into the clearing. His arms hung at his sides. His chest heaved as his lungs clamored for air.

"Um, Jackson?" Lexy said, careful not to startle her superior officer. "Are you okay?"

He shook his head.

"I found something."

CHARLIE, Lexy, Harlan, Mattie, and Jasper circled Jackson, who stood in a patch of snow tamped down by heavy foot traffic. Charlie looked from the snow to Jackson, to the snow again. Her expression, like that of her fellow expedition members, was one of bewilderment.

"You're sure this is the spot?"

Jackson nodded.

"Well, I don't see anything." Jasper impatiently shifted his weight from one foot to the other. "Why did you drag us out here?"

Charlie ignored Jasper and surveyed the area again. "What was it you thought you saw?"

"Nothing." Jackson's response was curt. He was still angry. "It's what I smelled."

Charlie inhaled. "I don't smell anything." Her voice was soft, yet held a hint of frustration.

"There is a trace of something." Harlan's eyebrows knitted as his high-powered brain churned. "Miss Battice, how much do you know about predator territorial behavior?"

Charlie tensed. Had she been a cat, her hackles would have raised. "A fair amount, but there could certainly be some gaps in my knowledge."

"I'm not questioning your knowledge." Harlan held up his hands in a gesture of peace. "I'm wondering whether any of the local predators establish territory using a pungent substance."

"Like a marker?"

"Yes. Is it possible that what Jackson smelled was a calling card?"

Charlie inhaled again, this time more deeply. "I don't smell anything...other than myself." She motioned to her brother. "Come take a whiff."

Mattie recoiled. "I'm not going to sniff you."

"Not me, you idiot. I want to borrow your nose."

Mattie joined her and took a tentative whiff. His expression immediately soured. "There *is* something here. Something funky." He turned in a circle and inhaled again. "Hold on." He left the circle, his head swiveling, then dropped to all fours a few yards away. With his face inches from the snow, he took a deep whiff and promptly dry heaved.

"Jesus!" He coughed violently, then, covering his nose, pointed. "Over there."

Harlan scanned the ground and kneeled next to a dark object the size and shape of a corncob. Lexy appeared next to him and studied the object. "Omigod, this can't be..."

"What is it?" Jasper demanded, inserting himself between the biologist and his former protégée. Lexy dipped a shoulder and shoved Jasper aside.

"What's it look like?"

Jasper looked again. "Looks like somebody didn't chew their food."

"Yes, there are pieces of bones and fur, but this isn't feces."

Jasper's nose wrinkled. "Sure as hell smells like it."

"Come on, Davy Crockett. You're supposed to be an outdoorsman. What kind of animal can't digest bones, feathers, or fur?"

Jasper's brow furrowed.

"Don't overthink it."

Embarrassment flickered across Jasper's face. His gloved hands tightened into fists—then relaxed. "Wait. This isn't shit. It's a gastric pellet!"

"And the color, deep black?" Lexy prompted.

"Means it's fresh."

Lexy rewarded Jasper with a pat on the back and turned to the surrounding snow. After a few sweeps of the area, her eyes brightened. "There!" She pointed to a shallow set of prints.

Jasper dropped to one knee. His eyes narrowed to slits. "Looks like gator tracks."

"Impossible," Harlan harrumphed.

"Relax, Doc. I said, they *looked* like gator tracks."

Lexy began her own inspection. "Jasper's right. Except alligators only have four toes on their back feet." She pointed to the closest set of tracks. "These have five."

"It's not an alligator," Harlan insisted.

"What else could it be?" Jasper snapped. "Look at the size and shape of those prints."

"*Varanus Komodoensis* comes to mind. They have five toes, front and back."

Lexy shook her head. "Komodo dragons and crocodilians couldn't survive these temps." Confusion etched her face. "Could we be dealing with some kind of warm-blooded reptile?"

"Like a dinosaur?" Mattie's inflection suggested he was kidding, but his voice indicated otherwise. When his suggestion met with blank stares, he gestured at the surrounding forest. "It's a big forest. Maybe it's something undiscovered?"

"Not likely." Harlan dismissed Mattie's theory with a wave of his hand. "Superior National Forest is big, but not Amazon Rainforest big. Hundreds of people hike this area every year. Someone would have seen such a creature before now."

He climbed to his feet and meticulously brushed the snow from his pants.

"Whatever this is, it's not native to the area."

JACKSON strode ahead of the pack, head down and hands clenched. Anyone with eyes could see from his body language that he radiated agitation. The animosity hung over the team like a fog, and everyone, even Jasper, kept their distance. Everyone but Charlie. She scrambled after Jackson, struggling to keep pace.

"Hey, wait up. Your legs are longer than mine." She'd meant it playfully, but when Jackson whirled, it was clear the effort had been wasted.

"Did you figure that out by observing my tracks?"

Charlie bent at the waist, struggling to catch her breath. "Okay, I deserved that, but can we at least talk?"

Jackson's jaw tightened, but he nodded.

"Look, not telling you wasn't the right call, but it was my call to make. Maybe I should have consulted with you, but you hired me to lead this effort. I'm responsible for its success."

Jackson licked his lips. "You may be responsible for the success of this effort, but I'm responsible for the safety of everyone out here."

"How are you responsible? You're an observer. I'm the—"

"What you are is a hired hand!" Jackson's words burst from his mouth in a torrent. "As such, *I* am responsible for what happens. If someone gets hurt or dies, that's on me. By withholding information, you compromised my ability to keep us safe—to keep *you* safe."

"I don't need you to keep me safe," she snapped. "We're not in any danger."

Jackson stared at Charlie as if she'd spoken a foreign language.

"This thing killed and skinned a bear, and gutted a full-grown moose with its bare hands." He jabbed a finger toward the rest of the group, who waited uncomfortably several yards away. "We're out here, unarmed, looking for some creature that you, Encyclopedia Brown, Nancy Drew, or Professor Dumbledore can't identify, and you don't think we're in danger?"

At first, Charlie looked as if she might explode. But after letting out a long, slow breath, she nodded contritely. "You're right. You have every reason to be upset." She looked past Jackson to the end of the procession. "Jasper! Bring me the TNW."

Jasper looked confused. "You said not to bring—"

"I know you have it. Get it. Now."

Jasper unzipped his backpack, dug out a long metal cylinder, and walked to Mattie. He positioned himself behind the perplexed young man and unzipped his backpack.

"Hey! What are you doing?" Mattie yelped as he tried to wriggle out of Jasper's grasp. Jasper held him fast and fished out a black triangle buried deep inside the backpack. With the two pieces in hand, he approached Charlie and motioned for her to turn her back to him. When she complied, he dropped to his knees, stuck his hand inside her rolled-up sleeping bag, and retrieved another cylinder, shorter and thicker than the first.

The team looked on as he reached under his coat and pulled what resembled a toy pistol from his waistband. Ignoring the amazed expressions of the rest of the team, Jasper quickly assembled a sleek black rifle from the pieces.

"Survival rifle." Jasper presented the finished rifle to Jackson. "Ever use one?"

Jackson accepted the weapon and admired its weight. "What kind of rounds does it take?"

Jasper produced two magazines, each the size of a deck of cards, from his pocket. "Four sixty Rowlands from a Glock forty-five ACP magazine." He handed the magazines to Jackson. "There's more where that came from." He nodded toward Harlan, who bounced his backpack.

"That's why it's so heavy," Harlan said good-naturedly. "I thought it was my pudding cups."

Jackson checked the rifle's chamber before jamming a magazine into the receiver. "I hate to admit it, Jasper, but you're growing on me." He motioned for Charlie to take the lead.

"You sure you're okay with me taking point?"

"Until I learn to read tracks, what choice do I have?"

Charlie adjusted her sleeping bag and backpack and started walking. Jackson followed, keeping his eyes forward and his head up.

"Looks like you and Charlie made up." Lexy pulled alongside him. "Is she going to be my new stepmother?"

Jackson smirked despite himself. "I wouldn't say we made up. I'd say we reached an understanding." The pair fell silent but continued to walk alongside each other.

"So... what about us?" Lexy asked, finally. "Are we good?"

"Why wouldn't we be?"

"Because I knew those weren't bear tracks... and I didn't tell you."

Steam rose from Jackson's nostrils in a rush of exhalation, but his expression remained calm.

"Sure."

"Is that 'sure' as in we're actually good, or 'sure' as in once we get back to the office, I should clean out my desk, turn in my badge, and lose your phone number?"

"If you think I'm going to lose a good employee over getting my feelings hurt, you're not as smart as I thought." He increased his speed, leaving Lexy to stare after him.

"You're kind of a dick. You know that?"

"Yep."

Lexy smirked as she fell several yards behind. She'd

taken only a few steps when Jasper's voice came from behind. "How are your feet?" He pulled even with her.

"What?"

"Your feet." He pointed at her boots. "You mentioned they were sore."

Lexy glanced down. "They still are, but not as bad as yesterday."

"Give these a try." He held up a pair of wool socks. "They're goofy looking, but they're better than what you're wearing."

"Thanks." Lexy took the socks. "I'll try them on when we set up camp."

"You'll have even more blisters by then. Probably want to put them on now."

Lexy looked ahead. Charlie and Jackson were already twenty yards away. "If I stop now, I'll never catch up."

Jasper put two fingers to his lips and blew a shrill whistle.

Charlie turned around.

"Take five?" Jasper yelled. "Equipment malfunction."

"Jesus Christ, Jasper."

"Sorry, boss." Jasper winked at Lexy. "You got five minutes." He tipped an imaginary cap and sat on a downed tree. Lexy sat at the opposite end of the tree and unlaced her boots. As she pulled off her first boot, she glanced in Jasper's direction, eyebrows knitted.

"You don't have some kinda weird foot fetish, do you?"

"That depends on your definition of fetish."

Lexy laughed and pulled off her blood-spotted sock.

He nodded toward Lexy's exposed foot. "I didn't peg you as a newbie. How'd you end up wearing the wrong gear?"

"Didn't expect to be out here this long." Lexy looked around. "I figured a day, day and a half at most."

"Yeah, I didn't figure on a two-legged, giant homicidal lizard either."

"And yet, you brought a rifle. Even though Charlie expressly told you not to."

Jasper sighed and climbed to his feet. "Guess that makes me an asshole."

"I didn't say that." Lexy smiled.

Mattie and Harlan leaned against the trunk of a Brobdingnagian ash tree, watching Lexy and Jasper from twenty yards away. "What do you think they're talking about?" Mattie asked.

"What else could they possibly be talking about?"

"I mean specifically. Where'd it come from? Did it escape from a lab? Is it a government weapon? How intelligent is it?"

"Have you ever considered that its point of origin might be extraterrestrial?"

Mattie chuckled, drawing a frown from Harlan.

"Sorry. I didn't mean to laugh."

"Please, enlighten me," Harlan prodded. "Obviously, something I said struck you as amusing."

"I'm just surprised a man of your intelligence believes in aliens."

"Given the circumstances, alien origin is every bit as plausible as a warm-blooded super predator going unnoticed in the Northwoods for hundreds of years."

"Is it? I mean, native legends of a cannibalistic animal roaming the forests have been around for hundreds of years."

Harlan laughed. "You mean the Wendigo? I doubt we're

dealing with a mythical harbinger of death, starvation, and disease."

Mattie scowled. "How is that any less plausible than life from another planet randomly showing up here?"

"I assume you're familiar with the Drake Equation?"

Mattie nodded.

"But the Drake equation only calculates the number of planets capable of supporting civilizations. It doesn't consider whether those civilizations would want to make contact with Earth. Also, it doesn't take into account the distances between habitable planets, the life spans of the members of those civilizations, or the fact that travel at or near the speed of light has yet to be proven possible."

Harlan gasped. "You don't believe in life on other planets?"

"I believe in aliens, Professor. I just don't believe they've traveled from where they are to where we are."

"Who's to say they haven't been here already?"

"Other than the vast distances?"

Harlan tsked. "Distance is hardly a barrier. One hundred fifty years ago, radio, television, computers, and space travel would have been inconceivable. A civilization only fifty or one hundred years ahead of ours could have a marked technological advantage."

Mattie rolled his eyes. "Yes, but what advanced civilization has ever encountered a less advanced one without inflicting cultural, biological, and environmental damage? If *they* were here, we'd know."

Harlan clapped his gloves together. "I'd forgotten how much I miss debating various theories with young people. You possess an inquisitiveness, intelligence, and confidence I haven't encountered since I left the university. It's delightful."

"So, you agree with me?"

"Of course not. Yours is a very human-centric perspective, Matthew. I prefer to think of our visitors as a benevolent species, looking only to advance their knowledge of the universe."

Mattie scoffed. "Who goes through the trouble of building a ship and risking life and limb without getting anything in return?"

Harlan grinned. "I see you've given this some thought."

"Usually after bongs and beer." A cocksure grin lit up Mattie's face. "And don't even get me started on the Cantina Dilemma."

Harlan cocked his head. "I'm not familiar with the concept."

"Have you seen *Star Wars*?"

"The Boba Fett tattoo on my left buttock would suggest I have."

Mattie's eyebrows arched. "Remember how there were all those different creatures in the cantina at Mos Eisley?"

"Of course."

"Well, what are the odds of beings from all those other planets breathing the same mixture of gases, tolerating the same atmospheric pressure and radiation levels, or even seeing the same light spectrum? Earth is likely to be just as toxic and hostile to a being from another galaxy as Jupiter or Saturn are to us. The distances are far too great and the odds far too remote."

"Interesting concept." Harlan scratched his chin. "But it has a bit of a flaw."

Mattie grinned. "Yeah, what's that?"

"The same flaw is present in the belief that Earth was *chosen* as the only place for life to exist. It isn't a mere coincidence that, of all the planets in the solar system, life only evolved on Earth. The same elements that were the building blocks of life on our planet likely spread to all the planets in the solar system. In other words, isn't it more likely the cantina's patrons visited Tatooine precisely *because* they could breathe the air, tolerate the pressure and radiation, and see within the available light spectrum, while those who could not, stayed away?"

Mattie's face went blank. Then the familiar grin made another appearance. "Spin it any way you want, Doc. Whatever we're tracking, I'd bet my life it's from Earth."

18

The Pilot woke from induced hibernation to a cacophony of alarms echoing within his elongated black helmet. The sounds should not have startled him. He'd run endless simulations in the time leading up to the mission. But few of the alarms he heard now were familiar, and those that were seemed out of context during the post-acceleration, pre-deceleration sequence.

The Pilot was unsure where he was. While the ship's black carbyne walls, sharply raked canopy, rounded bulkhead pegs that allowed the crew to pull themselves along in the absence of gravity, and the five sleek crew chairs, each with a slate gray console, told him he was still on the bridge of the *Deras*, the familiar confines of the ship provided no hint as to his *location*.

When he'd first peered through the smoked glass of his helmet through the *Deras'* canopy, he'd expected to see Karataj Station. The fact that neither Karataj Station nor Karataj itself was anywhere to be seen struck him as disconcerting.

Also, disconcerting was the matter of the *Deras'* current speed. The ship should have ignited its reverse thrust screen engines and decelerated to a velocity that allowed them to enter orbit around their home planet of Karataj safely. The engines were dark, which meant the *Deras* moved in excess of the intended orbital velocity, which would send the ship hurtling past Karataj, or worse, straight toward it. The *Deras* and everyone on it would vaporize.

Outside the *Deras'* many portals, the Vast's multitudinous planetary systems blinked but provided little insight. The Pilot tapped the featureless console in front of him with one gloved hand, and a collection of holographic gauges, meters, and dials appeared before him, presenting a series of flashing lights almost as unsettling as the alarms.

Before he had a chance to scan the display, a blue planet materialized in front of the ship.

"Something's very wrong," he said in a sibilant whisper that would have sounded to a human ear like the hiss of an angry cobra mixed with a series of grunts, chirps, and whistles reminiscent of a South American jungle at daybreak.

"You are correct." Adhara, the *Deras'* designer, chief engineer, and youngest crewmember, watched from her seat with her hands clasped in her lap. Like the Pilot, she wore a form-fitting black flight suit that kept her warm, provided water and nourishment, and administered the anesthetics that induced hibernation, as well as a cocktail of antibiotics, anticoagulants, and corticosteroids necessary to speed the healing process in the event of injury.

"Where are we?" He asked.

"Remain calm. Everything is fine."

"How can you say that?" The Pilot's voice rose to a shrill pitch matching the intensity of the alarms sounding within the ship. "We're headed toward that planet with no sign of slowing." He searched for his smoky brown home planet. "Where is Karataj?"

"You're looking at it."

"But that planet looks nothing like our home world."

"And yet it is. Look at the land masses. They are identical to those on Karataj."

The Pilot squinted at the blue planet. Adhara was right. The Great Masses were alike in every way, except that these were green with swatches of brown instead of brown with swatches of green. And the water was a brilliant blue instead of murky gray.

"How can this be Karataj and yet not Karataj?" He said, hiding his confusion and terror behind his helmet.

"Because it is our planet. But it is not Karataj."

Adhara unbuckled from her chair and floated upward. "The details would take time to explain. As we do not have time, I will say only that what you see outside this ship looks like our Central Star, our System, and our home planet. But it is not. Just as the Vast that surrounds the *Deras* is a Vast, but it is not *our* Vast."

The Pilot ached to challenge Adhara but wasn't sure the effort was worthwhile. In the time he'd known her, Adhara had never displayed a sense of humor. Not only did she not tell jokes, but she didn't understand them either. If Adhara said this Vast wasn't theirs, she believed that to be true. A renowned engineer and theorist, her more established rivals often challenged her theories, but never her computational skills.

"Have you told the others?" He gestured toward the rest of the crew: Raheel, the precise and dedicated navigator, who bore under his flight suit and helmet the red stripes and golden crest typical of his East Karatajan heritage; Solmeen, the gruff engineer and security officer, who stood a full two heads above all of them, and little Kechik, the clever and capable communications officer, whose small stature characterized his unionless birth from his mother's unfertilized egg.

"Certainly not."

"Why not?"

"They won't understand."

"I don't understand." The Pilot laced his fingers fretfully. "Why tell me?"

Adhara floated toward the nearest bulkhead, then pushed herself backward with one hand, spinning as she came to rest. "Because, my dear, Dito. I need a pilot."

"You have the autopilot."

"I require an actual pilot. A living, breathing, thinking pilot, capable of reacting to the unexpected; someone not reliant on a mere set of instructions." She reached out and tapped the Pilot's helmet. "I need you."

"But why?" He persisted. "The *Deras* flies itself."

"Because someone has to land the ship."

He frowned inside his helmet. "That isn't our mission. We are meant to dock with Karataj Station and take the ferry to Karataj's surface."

"Our mission has changed. We are now meant to enter this planet's atmosphere."

"But the *Deras* wasn't built for re-entry," he insisted. "It lacks shielding. It will burn up once we enter. Should we manage to survive entry, how am I supposed to control the ship? It has no wings, rear fins, or risers." The Pilot's voice rose again. "We'll tumble through the atmosphere and drop to the surface like a chunk of the outer belt."

"You're not listening, Dito," Adhara chided. "While the *Deras* has no true wings, it does have airfoils. They're merely hidden." Although younger by half than the Pilot, Adhara spoke as if she were the parent and he the child. "They don't have much lift, but supplemented by the attitude thrusters, they'll have enough."

He remained unconvinced. "I suppose there's no way to talk you out of this?"

He already knew the answer.

"There is no going back. Only forward."

"What if I refuse to pilot the ship?"

"Then..." She spun around like an ebony-clad ballerina. "Karataj dies, along with our culture, history, and achievements."

The Pilot looked at his sleeping companions. "Are you sure we shouldn't wake them? Surely, they will want to bear witness to the end of Ahliwarin society."

"No." Adhara waved him off. "They'll only complicate things. Besides, I have faith in you. Now, engage the screen engines before we crash into that planet."

He looked up from his console. The planet had moved closer without him realizing it. He located one of the console's many holographic buttons and pushed it. Persimmon-colored light from the ship's fission engines poured in from all sides.

"Screen engines initiated."

The Pilot squinted at the planet's mix of blue, green, white, and brown terrain. "Why is this planet so colorful? It hurts my eyes."

"What you see are the colors of life...and hope."

"Interesting..." He mused.

"What is?"

"That we find ourselves on a collision course, yet you see hope. If this was your plan, why did you not foresee this planet's location relative to the *Deras*?"

"This is another universe entirely," she huffed. "Many

things might have occurred here that did not occur on Karataj. Something that changed this planet's orbit, however slightly. A collision with another planet? A large asteroid?" She pointed to a pale, pockmarked moon orbiting the blue planet. "Perhaps the pull of the Great Satellite. Who knows?"

The shrill cries of the *Deras'* alarms suddenly resumed, startling the Pilot.

"Deceleration needs to occur in a shorter period! Much shorter!" He desperately scanned the console. "Perhaps we should revive our colleagues to verify your—"

"Enough!" Adhara snapped. "Give the *Deras* your full concentration, or we'll all die."

The Pilot fumed, but Adhara was right. Landing the *Deras* would require his full attention. He killed the alarms, then gripped the yoke tightly enough to make the handgrip creak. He glanced across the bridge at five bulbous buttons —the crew's life sign indicators.

Two of the orange-yellow buttons glowed, while the remaining three blinked, indicating the other crew members' state of suspended animation. He considered bolting for the buttons but talked himself out of it. Instead, he placed his free hand on the throttle and shoved it forward. The engines, silent in the Vast, roared inside the cockpit. Were it not for their sound-deadening helmets, the noise might have been unbearable.

He slowly let out his breath. While he was neither an engineer nor a scientist, he'd piloted craft of various types his entire adult life. They were in the planet's upper atmosphere, and he hoped that as they descended and the atmosphere grew denser, the impact of air against the *Deras'* nose and leading edges would combine to slow the ship. However, based on the rapidly dwindling distance between the ship and the planet's surface, impact appeared unavoidable. He released the throttle and grasped the small joystick that fired the retrorockets, creating a distinctive pop when the valves opened to release puffs of compressed gas.

In the Vast, the *Deras* would have flipped on its axis, but in the grasp of this planet's gravity, the ship barely reacted. He tried the maneuver again, this time firing the retrorockets for a longer duration. The *Deras* waggled before settling again. He had some semblance of control.

An orange glow enveloped the entire bridge. Fire. The result of intense heat on the *Deras*. As flames licked the canopy and portal windows, the craft shuddered, threatening to veer off course. The Pilot kept the nose down, even as the ship's rear danced and dodged.

"The atmosphere grows dense." He grunted through gritted teeth. "The increase in friction may tear the *Deras* apart, but we need the resistance to slow us down."

When Adhara remained silent, the Pilot glanced back to see her helmeted head flopped to one side. For all her intelligence, Adhara had no experience traveling in the Vast. She had passed out, buffeted by the warring forces of gravity and reverse thrust.

The Pilot grimaced, incensed that the young engineer would escape the stress of entry and avoid the horror of their impending death.

He alone would decide the fate of an entire people.

19

He stared at the crumpled form. It had followed him for almost a rotation, but moved at such a deliberate pace that he wasn't sure the thing was actually in pursuit. Apparently, when he dug into the snow to wait out the storm, his pursuer had continued to follow.

He'd considered putting some distance between himself and his pursuer, but curiosity won out, and he'd elected to wait. Not only had he wanted to see his pursuer up close, but he'd burned a great deal of energy trying to stay warm, and hunger had returned. He'd thought his pursuer might serve as a meal, provided he didn't expend his remaining energy trying to subdue it.

But he'd vanquished his foe with a single stroke, which was puzzling given the strength the thing must have possessed to track him for so long. Curious, he knelt and tugged at the thing's skin. The bright coloration seemed oddly ostentatious for a predator, as it made its presence obvious, especially in this expanse of white. Perhaps it wasn't a predator after all.

He nudged the odd thing. The outer skin made an

unusual sound when touched, as if made of some inorganic shell. Many creatures on his home world had shells, but those were of the organic variety, often made of some keratinous or chitinous material. This one's outer skin was thin and loose around its flesh.

He touched the thing's face with a nail almost as long as his finger. The outer skin fell away, causing him to shrink back. The face wasn't a face at all but another inorganic shell. Underneath the faux skin was its true face, wrinkled and of a different color than the outer skin. He marveled at how much the wrinkled animal reminded him of the Merebunta. Same flat face, same protruding ears, same deep-set forward-facing eyes. It and the Merebunta could have been distant cousins.

Sitting on his haunches, he pondered the fragile, wrinkled being. Was it intelligent? After all, it had fashioned weapons, albeit of a crude variety. Could this be the dominant species on this planet? If so, why hadn't the woolly horned beast, whose hollowed-out head he wore to keep out the cold, evolved to dominate?

A smell drifted in from behind, and he raised his head. There was something else. A sound, coming from a different direction, still behind, but not directly. It had come from—

Something hit him hard, knocking him forward with enough force to leave his back throbbing in pain.

He climbed to his feet to find himself surrounded by fur-covered animals, long-legged and low to the ground, sharp teeth bared, erect pointed ears flattened against the mottled gray, white, and black pelts of their lithe bodies.

The air vibrated with a low hum that emanated from the creatures' narrow mouths. Whatever they were, they were predators. Their stealthy attack suggested a less-than-friendly intent.

The snarling animals initially kept their distance, dodging toward him, then changing direction, moving in concert sometimes and without apparent coordination at others. As he presented himself, arms outstretched, he planted his feet in a stance wide enough to prevent him from being knocked off balance but close enough together to allow him to pivot.

Surmising the attackers sought a weakness in his defensive posture, the creature studied the beasts. The attackers' strategy impressed him. It was methodical and calculating. He wondered absently whether their strategy had resulted from years of hunting as a group or if the behavior was innate.

As he circled round and round, eyeing each of the fur-covered beings, it dawned on him their strategy was two-fold. Not only were they searching for a weakness, but they were also trying to wear him down. By forcing him to defend against attack, they forced him to use precious energy. Fortunately, they didn't know how quickly his metabolism burned fuel since he was as much a mystery to them as they were to him.

This lack of knowledge gave him a chance. He needed only to survive long enough for the attackers to grow impatient and make a mistake. He didn't have long to wait. One predator, a smaller, perhaps younger specimen, took an angle that brought it close to him, close enough for him to whip out one sinewy arm and rake razor-sharp claws along the animal's side. The animal howled in pain and retreated, leaving its comrades to complete the circle of attack.

He sensed his attackers' loss of confidence and went on the offensive. When one of the fanged creatures glanced after its departing associate, he unleashed a kick that launched the attacker into the air and headlong into the thick trunk of a massive tree. With a sickening crunch, the animal thudded to the ground, wheezing.

The quick loss of two of their raiding party left the three remaining predators less confident about their odds of success. In a last-ditch effort, the largest of the aggressors lunged forward. He sidestepped the strike and let the animal pass like a matador sidestepping a bull. It seemed almost too easy.

The would-be assailant scampered away from him and toward the "Merebunta" body. Only after it locked its jaws around one of the limbs did he understand his attackers' true intent. They never meant to make a meal of him. The crumpled body had drawn them to the area. They had arrived expecting a meal, only to find their prize guarded by an intruder.

He didn't care what his assailants' intent was. He was determined to ensure they understood that the crumpled body enjoyed his protection. When a second attacker locked its teeth into the body, he took two long strides and let out a snarl that burst from his throat with a roar that shook snow from the trees. The three remaining assailants scampered away in a chorus of yips, yelps, and barks.

Once the attackers were out of earshot, he re-assessed the crumpled body. The attackers' teeth had torn the brightly colored outer coat, exposing an underpelt. Leaning closer, he caught the glint of something metallic. A length of sinewy material encircled the creature's wrinkled neck. From that length hung a circle with two short appendages, perhaps legs.

He reached out and flicked the circle, spinning it along the length of material. Upon further inspection, he realized the circle was upside down. The two appendages weren't legs; they were more like horns, originating from a shared point at the base of the circle and rising in opposite directions until they extended beyond the circle at an acute angle.

Flicking the circle again, he noted it was made of a pliable material, soft enough to be shaped but hard enough to retain the shape given to it by its maker. He divined this was an artifact, a symbol of some kind, though a symbol of what he didn't know. It didn't matter. Symbolism hinted at a capacity for abstract thought, which denoted intelligence. He recoiled, shaking his massive head. The crumpled thing was no mindless animal driven by impulse and instinct, like the furred attackers. It was an intelligent, sentient being.

And he'd killed it.

20

Charlie slogged through the knee-high snow with fresh energy. Although the blowout with Jackson had been unpleasant, it had also been cathartic. The guilt she'd carried since leaving Nelson's place had weighed heavily, and now that her secret was out, she could focus on the task. Mostly.

Despite the danger the unidentified animal presented, Charlie let her mind drift, pondering the past days' events, specifically her interactions with Jackson. The man was flawed, but she liked that he seemed aware of his flaws and owned them.

On the other hand, she hadn't spent this much time around a man other than Mattie since she and Jasper broke up eighteen months earlier. Was her interest in Jackson due entirely to the fact that she hadn't gotten laid in almost two years? She was only human.

A tortured mewling carried on the wind, interrupting Charlie's inner monologue and causing the hair on the back of her neck to curl. She stopped and craned her neck, but heard nothing. When, after thirty seconds, she heard only the soft blowing of the wind, she licked her chapped lips. "Did you guys hear that?"

"How could you not?" Mattie's voice broke with fear.

"Did it come from the direction we're headed?" Lexy asked.

Charlie nodded, taking a tentative step.

"You think that was our space lizard?" Jasper asked.

"Possibly." Harlan's head swiveled. "It sounded a great deal like a crocodilian mating call."

"Great," Jasper said. "Horny *and* hungry."

Jackson sped up, overtaking Charlie. She saw him approaching and felt indignation rise. "What are you doing?"

"Taking point," he said as he rushed past her.

"Why are *you* taking point?" Charlie hoped her tone came across every bit as accusatory as she'd intended.

Jackson's eyes scanned the path ahead. "Because I'm the one with the gun."

THE CREATURE ACHED WITH EXHAUSTION. Using his hands and sharp claws to dig into the frozen soil had nearly depleted what little energy he had. Now finished, he picked up the crumpled body and gently placed it into the hole. Filling the hole with the displaced soil was easier than digging, and he covered the area with the freezing, white powder before plopping down on the burial site. As he contemplated the cold planet on which he found himself, his eyelids grew heavy. He could barely keep them open. He scoffed. Why fight the urge to sleep? Were the marauders to return, he could not fight them off again. It was merely a question of how he would die—at the fangs of the marauders or the icy fingers of the planet's gelid temperatures.

The realization should have filled him with dread, but he felt only relief. Death was preferable to this miserable existence. Had the muscles in his face been able to facilitate such an action, he might have smiled. Instead, he closed his eyes and settled in to await his fate.

Suddenly, his eyes flipped open. What if the marauders returned while he slept? He needed to dissuade them from returning and digging up the flat-faced creature's remains. But how? Then it came to him. The creatures had smelled the dead flat-faced creature's scent and come prepared to feast. They must have a heightened sense of smell. He would use their talent against them.

Summoning the last of his strength, he struggled to his feet. As his final deed, an act of atonement, he would prevent the desecration of the flat-faced creature's burial place. With a weary grunt, he positioned himself over the uneven ground and squatted.

He had slept what felt like only moments when a faint metallic smell floated on the wind. Blood. How had he detected the flat-faced creature's blood through the layer of snow and soil? Then he understood. The blood did not belong to the flat-faced creature.

It belonged to one of the attackers.

He unfurled his lanky frame and slogged to where the furred creature lay at the base of a tree. The animal's neck kinked at an odd angle. Its forkless tongue lolled out of its mouth. His belly rumbled at the thick fragrance of blood. To his dismay and disgust, he found himself craving the animal's remains.

His kind rarely ate other predators. Prey was still plentiful on his home planet, and as predators themselves, his kind seldom fell victim to other predators, except in the murky seas, where deadly behemoths more ancient than his own race patrolled with deadly relentlessness.

He experienced a pang of remorse, not for the dead marauder, but for the breach of etiquette necessary to survive. Then he remembered the animal had attacked without provocation. Guilt eased, he ripped a leg from the carcass and swallowed hungrily. The animal was mostly fur, bones, and stringy flesh, but he didn't care. He ate ravenously, shocked by how much he relished ripping off the remaining three limbs. Rip, eat, repeat.

Afterward, he sliced the animal's belly open with a flick of his index finger and picked out the vital organs. Within moments, he found his eyelids heavy again, this time from the somniferous sensation of a full belly. He dug a shallow den under a pile of downed trees and crawled inside. The irony of needing a nap wasn't lost on him. Moments earlier, slumber would have almost certainly meant death, but with a full belly to keep him warm, the cold wouldn't take his life, at least not that night.

JACKSON HATED THE COLD. Chicago was cold and snowy and endured brutal winds off the lake, but as a cop, Jackson was in and out of cars, the station, and courthouses all day. Exposure to the elements was frequent but brief. His gig as a

DNR officer was a different animal. There were long stretches where he and Lexy stood in the elements, inspecting illegal traps, roadkill, abandoned fish houses, and hastily constructed meth labs deep in the woods. Cold, especially in February, was as much a part of the job as coffee and acid reflux.

Here, the cold was a living thing, a spiteful spirit hell-bent on bringing misery and even death. Temperatures regularly dropped to twenty or thirty degrees below zero and hovered there for days. Even now, at a "balmy" ten below, the cold numbed Jackson's fingers and toes, burned his lips and skin, and turned the hairs in his nostrils into icy walrus whiskers.

At these temperatures, the slightest breeze knifed through his clothes, and every breath stung his lungs, filling his chest with a severe ache. *At least the tree cover kept the wind down.* Jackson lifted his boots clear of the snow while holding the TNW away from his body to prevent snow from lodging in the weapon's firing mechanism. While he believed taking point was the right thing to do, he found setting the pace while scanning for danger exhausting. He considered relinquishing both the rifle and the lead to Charlie when he heard Harlan's voice.

"Is anyone else enjoying this? Because I am having a blast." No one responded. "No one?" Harlan asked. "Just the fat guy? Okay."

"Harlan," Jackson's voice was husky with exertion, "it'd be a lot easier if you'd stop talking."

Harlan's breath streamed out in puffs and disappeared into the air. "Good point. I shouldn't waste what little breath I have talking when I could use it to breathe."

"That's not what he meant, Doc." Even Jasper's voice

strained with the effort of simple speech. "He means it'd be easier on all of us if you'd shut your yap."

Mattie patted Harlan on the back. "He doesn't speak for all of us, Professor."

Jackson thought about correcting Mattie when he heard the crunch of footsteps and glanced back to see Charlie approaching. "What's up?"

"Can't I just come up to say hi?" Charlie's tone was breezy, and her body language was open. She shoved her hands into her coat pockets and looked at Jackson.

"We've been walking for hours. This whole time you've never come up to say 'hi.'"

"Fair enough." She jabbed a thumb toward Harlan and Mattie. "Did you hear what they're saying back there?"

"They say a lot of things. Could you be more specific?"

"About what we're tracking. With it—the thing, being from another planet."

"I doubt they were serious."

"I think they were. At least they were considering the possibility." Worry lines creased Charlie's brow. "Aren't you the least bit curious about what we're up against?"

"Nope."

"What if it's some kind of super predator?"

"This is a pretty powerful rifle." Jackson patted the TNW.

"But what if the gun has no effect? We know nothing about this thing."

"We know plenty. We know it walks on two feet. We know it feels cold. We know it eats and shits. And we know it wails, which means it probably feels pain..."

"That isn't very scientific," Charlie replied, with a dubious look.

"I was a cop. I rely on instinct and experience." Jackson's head continued to ratchet back and forth as the pair walked.

"How long were you on the force?"

"Twenty-two years, ten as a beat cop, the rest as a detective."

"Did you enjoy it?"

He shrugged. "I was on the force for twenty-two years, so..."

"People do lots of things they don't like. Heck, people stay with people they don't like for longer than that, just because that's what they're—

"Hey!"

Jackson looked past Charlie to see Harlan at the back of the pack. "You okay?"

"Gotta pee." Harlan danced from foot to foot like a toddler in need of a potty chair. "Feels like I'm going to explode."

Jackson waved him on, and the little man waddled his way toward a cluster of ghost-white quaking aspen, several downed lengths of which littered the forest floor, their leafless branches poking through the snow cover at haphazard angles.

"We should wait," Jackson said. "He'll never catch up if we keep moving."

"Would that be such a bad thing?"

Jackson checked Charlie's face. She wore a tiny smirk. He pointed the TNW at the ground and squared his body with Charlie's.

"Why didn't you tell me we weren't tracking a bear?"

Charlie's eyes grew wide, and for an instant, Jackson felt bad that he'd ambushed her.

"I was afraid you'd cancel the gig if you knew," she stammered. "I need the money."

"No, you don't."

"Excuse me?"

"Tim said you're an elite tracker. You're in such high demand that *you* decide whether to take on a client. That doesn't sound like someone hurting for money. So, what is it?" Jackson's tone suggested he wasn't interrogating Charlie, but the intensity in his eyes made clear he expected an answer. When Charlie stayed silent, Jackson crossed his arms.

"When Mattie and Harlan said it could have come from somewhere else, I..." Charlie began, looking back at Mattie. "I know it sounds ridiculous, but the idea of aliens scares me."

"Why?"

Defiance raged behind Charlie's eyes and manifested itself in her set jaw. "Because *I* happen to believe God made us in His image."

Jackson raised his hands in a defensive posture. "Look, I get it. If this thing is real, it calls your whole belief system into question."

The muscles in Charlie's jaws relaxed, but her narrowed eyes indicated lingering wariness.

"I've seen some bad shit over twenty-two years," he continued, "but I've also seen things that make me think something or *someone* out there put all this together. I'm not saying I believe everything happens as part of some grand plan, but the odds of everything happening in the way necessary for the Earth to be here, for us to be here. They're too great to be an accident."

Charlie exhaled in obvious relief. "Thank you."

"For what?"

She looked away, like a bashful schoolgirl afraid to look her crush in the eye. "For not belittling my beliefs."

Jackson let out a soft snort. "Why would I—"

A blood-curdling shriek split the stillness.

Jackson and Charlie raced into the grove of aspens, where Lexy knelt next to Harlan, as Mattie and Jasper looked on. Scarlet splotches dotted the snow around the trio, creating a trail that terminated in a pair of quivering boots belonging to Harlan. The man hovered face down, his upper body held aloft by a jagged branch that protruded from his upper back.

"Harlan!" Lexy yelled again as she knelt next to the professor. Harlan's only response was to spasm intermittently between breaths, which came in gasps. "Get him up."

Mattie moved to grasp one of Harlan's arms.

"No!" Jackson grabbed Mattie by the shoulder and yanked him away from the fallen man. "We can't move him until we locate the wound."

Mattie looked at Jackson with wide eyes. "Look, but don't touch. See if you can find out where the blood is coming from."

Mattie nodded and scanned Harlan from head to toe. After a couple of passes, his brow knitted. "Shit." He pointed to Harlan's right shoulder. "It went right through him." He looked at Jackson. "What do we do?"

"We have to get his feet elevated," Charlie interjected. She stepped around Mattie and knelt next to Jackson. "We'll need to turn him over."

"We can't," Jackson replied. "He's stuck. The branch is still attached to that log." He pointed to a thick gray length of dead aspen.

Charlie looked under Harlan. "We'll have to cut the branch," she said solemnly.

Lexy leaned in. "Can't we just lift him? The branch will slide out."

Charlie shook her head. "The branch stays with him for now." She turned to Jasper, who stood behind her. "What do you have that's sharp?"

He stared blankly, and she snapped her fingers. "I need something to cut the branch."

Jasper swung his pack off his back. Without a word, he unzipped one of the pockets and dug through it. Within seconds, he produced a slender black object from the pack and tossed it to Charlie. She snatched the object from the air and turned it over in her hand. She pinched one end of the handle and pulled it carefully. A six-inch serrated blade unfolded from the handle. She offered the saw to Jackson. "You'll probably be faster."

Jackson took the saw and slid under Harlan like a mechanic angling underneath a car. Half his body disappeared under Harlan's, and soon, the sound of metal rending wood echoed in the clearing, accompanied by Harlan's agonized cries.

"How's it going?" Charlie's voice quivered as Jackson's arm jackhammered back and forth.

"Tough to get a good angle," he said. "It's coming, though."

Charlie checked Harlan's feet and legs. They'd stopped shaking. "Better hurry. I think he's going into shock."

Lexy covered her ears against Harlan's screams. Mattie's hands flew to his mouth, and Jasper closed his eyes.

Jackson kept sawing. "Hold him still. I'm almost there."

Harlan whipped one arm and both legs in an attempt to

get free of the branch, which shifted with every stroke of the saw.

Jackson kept sawing as Harlan screamed in a hoarse bellow punctuated by intermittent moments of silence. Tears streamed down Lexy's face as she threw one arm over Harlan and put her face next to his.

"It's okay, Harlan, it's almost over. You're gonna be okay." When Harlan's screams turned to full-on sobs, Lexy looked at Jackson, eyes pleading. "How much longer?"

Jackson ignored her question and shifted his weight, bracing himself against Harlan with one free hand as he increased the rate at which he sawed. Harlan screamed again.

"Almost got it…" Finally, mercifully, the protruding branch snapped, freeing Harlan, who let out one last scream before collapsing.

Charlie stood. "Now's our chance. Go."

Mattie and Jasper swooped in and rolled Harlan over, resting his head in a bed of snow-covered leaves. Charlie lifted the man's legs and rested them on Jasper's backpack. "Lexy, push down near the wound. Keep pressure on it."

Lexy placed both gloved hands near the blood-soaked branch. "For how long?"

"Until I tell you to stop."

"Somebody needs to go for help," Mattie whimpered.

Charlie shook her head. "No time. We have to get him out of here."

"How the hell are we going to do that? We're in the middle of nowhere."

"Why don't we call someone on your satphone?" Jackson asked.

"Like Mattie said, we're in the middle of nowhere. Who knows whether there's a rescue helicopter nearby?" Charlie fished her satellite phone from her pocket. "We need to get him to a county road or a highway. Somewhere where an ambulance can get to us."

CHARLIE, Jasper, Mattie, and Jackson watched Lexy transfer the contents of Harlan's backpack to hers.

"This is insane." Harlan was still on the ground but was awake and responsive, which meant he was alert enough to be his usual contentious self.

"Not at all." Lexy shrugged. "So, stop arguing."

Harlan huffed. "I can walk. If I can walk, I can carry a backpack."

"And what if you trip and fall?" Lexy countered. "You might dislodge the branch."

"I might do that with or without the backpack." The scientist scowled. "There's no point in you carrying my belongings."

"You're going to need your good arm to hang on to me. How are you going to get a backpack over that stick?" Lexy pointed at the branch protruding from Harlan's shoulder.

"Regardless, there's no reason for the rest of you to abandon the expedition. This is a once-in-a-lifetime opportunity. The chance to discover an unknown species. Why would you even think about giving that up?"

"We're not here for fame and fortune," Jackson said flatly.

"Precisely," Harlan said. "You're here to protect the citizens of Minnesota. If you abandon the search, you risk never finding the creature again, leaving a dangerous predator roaming the woods. What if it finds its way to a populated area?"

Charlie looked at Jackson.

"There's no one around for miles." Jackson addressed Harlan when he said it.

"And if it changes direction?"

"Then we'll call in the National Guard."

"And tell them what?" Harlan looked from Charlie to Jackson. "I doubt they'll just pile into their jeeps and tanks once you tell them a giant monster is on the loose. Even if they respond, are you willing to take the chance the creature won't encounter anyone before the Guard arrives?"

"He's right," Mattie agreed.

"He's not right," Jackson snapped. "He's manipulative and selfish. Harlan cares more about this mystery animal than he does about any of our lives, or his own."

Harlan appealed to Mattie. "Matthew. Can you honestly say you don't want to see this through? Alien or not, this is likely the most spectacular thing you'll ever experience. Ever. Do you want to miss out because I tripped over my feet while zipping my fly?"

"No." Mattie shot Jackson a sly grin. "Guess that makes me selfish, too."

Harlan clapped, which brought an instant gasp of pain. "That settles it. Lexy and I will head for the nearest county road."

Jackson shook his head. "I'm coming with you."

"We'll be fine." Lexy zipped her backpack and threw it over her shoulder.

"What if you run into trouble?" Jackson's tone was soft but firm. "You're unarmed."

"We're heading away from the trail. I don't need a weapon."

"Still, it's miles to the highway. You can't hold Harlan up on your own."

Lexy fixed Jackson with a hard stare. "Why are you treating me like a rookie?"

"What? That's not what I'm doing."

Lexy shook her head violently. "That's exactly what you're doing. I know you're upset about how Harlan and I treated you, and I'm sorry. But Harlan's my friend, and I'm the reason he's even out here in the first place." She stared Jackson down. "I should be the one to take him."

Jasper raised his hand. "I'll go."

"I don't think so," Jackson said flatly.

"Why not? At this point, I'd rather go with him than you."

Jackson flinched, taken aback by the anger in Lexy's voice.

"Let him go. They'll be fine," Charlie said, placing her hand on Jackson's shoulder.

Lexy grabbed Harlan under his armpits. The man grunted and gasped but managed to stand. Once steady, he held out his available hand to Jackson. "You're pretty handy with a saw." He nodded toward his injured shoulder. "I owe you one."

"It was nothing," Jackson said, still smarting from Lexy's fit of anger.

"Not to me."

Seeing the sincerity on his face, Jackson took the professor's hand, careful not to shake it. "I hate losing you from the team, Harlan."

"Let's get going." Lexy steered Harlan away from the rest of the group.

Charlie handed Jasper the satellite phone. "The map is on the screen. Once you get close to the highway, hit the emergency button, and the nearest first responder should receive the signal." She lurched forward and hugged him. "Good luck."

"I don't need luck," Jasper quipped.

"Oh, yes, you do." Charlie winked, indicating Lexy.

Jasper smiled. Not a grin, sneer, or smirk. A genuine smile.

"Any advice?"

Charlie pretended to think. "Just be yourself. But not too much," she added quickly.

21

Jackson and Mattie followed Charlie, who had retaken point. As usual, her head was down as she studied the snow. Jackson stole the occasional glance at her, partly because he found the tracker's ability to avoid obstacles without looking up fascinating. He also relied on his view of her boot heels to keep him on the trail while he kept watch. He still had the TNW, and while their expedition party had grown smaller, his responsibility to keep everyone safe had not.

"You like her, don't you?" Mattie said casually.

Jackson sputtered, considering blatant denial, but knew Mattie was no fool despite possessing a childlike innocence. "Is this the point where I say, 'Is it that obvious?'"

Mattie laughed. "It *is* that obvious. But I have to give you credit. You've done a great job of not staring at her like she's a piece of meat."

"Doesn't hurt that she's wearing a long coat, ski pants, and an oversized backpack."

"That wouldn't stop Jasper."

"Well, Jasper's a different breed, isn't he?"

Mattie nodded. His expression went from affable to serious. "So, what are your intentions regarding my sister?"

Although Jackson managed not to laugh, he failed to keep the amusement out of his voice. "Your sister is part of my team. Just like you, Lexy, Jasper, and Harlan. My only intention regarding her is to keep her safe and let her do her job."

"And after we find the Sleestak?" Mattie's grin returned.

Jackson chuckled. The kid was persistent, protective, and, apparently, a pop culture junkie. The Sleestak reference was decades before his time. "I don't know. She's great and all. Smart, funny, independent, tough…"

"*But?*"

"She used to date Jasper…"

"Which brings her judgment into question." Mattie let out a frustrated sigh. "I love my sister, but she's compelled to rescue stray animals."

"How does that usually work out?"

"Not great, but they tend to leave in better shape than she found them."

"Hey!"

Jackson and Mattie flinched. Jackson couldn't speak for Mattie, but he feared Charlie had overheard their conversation. He followed her voice and was surprised to see her on her knees up ahead. He and Mattie sprinted to her, arriving breathless from the effort.

"What's wrong?" Jackson rested his hands on his knees and gulped air into his lungs.

"These tracks." Charlie pointed at the snow. They were the same five-toed footprints the group had seen earlier.

"What about them?" Mattie asked.

"Not those." Charlie jabbed a gloved finger at a set of

prints obviously made by boots. "Those." Both men dropped to their knees.

"Whose prints are those?" Mattie asked.

"No idea," Charlie said.

Jackson compared the prints. They ran parallel, although the creature's prints were larger. Significantly larger. "Are they walking together?"

Charlie shook her head. "Doubt it. The boot prints are more recent."

Jackson frowned. "How can you tell?"

"See how the boot prints are well-defined?" She pointed to the larger prints. "Here, the surrounding snow melted, partially filled in the print, then froze over. These prints occurred hours apart."

Jackson's brows knit. "Like whoever made the boot prints was following the creature?" Charlie nodded. "How come we never saw the boot prints before?"

Charlie rubbed her face. "He could have come from another direction, and we angled in behind him. Maybe he passed us while we were sleeping."

Jackson didn't want to think about what would happen if the mysterious stranger caught up with the creature. "What else can you tell me?"

"He's locked in."

"Locked in?"

She nodded. "There's little deviation in the tracks. He was efficient with his steps. The stride, the shuffle—they're remarkably consistent." She climbed to her feet. "Like a machine."

"Like the Terminator," Mattie said.

Charlie shot Mattie a look, and his eyes dropped. She brushed the snow from her knees and addressed Jackson.

"Of course, it's just a theory. If you've got a better explanation, I'm all ears."

"It's not my job to speculate."

"Cop out," Mattie coughed into a gloved hand.

"What's the point of speculating? We'll find out soon enough." Jackson started walking, and Charlie and Mattie followed. They continued in near silence; the only sounds were those of their boots crunching in the snow. They had settled into a comfortable rhythm when the forest fell away, leaving the trio in yet another clearing.

The winter sun, hidden behind clouds most of the day, shone down from the clear blue sky with an intensity that forced Jackson, Charlie, and Mattie to raise their forearms against its rays. As their eyes adjusted to the increased light, they lowered their arms in unison. Their faces also went slack in unison, as if instructed by some unseen conductor.

Blood fanned out in front of them in a crimson semicircle, highlighting a host of helter-skelter footprints.

"What the fuck?" Jackson said breathlessly.

During his years with the Chicago Police Department, Jackson had seen numerous gruesome scenes and heard every conceivable description of blood and gore, with "Rorschach Test" and "Jackson Pollock painting" being two of the more common. This scene, however, was unlike anything he'd ever witnessed. The sheer volume and spread of blood reminded him of the time his pressure cooker exploded when his ex-wife Tanya had tried to make raspberry filling.

"What am I looking at?" Mattie asked, barely able to get the words out.

"Looks like a knife fight." Jackson looked to Charlie for confirmation.

"More like a dance marathon." She looked as if she were

watching a video of a chess match. Jackson and Mattie watched as Charlie knelt next to a cluster of prints. Her eyes darted left and right, taking in everything. "I think there are two sets of prints. Human and *other*. The human footprints end here. The others are all over the place."

Jackson nodded. "And the blood?"

"I'm guessing mostly human."

"How can you tell which is which?" Mattie's voice faltered.

"I can't. But our mystery creature's prints are all over the place." Charlie made another sweep of the clearing. "There are fewer human prints."

"Meaning?"

"Meaning," Jackson filled in. "Whatever we're looking for killed the person following it."

He looked at Mattie. The young man's brow was heavily creased. Charlie's explanation didn't seem to have sunk in. "Whoever loses the most blood tends to lose the fight."

"Not necessarily," Charlie said, more to herself than her brother. "Yes, most of the blood probably came from the human, and *some* might have come from our lizard friend, but some may have come from wolves."

Jackson perked up. "Wolves?"

"There are wolf tracks all over the place."

Mattie tightened his grip on his backpack. "This thing got into a fight with a wolf?"

"Not *wolf*, wolves," Charlie corrected. "I count at least three distinct sets of prints."

"Where'd the wolves go?" Mattie squeaked.

"Calm down. Their tracks head into the forest."

"And what about the thing?"

"I think it's still here."

"Fuck!" Mattie whirled, scanning the tree line. His rapid

movements caused the gear hanging from his backpack to clang like a set of pots and pans.

"Quit making all that noise," Charlie hissed.

Mattie froze, and the clatter of equipment subsided, only to be replaced by Jackson's sudden coughing fit. Charlie threw up her hands. "Are you kidding me?"

Jackson bent at the waist and continued to cough from deep in his lungs.

Charlie's expression went from anger to one of concern. "Are you okay?"

"The smell...," he wheezed.

"What smell?"

"Rotten..." He managed between coughs. "You don't smell it?"

"She never smells anything. Haven't you noticed that yet?"

Jackson pointed to a mound of discolored snow. "Reeks."

Charlie scooped a handful of the tarnished snow and held it to her nose. "This isn't just snow," she gagged. "It's musk."

"Snow. Mud." Jackson had recovered his voice but only enough to speak in short sentences. "Area dug up. Something's here."

Charlie poked the mound with a stick. "Mattie, can you get the shovel from my backpack?"

Mattie hurried to Charlie's backpack and began unzipping its many pockets.

Charlie presented her back to her brother. Her expression was grim, and her voice low. "Tell me this isn't as bad as it looks."

Jackson looked past Charlie at Mattie.

"It's every bit as bad as it looks."

• • •

MATTIE REACHED INTO A MEDIUM-SIZED POCKET, retrieved a black nylon pouch, then zipped the pocket. The cold teeth of the zipper responded with a high-pitched whine, and Mattie glanced upward at the soft blue sky as he climbed to his feet. The view seemed to calm his nerves.

And then he heard the sharp, pneumatic sound of air releasing.

"Come on, Matthew, get a grip," he chided himself. He stepped away from Charlie's backpack, his boot barely clearing the snow, when he heard the sound again.

His eyes grew wide as a snout—long, smooth, and white—poked out of the ground. Although the surrounding snow was also white, their difference was apparent. The snout had a dull, yellowish-ivory hue, contrasting with the snow, which was as white as a sheet of copier paper. Mattie squinted, trying to discern snow from snout, when a tangle of limbs and fur emerged from the ground and rose into the air.

Mattie craned his neck to take in the nightmarish creature towering over him. Years of ingesting video games, graphic novels, and science fiction movies failed to prepare Mattie for the flesh-and-blood incarnation of the beast. He found himself unable to move or speak even as the creature let out a sibilant hiss that warmed and humidified the air between them.

"Mattie! Down!"

Jackson's voice thawed the icy grip of panic, and the young man dropped to the ground an instant before a volley of bullets whizzed past, striking the creature in its gleaming snout. Impossibly, the beast remained upright and released a stomach-churning bellow as a whiplike forked tongue snaked from its mouth.

Mattie screamed, his hands digging into the snow as he

struggled to drag himself away. He belly-crawled a few feet before letting out a piercing shriek. He looked back, saw the creature gnawing on his leg, and passed out, oblivious to the second volley of bullets whistling overhead toward the snarling monster.

JASPER AND LEXY shambled through the forest, tethered by their arms to Harlan, who hung between them. The trio crunched with every step as their boots broke the thin layer of ice coating the virgin snow through which they moved. Harlan mostly moved under his own power but had to shift his weight from Jasper to Lexy to remain upright. As a result, he wore a near-constant grimace that coincided with the resounding thud of the foot on the same side as his injured shoulder impacting the ground.

Because the branch sticking out of Harlan's left shoulder made him favor his left side, Lexy bore most of his weight. Although she said nothing, the unbalanced cadence wrenched Lexy's body with enough force that her knees, hips, and lower back ached.

She noticed a glassy expression on Harlan's face and grew concerned. The man stared straight ahead, but when Lexy scanned the forest, she saw nothing unusual. "Are you okay, Harlan?" He nodded but didn't face her. She recognized his glassy expression as one he wore when confronted with a complex problem. Between the look on his face and his breathing, which came in short gasps, Lexy realized it took every ounce of Harlan's will not to cry out.

"Harlan?" She asked urgently. When he didn't answer, Jasper ducked behind Harlan's head and offered a reassuring smile.

"He's fine."

"He doesn't look fine."

"I told him to pick a point ahead and focus on it. It's a trick I learned in cross country. Kinda like a woman using breathing exercises to take her mind off the pain of childbirth."

Lexy came to a sudden stop, nearly causing Jasper to lose his grip on Harlan.

"What?" Jasper asked.

"Nothing. I just—I'm worried about Harlan." She frowned as Harlan continued to hobble without comment. "Do you think it's helping?"

"Doubt it. But he's taking it like a champ."

The trio continued through the snow, their footsteps and labored exhalations accompanied by the occasional gust of wind whistling through the tree cover.

Jasper glanced in Lexy's direction.

"Can I ask you a question?" He kept his voice low as if doing so would prevent Harlan from overhearing their conversation.

"Here we go," Lexy sighed. "I wondered when you'd get around to making a move."

"Wait. You think I'm making a move?"

"Right." She looked at Jasper with a dubious expression and made a sweeping gesture with her free hand. "The carefully orchestrated approach. Come on strong, offer an act of kindness, pretend to be an actual human being? Did you seriously think that was going to work?"

A wounded expression flashed across Jasper's face, leading Lexy to think she'd misjudged him. She was on the verge of issuing an apology when he laughed.

"Actually, I did," he admitted.

Lexy burst into laughter. "There he is. The true Jasper."

Jasper turned away. When he turned back again, he wore a thoughtful expression. "Can you keep a secret?" Lexy nodded, and Jasper leaned in conspiratorially. "My name isn't Jasper."

"Thank God. I mean, could you have picked a more ridiculous name?"

"That was my grandfather's name."

Lexy blinked.

"My real name is Clayton Shackleford III."

Lexy laughed again. "Come on. At least Jasper *sounds* real. Clayton Shackleford sounds like something out of a Gothic novel."

"Do you live in a cave?" Harlan's voice came from between them.

"Were you listening to us the whole time?"

"Yes, and frankly, it was the most insipid conversation I've ever heard. And I taught junior high school for two years."

"Aren't you supposed to be in a drug-induced stupor?" Lexy snapped.

"It was ibuprofen, not opium," Harlan said with a rueful sigh. "Thus, my only options were staring ahead or getting dragged into your painfully awkward conversation."

"What are you talking about?"

"Let me save you both the trouble of struggling to arrive at your respective epiphanies," Harlan said. "Jasper, aka Clayton, pretends to be a blue-collar ruffian. However, the Shacklefords are old money. Paper mill money. He obviously adopted the blue-collar persona not only to agitate his parents but also so people wouldn't judge him based on his extreme wealth and privilege. And then we have Officer Lexy, aka Alexandra Richards, only child of gynecologist parents, who threw away a promising academic career to hand out tickets to poachers while pretending to be shallow and vapid so her intelligence doesn't put people off. You two are a matching set."

"I liked you better when you were drugged up." She peered over Harlan at Jasper. "Sorry about that 'Jasper' thing."

"Fuck me," Jasper cursed under his breath.

"Hey. I said I was sorry."

Jasper pointed ahead to a clearing as smooth and white as a hospital bedsheet. Lexy squinted. The area was suspiciously devoid of vegetation.

"Is that a lake?" Lexy asked.

"Worse." Jasper surveyed the clearing in both directions. "A river."

THREE OF JACKSON'S shots found their mark. The force of the .460 Rowland slugs hitting home spun the creature's ivory head, leaving it to loll at an unnatural angle. Jackson kept the TNW at his shoulder, unsure whether the fight was over until the head rolled off the creature's massive shoulders and thudded to the ground. It took Jackson a moment to realize the "head" had been a hollow skull, little more than a helmet, and when his gaze returned to the creature, he saw intelligent eyes, forward-facing and deep set in a leathery green-gray head.

The situation was surreal. Between Mattie's screaming and the creature's bellowing and hissing, Jackson found it difficult to aim as he fired a second volley at the creature. This time, only one of the four shots connected, knocking the beast backward and dislodging its grip on Mattie's leg.

The angry beast locked eyes with Jackson, snarling and bellowing.

Jackson held his ground. He liked his chances now that the thick skull had fallen away, giving him an unimpeded shot at the creature's head. That was until the creature charged.

"Crap."

The creature cleared Mattie's prostrate body with ease, coiled muscle and aggression on a collision course with a target a fraction of its size and weight. Later, Jackson wouldn't recall the impact of the creature crashing into him at freight train speed, the feel of scratchy bear pelt against his chin, losing his grip on the TNW, or the air exiting his lungs as the creature bore down on him. He would, however, remember experiencing momentary weightlessness as he sailed through the air and crashed to the ground.

As he lay limp and inert, Jackson became vaguely aware that had it not been winter and the ground covered with snow, his return to earth might have resulted in death. The question of Jackson's survival, however, threatened to become moot as the creature stood over him, snorting and grunting with evident agitation. It glowered at Jackson as if looking for any excuse to rip him to shreds, but when Jackson remained immobile, the creature abandoned its attack, turning toward Charlie as it lowered its head. It meant to ram her as well.

"No!" Charlie yelled in a commanding tone, jabbing an index finger at the beast. Miraculously, the tactic worked, and the creature hesitated. "No," she repeated in the same tone, as she moved toward the creature, arms raised, palms turned upward.

The creature shifted its feet and let out a muted roar, but Charlie continued, angling away from the creature and drawing its attention from Jackson while putting herself on a path toward the discarded TNW. She kept her hands up as she moved, which seemed to hypnotize the creature. It watched her with interest. "Just a little longer..." Charlie muttered in a soothing voice. She was only a few feet from the rifle, almost within arm's reach.

"Don't do it, Charlie." Mattie's voice came in an urgent whisper.

"Be quiet," she hissed.

"He's intelligent, maybe more so than we are. He's traveled millions of miles to get here. Why would he want to hurt us?"

"Because he's a monster, Mattie."

Mattie gestured at the bearskin wrapped around the creature. "He's not a monster. He's just cold and alone."

The creature whirled at the sound of Mattie's voice. As it turned out, the muscles in its face relaxed. "You just want to go home, don't you?" Mattie cooed. He sat up, and the creature grunted in warning. Mattie held up his hands, just as Charlie had done. "Whoa, whoa. Calm down, big guy. It's okay. We're all after the same thing."

Jackson shifted in the snow, and the creature let out another roar.

Charlie dived the last few feet for the rifle, grabbed it, and rolled into a shooting position. She squeezed the trigger, and the weapon erupted. Unfortunately, the shot went wide, and the creature wheeled in Charlie's direction.

She fired a second shot, missing again. The errant shot struck the snow near the creature's feet, sending a cloud of fine powder into the air. The round's proximity seemed to spook the creature, and before Charlie could fire again, it bolted into the woods.

LEXY, Jasper, and Harlan moved quickly, at least compared to their previous pace. Although the snow was just as deep on the river as it had been in the forest, aided by the frozen river's smooth surface and the absence of foot-snaring weeds, the trio made good time.

"I would like to go on record as not being a fan of this plan." Harlan was now wide awake, full of complaints and grievances.

"I told you. It would have taken longer to go around."

"How much longer?"

Lexy shrugged her one free shoulder. "I don't know. An hour. Maybe two."

"I wasn't talking to you. You have an incentive to lie." Harlan whipped his head around to look at Jasper. "How long to go around?"

Jasper looked up and downriver. "Actually, it's more like three hours."

"Nevertheless, we should have gone around." Harlan pouted like a hungry toddler. "I vote we turn around and head downriver until we find someplace safe to cross."

Lexy shook her head adamantly. "We don't have time. We need to get you to a hospital. Besides, it's barely above zero." She looked at Jasper. "The ice will hold. Right?"

"Probably. But I wouldn't worry about it. If one of us falls through the ice, even if we made it out, we'd probably die of hypothermia."

Harlan's eyes nearly bugged out of his head.

Lexy shot Jasper an exasperated look.

He smiled, not the least bit repentant. "You two are an odd couple." When Lexy didn't respond, he continued. "I never would have pegged you two as friends."

Lexy gave a nonchalant shrug. "We get each other. He doesn't cut me any slack because I'm a girl, and I don't hold his incredible nerdiness against him. He's a brilliant man and an excellent teacher if you ignore his personality."

Jasper couldn't hide the grin spreading across his face.

"I guess you'd have to know him," Lexy snapped.

"Guess so." They walked on, silence enveloping them until Jasper turned to Lexy. "So, what happened to you?"

Lexy puzzled. "Happened?"

Jasper nodded. "Yeah. If Harlan is as brilliant as you say, you must be brilliant yourself."

"I don't know if I'd say *brilliant*. Capable. Gifted even. Brilliant might be a stretch." Lexy kept a straight face as long as she could, then a laugh burst from her mouth in a snort. Jasper joined in, although it wasn't clear whether he was laughing at her faux modesty or the donkey-like sound that had escaped her nose.

"Seriously. How do you go from teacher's pet to sidekick to a washed-up cop?"

Lexy's eyes, already lidded against the cold temperatures and blowing wind, narrowed to slits. "Let's not do this."

"I'm just saying—"

"I know exactly what you're saying." Lexy fixed Jasper with a penetrating stare. "You want to know what colossal fuck up resulted in me being banished to this frozen purgatory?"

"Well, yeah. It's gotta be one hell of a story."

"It's not."

"How about you let me be the judge of that?"

Lexy exploded. "You're so goddamned eager for a story? How about we start with yours?"

"Huh?" The word tumbled out of the startled man's mouth like a forgotten cigarette.

"Why are *you* here?" Lexy pressed. "You've got money. Why are you stomping around the woods with Charlie and Mattie when you could be partying in the South of France?"

The familiar grin returned. "We don't do the South of France. We're 'Lake Geneva' people."

"Answer the question, Richie Rich."

"I killed a guy."

Lexy waited for Jasper to reveal his comment as yet another joke, then felt a pit in her lower intestine when his grin failed to reappear.

"Too many beers and not enough common sense." Jasper's eyes turned downward. "I was fucking around with my buddies at the cabin and assumed the Remington was empty." His Adam's apple twitched in his throat. "My buddy took a hull of double-aught buckshot to the chest at point-blank range. Blew his insides out his back."

Lexy had a thousand questions, but settled on one. "Did you do time?"

Jasper let out a braying laugh. "People like me don't do time. We get sent to a posh rehab center to reflect on the error of our ways." He shook his head ruefully. "They treated me like the heroine of a Victorian novel, sent away to live with an 'uncle' for nine months."

Had it not been brutally cold and the fur-lined hood of her coat not hidden most of her face, Jasper would have seen what little blood hadn't already retreated from Lexy's face. No matter. Her enlarged eyes and audible gasp told Jasper he'd struck a nerve.

Lexy shrugged Harlan off her shoulder and stomped away, leaving Jasper to adjust to the shifting weight. Gravity reasserted itself, and both men lost their balance.

Harlan crashed to the frozen surface, emitting an agonized wail. He lay on the ice, clutching his shoulder, then suddenly rolled on his side and ejected the watery contents of his stomach.

Jasper scrambled to Harlan's side and tried to place the man on his back, but Harlan curled into a ball and let out a second scream so loud Jasper covered his ears.

Lexy heard Harlan's screams but ignored them. Jasper's words replayed in her head like a skipping record, leaving her furious and devoid of empathy. She had trusted Charlie and thought they'd bonded, only to have the woman share her secret with Jasper, of all people. And the way he'd hinted at Lexy's past, "like the heroine in a Victorian novel."

Her rage soared, fueling a burst of energy that propelled her across the river. It was at that moment that her brain injected a kernel of doubt. *What if it wasn't Charlie? What incentive did she have to break my confidence after sharing such intimate parts of her own past? And when would she have? Charlie and Jasper were never alone together, not in the entire three days of the expedition.* Lexy stopped as the answer came to her: *Jackson.* He'd spent the better part of the trip bringing up the rear with Jasper, not to mention two nights sharing a tent.

Lexy thought she'd been angry when she'd suspected Charlie of betraying her trust, but now she was livid. Jackson, her friend and mentor, must have told Jasper how Lexy had gotten pregnant her sophomore year and been sent—no, exiled—to stay with her mother's sister in Portland. The most soul-wrenching time of her life, and Jackson had cavalierly shared the sordid details like they were his to tell.

Except he couldn't have. Lexy could tell Jackson anything, but not that. Other than her parents and Charlie, she'd told no one she'd dropped out of college, let alone why. Not Jackson, not Harlan. No one. Lexy's anger drained away. Her intestines tied themselves in knots, sending acid into her throat. Her fury had been misplaced and unwarranted.

She spun and looked across the ice. Jasper kneeled at Harlan's side, trying without success to stop the writhing man from further injuring himself.

Lexy sprinted toward them, mounting guilt threatening to squeeze the air from her lungs with every step, but as she approached, Jasper held up one hand like a traffic cop and shouted something she couldn't make out. She tried to slow down, but only skidded on the ice.

Not until she heard a sharp crack did she understand. Too late. The ice beneath her gave way, and she disappeared into the river, launching a geyser of water into the air.

As WATER CLOSED above her head, she experienced a thousand sensations at once: gravity pulling her down like enormous ankle weights; the muffled sound of water sloshing in her ears; flashes of refracted light; bitter cold attacking her skin with the insistent sting of a million angry ants; and a mixture of flavors, equal parts earthy and piscine, as water found its way into her mouth and washed over her tongue. The converging sensations threatened to overwhelm her until her mind, in a desperate attempt to preserve her sanity and life, eased her into darkness.

JASPER SAW terror in Lexy's eyes as she slipped under the river's surface. One moment she was there, the next, gone. It happened so quickly he wasn't sure he hadn't imagined it, but Harlan's urgent voice confirmed that what he'd seen was no mere trick of the light.

"Go! Go! Go! There's still time!" Harlan urged from his prone position.

Jasper scrambled to his feet and scampered across the snow, slipping and sliding as he struggled to keep his balance. Despite his efforts, he lost his footing and pitched forward, falling short of the spot where Lexy had gone under. Rather than stand, he stayed down and belly-crawled frantically until snow gave way to cloudy ice, and cloudy ice to clear. There, amidst a spider web of cracked ice, was the jagged hole.

He peered into the dark hole and gasped when he saw Lexy staring at him from beneath the ice, maddeningly close yet separated by a six-inch opaque barrier. She was as pale as anyone he'd ever seen in his life. Her blue eyes bulged in their sockets, and her blonde hair framed her face with Medusa-like undulating wisps. Lexy's hands, rendered gloveless during the fall, scratched at the ice in a frantic search for purchase.

"Fuck!" Jasper punched the ice with his elbow but gave up after a single blow, wincing in pain and having hardly made a dent. He searched for something to break the ice, aware of the ticking clock marking time in his head. Finding nothing, he glanced at the hole again and saw, to his horror, Lexy floating, arms outstretched, her head bumping lazily against the ice.

"No, no, no, no..." Jasper pleaded, spinning on his stomach in a fruitless search for something of use. With a scream of frustration, he crawled to the fissure, arms and elbows flared out like duck wings, the tips of his boots propelling him forward.

He jammed an arm into the water. The ice creaked in protest as six inches of the hole's edge gave way. Jasper fished the water with his submerged arm, barely able to ignore the cold that penetrated his clothes and seared his skin. Just as he felt he had no choice but to submit to the icy water's frigid grip, something brushed against his hand, and he spread his fingers, grasping until he latched on to something more substantial than an errant weed—a *handful of hair*.

Jasper pulled with all his strength. With a rush of splashing water and brackish froth, Lexy's head breached the water's surface and lolled to one side. Jasper grabbed Lexy by her coat and pulled her head and shoulders onto the ice, but lacking sufficient leverage and full use of his numb arm, she threatened to slip from his grasp and slide back into the water.

He tried to dig in, but the tips of his boots skidded across the slick ice as Lexy's dead weight pulled him toward the gaping hole. For an instant, he considered letting go to save himself, but forced the thought from his mind and doubled his efforts. "I got you," he spat through frozen lips, not sure his words, meant to reassure whatever part of Lexy's brain remained capable of being reassured, were truthful. He could feel his grip on Lexy growing less secure by the second.

"Jasper!" Harlan's cry came from behind him, and he twisted to see the injured man propped up on one elbow, holding a length of birch like a javelin. Jasper was unsure of Harlan's plan, but understood when he saw Harlan draw back his arm. Harlan swung his arm with a grunt and a piteous yelp, propelling the branch across the ice. The attempt fell short as the stick came to rest beyond Jasper's reach. Harlan groaned. "I'm out of sticks. Can you reach it?"

Jasper stretched out one leg and laid the tip of his boot on the branch. With teeth clenched, he pulled his foot toward him and the branch along with it. Within seconds, he'd dragged the branch close enough to grab. Holding on to Lexy with one hand, he stretched his arms as far as they would go and grabbed the branch with the tips of his outstretched fingers. Still holding Lexy, he pulled the branch toward him and laid it across the hole, bridging the gap.

Careful to maintain his grip on Lexy, he spun on his buttocks until his legs pointed in a V, locking the branch against the soles of his boots. He leaned back, pulling Lexy over the branch and toward him. The branch bowed, and his plan seemed destined to fail until Lexy's upper chest cleared the water and rested on the branch. Jasper adjusted his grip and heaved again, moving his arms in a rowing motion that pulled Lexy further out of the water. He repeated the motion, gaining an inch with each agonizing pull until Lexy's entire body was free of the water, then collapsed, exhausted and panting.

"What are you doing?" Came Harlan's voice again.

"Catching my breath."

"While you're doing that, Lexy could be suffering irreversible brain damage."

Jasper forced himself into a sitting position and then straddled Lexy.

"What are you waiting for?" Harlan urged Jasper on with a feeble wave of his good arm.

Jasper suspected the woman's chances of survival were even at best. Even if she survived, brain damage, as Harlan suggested, was a possibility.

"Fuck it."

Jasper laced his fingers, placed his hands on Lexy's chest, and pushed down in short strokes. As he lowered his lips to hers, all he could think was *She's gonna be pissed.*

22

Sunlight that had been blinding earlier in the day now left only the faintest hint of its presence in the form of pink streaks across the sky. Mattie sat on the ground, his back against the slender, pale trunk of a scarred and peeling tree as Charlie tightened a leather belt around his leg above the knee. Mattie flinched and sucked air through his teeth.

"How are you doing, kiddo?" Charlie tried to sound as cheerful as possible.

"It's only a flesh wound," Mattie said, in his best Monty Python accent. "I lost more blood when the neighbor's cocker spaniel bit me."

"If I remember correctly, you bit Toby first."

"Details..." He shooed her away, nodding toward Jackson, who was propped against his own tree trunk, several yards away. "You should be checking on him. He got it worse than I did."

Charlie sighed. Her brother was right. The Erickson's asshole cocker spaniel had taken a pretty good chunk out of Mattie's shin when he was ten. The wound had required plastic surgery to repair the damage, but a scar remained to this day. By contrast, the thing that bit Mattie had made a relatively clean wound. The creature's teeth punctured rather than tore Mattie's skin, and she had cleaned the wound easily. More importantly, there hadn't appeared to be any muscle damage or significant loss of blood.

She stood up and headed toward Jackson. As she drew closer, she saw he'd shut his eyes tightly. She knelt next to him.

"You in there?"

His eyes opened but reflected neither surprise nor recognition. Charlie moved closer and peered into them.

"What are you doing?" Jackson waved her away with one limp hand. Charlie ignored his feeble attempt and continued to stare into his eyes. This time, she saw recognition, but he still seemed somewhat unsure of his surroundings.

"Checking to see if you have a concussion."

"I didn't hit my head."

"Good. Because I had no idea what I was looking for." She looked the rest of him over. One hand rested on the TNW, the other lay across his lower chest. "How are your ribs?"

"They hurt like hell. But they're better since you gave me that aspirin."

"I hate to tell you," Charlie said, laughing, "but those were Midol."

Jackson laughed, then moaned. "Oh God, don't make me laugh."

Charlie got to her feet, smiling, and offered her hand. "Can you walk?"

Jackson waved her away a second time, nodding as he checked the TNW's safety was on before planting the stock in the snow. He leaned forward and tried to "walk" himself up the rifle to a standing position, but barely got off the ground before falling against the tree and sliding down the trunk until he hit the ground with an anguished grunt.

Charlie winced. "You seem attached to that gun. You think it's coming back?"

Jackson sat against the tree, eyes closed, a pained expression on his face. "Don't know why it wouldn't. It's clear one of us couldn't hit the broad side of a barn."

Charlie clasped her hands against her chest in a faux display of offense. "Yeah, well, it's also pretty clear one of us can't take a hit."

Jackson opened his eyes to meet Charlie's gaze. "You got a bit of a mean streak, Charlie Battice. I like it."

As Charlie laughed, Jackson held out his free hand without relinquishing his grip on the TNW. Charlie grabbed hold, placed her feet toe-to-toe with Jackson's, and leaned back. Although a struggle between Charlie's weight and Jackson's use of the TNW as a crutch, Charlie lifted him to a standing position, with Jackson grimacing the entire time.

"Are you sure you're okay?" Charlie asked.

"Yeah." Jackson swayed unsteadily. "Once we get moving, I'll be fine."

Charlie fixed him with a disapproving stare, then turned toward Mattie. "Are you ready to..." She trailed off upon seeing Mattie behind her, leaning against a shoulder-high stick. He gave her an enthusiastic thumbs-up as he presented the stick for Charlie's review.

"Check out my staff. I'm Gandalf."

"You're an idiot." Charlie shook her head and headed across the clearing.

AN ORANGE SNOWPLOW rumbled along the highway like a giant beetle as it tramped over bumps, potholes, downed branches, roadkill, and any other object it encountered.

Auggie, a slender man with a patchy beard, narrow eyes, and the persistent scent of dried sweat, peered at the rearview mirror from the driver's seat. He gazed at the trio of passengers huddled in the sleeper portion of the plow's cabin. A tall blonde woman, flanked on either side by a young guy with a bruise under one eye and an older guy who kept his eyes tightly shut and, incredibly, appeared to have a foot-long stick poking out of his shoulder, huddled like penguins in a snowstorm. The three had been mostly silent since they'd gotten into his rig, except for the old guy. He kept making a low groaning sound that turned into a high-pitched yelp whenever Auggie's snowplow hit a bump in the road.

"You sure one of you don't want to sit up front? It'd be way more room," Auggie offered. Although he'd hoped the blonde would accept his invitation, he was relieved when no one took him up on the offer. He'd intercepted the strange trio's distress call while plowing a client's quarter-mile-long driveway, and while happy to help, his passengers made him uneasy.

The younger guy was the only one of the three who seemed to hear Auggie's offer. He leaned forward and presented a polite smile. "No, thanks. We're fine. We need the body heat."

"You sure?" Auggie insisted. "I've got the dashboard heater on full blast."

The older guy's eyes fluttered open like those of a cadaver coming to life. "Our friend's core temperature is dangerously low. The body heat from the three of us in close quarters is more beneficial than circulated warm air."

"Hypothermia?" When the older man nodded, Auggie added, "Rough way to spend an afternoon."

The older man laughed, then immediately yelped. "Yes, except in this case, her near-frozen condition kept her from entering a permanent vegetative state. Although I suspect at some point, she may have been clinically dead."

Auggie looked at the woman in his rearview mirror. On second inspection, she was unusually pale, even for a blonde. "Guess that explains the rush to get to a hospital."

The old guy closed his eyes again, and Auggie returned his attention to the road. He had nearly settled in when he heard the blonde say in an angry whisper, "You never said I *died*."

"I didn't have a chance," the younger guy responded between clenched teeth. "You came to and punched me in the face."

"I woke up with you straddling me. How was I supposed to know you were doing chest compressions?"

Auggie's eyes bugged. He couldn't get these people out of his rig fast enough.

JACKSON, Charlie, and Mattie marched through the woods like the three soldiers in Archibald M. Willard's "Spirit of '76". Unlike Jackson and Mattie, both of whom walked with a limp, Charlie moved unfettered and easily kept pace with her injured companions. She looked back and forth between the two men with a bemused expression. "Isn't anyone going to comment on what happened?"

"Where would we even start?" Mattie responded.

"How about the fur coat and skull for a head?" Charlie suggested. "What was that about?"

"It was just trying to stay warm."

"It *ate* them, Mattie."

Mattie dismissed Charlie's argument with a roll of his eyes. "So, it was hungry? How is that any different from making a leather jacket from a cow?"

"The important thing is we confirmed what killed the moose and the bear," Jackson interjected, shooting Charlie a devious look. "Then again, you already knew that."

Charlie responded with a raised middle finger.

"I think we were right about it being warm-blooded," Mattie said.

"Looked like a reptile to me." Charlie countered. "It had claws. And that head. It looked like a giant lizard."

"Did you see how fast it moved?" Mattie scoffed. "It was quick. Cat quick. It has to be warm-blooded."

"Cobras are quick," Charlie insisted.

Mattie sighed. "I wish Harlan were here. The Doc would say he's warm-blooded."

"He?" Charlie squinted at Mattie. "Is that thing just a lost pet to you? Should we hang up pictures of it on telephone poles?"

"I'm just saying—"

"This thing is dangerous, Mattie. Did you forget what it did to that moose, or the bear, or Jackson? Did you forget that thing *bit* you?"

Mattie's eyes dropped initially, but he soon lifted his head. "It's a small price to pay to be a part of the most important discovery in the history of the world."

"You were almost part of its evening meal," Charlie snapped.

"You know what? Never mind." Mattie gripped his staff and lurched away. As soon as he turned his back, Charlie stuck out her tongue.

"Cut him some slack." Jackson chuckled. "A space lizard attacked him, and you're taking all the fun out of it."

Charlie laughed as Mattie grew small in the distance. "He's fine. He knows I'm only a pain in the ass because I love him." She smiled at Jackson. "What about you? How are you doing?"

"Honestly? Not great. I haven't been hit that hard since high school."

Charlie puzzled.

"During a football game." Jackson winced as he re-lived the moment. "Devon Smithers ran over me like I wasn't even…"

Charlie saw alarm register on Jackson's face and followed his line of sight.

Mattie knelt in the snow, fifty yards ahead, swaying from side to side. She thought he was messing around again until he teetered one last time, then fell over.

"Mattie?" Charlie left Jackson to lean against the TNW and sprinted toward her brother. By the time she reached him, he lay motionless in the snow. She yanked off one of his gloves and grabbed his exposed wrist. She held it for several seconds before placing an ear to his mouth. "He's not breathing."

Jackson staggered over. He put his ear to Mattie's lips as Charlie had done, then unzipped Mattie's coat. He placed his hands on Mattie's chest and pumped four beats several times, then lowered his head to listen. Detecting no heartbeat, he tipped Mattie's chin up and pinched the younger man's nose before blowing two quick breaths into his mouth. He lowered his ear to Mattie's chest, then resumed compression until the pain in his ribs forced him to stop.

"Sorry…"

Charlie shoved him aside and took over the compression

strokes. Mattie rewarded her efforts with a sputtering cough. Once sure he could breathe, Charlie stepped back.

"Is he okay?" Jackson asked.

"I don't know, but he's breathing."

"Thank God." Jackson sat back in the snow and crossed his hands over his chest, letting out a low moan as he closed his eyes.

"What do you think made him collapse?"

"Any number of things," Jackson began, his voice little more than a croak. "The cold, exhaustion, dehydration, and a drop in blood pressure. I don't know."

Charlie took Mattie's hand and pressed two fingers against his wrist. "His pulse is still weak."

Jackson propped himself up on one elbow, grunting. "That thing had a mouth full of teeth. Maybe he lost more blood than we thought."

Charlie shook her head. "I tied off his leg with a belt. He shouldn't be losing blood." She peered at Mattie's wounded leg. "Maybe there was something about the bite." She pushed aside a clump of her long black hair that had fallen into her eyes. "Maybe it's infected or something." She turned to Jackson again and saw that his eyes were wide. "What?"

"Your face." He pointed.

Charlie ran her palm across her cheek. "There's nothing there."

"Forehead," Jackson said, pointing again. She ran her hand across her forehead. It came away streaked with blood.

Charlie checked her other hand. It too was covered in blood. She bent to inspect the rest of her body, but she cut her examination short when a bright light lit up the entire area. Instinctively, she held her arm in front of her eyes but lowered it when Jackson gasped.

"Jackson?"

She squinted into the light source and saw Jackson shining his cell phone light on Mattie. Blood soaked the snow around the young man, turning it red.

Charlie lunged for the belt encircling Mattie's leg.

"No!" Jackson yelled. "That could be the only thing keeping him alive." He lifted Mattie's feet and slid a backpack under them while Charlie alternated between caressing Mattie's forehead and holding his hand. "This should help for now, but we can't stay here."

Charlie looked at Jackson as if he were crazy. "We can't move him. He won't survive."

"We don't have a choice." Jackson was adamant. "The blood will attract predators."

Charlie sat in the snow, disconsolate. "This is all my fault."

"It's nobody's fault." Jackson grabbed the TNW and checked the chamber before pulling the magazine and counting the rounds.

"How are we going to get him out of here? I can't carry both of you."

Jackson opened his mouth to respond when a distant reverberation caught his attention. The sound was faint but steady. Rhythmic. Familiar.

"Is that what I think it is?" When Charlie didn't answer, he looked skyward. There it was again. "Tell me you have the flare gun." Charlie returned a blank stare. "The flare gun," Jackson barked. "Where is it?"

"My backpack." Her response came as a whisper.

Jackson located Charlie's discarded backpack and lumbered over to it. "Which pocket?"

Charlie hesitated, preoccupied with Mattie.

"*Which pocket?*" Jackson demanded. His sharp tone snapped her back into the moment.

"The small one on top."

Jackson ripped open the backpack and dumped its contents out. "It's not here." The steady *whup, whup, whup* grew louder by the second.

"Try the second from the top."

Jackson yanked open another pocket and plunged his hand inside, retrieving a bright orange flare gun. "Which direction?" He turned the flare gun over in his hand.

Charlie cocked her head. "East."

Jackson spun, trying to locate the helicopter. "Which way is east?" Charlie pointed, and Jackson aimed the flare gun upward. He pulled the trigger. Nothing happened. "You've got to be kidding me! It's empty!"

"You think I keep a loaded flare gun in my backpack?" Charlie shouted. She let Mattie's head drop and sprinted to Jackson. She grabbed the backpack, dug in the second pocket, and pulled out a flare. "Here!" She tossed the flare to Jackson, who fumbled to get it loaded.

"Hurry!"

Jackson loaded the flare, aimed the gun skyward, and pulled the trigger. The flare streaked into the darkened sky, leaving a red-orange trail as it soared.

JACKSON STARED through the bulbous glass front end of the MD500E rescue helicopter, marveling at the moonlight reflecting off Lake Superior. It'd been almost two years since his return to Minnesota, and he'd been all over the area chasing poachers, escaped prisoners, and drug runners, but never ceased to be stunned by the beauty of the North

Shore. Despite the cluster of iridescent dials lighting up the MD's instrument panel, the din of the helicopter's engine, and the *whup whup whup* of rotors spinning, Jackson was oblivious to almost everything but the view until Charlie's anxious voice came from the back seat.

"How much longer?"

Sam McLaren, a thin man with salt and pepper hair and a Magnum P.I. mustache he wore unironically, glanced over his shoulder. "Any second now," he announced and banked the helicopter.

Jackson saw the lights of the Grand Marais Health Center below. The facility had a heliport equipped for emergency landing. Once Sam realized one of his passengers was injured, he radioed ahead to alert the Health Center to their arrival. As the chopper descended, Jackson spotted a team of medical providers waiting with a gurney, their blue scrubs and white masks flapping in the wash from the chopper's blades.

The helicopter set down with one skid hitting the ground an instant before the other, but far enough apart to be jarring. Sam killed the engine and was out of the cockpit before the rotors stopped turning. Jackson tried to swivel at the hips to check the back seat, but his ribs had grown even more sore during the short ride to Grand Marais, and he had trouble moving, let alone pivoting.

The rear door opened, and a sudden rush of wind hit Jackson.

"Easy, easy," Sam said.

A commotion came from the rear compartment as Charlie moved about. Several unrecognizable voices, encouraging but commanding, joined in, then faded as Mattie was extracted from the helicopter and whisked away.

The front and rear doors of the chopper slammed shut,

and Jackson found himself alone after the flurry of activity. It was strange to be alone after three days in close quarters, but he was content to ponder the events of the last few days when the door to his right opened and Lexy peered in.

Jackson stared.

"What the hell are you doing here?"

"This is the only medical facility for miles with a helipad. Where else would I be?" Lexy looked Jackson up and down, her gaze lingering on the bloodstains on his clothes. "Besides, it's a good thing I'm here, old man. You look like you could use some help."

He nodded dumbly, and Lexy lifted his legs, one at a time, turning him toward her. She took both his hands and leaned away from the helicopter, using her weight to spin him the rest of the way. He used his foot to feel for the passenger step extending from one skid. His foot found the step, and he groaned as he settled onto the ten-inch-wide piece of metal.

"Take your time," Lexy warned, but he moved too quickly, and his weight shifted, dropping his left foot to the ground faster than expected. He yelped as his ribs protested the jarring impact.

"Sorry." Lexy's voice was so full of sympathy that Jackson hesitated, momentarily taken aback. His junior officer exhibited many fine qualities, but tenderness was rarely one of them. She helped him lower his right leg off the step and gripped his pant leg to ease the impact of his other foot hitting the ground. "I leave you alone for five minutes, and all hell breaks loose." She sported a mischievous grin. "Told you I was the brains of this outfit."

"When have I ever denied you were the brains?" Jackson countered. "You're the smart one. I'm the good-looking one." Lexy let out a derisive pfft and put an arm around his waist.

He snaked an arm around her shoulder, and they shuffled toward the hospital entrance.

Jackson moved slowly, and the walk across the plowed but still slick parking lot gave him time to notice his surroundings. The first thing he saw was Lake Superior. Despite the absence of much light, the lake's presence and location were strangely apparent. It was as if Jackson were a lodestone on a string and Superior was the Earth's magnetic field. He just *knew* where the lake was. He'd experienced the feeling before, mainly during the day, when the sun reflected off the lake's surface, alerting every creature blessed with the gift of sight to its presence, but this was the first time he'd felt the lake's weight without relying on his "normal" senses. The feeling comforted and unnerved him, and he dismissed it with a shake of his head.

The second thing Jackson noticed was white material sticking out from underneath Lexy's coat and fluttering around her knees. While he needed several seconds to identify the material as a hospital gown, it took him only a moment to recognize the ill-fitting coat. "Why are you wearing Jasper's coat?"

"Long story. I'll tell you later."

Jackson was in no mood to wait. "And why are you wearing a hospital gown? Where are Jasper and Harlan?"

"I said, 'later'." We need to get you inside."

"Lexy!" Jackson's outburst rattled his ribs, and he growled against the intense pain.

Lexy stopped and turned to Jackson, lips pursed. "On our way to the highway, we came across a river. Instead of going around, we decided—*I* decided we should cross. I was wrong."

Jackson had heard enough. "Are you okay?"

"No." Lexy shook her head solemnly, tears welling in her

eyes. "I died, Jack. When Jasper pulled me out of the water. I was fucking dead."

Jackson felt his throat tighten.

"You should be in a hospital bed, Lex."

"I needed to see you." The statuesque blonde woman's eyes welled with tears. "Between Harlan and Mattie... I needed to know that you were okay."

"I'm fine. A little beat up, but fine."

Jackson opened his arms, and Lexy collapsed against him, her body convulsing as she sobbed. The pain in his ribs was excruciating, but it was nothing compared to his emotional anguish. In almost two years, he'd never seen a hint of a tear from Lexy, not when they watched videos of soldiers returning home from war, not even when the father in the horror film *A Quiet Place* sacrificed himself to draw a monster away from his children. While the scene never failed to draw tears from Jackson, Lexy had remained unmoved. Now, his friend's unfamiliar sobs cut him as deeply as if she were his child.

They held one another, quaking as they cried. They might have stood there forever had the hiss of doors opening not interrupted them. Jackson peered past Lexy to see Sam emerging from the clinic.

"Everybody okay?" Sam asked.

Jackson reluctantly released Lexy. "We're fine, Sam. Thanks to you."

"Don't thank me. We didn't have any idea where you were." He nodded at Lexy. "It was her idea to head west. Ballsy move if you ask me, but she insisted on it." Sam gave Lexy a two-fingered salute and headed for the chopper.

"How'd you know we were in trouble?"

"I didn't." She smiled a devilish smile. "Jasper did. He insisted on a flyover."

Jackson scoffed.

"Admit it. You misjudged him. We both did."

"I'm pretty sure he's an asshole...but that doesn't mean he isn't a useful asshole."

Lexy offered Jackson her shoulder, and they shuffled toward the clinic's double doors.

JACKSON SAT ON AN EXAMINATION TABLE, shirtless and swinging his legs as he looked around. The small, white room might have been considered boring had the walls not been adorned with photographs of Lake Superior, Gooseberry Falls, Split Rock Lighthouse, and Isle Royale.

A sharp knock at the door startled Jackson, and he jumped, drawing a wince.

The door opened, and a petite, bespectacled woman in scrubs stepped in. "Hi, Officer Jackson, I'm Dr. Halpern. I have—"

"It's Bennett, actually. Conservation Officer Bennett."

Dr. Halpern looked at the chart in her hand and pushed her glasses up on her nose. "So, it is. My apologies."

Jackson waved her off, drawing another wince.

"Still pretty tender, huh?"

"That would be an understatement, Doc."

Dr. Halpern made a note on the chart. "Well, the good news is they aren't broken."

"And the bad news?"

"The bad news is you have several cracked ribs." Jackson frowned as the doctor hugged the chart to her chest and offered a smile that crinkled the corners of her eyes. "A cracked rib hurts almost as much as a broken rib, but the pain prescriptions aren't as good."

Jackson laughed at Dr. Halpern's joke and instantly regretted it. His face contorted in a mask of pain that went beyond the previous wince. Dr. Halpern's eyebrows knitted. "Officer Bennett, may I ask how you suffered your injuries?"

"Car accident." Jackson had had plenty of time to concoct a cover story while awaiting Dr. Halpern's arrival. "Hit a patch of ice and lost control of my vehicle." Dr. Halpern's mouth twitched, and Jackson shifted. "May I put my shirt back on? I've gained a few pounds, and I'm a little sensitive about it."

"Of course." She turned toward the door.

As Jackson dressed, he noticed Dr. Halpern lingering. "Is there something else, doctor?"

"I used to live in Mesquite, just outside of Dallas. Fun fact: Mesquite is the rodeo capital of Texas. I treated lots of cowboys for lots of injuries. Rodeo clowns, too. Cracked ribs were pretty common among those fellas. That sort of thing happens when you get broadsided by a two-thousand-pound Brahman bull." She leaned against the door frame. "What's unique about cowboy injuries is they rarely have just one or two cracked ribs. They tend to get them up and down, on both sides of their torso. Just like you."

Jackson listened, but the pain in his ribs had reached critical levels, and he was eager to get the pain meds the intake nurse had promised. "With respect, Doctor. What's your point?"

"I've been doing this a long time. Long enough to know car crash injuries from rodeo injuries. Yours suggests a bull ran you over, but you don't strike me as the rodeo type."

"I certainly don't look good in chaps," Jackson replied with a smirk.

Dr. Halpern's mouth curved into a smile, but her eyes reflected more than a bit of skepticism. "Since you're with law enforcement, I'll give you the benefit of the doubt, but I'm curious why you and your friends suffered such different injuries. Hypothermia, anaphylactic shock, and puncture wounds? Something's rotten in the state of Denmark, Officer Bennett."

Jackson hadn't expected the physician to tie Lexy, Mattie, and Harlan together, and his mind raced to fabricate a plausible excuse when a dour-faced nurse hurried in.

"Dr. Halpern? We have a problem with a patient."

The doctor smirked in a way that said, "Consider yourself lucky," and followed the nurse out of the room.

JACKSON PEEKED into a patient room and saw Harlan propped up in bed, his arm in a sling, mouth open as he slept. Lexy lounged in a chair, her nose in a magazine. "I hardly recognized him without the broom handle sticking out of his shoulder," Jackson quipped.

"I know, right?" Lexy put down her magazine. "What's the word on your ribs?"

"Cracked but not broken." Jackson lowered himself into a nearby chair.

"Is that good or bad?" Lexy asked.

"A bit of both."

Harlan opened his eyes and looked Jackson up and down. "It's good because it means he didn't puncture a lung, but it's bad because he won't get the good drugs." He sat up, apparently drugged beyond feeling pain in his injured shoulder. "What the hell happened out there?"

"We saw it," Jackson said.

"So, I gathered." Harlan grinned. "And apparently, it saw you."

"Hey, I got in a couple of good licks with the rifle."

Horror clouded Harlan's face. "Please tell me you didn't kill the most important discovery in the planet's history."

Jackson cocked his head to one side, amazed by Harlan's use of almost the exact words as Mattie. "Don't worry. It's still out there. And it's probably pretty pissed off."

"What did it look like?" Harlan stared like a child hanging on every word of Grandpa's bedtime story.

Jackson held his hands out in front of him. "It was big. And lean. Seven, eight feet tall, with a moose skull and brown fur. Its arms were long and muscular, and its hands…" Jackson spread his arms wide and let his fingers dangle. "They were long and thin, with claws at the ends. Daggers, really, like the comic book character Wolverine. And the smell. Its breath was hot and…" Jackson paused, searching for the right word.

"Fetid?"

"Yes!" Jackson pointed at Harlan. "Like a bag of meat left out in the sun for a week."

Harlan's brow furrowed. "Wait. Tall, thin, furry skull for a head. Long arms and long claws. You're describing a Wendigo."

Jackson puzzled. "A what?"

"A Wendigo. A spirit of First Nation and Indigenous lore. They're often described as being of incredible height, clawed, covered with fur, and having the head of a deer or moose."

"Sounds about right. Except for the deer head."

"You just said it had the head of a moose."

"No, I said it had a moose *skull*."

"I fail to see the difference." Harlan looked at Lexy, who shrugged in agreement.

Jackson huffed. He'd been the target of their tag team

before and didn't care to revisit it. "It didn't have a moose skull for a head. It was wearing a moose skull *on* its head." He paused, allowing Harlan and Lexy to digest his words. "Like a helmet."

"How do you know it was wearing the skull?" Lexy asked.

"Because it fell off when I shot it."

"You shot it in the head?"

"Twice. The rounds just bounced off. But the second shot knocked the skull off its head."

"And what, pray tell," Harlan spoke through clenched teeth. "Was underneath the skull?"

"I don't know."

"Why not?" Harlan was fit to be tied.

"Because it ran over me." Jackson's voice dropped to a whisper. "I don't remember much after that."

Harlan and Lexy looked at each other and giggled.

"Wait. You're saying it ran over you, like in a cartoon?"

"No, Alexandra, not like in a cartoon." Jackson's voice rose with indignation. "Like in the real world, when you get trucked by a two-thousand-pound Brahman bull. It may sound funny, but when it happens to you, it's not funny at all. It hurts like a motherfucker."

"So, you're saying it trampled you?" Lexy and the doctor looked at each other again.

"Am I not speaking English?"

"Extraordinary." Harlan sat back in his bed.

Jackson glowered. "Not the word I would have chosen."

The door to Harlan's room opened. A burly, bearded orderly in snug-fitting blue scrubs entered, pulling a cart loaded with meds. "Time for your meds, Dr. Farley." The orderly didn't wait for Harlan to respond and moved his cart between Lexy and Harlan, forcing Lexy to leave her seat and move to the other side of the room.

Jackson turned away to give Harlan some privacy. As he faced the nearest wall, he saw a cream-colored map of the Minnesota side of Lake Superior encased in a thick piece of plexiglass. Like everything else in the room, the map seemed oversized in the small space, but offered impressive detail.

The map displayed terrain and forest density in brown and green shading, cities and towns in 10-point italicized type, creeks and rivers in blue, and federal, state, and local highways in red, blue, and gray. Lake Superior, represented in stark white, occupied fifty percent of the map. The lake's northwest shoreline bisected the map in an ambling hypotenuse that ran from the bottom left corner of the frame to the top right.

Lexy noticed Jackson staring. "What's up, boss?"

"Just looking at all the places I've been in the last two years. Except for trips to the airport, I hadn't been outside a one-hundred-mile radius of Two Harbors until that thing showed up." Lexy snickered, drawing Jackson's gaze away from the map. "What's so funny?"

"As far as we know, that thing's been to more places in Minnesota than you."

"Can we stop calling it 'that thing'?" Harlan snapped. "It's probably more intelligent than the three of us."

"Fine. What should we call it?"

Harlan considered. "How about... Fred?"

"Random." Lexy pointed at the map. "Clarksville, where he broke into Remy Nordgren's cabin; Massasauga River, where Kirk's kids found the cave; Denmark Falls, where it killed that poor horse; Mr. Nelson's property in Welterton Township, where it slaughtered the moose; and just outside

Stavanger, where Jackson *claims* to have gotten in a lucky shot."

She turned to Jackson, whose brow furrowed. "What are you thinking, boss?"

Jackson left the room, leaving Lexy and Harlan to stare at each other while the orderly packed up his supplies. He returned a moment later, holding a marker, and approached the map.

"Hey, is that erasable?" The orderly demanded.

"Go through the cities again," Jackson said, ignoring the orderly. "All the places it's been."

Lexy listed each city, and Jackson marked them on the map.

"His path follows the shoreline," Harlan noted. "But he's never closer to the lake than a few miles or farther away than ten or so miles."

"All the population centers are on the shoreline," the orderly said matter-of-factly. "Between tourist traps and tourists, it would be tough to stay out of sight if 'it' followed the shoreline."

Jackson, Lexy, and Harlan stared at the man.

The orderly lowered his eyes. "I do a little hunting on the weekends." He looked up again, interested. "You guys tracking a deer or something?"

"Something like that." Jackson glanced at Lexy.

Harlan squinted at the map. "What animal moves like that? With a purpose?"

"Migrating?" Jackson asked.

Harlan shook his head. "Not this early. Not to mention, a cold-blooded creature has no reason to be active in February."

"Mattie doesn't think it's cold-blooded," Jackson added,

mostly to see Harlan's reaction, but also because he wanted the scientist's opinion.

Harlan blinked. "Based on what?"

"The speed. He said Fred moved like a warm-blooded animal. He was certain you'd agree."

Harlan grinned from ear to ear. "He's a fine young man. Once this is all over, he should—"

"Maybe it's headed for the Mountain."

Jackson, Lexy, and Harlan turned to see the orderly eyeing the map.

"What mountain?" Jackson asked.

"*The* Mountain."

"Near Grand Marais?" Lexy frowned. "Why would he head there?"

The orderly reached for the marker in Jackson's hand. "May I?"

Jackson reluctantly relinquished the marker, and the orderly drew a line through each point Lexy had identified. He stopped near the top of the map and circled the area with a flourish.

"The Mountain's the highest point in Minnesota," the orderly boasted. "Which isn't saying much considering it's only two thousand feet above sea level."

"Two thousand, three hundred, one. But who's counting?" Lexy added.

The orderly pointed at Lexy and winked. "If you ask me, I'd say he's headed for high ground."

Jackson studied the map. "Why?"

"I would have guessed he's looking for protection, but it's not deer season." The orderly shrugged. "And, hunting isn't allowed on the mountain, so it's not like he's behind enemy lines."

Realization crept across Jackson's face. "It's an extraction point."

Harlan perked up. "Of course, it is!"

The orderly puzzled. "An extraction point?"

An overhead speaker chimed. "Ron, to the front desk. Ron to the front desk." The orderly checked his wristwatch. "Crap, I'm late with Mr. Loomis' meds. He's gonna chew my ass." The orderly bolted for the door, dragging the cart behind him. "Good luck with that buck." He hurried out and pulled the door shut, leaving Jackson, Lexy, and Harlan to look at each other.

Lexy broke the silence. "So...what now?"

"What are our options?" Jackson asked.

"You tell us," Harlan replied. "It's your expedition."

Jackson had forgotten the expedition was his idea. He thought momentarily, then raised one hand, index finger extended. "Option one, just let him go. If we're right about where he's headed, he should be there in a few hours. If it is an extraction point, someone or *something* will probably be there waiting to take him home. Problem solved."

Harlan gawked. "You'd let Fred slip away without knowing where he came from?"

"I don't care where he came from as long as he leaves."

Lexy shook her head. "Can we really know the problem is solved if we're not there when he reaches the extraction point?"

"Which brings me to option two." Jackson held up a second finger. "We beat him to the top of the mountain."

Harlan's head yo-yoed up and down in agreement. "I very much support option two."

Jackson looked at Lexy. "What about you, Lex?"

"I don't know. There's no guarantee he makes it to the

top. Charlie said there were wolves out there, and that thing—"

"Fred," Harlan corrected.

"And *Fred*," Lexy said with a huff, "is injured. They might finish him off before the other Freds have a chance to pick him up."

"Which brings me to option three. I escort him."

"Absolutely not." Lexy shook her head violently. "We can't risk anyone else getting hurt."

"Which is why I'm going alone."

Before Lexy could argue, the door opened, and Jasper walked in. Lexy shot Jackson a look that said, "This isn't over."

"How's Mattie?" Jackson asked.

"Stable, but not out of the woods yet." Jasper smiled. "Want to go see him?"

JASPER HELD open the door to the recovery room as Jackson wheeled Harlan in, followed by Lexy. Charlie sat in a chair next to Mattie's bed, nearly hidden by the tangle of tubes from the ventilator humming nearby. Focused on the monitor displaying her brother's vitals, she looked up only after Jasper let the door swing closed. Her eyes were puffy and red, her face pallid. Although she'd been in the hospital only a few hours, she looked as if she hadn't slept in days.

Lexy embraced Charlie in a long hug, after which Charlie bent at the waist and gently squeezed Harlan's hand before looking at Jackson. She attempted a smile but failed. Her lip quivered, and she gripped Jackson around the neck with both arms and buried her face in his shoulder. Jackson tightened his grip, not letting go until she regained her composure and stepped away, revealing a face wet with tears.

"I need you to do something for me."

Jackson nodded eagerly. "Of course."

"Kill it."

He let out a small laugh, assuming she was joking.

"Seriously." Charlie's voice was cold and dispassionate. "I want you to find it and kill it."

Jackson glanced at Mattie.

"You know that's not what he would want."

Charlie's mouth tightened to a thin line.

"I don't care."

"We should go." Jasper ushered Lexy, Jackson, and Harlan toward the door as Charlie collapsed into her chair.

Lexy pushed Harlan out of Mattie's room, into the hallway, where she parked Harlan's wheelchair and waited for Jackson and Jasper, who pulled the door closed behind them, to follow. Once all four were present, Lexy started down the hallway, unaware that Jasper and Jackson lingered behind.

"Listen," Jackson began. "I realize the two of you have a history, and you're protective of her, but—"

Jasper cut him off. "It's pretty clear she's moved on." He looked down the hallway at the departing Lexy. "And I'm trying to do the same."

"Great," Jackson said. "Then we don't have a problem?"

"Actually, we have a *big* problem." Jasper took a deep breath. "Charlie's set on killing that thing, regardless of what you, Mattie, or anyone else thinks."

"We know where it's going. It'll probably be gone by nightfall."

"We may have that long." Jasper glanced over his shoulder toward Mattie's room, lowering his voice as if suddenly remembering Charlie's presence nearby. "Mattie's body is shutting down."

"What? Why?

Jasper shook his head. "His blood won't clot. They don't know why, and they're afraid to move him. If they don't figure it out soon..."

Jackson didn't need Jasper to complete the sentence.

"When that happens, Charlie's gonna go nuclear. Without the rest of us to slow her down, she'll find that thing, and she'll put it down like a rabid dog."

Jackson studied Jasper's face. The young man appeared to have aged ten years.

"What do I do?"

"I don't know, but you better do it quick."

Jackson nodded and stuck out his hand. "Thanks for the heads up, Jasper."

Surprise lit up Jasper's face. He seized Jackson's outstretched hand as if afraid the conservation officer might change his mind and rescind his offer.

"So... we're good?"

Jackson smiled.

"You brought Lexy back from the dead. We're more than good."

LEXY FOLLOWED Jackson out of the hospital as he lumbered to a waiting Toyota Prius. "This is insane," she argued as he opened the car's back door. "You can barely walk."

"I know," Jackson agreed. "But I'm down to option three."

Lexy poked Jackson hard in the ribs, and he wailed. "You can't go out there on your own. You're injured and unarmed. Even if you don't find that thing—"

"Fred," Jackson smirked.

"This isn't funny, Jack. Do you want to die out there?"

"Wasn't planning on it."

The stern look on Lexy's face indicated the time for jokes had passed.

"Do you even have a plan?"

Jackson put one foot in the Prius and rested his hand on the roof. "I do." He forced a smile. "It's not great, but it'll have to do."

Lexy glowered, but when Jackson didn't relent, she threw up her hands. "How can I help?"

"Have Jasper call Dale Dempster at the Grand Marais office and tell him I'm coming." He lowered himself into the tiny car. "I'll need access to a vehicle, weapons, and roadkill.

23

Dale Dempster idolized Ronald Reagan, John Wayne, and Charlton Heston. He also liked guns, hunting, country music, pickup trucks, and beer, inclinations that made him the perfect demographic for the Grand Old Party, of which he was a card-carrying, lifetime member. Dale also liked Jackson Bennett.

The two had struck up a friendship shortly after Jackson arrived in Two Harbors. The ex-cop had been in his new position just over a month when he'd done a tour of nearby DNR offices to get a lay of the land and pick the brains of his more seasoned peers. That move alone had endeared him to Dale. Few people admitted they lacked knowledge, and fewer still called attention to their ignorance by seeking advice.

Some of Dale's colleagues considered Jackson's overture evidence that he was unqualified for a senior position and dismissed him as an example of what was wrong with the DNR and the country in general. Dale believed Jackson was one of the good ones. He knew how that sounded, but he didn't mean it in a coded, back-handed way. He was referring to Jackson's competency as a law enforcement officer.

Jackson reminded Dale of John Lyght, Cook County's first and only black sheriff, and he suspected both men struggled with the complexities of enforcing the law in a predominantly white district. He also found Jackson, like Sheriff Lyght, fair in his application of the law.

Other than an isolated incident in which Lexy broke the hand of a drunk camper who'd slapped her on the rear end, in the two years since Jackson took over the Two Harbors office, there were no lawsuits, accusations of corruption, or complaints of police misconduct. The results spoke for themselves. So, when Lexy called, asking Dale to provide Jackson access to equipment, weapons, and roadkill, Dale was happy to oblige.

As Dale sat at the front desk watching the closed-circuit feed from the parking lot camera, he saw a car's headlights turn into the lot. The car pulled up in front of the building and put on its hazards even though there wasn't another car in the lot except Dale's.

The old man rose from his desk when he saw Jackson heave himself out of the back seat of the Prius. He noticed his friend was slow to get out of the car and chalked it up to the car's diminutive size and perhaps the cold weather, which always made leaving a warm vehicle difficult. Dale waited at the entrance for Jackson to get close, then pushed open the glass door.

Jackson stepped inside, and Dale was startled to see him in civilian clothes and sporting a beard at least twenty-four hours past a five-o'clock shadow. Jackson was usually clean-shaven and, while Dale wouldn't have described him as dapper, was always at least presentable. Nonetheless, Dale offered his hand, and the two men shook.

"You look like crap," Dale said with a smirk.

"Been a tough couple of days."

"Couple of days? You on a stakeout or something?" Dale walked as he talked, leading Jackson to the front desk, where paperwork awaited them in two neatly stacked piles.

"Something like that. We're tracking a rogue bear."

Dale frowned and handed Jackson a pen. "Seems like a lot of work for one bear," Dale said, his voice steeped with disapproval.

"It is." Jackson signed where Dale instructed, not even bothering to read the documents. "But he's already killed another bear, a moose, and tangled with a pack of wolves. We're hoping to catch him before he comes across a human."

Dale nodded and walked away from the desk.

Jackson followed. "So, how's Maria?"

"She has her good days and bad." Dale was careful to omit any trace of sadness despite his wife's difficult battle with MS. Maria was a proud woman and would have considered Dale's pity an insult.

"More good than bad, I hope?"

"The fact that Conservation Officer Bennett asked after her will make this a good one." Dale glanced back over his shoulder as he shuffled down the hallway. "I take it you're not getting anywhere with the ex?"

"Sure. I'm getting further away from reconciliation," Jackson quipped.

Dale chuckled and stopped in front of a black chest-high safe. He entered a code into the keypad, and the safe's door swung open, revealing three sleek M4 Carbine rifles nestled into custom inserts that kept the weapons upright. Next to the M4s were various sidearms and several not-so-neatly stacked ammunition boxes. Dale retrieved a rifle, verified it didn't contain a magazine, and then checked the chamber before handing the weapon to Jackson. "Don't lose this. We only got the three."

"Why do you have any?" Jackson asked as he gauged the compact but formidable weapon's weight. "You're a fisheries office."

Dale eyed him. "You ever come across a bunch of fellas taking more than their share of walleye? They're liquored up and already counting all the money they're gonna make, and I show up to tell them they spent the whole day netting fish for nothing." He nodded toward the M4. "They get a look at that baby and offer to throw the fish back for you."

"Maybe so, but I'm not sure the bear cares."

Dale scoffed. "Set that weapon to burst, and I guarantee Yogi will sit up and take notice." The old ranger grabbed two boxes of 64-grain soft point .223 caliber ammo, closed the safe, and motioned for Jackson to follow. As they walked, Dale reached back and handed the ammo to Jackson. "Moving kinda slow. You get hurt out there?"

"Nothing a little aspirin won't fix." Despite his bravado, Jackson struggled to keep up with Dale, a man twenty years his senior.

DALE SHUFFLED into the carport toward the department's well-worn Chevy Silverado but changed direction when he saw Jackson make a beeline for a shiny Ford F-150 truck. "How about you take the Silverado? It's got an ATV in the back."

Jackson didn't so much as glance in the Chevy's direction. "I can barely walk, Dale. What am I going to do with an ATV?"

"We can take it out."

Jackson tore his attention from the Ford and faced Dale. "Right. And who's going to take care of Maria after the ATV turns you into a pancake?"

Dale sighed as he lifted the Ford's keys from the board and tossed them to his friend. "Just promise you won't put that deer carcass in the cab."

~

DALE STOOD next to the idling truck as Jackson sat behind the wheel, fiddling with the dials and buttons. "Remember, not a scratch." Jackson crossed his heart but was already distracted by the overabundance of controls on the truck's dashboard. "You never said what you needed the deer carcass for," Dale said.

Jackson looked up. "Fishing." He grinned.

"More likely to catch a pack of wolves than a bear," the older man grumbled.

"You have no idea." Jackson turned on the stereo, and Dale moved away from the truck, driven back by the wall of EDM booming from inside the cabin. Jackson leaned out of the open window. "Tell Maria I'm looking forward to dinner again sometime soon."

Dale nodded. "Sure thing. Long as you bring Lexy along with you. If Maria is going to spend the whole evening fawning over you, the least you could do is bring along that delightful young lady for me to flirt with."

Jackson offered a thumbs up and stomped on the gas pedal. The truck's tires gripped the pavement and launched the vehicle forward. Dale watched with dismay as the Ford fishtailed out of the parking lot and onto the highway.

~

JACKSON GUIDED the F-150 down Gunflint Trail with both hands on the steering wheel, his eyes on the dark road ahead, and his mind focused on his plan. Although the distance between the Mountain and where he and Charlie had encountered Fred was short, the odds of finding one creature, even an eight-foot-tall one, were slim.

Jackson accounted for the long odds by bringing the deer carcass. He hoped Fred would be hungry enough to walk into what he likely would understand to be a trap. This was the reason for the M4 Carbine. Things would get ugly if Fred showed up unhappy to see Jackson again. Even if Fred proved too intelligent to be enticed by the carcass, Jackson might encounter wolves, in which case the M4 would still be a welcome ally. Either way, he had to be ready for a fight.

Where Jackson would fight was another concern. Placement of the carcass was vital. If he set the bait too far from Fred's path, he might not pick up the scent. If he put the bait downwind of his quarry, the wind might carry the smell of the carcass away from Fred, making it difficult for him to detect it regardless of proximity.

Jackson chuckled at the thought of the creature as quarry. Harlan had said Fred was most likely a predator and an intelligent one. If that were true, Jackson would be more likely to be Fred's quarry than vice versa.

Great. A giant lizard with razor-sharp teeth and claws has a score to settle.

He was reconsidering the solo endeavor when the F-150's in-dash GPS directed him to veer off Devil's Track Road. Unfortunately, Jackson was so busy pondering the wisdom of his undertaking that he missed the turn and found himself driving off the pavement and onto the shoulder.

He yanked the wheel but overcompensated, and the truck's rear came around. Knowing better than to slam on his brakes, Jackson steered into the slide and allowed the vehicle to straighten before applying the brakes. Once the truck skidded to a stop, he waited for his heart to leave his throat and return to his chest.

Jackson killed the engine, grabbed his phone, and tapped the weather app. Although the mountain was still miles away, he figured he was close enough to get an accurate reading. According to the app, the wind speed fluctuated between ten and fifteen miles per hour in a southwesterly direction, which meant the wind was blowing in the direction Fred was most likely approaching the mountain. Jackson pocketed his phone and retrieved the M4 and several feet of nylon rope from behind the passenger seat.

He stepped out of the truck onto the dark pavement. The lingering scent of hot rubber on asphalt tickled his nostrils as he walked to the rear of the vehicle and lifted the bed cover. Dale had field-dressed the deer before freezing it, removing the head, entrails, and skin.

Jackson gazed at the carcass, unsure how he would carry 100 pounds of flesh and bone into the woods in his current condition. A quick scan of his surroundings revealed a classic Saltbox home not far away. More common in the Northeast, the house, with two stories up front and a dramatically slanted roof that sloped to a single story in the back, was suited for Minnesota. The sharp roofline encouraged the melting of snow and deflected the unremitting wind that blew in from Lake Superior.

But the home wasn't what held Jackson's interest. It was the lime-green plastic sled in the front yard that caught his eye.

Jackson considered his options. He had no desire to lug the deer across the snow but was keenly aware of the optics of a man with a three-day-old beard and grimy clothes sneaking up to the house at night. However, the pain in his ribs overcame any trepidation, and Jackson headed for the home, intent on claiming the sled.

Jackson fought through dense tree cover at a snail's pace. Besides sore ribs, he suffered the effects of the painkillers he'd "borrowed" from Harlan. His breath came in a rasp, interrupted by the occasional cough that he struggled to kill before it caused his ribs to burn.

The sled had proven useful, but like the M4 and his own feet, seemed much heavier now than when he first loaded the carcass. The wind didn't help as it created drifts into which Jackson sank up to his crotch. After the fifth such drift, Jackson paused in the thigh-high snow. Exhausted and gasping for breath, he let the nylon rope slip from his hand.

He scanned the clearing ahead, trying to figure out a path, but no one direction promised an easier route than the others. Instead of throwing the rope over one shoulder as he had before, he looped it over his head and shoulders and under his arms like a harness around a sled dog and steeled himself against the wind.

That was when he noticed the maple tree. It was old, twisted, and nearly dead. It sported several thick branches and a trunk that split into a V, creating a crotch that would have been the envy of any tree-climbing adolescent. Jackson looked from the rope to the twisted tree. A plan sprouted in his brain.

He pulled the rope over his head and was about to loop it over the crotch of the tree when he felt a vibration. He checked his phone, but it wasn't on. Why would it be? He hadn't gotten a signal in days. He felt the vibration again. "What the hell?"

He ignored it and took a step, but there it was again. It was coming from his side pocket. Puzzled, he reached into his pocket and pulled out Charlie's satellite phone. He didn't recall using the phone, let alone putting it in his coat pocket, but there it was. Jackson looked at the glowing LCD screen and saw a number with a 218 area code. He recognized it as the code for the northern half of Minnesota. He fumbled with the unfamiliar phone for several rings until he snatched off his glove and answered.

Lexy's urgent voice blared from the handset. "Jackson?"

"Did you put Charlie's satphone in my pocket?"

"I told you I had your back."

"What's up?" Jackson tried to sound nonchalant but knew Lexy wouldn't have called unless something had gone wrong.

"Charlie knows what you're up to."

"So?"

"She called Tim Frieda and asked him to talk some sense into you. He laughed it off at first, but when she told him you were alone, he said he'd call a friend down in St. Paul."

"What friend?"

"Some bigwig in the National Guard."

"Who'd be crazy enough to come out here? It's fifteen below."

"You're right," Lexy agreed. "They told him the National Guard isn't in the business of spending tax dollars on lost hikers. Especially DNR officers, who should know better."

"Great. Crisis averted." Jackson turned the phone in his hand, looking for the "off" button.

"Crisis *not* averted," Lexy shot back. Her angry voice

continued to blare through the speaker. "Charlie told Tim why you were out there, and he told the bigwig."

Jackson laughed. "And who are they going to get to take point? No one with a brain and a pension would run the risk of this whole thing turning out to be a hoax."

"What about your friend Campbell? He's tight with the brass in St. Paul."

"Kirk?" He scoffed. "He just got home after eighteen months overseas. There's no way they'd send him into the field again so soon."

"I hope you're right," Lexy finally said with a sigh.

"One hundred percent. Now go get some rest." He canceled the call and returned the phone to his pocket. He knew it was wrong to downplay Lexy's concerns. She was just looking out for him. But the call was a waste of time and energy, and he had little of either. Besides, he knew she was right. If the Guard told Kirk to saddle up, he'd saddle up. No questions asked.

He shook his head. Kirk didn't have the last word on the subject. The final say belonged to his *real* commanding officer, Marnie. And she'd never allow it.

MARNIE'S SHOULDERS slumped as she climbed the stairs to the second-floor bedroom. She was exhausted after a long day of sitting with Scottie while returning phone calls from anxious sellers and buyers concerned that spring would come and go without a sale or purchase. Never mind, it was only February, and the real estate market wouldn't kick into high gear until March.

This is why real estate agents earn a percentage instead of a fixed fee.

In addition to showings, she played the roles of coun-selor, unofficial legal advisor, and therapist to her clients. She found the hand-holding and constant reassuring rewarding, financially and emotionally, but it was exhausting.

What she also found exhausting was sex. Since Kirk returned from Afghanistan, they'd been going at it like a couple of college kids. Whenever they had a moment alone, he was all over her. At first, it had been cute. She'd missed him as much as he'd missed her, but the novelty was wearing off.

As she walked down the hallway toward their bedroom, she knew Kirk was waiting, clean-shaven and wearing little more than a splash of cologne. It might have been adorable, but she was still angry at him for bailing on Scottie the other night. He'd finally come clean and admitted seeing his son lying in a hospital bed made him feel helpless, but Marnie had little patience for male fragility where the welfare of their children was concerned, and her attraction to Kirk had dimmed the last few days. Besides, she was beyond tired.

She paused at the door, then turned the knob. The door swung open, and there was Kirk, posed on the bed like Hugh Hefner. He grinned and reached for the bedside lamp. Mercifully, a shrill cry from the nightstand startled them both. Marnie recognized the high-pitched tremolo as that of a common loon, the state bird of Minnesota. Sarah must have stolen her father's phone and changed the ringtone.

Kirk frowned at the interruption, but Marnie was thrilled. She might have laughed had it not been so late in the evening. Phone calls at this hour meant only one thing: the Guard.

Kirk raised the phone to his ear. "Kirk here..." A crease

bisected his forehead. "I'm sorry. Who is this?" He sat up arrow straight. "No, sir. Not at all. What can I do for you, sir?" He glanced at Marnie, and she shot him a questioning look.

He ignored her nonverbal inquiry and frowned even more deeply. She giggled inwardly. He must have noticed she'd slipped out of her work clothes and into her "not tonight" uniform of baggy sweats and an even more baggy UW-Superior sweatshirt. He opened his mouth in protest, and she prepared herself for the inevitable sad dog eyes and pouting, but was spared the guilt trip when Kirk's mouth snapped shut.

"Jesus Christ...Of course, sir...Yes, sir. Thank you for thinking of me, sir." Kirk hung up and bounced from the bed.

"What's going on?"

"That was Commander Wirth down in St. Paul. Something's going on near the BWCA."

"*Something*?" Marnie's voice had an edge that filled in the words she didn't verbalize.

"Wirth didn't want to give specifics over the phone," Kirk hurried to the closet and sifted through his clothes.

He avoided eye contact as he scurried about, but Marnie joined him at the closet. He pulled out two sets of fatigues, one of which he shoved into a rucksack; the other he pulled onto his lean frame. "I don't have time for a stare-down, Marnie. I gotta get on the road. I'll call you as soon as I get there."

Marnie tapped her foot, and Kirk's shoulders slumped. "Fine, we'll be near Grand Marais, but that's all I can tell you." He grabbed his boots and rucksack and hurried from the room.

. . .

MARNIE TRAILED Kirk out of the room and down the stairs. They weren't done with their conversation, even if he thought they were. Kirk took the stairs two at a time, but a stop at the hallway closet allowed her to strategically position herself in the foyer. She was already organizing her talking points in her head when she heard Sarah's call from down the hall.

"Mom? What's going on?"

Kirk squeezed past Marnie, not even bothering to put on his coat as he gave her a quick peck on the lips and yanked open the front door.

"You dodged a bullet, mister," Marnie called after him.

"Don't wait up." Kirk grinned and disappeared out the door.

She wanted to go after him, but settled for wrenching the front door deadbolt behind him.

"Mom? Didn't you hear me?" Sarah's insistent voice came from down the hall.

"I'm coming. Keep your pants on!" Marnie killed the foyer lights and headed down the dark first-floor hallway.

MARNIE ENTERED the room to see the faint outline of Sarah curled up in Scottie's bed with her tablet. Marnie's heart melted. The girl had taken to sleeping in her brother's bed in his absence. Tough as she pretended to be, Sarah was a kind-hearted child who adored her big brother.

"What's wrong, sweetheart?" Marnie asked as she sat next to Sarah.

"Who was on the phone?" Sarah demanded.

"Nobody."

"You mean the National Guard."

Marnie swore she *heard* her daughter frowning in the darkness.

"What did they want?" The teen sounded more annoyed than afraid.

Marnie couldn't blame her. Kirk had just returned from one of the most dangerous spots in the world, and they couldn't give him a couple of days of peace? She kept her thoughts to herself, reluctant to feed into her daughter's already considerable disdain for Guard command. "Your father didn't give details, but promised to call later."

"Did he say where he's going?"

"That's classified information."

Sarah responded with a feral growl.

Marnie couldn't keep anything from Sarah. The girl was too clever and persistent. She would pepper Marnie with questions until she got what she wanted. Marnie could usually hold out for a few hours, but she was exhausted, and Sarah's relentless assault weakened her defenses. "All I can tell you is it rhymes with *Green Beret*." Marnie pressed her index finger to her lips with a devious smile.

"Why would he go to Grand Marais?"

"I don't know, sweetheart." Marnie sighed. "At least he's not in any danger."

"That you know of."

Marnie aimed in the direction of her daughter's voice and thunked her on the forehead with her index finger. "Now you're just being dramatic." That was shorthand for *I'm too tired to argue,* but Sarah had a point. Local deployments such as chemical spills or prairie fires sometimes involved an element of danger, but the details of similar deployments weren't usually shrouded in such secrecy.

"Are you sure he's safe?" Sarah sounded like a little girl

worried about her father instead of her usual impudent pre-teen self.

She *felt* her daughter scanning her face for any hint of concern and forced a smile. "There's no industry up there. What could have gone wrong?" Marnie climbed under the covers. "Besides, he's only two hours away."

Sarah curled up next to her, and the pair lay quietly.

"It stinks in here," Sarah said, breaking the stillness.

"Yes, it does. We should wash Scottie's sheets before he gets home."

"Burn them is more like it."

Mother and daughter giggled, then lapsed into a comfortable silence. Marnie closed her eyes and dropped into a deep sleep.

JACKSON SAT in the maple tree's crotch, panting. The drugs had worn off, and the pain in his ribs was so sharp the bite of below-zero air no longer registered. Except for his ribs, he was numb. The only other thing he felt was a sense of disappointment. Disappointment that Mattie had been hurt, and in his conclusion that he and Charlie would never forge a relationship.

He was sure any interest the woman might have had in him would evaporate once she discovered he'd left the hospital in Grand Marais, intent on aiding the very creature that had injured her brother. On top of that, there had been no sign of Fred. It was a shit day all around.

Jackson adjusted his position to allow the blood in his legs, feet, and buttocks to circulate. As the pinpricks of poor circulation moved throughout his extremities, he wondered what he was doing in the woods in the middle of the night, in a tree.

A wry smile threatened to crack Jackson's frozen lips. Tim Freida was fond of pointing out that Jackson, despite his supervisory position with the DNR, knew almost nothing about wildlife and even less about tracking or hunting. He was right. For all Jackson knew, he'd fouled the deer meat when putting it on the sled. Even if he hadn't, the deer meat's frozen state might have prevented the scent from reaching Fred, no matter how acute his sense of smell.

In hindsight, Jackson shuddered at how little he'd thought this through. All he'd cared about was reaching the creature before Charlie, but what was the goal? Luring Fred into the open to do what? Warn him? Rescue him?

Lexy was right. He had no plan—at least not a good one.

24

Kirk looked through the Humvee's windshield into the forest. With the vehicle parked on an incline facing downward, he had an enviable view of Superior National Forest spread out beneath him. Although it was night, the moon shone brightly enough that the view was breathtaking, but Kirk wasn't interested. To him, nature was a thing to overcome, not to behold. He didn't mind the outdoors; he'd enjoyed camping as a child and teen and had tried to instill respect for the outdoors in his children. But it held no special place in his heart as it did for many Minnesotans.

He chuckled, thinking about Jackson out there in the forest. The woods represented everything Jackson hated: the outdoors, the cold, separation from the creature comforts of the modern world. On the other hand, this was very much Jackson's style. The man had a knack for complicating his own life and the lives of those around him.

As he had several times over the years, Kirk marveled at their friendship. In many ways, they were complete opposites. Kirk was from a sleepy Minnesota town, while Jackson was from South Side Chicago. Jackson was a Democrat; Kirk, a Republican. At age fifty, Jackson still listened to rap music, which Kirk found unseemly, while he preferred country and classic rock and roll. And then there was the matter of faith. Kirk cherished his strong ties to the church. Jackson, by contrast, had joked at Kirk and Marnie's wedding that he was surprised he hadn't burst into flames upon entering the chapel. Jackson was a good guy and a great friend, but at times, he lacked direction or conviction.

Kirk had always endeavored to provide such direction, taking Jackson under his wing after assuming the freshman would struggle with a college curriculum and being away from home for the first time. He'd been wrong on both counts. Jackson had taken to college-level courses and shared a rapport with his teammates and classmates that Kirk envied. He had to admit, up until recently, Jackson had managed a fair amount of success despite the obstacles placed before him.

That was the thing he admired most about Jackson—his ability to overcome his shortcomings, or at least what others perceived as shortcomings. When Jackson stepped on campus as a skinny freshman, Kirk noted his lack of size or elite speed and dismissed him as a benchwarmer destined to serve as practice squad fodder. Within days, the kid displayed a nose for the ball and an uncanny ability to anticipate what play was coming before the opposing offense even broke the huddle. He'd also displayed heart, intelligence, and a talent for making those who underestimated him pay for their mistake.

Kirk squirmed. Was he guilty of making the same mistake now? When Tim Freida had called to let him know Jackson was in Superior National Forest, alone and injured, Kirk dismissed it as "Jackson being Jackson" and assumed his friend would return to Two Harbors after a few hours, frostbitten and humbled. Yet, here he was, going on three days in the sticks.

"No." Kirk shook his head. Regardless of his motives, Jackson had no business out here by himself, no matter that the thing had attacked livestock and frightened Kirk's kids. "The guy was out of his depth," he thought angrily, "and now I have to bail him out."

"Lieutenant!" Kirk barked, startling First Lieutenant Paul Cooper, the thin-faced twenty-eight-year-old with a receding hairline and pale blue eyes too close together, who occupied the Hummer's driver's seat. "What's the ETA on that Lakota?"

"Twenty-two thirty hours, sir," Cooper responded without checking his watch. "They should be here any minute."

Kirk barely nodded. He didn't care for Lieutenant Cooper. The young man was an insufferable kiss-ass and a bit of a know-it-all. He was also competent and followed orders without hesitation. That was a rare commodity in the Guard, one that outweighed the lieutenant's negative attributes. While Kirk felt the Guards' reputation as incompetent slackers was undeserved, he recognized that most wouldn't have survived in the Army, Navy, Marines, or Air Force, especially people like Cooper, a corporate lackey during the week and a Guardsmen lackey one weekend a month, two weeks a year.

Kirk looked out at the forest again. *Talk about a needle in a haystack.* The task of finding that thing seemed impossible. Superior National Forest encompassed nearly four million acres of trees, rocks, and water. That thing could be anywhere. Jackson could be anywhere. Kirk's squad could search for days without finding a trace of either of them.

If it weren't for that tracker, he'd have no idea where to begin. She'd been full of attitude but knew her business and had given Kirk the last known location based on where she, Jackson, and her brother had been rescued.

Still, there was a shitload of terrain to cover. Thank goodness for the choppers. The Lakota could cover several times the area his six Humvees could, in a fraction of the time. The little aircraft also had the advantage of a powerful searchlight that lit up the ground like daylight. The only drawback was that if the light didn't fall directly on the target, they might as well not have been there at all.

Kirk, however, had an ace in the hole: National Guard Commander Ryan Wirth. The two had crossed paths in Afghanistan before the hasty withdrawal, and the Commander had taken a liking to Kirk. Like Kirk, Commander Wirth had grown up on the North Shore, and they knew many of the same people. They also shared similar views on the essentials: football, faith, and family.

Commander Wirth recognized Kirk not only as a good soldier, but a good Christian, which was why he'd agreed to send a National Guard Black Hawk outfitted with FLIR, Hydra missiles, and a door gunner to help with the search. While disappointed by the time required to kit out the Black Hawk and make the two-hundred-thirty-mile trip from St. Paul to Grand Marais, Kirk secretly hoped the Black Hawk wouldn't be necessary. The chances of someone getting hurt would increase exponentially once the Black Hawk entered the fray.

Kirk checked his watch. The Lakota couldn't arrive soon enough.

25

Jackson wondered how deer hunters managed not to fall asleep in their blinds. The tedium of sitting in a tree awaiting the arrival of prey seemed only slightly less painful than the pain in his frozen extremities. Ironically, it was that same discomfort that kept him from falling asleep and plummeting to his death or sustaining a substantial injury. That, and his brain, which insisted on replaying events, recent and old, over and over in his mind.

He'd always been the sort to ruminate over past mistakes, but in the last three days, he'd had more time to dredge up a list of his failures. As he shifted into a more comfortable position, he scanned the clearing for signs of Fred. He found none. Just the lime-green sled dangling from the tree. It was a ridiculous sight: one hundred pounds of deer steaks piled high on a child's toy and suspended ten feet above the earth by a creaking length of electric blue rope. *My life has become a cartoon. The only thing missing was an ACME anvil.*

Something moved just beyond the sled, breaking up Jackson's pity party. It might have been the wind, but the movement was too localized. Wind would have disturbed the entire clump of trees. A single tree had moved, as if something had brushed or leaned against it. He held his breath and waited for the phenomenon to recur. He had only seconds to wait before the tree stirred again; the branches parted just enough to allow a long, pointed head to poke through.

"Fred...," Jackson whispered breathlessly, then immediately regretted it. He didn't know how well Fred could hear, but it would have been better had he not made any sound at all.

If Fred heard Jackson, he didn't let on. Jackson watched as Fred looked around and, lifting his snout, poked out his forked tongue, swirling it in the air like a child waving a pinwheel. The long tongue retreated into Fred's mouth and disappeared. Fred also retreated, disappearing into the darkness with no rippling of the surrounding trees.

"Maybe after tasting my scent on the wind, Fred decided the deer-sicle wasn't worth getting shot a third time," Jackson thought. As he resettled, preparing for a long wait, he saw more movement. This time it was a set of trees, twenty yards from where Fred had stood. The lower branches, only a few feet off the ground, quivered. Whatever caused these branches to flutter was stealthier than Fred.

Had Jackson not been looking at that specific clump of trees, he might never have noticed the two wolves that materialized in the clearing.

Jackson was awestruck. In almost two years with the DNR, he'd never seen a wolf in the wild. The animals were elusive and wary of humans, and while they sometimes ventured as far south as Duluth to pick off house pets or livestock, they were rarely seen other than in the grainy greenish-black footage of a hunter's trail camera.

He watched the wolves inspect the spot where Fred once stood. They appeared relaxed and unhurried, but their ears twitched, and their eyes scanned the forest for any hint of movement or the faintest sound amidst the quiet.

An ache spread throughout Jackson's torso, and he shifted to relieve the throbbing in his ribs. As he moved, the wolves turned, and he froze, worried they'd spotted him. Concern turned to outright fear. Two more wolves had appeared. Fortunately, the new arrivals either didn't know he was there or didn't care, and they slunk toward the crooked tree, tails and ears low. As they moved closer to the tree, the wolves appeared to gain confidence and loped toward their prize.

Fred burst from the trees, bellowing as he charged. The wolves didn't deviate from their path. Instead, the rangy canines glanced at each other, ears twitching and mouths falling open in a relaxed manner that gave them an almost bemused expression.

Fred looked from one pair of wolves to the other, and his body tensed. The wolves continued their slack-jawed gaze. One even yawned, its warm breath rising lazily into the cold night air. Fred took one more unsteady step. No response from the wolves. He took another—still nothing.

Jackson realized Fred wasn't exercising caution. He was limping. One of Jackson's shots must have hit Fred.

The creature limped to the tree and posted up underneath the sled. The sled twisted in the breeze, presenting its fleshy cargo. He hesitated, then retrieved the knife from his bearskin "cloak" and followed the nylon rope over the tree branch to the trunk where Jackson had tied it. Grabbing the rope, he sliced through it with a single slash of the knife. The sled plunged downward, destined to scatter meat in the snow, but Fred dropped the knife in favor of the venison, catching the sled before it hit the ground.

The wolves immediately fanned out and surrounded the creature.

Fred spun on his one good leg and faced bared fangs in every direction.

Jackson had seen wolves in action, albeit on video, and been impressed by their hunting prowess. Watching Fred move, however, was surreal. He held the sled under one arm, holding it as easily as one might a loaf of bread. Jackson's brain struggled to comprehend a creature of Fred's size moving with such dexterity.

While Fred's speed and strength impressed Jackson, so did the wolves' patience. They had remained focused on Fred while the suspended deer meat swung only a few feet away. Was it possible they had been holding back until Fred brought the meat down to their level?

Even more impressive was the wolves' coordinated attack. They dodged Fred's advances and foiled his defenses as if anticipating his every move. Had the wolves learned from their previous encounter and come to the rematch prepared?

Jackson wasn't confident Fred could fend off the wolves a second time. He appeared tired and hurt. With his injured leg, the pack danced effortlessly beyond the range of his dangerous claws. It seemed to Jackson that the wolves' revised strategy was to get Fred away from the meat, leaving it open for a quick mouthful before he could return. Fred's apparent inability to pivot on his injured leg left him vulnerable on one side.

Jackson debated. Wolves no longer enjoyed protection under Minnesota law, but he had reservations about shooting or even injuring one of them. The animals were a vital part of the Minnesota ecosystem, and the decision to kill them was not to be made lightly, especially when the animals were acting out of instinct.

The wolves attacked. Fred stepped left on his injured leg, which allowed him to face his attacker and hold it at bay. But he neglected to lift his foot clear of the nylon rope coiled next to him, and as he stepped, the rope hooked on the toe of his left foot. When Fred planted the foot, it tugged the rope with it.

The more Fred moved, the tighter the rope grew. Finally, without an inch of give, the rope yanked Fred's leg backward. Emitting a bloodcurdling yelp that echoed throughout the clearing, the giant lizard went down spectacularly, one hundred pounds of deer meat clutched to his chest. The lime-green sled split in half upon impact, ejecting frozen deer meat like candy from a ruptured piñata.

The wolves pounced, gobbling the scattered meat in chunks.

Entangled in the length of rope, Fred couldn't stop the first two assailants from feasting on the meat, safe from his deadly claws. The third wasn't so lucky. Fred grabbed its tail with two fingers in a grip powerful enough to make the fleeing creature yelp in pain and drop its prize. He speared the meat with one claw and dragged it toward him, but had little time to appreciate the small victory as the largest of the animals bared its teeth. Fred tried to roll away but was too slow. The wolf fastened itself to Fred's neck.

The wolf's companions, having devoured their snacks, returned and nipped at Fred's hands and arms, impeding his ability to fend off his attackers.

The large wolf tightened its hold on Fred's neck. As his body jerked and yanked under the persistent pull of the attackers, Fred's gasps for breath grew raspy and labored.

Jackson fired a warning shot into the air. Although the shot sent two wolves running for cover, one, the largest of the pack, refused to release its grip and clung to Fred's throat.

Jackson absently noted the wolf's beauty. The animal was large and lean, with a muscular neck and shoulders; a strong and cunning leader who'd likely survived bears, disease, hunger, other packs, and the ire of humans. It would be a shame to kill such an animal, but it would be criminal to let Fred die. Harlan would never forgive him.

Charlie, however, might be pleased to hear Fred died a slow, agonizing death.

Jackson dismissed the idea. Fred was as intelligent as any human, and he would never have stood by and let a wolf kill a person. He flicked the M4's firing lever from "auto" to "semi," leveled his eye with the rifle's sight, and squeezed the trigger.

Fred had flinched at the sound of the M4's report. Jackson saw him do so again as the enormous wolf collapsed on top of him. Finally able to use his arms and hands, Fred squirmed under the dead wolf and pushed it off his chest. He tried to get up but found himself entangled in the rope.

Jackson shimmied down the tree trunk until he reached what he thought was a safe height from which to drop. He was mistaken. The force of the two-foot drop sent waves of pain through his ribs, causing him to collapse to the ground, which sent a second wave of pain through his ribs and the M4 flying. Once the pain subsided, Jackson searched for the rifle and spotted it several feet away, half buried in the snow. He still ached from the fall and didn't relish the idea of moving, but the wolves might return, and he wanted to be armed if they did.

He crawled through the trampled snow toward the weapon, receiving another jolt to his ribs with each movement. Although only fifteen feet, the distance had seemed longer, and after five agonizing minutes, he grabbed the rifle and pushed the stock into the snow until it hit solid ground. Using the upright M4 as a crutch, he was able to stand with surprisingly little effort or pain. He smiled at his ingenuity until he realized he had "walked" himself up a loaded rifle without moving the selector switch to Safe. "Fucking idiot," he mumbled to himself as he cradled the weapon under his armpit and turned toward Fred.

FRED STARED at the flat-faced creature. He was sure it was the one he'd encountered the cycle before. He recognized its scent and the crude weapon tucked under its arm. As the creature moved toward him, Fred noticed, with grim satisfaction, that it moved with a limp. Like him, it had sustained an injury. His satisfaction evaporated when he remembered he was unable to move.

Thoughts raced through his mind. Perhaps the flat-faced creature was the furry animal's caretaker and was coming to exact revenge or finish what it had started in their previous encounter. But this creature killed the large attacker. He wouldn't have done so had they been allies. Then again, perhaps the flat-faced creature was also a predator and wanted Fred for itself. After all, Fred knew he was a formidable foe and would make an impressive trophy.

He shuddered at the idea of being killed for display, then shuddered at the alternative. What if the flat-faced creature meant to take him alive and imprison him for the amusement of other flat-faced creatures? The idea of captivity and a life of poking and prodding by younglings scared him more than death, assuming the flat-faced creatures had younglings.

JACKSON PROCEEDED SLOWLY. While he meant Fred no harm, the creature didn't know that. As he drew nearer, Jackson heard Fred's rapid breathing. Despite its superior size, strength, and perhaps intellect, Fred looked afraid. Jackson felt sorry for him, but there appeared to be no way to convince Fred he was an ally.

Jackson kicked at the snow and walked a serpentine pattern. After half a dozen passes, his boot clanked against something hard. He kneeled, biting his lip against the pain as he retrieved what he was looking for. Fred's knife. He turned it over in his hands, noting the serrated blade and tan wooden handle, which appeared to have been fashioned in place of the original. In the moonlight, he could just make out lettering carved into the knife handle. "R. Nordgren." Jackson smiled. So, Fred was Lexy's "pissed-off raccoon."

Alarmed by the sounds of a struggle, Jackson whirled to see Fred laboring to free himself. The creature snorted and bellowed like a wild boar. Froth dripped from his jaws, and his eyes were wide. Jackson hadn't noticed the white portion of Fred's eyes. He'd assumed they were black, cold, and lifeless, like those of a shark, but they reflected fear.

"What the hell's gotten into you?" Jackson asked aloud, then realized he was brandishing a rifle in one hand and a knife in the other. Fred was right to be frightened. The man who'd tried to kill him was looking down at him while holding not one but two weapons.

"Easy, big guy. I'm not going to hurt you." Jackson laid the M4 on the ground and knelt next to Fred, but kept a close eye on Fred's claws and legs, having surmised that one kick from Fred's muscular legs meant instant death. With a guttural grunt, he climbed to his feet and hobbled to the base of the crooked tree. He took the nylon rope in one hand while using the knife to saw at it. The fearsome blade quickly cleaved the rope in two long pieces. Jackson picked up the end attached to Fred and tossed it at the bellowing creature.

Fred stopped protesting long enough to notice he'd been cut loose but watched Jackson with suspicious eyes. He wiggled his upper body, and the coils ensnaring him loosened, allowing him to free one hand, which he used to pull the end of the rope toward him and work it through the coils until they were slack enough to free his other hand.

Jackson grabbed his rifle and watched Fred struggle to sit up. His hand tightened around the M4 as the creature unraveled the rope from its lower body, climbed to its feet, and then shook itself like a dog shedding water.

Jackson suspected Fred had lost circulation in his extremities by the way the creature pranced about. The display amused Jackson, and he laughed, drawing Fred's attention.

"What? You look ridiculous."

Fred let out a petulant bark, like that of a seal, and kept prancing, adding vigorous rubbing of his muscular arms to the already comical spectacle.

Jackson shook his head. "Superior intelligence, my ass."

Fred finished his calisthenics and tiptoed around the tree, snapping up meat left behind by the fleeing wolves. The remnants were little more than scraps, and Fred gobbled them up in seconds. When the meat was gone, he looked at Jackson, licking his lips.

Jackson bounced the rifle under his arm. "Don't even think about it."

Fred snuffled and circled, stopping only when he spotted one of the two dead wolves lying amidst the tangles of rope. He stared at the carcass, let out what Jackson swore was a sigh, then dropped to all fours. He nuzzled the dead wolf with his snout before lowering his head to eat.

Jackson recoiled at the sight and sound of Fred devouring the dead wolf. The blood had mainly congealed in the frigid night air, but the crunching of bone and cartilage turned Jackson's stomach.

It was the *thought* of Fred consuming the wolf he found most repugnant. Something in Jackson bristled at the sight of the noble animal gobbled up like so much roadkill. He resented the apex predator's undignified demise, aware his resentment made little sense. Plenty of predators were on the human menu: walleye, shark, and even bear and alligator in some parts of the country. Still, it bothered Jackson to his core, and he looked away.

I guess it's now or never. He's eaten, so he might not kill me out of hunger. I untied him, so he may no longer see me as a threat.

Knowing the idea was optimistic, perhaps dangerously so, he nonetheless started toward Fred, who hunched over the remains of the wolf in a manner that made him appear both embarrassed and gluttonous. As Jackson inched closer, Fred resorted to snuffling, snorting, and twitching before letting out a fierce bellow that stopped Jackson in his tracks.

"All right, all right. I get it." Jackson held up his hands. "I'm an uninvited dinner guest. But I'm not here to hurt you again."

Fred resumed feeding but kept a watchful eye on Jackson's rifle.

"Are you afraid of this?" He held up the rifle, and Fred let out a warning growl. "Fine." Jackson pulled the magazine from the M4 and tossed it away. The gesture was a hollow one as Jackson carried another full magazine in his pocket. Also, the creature might not have made the association between the magazine and the bullets that had ripped into its leg.

Jackson pointed the rifle toward the sky and pulled the trigger. Nothing happened. "See? No more bullets. No more bang-bang." He started forward again but froze when Fred threatened to charge, as he had the day before. "Okay, okay, you don't like the gun." Jackson turned the M4 over in his hands... then tossed it as far as he could.

Fred rose on two legs.

"Here we go," Jackson said under his breath, knowing he was at Fred's mercy if the creature charged. He reached into his pocket.

Fred let out a soft snort and craned his neck.

"Nothing dangerous," Jackson cooed. He withdrew a piece of paper and unfolded it, careful not to make any sudden moves. The paper expanded, growing into a four-foot-by-three-foot poster-sized sheet. It wasn't a poster but the Lake Superior map from the Grand Marais hospital.

"Just a piece of paper." Jackson had Fred's attention. The creature seemed fascinated by the crisscrossing lines and colors, and when Jackson turned the sheet toward him, he crept forward. "Must have left your glasses at home," he joked, amused that Fred might need spectacles.

Encouraged by Fred's interest, Jackson pointed to himself, Fred, and then the map. Fred cocked his head again, and Jackson repeated the motion. Fred took a cautious step and peered at the map again. He took yet another step, and Jackson gently laid the map on top of the snow. Again, he pointed to himself, then Fred, then at the same spot on the map.

As Fred studied the map, Jackson thought he saw recognition in the creature's eyes. It looked up, made a broad sweep with its arm as if referencing the surrounding area, then pointed to the location Jackson had pointed out on the map. "Yes!" Jackson nodded excitedly. "That's us!" He pointed to himself and Fred again, mimicking Fred's sweeping motion before pointing to the map. Fred grunted in apparent understanding.

Jackson pointed to the map yet again, drawing his finger across the damp sheet as he traced a route from their current location to the spot marked "The Mountain."

Fred cocked his head again.

Jackson pondered, then pointed to himself, then to Fred, and finally to the map, drawing an imaginary line to the Mountain.

Fred let out a huff that was almost certainly an expression of boredom, but when Jackson pointed his middle and index fingers downward and made a walking motion, Fred re-engaged, leaning in and startling Jackson, who took a quick step back. The creature ignored Jackson and, pointing to the map, drew one clawed finger from their location to the Mountain. He looked at Jackson, pointed to himself, then Jackson, and mimicked Jackson's walking motion with two of his long digits.

"Yes! We're walking." He pointed into the distance. "We're going to that mountain!"

Fred slowly backed away, careful not to turn his back.

"Great, now he thinks humans are dorks."

Fred coughed and sputtered. He bent at the "hips" and

lowered himself to the ground. Jackson puzzled as the coughing turned to gagging and the gagging to choking.

Jackson recoiled as the creature ejected a torrent of spittle from its mouth, shuddered from head to toe, and then regurgitated a softball-sized silver orb onto the ground.

"What in the...?"

The creature wiped its mouth on its bearskin and stood upright. The eight-foot-tall lizard actually looked proud of itself.

Jackson felt bile rise in his throat and turned away, sucking air through his nose and mouth. Once confident he wasn't going to retch, he turned to see Fred holding the orb.

"What the fuck?"

Fred grunted and twisted the top half of the orb clockwise. The orb levitated from Fred's palm into the air, then blinked green. Jackson dropped to the ground and covered his head.

Fred *chortled* and motioned for Jackson to stand as the orb hovered, projecting blue, green, and yellow lines into the air.

Jackson struggled to his feet, blinking as he recognized the tri-colored lines as a three-dimensional topographical map. A single pixel on the map blinked red, then moved, leaving a dotted line in its wake. Jackson gawked as the pixel crossed uneven terrain until it encountered a soft rise that angled into an incline. The pixel scaled the inclined, rising until it reached the top, where it turned a pleasing blue.

"Holy crap. Three-dimensional maps."

Fred looked at Jackson, hands on his hips.

Jackson laughed. "Fine. You win. You have better toys."

Fred grasped each of his arms at the elbow with the opposite "hand" and looked into the sky.

"What does that mean?"

The big lizard nodded toward the hologram and then looked to the sky again. This time, he grasped his arms as if securing his grip on each elbow.

Jackson shook his head. "I still don't understand."

Fred snuffed, jabbed one claw at the sky, and lowered his arm until his claw hovered over the flashing pixel. He waited a moment, then repeated the gesture. This time, after his claw hovered over the pixel, he clasped his arms at the elbow again and stared at Jackson.

"I'm sorry, I still don't…"

Fred grunted with agitation and thrust one arm at the sky. Instead of lowering his claw as he had before, he stuck out both arms and waggled them like a bird in flight. With a flourish, he brought his outstretched arms together in a crude breaststroke that ended with both claws pointing to the still oscillating orb.

Jackson frowned at the sight of the reptile, bent at the knees, arms pointed like a swimmer preparing to dive into a pool. He felt another laugh coming on when it hit him.

"Your friends are coming to meet you."

Fred cocked his head. If he'd had visible ears, they would have perked up.

Jackson raised a hand into the air and then let it flutter downward until it hovered over the Mountain. "They're going to pick you up there."

Fred trilled excitedly. The sound reminded Jackson of a cat peering through a window at an unsuspecting bird.

"Got it. You have a plane to catch. Let's get going." He made the walking motion again.

Fred grabbed the orb out of mid-air and looked at Jackson with a sheepish expression.

"What?"

Fred offered the orb to Jackson.

"Oh, I see. Your people have hovering map balls but haven't invented the backpack?" He held out his hand and took the orb from Fred, aware the creature had regurgitated it moments earlier. He turned the object in his hand and twisted it counter-clockwise, as he thought he'd seen Fred do moments earlier. The orb throbbed but didn't rise. Instead, it blinked an ominous red.

Fred released a startled squeak and snatched the orb from Jackson.

"Hey!" Jackson yelped. He wasn't sure why Fred reacted as he did, but felt chastised by the creature as it touched the orb in a pattern of long and short caresses.

The orb went silent, and Fred relaxed. He stared at Jackson with narrowed eyes, the slits of his nostrils shrinking until they were almost closed. Jackson wasn't sure but suspected the creature was scowling.

"Whatever." Jackson folded his map and stuffed it into his pocket. "See that? It's called a pocket. Now *that's* technology."

Fred held out a claw and nudged Jackson's coat pocket.

"What?" Jackson looked down at his coat and saw nothing there.

Fred nudged the pocket again, then held out the orb.

"You sure you're okay with me holding it? Because a few seconds ago, you were acting like a jealous toddler." Jackson extended his open palm. Fred relinquished the orb, but when Jackson withdrew his hand, he emitted two sharp snorts.

"I'll be careful," Jackson snapped as he placed the orb in his coat pocket. He checked his watch. "We gotta go." He started walking and got only a few feet before realizing Fred wasn't behind him. He turned to see Fred down on all fours.

"Um, what's going on?" Jackson inquired. Fred started gagging again, this time more violently. "Not this again."

Fred's previous coughing fit was alarming, but this episode was disturbing. The creature's body undulated as a wet gulping sound rose from deep inside its gut. He shook his head back and forth as if trying to dislodge something. Jackson stood by until he couldn't watch anymore.

Knowing first-aid procedures made zero sense, Jackson positioned himself behind Fred. He was about to grab the creature around the waist when Fred upchucked a wet, slimy object the shape of a hot dog. It was one of the pellets Charlie and Jasper had identified two days earlier.

Jackson's face scrunched, and he gasped, covering his mouth. "Fuck!" He exclaimed through cupped hands. "That's seriously nasty."

Fred stood and stretched, unfazed by the episode or the pellet. He seemed almost energized.

"Can we go now?" Jackson's face was still contorted with disgust as he avoided the steaming pellet. His pocket vibrated, and Fred let out a bark and backed away. "Calm down." Jackson pulled the satellite phone from his pocket, checked the number, and then answered.

"Hey, Lex." He frowned. "Yes, I'm still alive." His eyebrows arched as he shifted the phone between his hands. "How far out?" He returned the phone to his pocket and turned to Fred.

"We're going to have visitors."

26

Jackson struggled to breathe. His lungs rebelled at the introduction of frigid air, but his brain overruled them, demanding oxygen. Taxed after limping up a snowy incline, he bent over, ready to vomit, but there was little in his stomach to expel. He needed air more than anything, and the best way to get it was to drop to his hands and knees and breathe as deeply as possible.

Five minutes passed before his breathing slowed to something approaching normal, and even then, he had to use the slender trunk of a tree to lift himself into a standing position. He was upright for another five minutes before noticing Fred was watching.

"Out of shape," Jackson said between breaths. "Last time I saw the inside of a gym was in a TV commercial. Not that you'd know what those are."

Fred blinked and turned away.

Jackson cursed under his breath and limped after Fred, who staggered up the trail, crashing through the underbrush and crushing snow and foliage underfoot. At first, he resented Fred's bull in a china shop approach as everything the creature dislodged rolled downhill, but he realized the creature acted as a road grader, clearing a path that made it easier for Jackson to climb.

"Hey! I'm supposed to be leading you, not the other way around."

Fred glanced over his shoulder and snorted. Jackson noticed for the first time that his companion, despite blazing a trail through brute force, also limped. And why wouldn't he? He'd been shot with .460 Rowland slugs and attacked by wolves, both of which had occurred because of Jackson's presence or when initiated by Jackson himself.

Guilt racked Jackson's conscience, momentarily eclipsing the pain racking his body, but this was not the time to dwell on fault. The truth was, *not* thinking about the events of the last three days was all that kept him going. He gritted his teeth, prepared to focus on the terrain ahead, when he heard the staccato *THUMP, THUMP, THUMP* of blades slicing the air.

THE LAKOTA UH-72A helicopter flitted over Superior National Forest like a dragonfly buzzing an overgrown lawn. Like the MD500E that picked up Jackson, Charlie, and Mattie, the UH-72A was a multi-purpose helicopter designed to fill many roles, including search and rescue. Unlike the MD500E, the Lakota sported four blades on its main rotor and a set of twin vertical stabilizers mounted on twin horizontal stabilizers, which made the diminutive chopper noisy but gave it uncommon stability for a craft of its size and shape.

The Lakota's current load-out made Captain Harrison Dinwiddie's job easier as he guided the chopper over the treetops at a brisk but safe speed. Not that the baby-faced pilot, who looked younger than his forty-three years, lacked the daredevil attitude required of anyone crazy enough to strap themselves into a machine and soar above the clouds in defiance of God's will. Dinwiddie simply didn't feel the need to be reckless about it.

Prudence made Dinwiddie and his co-pilot, First Lieutenant Kayla Matthews, an effective team. They made a habit of avoiding unnecessary risk. It was the reason Command rousted them in the middle of the night to fly one hundred twenty miles from Duluth to the Mountain. Command knew they could count on Dinwiddie and Matthews to be discreet and efficient. Rather than dwell on the possibility they'd received the mission as a slight, the pair embraced the opportunity to take part in an important, low-profile mission.

As an inter-gender flight team, Dinwiddie and Matthews received constant ribbing and questioning of their abilities. The barbs didn't bother them. They needed only to point to their impressive accumulation of flight time and exemplary flight records to justify their existence.

Matthews was thirty-two with piercing green eyes and an icy disposition that prompted ground crew and fellow pilots to refer to her as the T-1000, after the superhuman shapeshifting science fiction movie antagonist. The lean woman served in the U.S. Army before joining the National Guard and had spent time in Eastern Europe, training to spot enemy troop movements in heavily forested areas. The skill wasn't easily mastered, especially from a helicopter, as the wash from the rotors often created false positives in the trees below. But there was a rhythm to the motion of trees caused by the downward flow of wind from whirling blades. Once she'd learned to differentiate between movement caused by helicopter blades and that caused by natural factors, the job became simpler. Of course, tracking a circle of light as it followed a moving target across mottled arboraceous terrain wasn't simple, even with the powerful LS16 searchlight lighting up tree cover like the opening night of a Broadway show.

"Hold her steady," Matthews said into her headset.

"Did you see something?" Dinwiddie asked.

"Not sure. Maybe if you'd hold her steady, I could confirm."

Matthews' grumpiness didn't bother Dinwiddie any more than his penchant for unnecessary questions bothered her. His co-pilot was only grumpy three times a day: morning, noon, and night. Once her coffee kicked in, she was as personable as a Walmart greeter.

Dinwiddie put the Lakota in a hover while Matthews moved the searchlight back and forth over the area. "Pull back a bit," she requested. "I think it's below us." Dinwiddie reversed a few yards so Matthews could angle the searchlight at an angle, obviating the need to peer through the glass-bottomed cockpit. She made several passes, not expecting to find anything so early in the search, but as luck would have it, the spotlight chanced upon a shadowy figure moving branches aside with swipes of its long arms.

"Holy shit!" Matthews exclaimed. "I see it!"

The helicopter shifted suddenly, causing Matthews to lose sight of the creature. She scanned the trees, struggling to reacquire her target as the Lakota swayed. "Keep still. I'm losing him!"

"I'm taking wind off the mountain." Dinwiddie offered the insight as calmly as ordering an iced tea.

"Dammit! I still can't—wait, there it is." Matthew's eyes widened. The thing had to be eight feet tall and looked like a mix between a buffalo and a dinosaur. "It's staring at us." She ignored the impossible image her brain presented. "It's got something in its hand. A rock, I think."

"A rock?" Dinwiddie scoffed. "Who does it think it is, Fred Flintstone?"

Matthews saw the creature rear back. "Get us out of here."

"Why?" Dinwiddie asked.

"Pull up, pull up!" Matthews yelled.

Dinwiddie yanked back on the cyclic stick, and the Lakota rose.

The rock shot out of Fred's hand like a missile.

"Bank left! Bank left!" Matthews screamed. Dinwiddie jerked the cyclic stick again, but it was too late. The rock smashed into the Lakota's tail section, severing the rotor and stabilizers, and throwing the helicopter into a wild spin.

JACKSON WATCHED in horror as the damaged helicopter plunged below the treetops. The sound of splintering trees, metal scraping against metal, followed by a bass-laden WHUMP, replaced the beat of rotor blades. A cloud of swirling snow rose above the treetops, then descended in sync with the dying whine of the helicopter's engines.

Jackson glared at Fred. "*You* did that!" He was furious. But when Fred looked downward like a chastised puppy, Jackson's anger melted away. Fred was only protecting himself. Besides, the lack of an explosion was a good sign.

Jackson estimated the Lakota at more than a mile away, but it took him only half an hour to locate the downed helicopter. Most of the Lakota was a twisted mass of smoking metal, but the cockpit appeared intact, which was another good sign, given that the impact of the crash alone could have killed or injured the crew. Jackson steeled himself against the possibility of carnage and peered through the bulbous canopy. The helicopter's configuration supported up to five occupants, but Jackson counted only two.

Jackson tried the Lakota's pilot-side door. It creaked but didn't give. The door frame was out of alignment, making it difficult to open the door. He pulled on the door again, putting all of his weight into the effort. This time, the door gave way but refused to come free. He was about to try one of the other doors when the door suddenly came off in his hand. He puzzled at the broken hinges, then noticed Fred holding the door aloft by the top edge.

"I told you to wait!" Jackson hissed. Fred ignored him and released the door, which fell to the snow. He should have realized the extent of Fred's strength when he heaved the medicine ball-sized rock into the air, but it truly struck him when Fred widened the bent doorway with his bare hands as if using a hydraulic rescue tool.

Jackson expected Fred to squeeze into the helicopter after widening the door, but the creature stepped aside and allowed Jackson entry. As he climbed in, he understood why Fred had let him enter first. Fred knew nothing of human physiology, so it made little sense for the creature to provide aid beyond freeing the pilots of physical restraint.

He started with the pilot and was relieved after inspection that the guardsmen suffered only minor injuries, displaying a solid pulse and clear, unobstructed breathing. Given neither pilot moved, it was fair to assume they had been knocked unconscious during the crash, but Jackson was reluctant to wake either of them. A sudden return to consciousness might send them into shock, as might the sight of a giant, rock-throwing bipedal lizard towering over them. Jackson moved to the co-pilot and unhooked her safety harness.

Fred grunted, motioned toward the door, then the co-pilot. It took Jackson a moment to understand what Fred was asking, but when he did, he shook his head. "No." Jackson cradled himself in his arms and pretended to shiver. Fred wanted to know if he should remove the co-pilot from the helicopter. Jackson figured the cockpit protected the crew from weather and animals and felt it best to leave them where they were. "Cold. Brrr." He pretended to shiver again. Fred made a sound like an old man dislodging phlegm and squeezed out of the helicopter.

Jackson took the co-pilot's hand in his. He waited for the telltale pulse on her wrist, but, finding nothing, calmly reset before taking her hand again. Still nothing. Jaw clenched, Jackson released the co-pilot's hand and placed his index and middle finger on her neck. After four long seconds, a faint but detectable twitch rewarded his patience. His knees nearly gave out as he waited for another twitch. That twitch came two seconds after the first. Low, but there.

He allowed himself to breathe again and checked the co-pilot over for other signs of injury. Other than a few scrapes and bruises, she appeared fine. "Nice job sticking the landing." Jackson patted the instrument panel affectionately. While considerable skill and some degree of luck likely contributed to the crew's survival, the fact that both guardsmen were still breathing was a testament to the helicopter's build. The Lakota was one tough little son of a bitch.

The pilots' stable condition re-energized Jackson. He reached between the seats and felt around in the darkness. After a few seconds of fruitless groping, he retrieved a plastic box and opened it to find a flare gun inside. Grinning, he looked outside to see Fred pacing. Fred caught Jackson's eye and grunted. "All right, all right, I'm coming."

Jackson squeezed through the cockpit's twisted doorframe and looked back at the mangled helicopter. His face darkened. He yanked the satellite phone from his pocket.

SOME MIGHT HAVE DESCRIBED Lieutenant Cooper as unremarkable. They would have been wrong. Although of average intelligence, Cooper possessed a knack for anticipating his commanding officers' needs before they asked, along with a smarmy disposition. The former made him invaluable to his superiors, while the latter alienated him from his fellow guardsmen.

At the moment, Kirk regretted selecting Cooper as his chauffeur and valet. As he sat in the Humvee's passenger seat, his head smacking against the roof, Kirk wondered if the lieutenant was intentionally hitting every bump in the road. If it weren't for the need to reach the downed helo as soon as possible, he would have taken the wheel himself.

Instead, he would have to settle for berating the eager young man. He opened his mouth to accuse Cooper of trying to give him a concussion when his National Guard-issued satphone rang. He pressed the device against his head, looking forward to tearing whoever dared call him at this time of night a new one.

"Who is this?" His eyes widened. "Jack? Where are you?" His eyes narrowed. "What do you mean, you're with it?" He struggled to digest what he was hearing. "You're with that thing?" He was yelling now, partly out of anger and partly to be heard over the growl of the Humvee's diesel engine and the intermittent noise of the vehicle's tires on snow, mud, and gravel.

"Don't tell me to calm down! I swear to God, Jack, if that thing hurts my people..." Kirk pressed one hand against the dashboard and glanced at Cooper. The lieutenant's eyes were on the road, but Kirk was sure he was listening. Kirk wasn't sure whether he admired or detested the man's multi-tasking. It was one thing to keep himself apprised of the situation; it was another to eavesdrop.

"You need to stand down, Jack. Right now!" Spittle flew from his mouth. "Because you have no business tooling around the woods. Stand down before you get someone else killed."

JACKSON BLINKED. "Somebody else? What are you talking about?"

The satellite phone whispered Kirk's response, and Jackson sank into the snow, legs splayed in front of him. Tears welled in his eyes. Only the pain from his cracked ribs kept him from curling into a ball on the forest floor. Instead, he let out a guttural scream so full of frustration and fury that the forest fell still. Even the once-ceaseless wind seemed to have stopped blowing. It was as if the whole of the forest offered a moment of silence.

"Jack?" Kirk's voice crackled from the phone. "Jack, are you there?"

Jackson wiped frozen teardrops from his eyelashes and took a deep breath before holding the phone to his ear. "Give Charlie my condolences." He squeezed the phone until it creaked, then launched it across the clearing, where it shattered against the trunk of a maple tree.

Fred offered a concerned grunt.

"Give me a minute. Okay?" Jackson climbed to his feet, laced his fingers on top of his head, and paced back and forth. After several laps, he pulled the flare gun pilfered from the downed UH-72A from his pocket and fired into the sky.

THE MOUNTAIN, while technically a mountain, was more of a hill. Despite rising to only twenty-three hundred feet above sea level and a prominence of only one thousand three hundred one feet, the mountain nonetheless stood out against the surrounding terrain. It was, as Ron the orderly had proclaimed, the highest point in Minnesota.

Located in the southernmost portion of the Boundary Waters Canoe Area and Superior National Forest, the Mountain and the immediate vicinity radiated with arboreal beauty, even at night. The micro full moon, amplified and reflected by the snow, cast enough light to bathe the rolling landscape in a hazy glow—a tapestry of twinkling stars added to its beauty.

KIRK'S HUMVEE idled near the base of the mountain. He stood next to the vehicle, looking through night vision goggles and ignoring Lieutenant Cooper, who stood beside him.

"Any sight of the chopper, sir?" Cooper asked.

"Not yet, but at least there's no smoke or flames."

"That's a good sign... right?"

Kirk debated whether to answer when a flare streaked into the air, bathing the area in a soft red-orange glow. "Son of a bitch," Kirk griped, yanking off the goggles.

"What's the matter, sir?"

"Just caught a flare through the goggles." Kirk blinked angrily and rubbed his eyes. "What's the ETA on that Black Hawk?"

Cooper checked his watch. "Twenty minutes, sir."

Kirk raised the goggles and scanned the mountain again, but the exercise was interrupted when an aging Ford Explorer turned off Bally Creek Road at high speed and skidded to a stop. The door of the vehicle opened, and Charlie leaped out. Her boots had barely hit the ground when Cooper yelled, "Ma'am, this is a restricted area, National Guard business only."

Charlie stormed past Cooper to Kirk. "Was that a flare?"

Kirk didn't bother to turn. "You must be Miss Battice."

"Was that Jackson?"

"How'd you find us?" Kirk demanded of Charlie, his face pinched with annoyance.

"Your people are barreling around in two-ton diesel-powered trucks in the middle of the night. You're not exactly operating incognito."

Kirk returned the goggles to his face, drawing an exasperated huff from Charlie.

"Don't you care what happens to him?"

"Of course I do. But I have my orders, Miss Battice. Besides, I just spoke to him. He's fine."

"Thank God." Charlie took a long breath and let it out slowly.

"And while we're asking questions." He lowered the goggles again, this time resting them on the hood of the Humvee. "Did you know Jackson is helping that thing?"

Charlie flinched. The amber glow of the Humvee's side marker lights provided enough light to display the disbelief on her face. "That's ridiculous," Charlie scoffed. "I sent him to kill it."

"Really?" Kirk's eyebrows arched. "I figured you for the 'catch and release' type."

"I am." She swallowed hard. "Was."

"Major Campbell?" Cooper interrupted. "The Black Hawk should be here any minute. Should I direct them to the Lakota, sir?

"Negative, Lieutenant," Kirk said sharply. "Direct Murphy and the other units to the Lakota. The Black Hawk's infrared will come in handy." He caught Charlie's eye. "And Lieutenant? Confirm the Black Hawk's carrying plenty of ammo."

Cooper scrambled into the Humvee.

"You're a real asshole, you know that?"

"Like I said. Orders are orders." A smug smile lifted the corners of Kirk's mouth as he crossed his arms against the cold. Charlie gave him a withering glare and stomped to the Explorer, but as he watched her go, the smile disappeared.

"Miss Battice?"

Charlie stopped at the Explorer, her hand on the door.

"Would you do me a favor?"

"You're kidding, right?"

Kirk looked over his shoulder and saw Cooper in the Humvee barking orders into the radio headset. When the lieutenant gave him a cheerful thumbs up, Kirk sighed and turned to Charlie.

"Find Jackson before that Black Hawk does."

Charlie climbed into the idling Explorer without a word. The SUV fishtailed away, sending up rocks, mud, and snow as its taillights disappeared into the night.

27

Sarah climbed out of Scottie's bed with little concern that her mother would wake. Marnie was usually a light sleeper, but the snoring that rocked Scottie's room suggested she was exhausted. Once confident Marnie was indeed dead to the world, Sarah slipped out of bed.

She couldn't shake the feeling that her father was in danger. She had no evidence to support her suspicion, but her father had been home from Afghanistan only a few days, and she couldn't bear the thought of something happening to him after he'd survived eighteen months in the Middle East.

Once out of the house, Sarah made her way to Shepard's on foot. The family restaurant on the outskirts of town had once been part of a national restaurant chain and kept the twenty-four-hour operating schedule and familiar green trade dress, but all other signs of the chain's existence had been removed to avoid lawsuits.

The walk hadn't been long, but it was cold. Fortunately, this meant the streets were mostly free of cars, and few people milled about. The weather, along with the late hour, also meant fewer people at Shepard's.

Sarah glanced around the dim dining room. While the cold had scared some potential diners away, there were enough intrepid customers that she didn't stand out. On this night, the "crowd" consisted of the usual smattering of teens and twenty-something students.

It wasn't uncommon for college and even high school kids to study at Shepard's.

They'd commandeer a booth or table and spread out their books and laptops. The wait staff turned a blind eye to such homesteading, provided the students only did so late at night or during slow nights. The unspoken agreement benefited both parties. While the students tended to only to order coffee or soda while occupying tables for hours on end, the wait staff was free to ignore them in favor of the occasional families who let their children run amok inside the restaurant, but assuaged their guilt by tipping well.

Sarah had found a small, two-seat table in the restaurant's rear, next to the restrooms, and spread out her books. Though only fourteen, she had been careful to make herself appear as old as possible. She'd applied a touch of makeup in the bathroom to give the impression she was old enough to wear makeup. She also wore one of her mother's worn UW Superior sweatshirts to suggest she was, if not college-age, old enough to be considering the school among her potential college choices.

When her matronly waitress asked how Sarah was going to pay for her meal—homelessness was prevalent in the area, and dining and dashing was a frequent occurrence—Sarah pulled out a crisp twenty-dollar bill, tossed it on the table, and promised the woman "a healthy tip if she kept the pop coming." Sarah claimed to have a big test on

Monday for which she wasn't quite prepared. Her textbooks, however, were a ruse. She spent most of her time peering at her phone, hidden between the pages of the textbook she'd stolen from her mother's bookshelf, and hoping the waitress didn't realize almost no one used textbooks anymore.

When not looking at her phone, Sarah watched the Shepard's entrance. Finding the right family was crucial for making it to Grand Marais. Caution was not only warranted but required. She dared not travel with a single adult, especially a single male. Even a single female posed a danger, as there were bound to be conversations and the inevitable questions during the two-hour trip—questions she didn't want to answer.

But by ten o'clock, after consuming three colas, a plate of French fries, and the top half of a banana chocolate chip muffin, a single family had yet to enter the restaurant. She'd missed prime family time, and the odds of locating her prey this time of night were rapidly dwindling. She'd been in the booth for more than an hour, long enough for her toes and fingers to thaw from the cold walk, when she decided to call it. She conceded it had been a risky plan, but if she was lucky, she could get home before her mother realized she was gone.

Sarah gathered her things and was about to surrender her table when a kid, six or seven years old, burst into the restaurant and headed for the restrooms, trailed by his father, a guy in his mid-forties wearing an Atmosphere T-shirt.

Sarah recognized the band as a popular rap group out of Minneapolis. Both her dad and Scottie were fans. She wouldn't have paid any attention to what either her father or brother listened to, but the fact that they agreed on this band was noteworthy because it was one of the few things they had in common.

She sized up the father, taking in his shoes, pants, and hair. He was close to settling into his status as a dad, but his T-shirt and longish haircut screamed, "I'm not ready to relinquish my youth." The shirt also suggested that under the right circumstances, the right person might lure him from familial bliss, at least long enough to experience one last fleeting moment of freedom before old age made him less desirable.

She smiled, but not at the dad. It was the son who caught her eye. He wore a wrinkled Toronto Maple Leafs T-shirt smeared with chocolate sauce. *Canadians.* While the shirt didn't explain why they'd stopped for a meal so late at night, it explained why they'd been willing to brave the cold weather to dine at Shepard's.

Sarah's anticipation grew. In her experience, Canadians were not only impervious to cold but also kind and unfailingly polite. If they were on their way back to Canada, they would likely be traveling even farther than Sarah and would find it impossible to deny a well-mannered college student a ride to Grand Marais.

After father and son passed on their way to the bathroom, Sarah glanced back in the direction from which they'd come. At a four-person table in the middle of the restaurant, located midway between the bathrooms and the register, a short-haired, petite woman, closer to forty than thirty, gathered the remnants of the previous diner's meal and moved them to the table's edge. As the woman wearily stacked plates and gathered utensils, she glared at a disinterested redhead girl about Sarah's age who scribbled idly on a kid's menu with a broken crayon.

Mom is about to lose it, and her daughter doesn't realize it.

Sarah considered this bad news. If mother and daughter were at each other's throats, the ride to Grand Marais would be tense, and the family might decline to give Sarah a ride.

She wanted to go over to the table and shake the girl, but calling attention to herself would be counterproductive. Even if the family were to give her a ride, every person in Shepard's was a potential witness who could identify Sarah, the family, and whatever car they were driving, especially if the vehicle had Canadian plates.

SARAH SCANNED the parking lot in search of Canadian license plates. Of course, with the Canadian border only one hundred fifty miles away, there were several cars with such plates, but Sarah bet on the family having an SUV of some sort. The space requirements for sports equipment or other kid-related paraphernalia made sedans all but obsolete.

Sarah eliminated three sedans and one SUV with a car seat, as neither of the two kids needed one, leaving only the burgundy Nissan Murano and the black Toyota Highlander with the Northdale Cross Country bumper sticker.

She checked the restaurant windows facing the parking lot to ensure no one was watching and sauntered to the Nissan. Peering inside, she saw that the vehicle was immaculate. There was no way a vehicle stayed pristine while carrying a family of four, especially when one family member was a six-year-old boy streaked with chocolate.

This left the Toyota. Sarah stayed close to the Nissan, using it as a blind from which to await her quarry. She'd paid her bill and gone to the bathroom ten minutes earlier and expected the family to emerge from Shepard's soon. The hour was already late, and the family had no incentive to linger with a two-hour-plus road trip ahead of them.

Within moments of crouching behind the Nissan, the front entrance to the restaurant burst open, and "Chocolate Boy" ran out at full speed. Sarah cringed at the child's reckless scamper into the parking lot and had to hold herself back from sprinting across the lot to grab him when the mom emerged, hot on Chocolate Boy's heels, and halted him with a stern "Ben! Parking lot!"

Ben skidded to a stop. The woman stormed up to him, but neither grabbed his arm as Sarah expected nor yelled at him. Instead, she gave the boy a look of disappointment that would have shamed the most obstinate floor-wetting Corgi.

Ben smiled at his mother and shrugged. "Sorry."

Her look of disapproval softened, and Sarah guessed the mom wasn't the disciplinarian of the two parents. This was good. It was time to act.

Sarah stepped out from behind the Nissan. "Excuse me."

The mom snapped to attention at the sound of Sarah's voice. Eyes narrowed, she pulled Ben toward her, putting one arm around him. "Yes?" She looked Sarah up and down.

Sarah offered a smile and a squint of her eyes. Her smile, tempered so as not to come across as psychotic, suggested friendliness, and squinting eyes projected urgency without revealing that Sarah was delivering a practiced pitch. "I was wondering if you were headed north."

The woman nodded reluctantly, glancing over her shoulder at the restaurant. The front door remained closed, and she faced Sarah. "Are you headed to Winnipeg?"

Sarah shook her head, dejected. While no Canadaphile, she knew enough about Canada to know Winnipeg was northwest of Duluth, and the family's path would take them off Highway 61 long before they reached Grand Marais.

The mom bit her lip. "Actually...we're headed to Thunder Bay tonight." The words came out in a rush.

Sarah's head jerked upward. "Then you're passing through Grand Marais?" Her eyes were wide with hope. Before the mom replied, the restaurant door opened and Mr. Atmosphere emerged, with the sullen redhead in tow.

Mr. Atmosphere looked at his wife and son, then at Sarah. His gaze returned to his wife, eyebrow raised. "Natalie?"

Natalie offered a weak smile. "She needs a ride." Natalie's statement sounded more like a question.

Mr. Atmosphere's brow creased. "A ride where?"

Natalie looked to Sarah for confirmation.

"Grand Marais, or as close to it as you can get me." She had not made the same request of Natalie, but sensing Mr. Atmosphere had no compunction about overruling his wife in front of a stranger, she thought it best to give him options.

"Unfortunately, we're headed back to Winnipeg." Sympathy crossed Mr. Atmosphere's face. "That will take us off 61 before we reach Grand Marais. Sorry." He offered Natalie a caustic smile that said, "See how easy that was?" but when Natalie's nervous expression remained, the smile evaporated.

Sarah pounced. "Your wife mentioned you're stopping in Thunder Bay for the night." Her tone was both innocent and unassuming despite a triumphant grin. "Highway 61 runs right through Grand Marais on the way to Thunder Bay. I bet you could gas up without even getting off the highway."

Mr. Atmosphere glanced at Natalie, silently conveying an apology with a tilt of his head.

Sarah smiled inwardly. The dad was stuck. He had to agree to give Sarah a ride, or it would be a long drive to Thunder Bay. She tightened her grip on her backpack and shifted her weight, preparing to head for the Toyota.

"Sorry. We don't do hitchhikers, especially underage

ones." Mr. Atmosphere saw Sarah's deflated expression and hastened to soften the blow. "It's a safety thing. If we were to have an accident..."

"Eric..." Natalie's voice hovered on the edge of pleading. "We can't."

Natalie crossed her arms over her chest, but Eric didn't give her a chance to respond. "What if that were Chelsea?" He pressed. "Wouldn't you rather she came to us with her problems and not run away? Wouldn't you rather she didn't climb into a car with strangers?"

Natalie set her jaw. "She's not climbing into a car with strangers. She's climbing into a car with *us*. We're good people."

"Yes." Eric pointed at Sarah. "But to her parents, we're strangers. If I were her father, I would want a stranger to tell my daughter to go home."

Sarah had been willing to accept a little tension as part of the ride, but this was turning into a full-on battle. Eric wasn't wrong. Paranoid? Sure. But not wrong. Sarah's parents would never have given a strange girl a ride, not even across town. They would have called the authorities without hesitation. Fortunately, these people were so busy debating among themselves that they hadn't thought to involve the authorities.

SARAH HUDDLED on a street corner across from Shepards, head down against the cold. Even though she'd dressed warmly, without the protection of an enclosed bus stop, Sarah would have to head home or resort to hanging out in the convenience store across the street. While she found the idea of taking shelter in a gas station appealing, the chances of a well-meaning clerk calling the cops on the little girl trying to scam a ride at this late hour were high.

She clenched her jaw. Although not spoiled, Sarah usually got what she wanted when she set her mind to it. Of course, her father's safety remained her primary concern, but the idea of failure gnawed at her. In her mind, success was often an act of sheer will. If she didn't find a way to Grand Marais, the failure would eat at her.

The cold was already too much, and it was growing colder and later. She had to make a decision. Return home, or try to find another ride. Returning home was the wise decision, but as a Campbell, failure was unacceptable. Besides, if she returned home to find her mother awake, she'd be in a ton of trouble with nothing to show for it.

A car horn blared, jolting Sarah from her thoughts. A white pickup idled in front of her. The passenger side window rolled down, and a thirty-something man, clean-shaven, with medium-length brown hair, peered out, smiling. "Hey! Need a ride?"

Sarah's heart skipped. Sometimes, luck was better than sheer will. Then she realized the man looked familiar. "What?" Sarah stalled while she tried to recall how she knew him. That she recognized him, a fact that should have brought comfort, made her even more cautious.

The man glanced around, then smiled even more brightly. "I saw you in the restaurant and assumed you were a townie. Guess I was wrong. Where are you headed?"

He had smiled at her in the restaurant while he bussed tables. She had nodded out of politeness but hadn't paid him much attention. He was at least twice her age, even assuming she presented as seventeen. Sarah's mind, sharp despite the cold, provided an answer before she had time to consider. "South." Grand Marais was ninety miles north, but the man didn't know that.

He nodded and slapped the dashboard as if he'd just scratched off a winning lottery ticket. "Cool! Me too!" He opened the door and held it open for Sarah. "Hop in."

Sarah froze. She hadn't thought that far ahead. He was trying to entice her into his truck for reasons other than the goodness of his heart, but she hadn't prepared a script in the event he answered incorrectly. "You know what? I'm confused. I'm heading north. The jog in the road back at the stoplight got me turned around. Thanks anyway."

The man's face darkened. As she scanned his face, burning every feature into her memory, she suspected that his medium-length hair, beardless face, and lack of glasses were intentional. That was why it had taken her a moment to remember where she'd seen him. The man had no unique features, at least none that she could see, and she wondered if the nondescript pickup truck was a continuation of the theme, chosen for its generic appearance.

"I have money," he said in a rush. He squeezed his eyes shut. He'd played his hand. There was no way she was going to get into the truck willingly.

"I'm good. Thanks." Sarah turned on her heel and started walking. She'd head south, reasoning that if he wanted to follow, he would have to pull a U-turn. She glanced over her shoulder and was relieved to see the truck's brake lights flicker and fade as the vehicle drove away. Her relief quickly faded as the truck's red brake lights lit up again, followed by white lights as the truck reversed.

"Crap." Sarah increased her speed, hoping to outpace the truck but not wanting to call unnecessary attention to herself by breaking into a run. The plan didn't work, and the truck overtook her, skidding to a stop ten feet away. The passenger side door opened, and one booted foot issued from the truck.

Sarah bolted past the truck and into the street, her heart beating in her throat. A horn bleated, and she whirled to face a blur of headlights. She screamed and threw up her arms against imminent impact. When the impact didn't happen, she lowered her arms to see a black SUV idling inches away. Eric jumped out of the driver's door, and Natalie circled from the other side. "Get into the truck!" Natalie demanded.

Sarah hesitated, confused, until the rear door opened and Ben poked his head out. "Go!" Natalie barked, pointing to the open door. Sarah sprinted for the truck and dived inside. Safe inside the SUV, she watched as Eric placed himself between his SUV and the busboy.

"We have your license plate number," he threatened. "And your description."

The terrified busboy sprinted to his truck and scrambled inside. The engine howled as the truck crossed two lanes of traffic before disappearing into the night.

28

Dense forest reached for the underside of the long, lean UH-60 Black Hawk as it sped toward the Mountain. At a cruising speed of just over one hundred fifty knots, it had taken the helicopter fewer than ninety minutes to make the two-hundred sixty-one-mile trip from its home base in St. Paul to Grand Marais.

Captain Doug Carney wore a slight frown on his clean-shaven face under the visor of his helmet. He looked every bit the part of a pilot, from the piercing blue eyes to the strong jaw. Even with bags under his eyes, he could have been a model or actor.

When he and his crew received word that the Duluth unit needed air support, they received no explanation. All he knew was the Black Hawk would lift off with an M240 .50 caliber machine gun and half a dozen Hydra missiles. It was a testament to the ground crew that they completed the load-out in record time, and the Black Hawk was airborne eighty minutes later, with the flight crew cruising over the forest with little sleep and even less intel.

Carney suspected the whole exercise was a waste of time

and taxpayer money. He felt their mission was little more than a favor to Kirk Campbell, who was friends with the base commander in St. Paul. But sixty minutes in, they'd received an update. Not only were they looking for an unidentified entity on the run in Superior National Forest, but Command had also informed them that a National Guard helicopter had gone down near the Mountain. Carney remained confused as to why they'd needed to outfit the Black Hawk with the M240 and Hydras to search for a lone individual and a downed chopper, but flight time was flight time, even at night. Besides, it gave the team a chance to get in some work with their "toys".

Carney glanced at First Lieutenant Kyle Peterson, whose eyes scanned the Black Hawk's embedded display. "Anything yet? We're approaching last known."

Peterson, a weasel of a guy, the sort who might torture animals if he thought he could get away with it, shook his head without taking his eyes off the screen. The helicopter's forward-looking infrared system, or FLIR, displayed images of the ground below. FLIR detected heat and converted it into a visual image based on temperature. Unlike cameras, which required light to record usable images, FLIR relied on the delta between the heat radiated by its targets and their surrounding environment, making the system effective both from long distances and in low-light situations.

"Hold on. I think I saw something," Peterson said into his headset. Although Carney sat only feet away, the Black Hawk's four 25-foot-long blades and pair of powerful turbine engines made it nearly impossible for Carney and Peterson to hear each other without radio headsets.

"There's the Lakota." Peterson pointed to the display, where a gray/white blob shimmered on the screen. "Circle around so I can get a better look."

"Copy that." Carney banked the Black Hawk and pulled a tight, efficient circle that would put them back over the area in seconds. As he brought the chopper around, Carney saw guardsmen spilling out of a pair of Humvees. He hovered over the site until a guardsman attending to the downed pilots looked up and gave a thumbs-up.

"Looks like they've got it handled," Peterson said.

"Shouldn't we check in with Major Campbell? He might have more intel on our 'unidentified entity'."

"Whatever. It's probably just some drunk assholes lighting off fireworks. Let's just go."

"Copy that." Carney pointed the nose of the Black Hawk forward.

Jackson and Fred made their way along a dirt road. Between Jackson, with his hood over his head against the cold, and Fred's bulky bear skin hanging off his broad shoulders, they looked like a pair of Shaolin monks on a pilgrimage. Jackson limped along, while Fred, despite his injuries, strode on long, powerful legs, head bobbing in rooster-like fashion, arms and neck moving rhythmically. Jackson noted, with no small amount of jealousy, that the big creature seemed to be gaining strength with every step.

Jackson glanced back to check their progress and, seeing how little they'd made, stopped to rest. Fred grunted, urging Jackson on.

Jackson ignored his companion and followed the road with his eyes. The glow of the watchful moon lit the road as bright as a row of electric lights. He shook his head. "We can't follow this."

Fred angled his head toward the sky, then considered

the dirt road ahead. He tracked the road's winding path up the mountain, looked at Jackson, and then made the same two-finger walking motion Jackson had made earlier.

"Yes, we'll keep going." Jackson indicated the road with a nod of his head. "But if we stay on this road, we're sitting ducks."

Fred pointed his enormous snout toward the mountain and grunted.

"We have to go into the woods." Jackson pointed to a patch of trees hugging the road's edge. "The road is too dangerous."

Fred expelled air through his teeth. The result was a noise like the hissing of a semi-truck bleeding its brakes. Jackson stepped back, never having heard the creature issue such a sound.

"Bitch, all you want. We won't make it if we stay on the road."

Fred repeated the hissing sound and wandered away, determined to walk the road.

Jackson couldn't help but chuckle. The sight of the towering lizard, no matter how intelligent, stomping away in a huff was funny. "Suit yourself." Jackson hobbled toward the woods. He'd almost made it to cover when he heard a familiar sound.

THUMP, THUMP, THUMP.

Jackson stiffened, recognizing this was no small surveillance chopper. The chop of the approaching aircraft's blades was deeper, the whine of its massive turbine engines more menacing. "How many damn helicopters does Kirk have?" Jackson looked up the road where Fred moved lackadaisically. "Get off the road!"

Fred whirled as the sound of the helicopter reached him. His reptilian eyes widened when he spotted the approaching chopper. Like Jackson, Fred must have recognized the incoming vehicle, although similar to the previous one, it had a different purpose. This was an instrument of war.

"Into the woods! Go! Go! Go!" Jackson pointed to the trees. Fred blinked, shifting his weight from one foot to the other. Jackson gesticulated wildly. "Trees! Now!"

Fred bolted and quickly disappeared into the nearest cluster of trees.

Once Fred was safely out of sight, Jackson searched the sky. His face fell at the sight of the approaching helicopter. "A fucking Black Hawk."

CARNEY LOOKED over the top of the Black Hawk's wide instrument panel at the sea of trees swaying below. He didn't know what his co-pilot saw and didn't have to. He trusted Peterson to identify whatever it was they were after so that Butters could get a bead on it.

"There he is!" Peterson whooped, glimpsing an image on the dirt road. The image was a lighter shade of gray and stood out from the trees and the road. "Butters, you ready?"

"Give me a sec." Crew Chief Austin Butters, tall and wide like a heavyweight collegiate wrestler, squatted next to a tripod, on which rested a four-foot-long M240 machine gun. The elder statesman of the crew at thirty-eight years old, he nonetheless moved with the speed and agility of a wet-behind-the-ears recruit as he fed the belt of 7.62-millimeter rounds into the machine gun's receiver and slapped the feed cover into place.

"Hurry up, man!" Peterson barked as he checked his screen.

"Almost there." Butters slid into place behind the M240 and grasped its dual spade grips before disengaging the safety and peering through the sights down the length of the weapon.

"Clear to engage?"

"Fire at will." Peterson steeled himself in anticipation of the staccato pop of machine gun fire, but there was no popping, just the relentless chop of helicopter blades.

"I said 'fire at will.' " Peterson whirled to see Butters squinting.

"What the hell is that?"

"What is what?"

The crew chief pointed toward the ground.

"It's huge. It's the size of a polar bear."

"So what?"

"It's too brown to be a polar bear." He shook his head as if trying to reposition his eyes. "It's also too big to be a black bear and too skinny to be a grizzly."

"I don't care what it is," Peterson snapped. "Our orders are to locate and terminate."

Butters shrugged and looked down the barrel again.

"Hold tight. I'm going to make another pass," Carney replied.

"Negative," Butters commanded. "I can get him from here."

"No can do." Carney was adamant. "I'm getting a wicked crosswind. Having a hard time keeping her steady."

"Try using both hands." Peterson leered at Carney.

"Don't listen to him." Butters rested his thumbs on the M240's whale-tail-shaped thumb-activated trigger. "Just keep this bird steady." He pressed the trigger, and the rapid thud of machine-gun fire filled the cockpit.

Dozens of rounds riddled the ground below, sending up

puffs of snow, but when the air cleared, there was no sign of the target. The crew chief scanned the trees as the Black Hawk swayed. "Fuck! I lost him."

"How did you miss at this range?" Peterson barked.

"There's a shitload of trees down there," Butters objected. "They're blocking the rounds."

"Screw it. I'll find him." Peterson searched the display. "How did he just disappear?"

TWO LUMPS LAY on the ground, half-buried in the snow. One was a mass of brown fur; the other a smaller mass of shimmering silver. Although snow, branches, and pine needles swirled around them, neither moved. Only after the sound of the Black Hawk grew faint did the brown mass stir.

Fred's large, angular head poked out from underneath his bearskin. His nostrils flared as he stuck out his tongue to taste the air. He searched the sky, his gaze lingering on the area from which the muted sounds of a departing helicopter had come. Satisfied, he grunted.

Jackson climbed out from under a shimmering silver sheet and took a deep breath. "Jeez," he exclaimed, in between gasps for air, "I'm not exactly fresh, but you stink."

Fred paid Jackson no mind and reached out to touch the fluttering silver sheet.

"Mylar. It's an insulator," Jackson said as he touched Fred's bear skin. "Just like your bear skin. That's why they saw me, but it also kept their infrared sensor from seeing my heat signature." He tried to help his companion understand by touching his arm, then yanking his hand away and shaking it as if he'd burned himself. "Warm." He felt Fred's bare hand, then drew back and shook it again. "Warm."

When Fred didn't seem to understand, Jackson touched the snow with his bare hand, then drew it back, wrapping himself in his arms and shaking. "Cold." He draped the Mylar blanket over one arm and touched it with his finger, as he had before. This time, he drew his hand back and wrapped himself in both arms, shivering as he did so. "Cold." He covered himself in the Mylar blanket, pointed into the sky, then at his own eyes, then at Fred and himself, and said, "Cold."

Fred snuffled and walked away.

"Hey, you asked."

CHARLIE SQUINTED through the windshield of the Explorer. Although her headlights were on high and the moon was full, driving on the dirt road at night was still tricky, especially at the speed she was going.

She wiped her hair from her eyes and instantly regretted it. In the fraction of a second she lost sight, the Explorer lost footing on the uneven path and threatened to skid into a wall of trees.

Pay attention, Charlie! You know better than that.

She took a deep breath and calmed her nerves.

"He was a cop. He can take care of himself." Her pep talk seemed to work. "Besides, I can barely see, and I'm on the ground. Imagine trying to see with all the snow blowing around a chopper." Charlie considered momentarily as the needle on the SUV's speedometer dropped to a slower yet steady pace.

"Unless they have infrared…"

29

Jackson scrambled up the mountain as best he could, but based on Lexy's recitation of the mountain's elevation as twenty-three hundred feet, he'd figured the climb would be easy. Healthy, that might have been the case, but in his current condition, scaling the diminutive mountain proved treacherous. Jagged broken rock debris littered the trail, preventing stable footing, and the recent snow made avoiding even the few downed branches and lunch pail-sized rocks that weren't buried by snow nearly impossible. Every lift of his knees and reach of his hands in search of purchase sent a stabbing pain through his injured ribs. Each of his many breaths brought more pain. He wasn't sure how much longer he could go on. Harlan's stolen drugs had worn off long ago, and he'd already taken double the recommended dosage. He had two choices: stop climbing or risk an overdose.

As he watched Fred scale the terrain with relative ease, he realized neither choice made a difference. He was more of a hindrance than a help to Fred.

Jackson was sure it was *his* red coat the Lakota co-pilot

had seen and *his* heat signature the Black Hawk had locked onto before he'd thought to cover himself with the Mylar blanket. That realization sapped his remaining strength and compelled him to collapse onto a rotting log.

"Hey!" Jackson said in a hoarse whisper. When Fred didn't respond, he put two fingers in his mouth and blew a shrill whistle.

Fred turned, and Jackson almost laughed at the frustration evident on the creature's narrow face. "Go." He waved his companion on. "I can't go any farther." Fred inclined his head and let out a sharp bark, his already narrow eyes reduced to slits. "Just fucking go!"

Fred peered at Jackson. The massive creature rocked on its heels and knitted its claws, making a clacking sound.

He's pissed. And why not? He might already be at the top of the mountain if I hadn't slowed him down. Every moment he waits for me decreases his chances of survival.

An explosion ripped through the air, sending dirt, snow, ice, and shards of trees into the air. The already dark forest went completely black.

PETERSON PUMPED HIS FIST. "Direct hit! Base, this is Chopper 2, we got him!" He glanced at the crew chief. "Told you we should have gone with the Hydras first," he teased.

"Rounds are cheap. Those Hydras are three grand apiece. You want to explain to the quartermaster why we blew six grand on target practice in the middle of a recession?"

"We got him. That's all that matters."

"Nice shooting, guys." Carney's voice resounded through their headsets. "What do you say we head over to Grand

Marais for a couple of beers? We could set down on a rooftop bar and scope out the local talent."

"It's 0300, man," Peterson protested. "Everybody's paired up for the night. Besides, for a pilot, your game's pretty weak."

Carney let go of the collective stick long enough to flip off Peterson.

The co-pilot smirked under his visor and scanned the charred trees and rising smoke, enjoying the carnage, when Lieutenant Cooper's voice squawked in his ear.

"Chopper 2, this is base, please confirm."

Peterson checked the forest below again as Carney held the Black Hawk steady. "Base, I see a body down. It's definitely not moving."

"Is it human?" Came Cooper's reply. Peterson frowned.

"Say again?"

"Can you confirm whether the body is human?" Cooper repeated. "We have reason to believe DNR personnel may have been traveling with the target."

Peterson's eyes widened. "Uh, we can't confirm from this height, Base."

"Understood, Chopper 2. Can you get in closer and check it out? Command requests confirmation."

Peterson hesitated, but when Carney made a rolling motion with his free hand, he cleared his throat. "Say again, Base?"

"Set down and confirm the target has been neutralized." Cooper's tone had taken on an edge. Peterson looked to Carney, who shook his head.

"Negative, Base," Peterson stammered. "Uh, we have no place to sit down. Tree cover is too thick." His headset remained silent, and he relaxed. "Base? You still there?"

"Chopper 2, topography shows your location as adjacent

to a dirt road. Set down and confirm you've neutralized the target." Cooper was telling, not asking.

Peterson looked at Carney. "I'm not leaving this chopper. That's what ground troops are for." Carney nodded vigorously. "Negative Base," Peterson said into his headset. "I'm sure the topography is accurate, but we're in real close quarters here. We can't risk—"

An angry voice blared in Peterson's ears. "This is *Major* Kirk Campbell. You set that goddamned bird down right now, or I'll see to it you never fly again. Are we clear?"

Peterson and Carney exchanged a look. Peterson sighed. "Crystal, sir."

THE BLACK HIGHLANDER had traveled up Highway 61 for half an hour before anyone said a word. Even Ben, the young boy, ignored Sarah, as he was more interested in the handheld video game on his lap.

Chelsea, who was close to Sarah's age, had re-immersed herself in social media. Although it'd have been nice not to travel in total silence, Sarah was relieved that the girl seemed to be scrolling and wasn't posting anything about what she'd witnessed.

She saw Natalie glance at her husband, Eric, and winced. The adults hadn't spoken to each other for the last thirty minutes, and Sarah hoped she hadn't caused permanent damage. From the back seat, she heard Eric whisper, "Go ahead," to his wife. Natalie smiled at him before whirling toward Sarah. "How are you?"

Sarah met Natalie's eyes. "Good. Thank you. And thank you for coming back."

"It was the right thing to do."

Sarah swallowed hard, tears forming at the corners of her eyes. "So was leaving."

Natalie patted Eric on the shoulder. "And so was changing our minds."

Eric glanced in the rearview mirror. "What's your name?"

Sarah was careful not to hesitate for too long. "Olivia."

"What's in Grand Marais, Olivia?" Eric spoke as if they were fellow travelers on a shuttle bus headed for the airport terminal.

"My father." That part came easily, as it was true.

"And your mother?" Natalie asked.

Sarah had to keep from smiling. They were going to tag-team her. That was fine. She'd already anticipated that inquisition might be a cost of receiving a ride. "She's in Duluth." Sarah figured it was best not to give them too much truthful information in case they called the police. That issue had not yet been addressed, and she wanted to provide as few details as possible.

"Is there a reason you didn't have your mother give you a ride?" Eric had a hint of accusation in his tone.

"My parents are divorced." She had rehearsed her story in her head and was confident she could ace the interrogation.

"And I suppose your father doesn't have custody?" Natalie's snark seemed aimed more at Sarah's fictional father than at Sarah.

"Sexist," Eric remarked with a chuckle.

"Ain't sexist if it's true," Natalie said. "Isn't that what your dad always says?"

"He has shared custody, just not this weekend," Sarah interjected. She caught Eric's eye, and the pair shared a conspiratorial wink.

"Then why the hurry to go up this weekend?" Natalie asked.

"It's his birthday." Sarah lowered her voice, aiming for a dejected tone.

Natalie and Eric shared a look. Sarah noticed but kept her head tilted down, not wanting to tip her hand. Natalie faced Sarah again. "Sweetheart, I love that you want to surprise your dad on his birthday, but isn't your mom going to worry?"

"I plan to call her once I get to my dad's house."

"But that won't be for hours," Eric argued. "What if you called your dad, and *he* called your mom?"

"If I call my dad, he'll call my mom, and she'll make me come home or drive up to get me." She lowered her eyes again. "And I won't get to spend the weekend with him."

"What if we called him once we get closer to Grand Marais, just to give him a heads up?"

Sarah shook her head. "He's at work."

Natalie checked her watch. "Now? It's almost midnight."

"He's a chef at a restaurant. He just started last week, and I'm afraid that if I bother him, he'll get in trouble and maybe get fired." Sarah widened her eyes to indicate fear. The ploy had the desired effect, and Natalie held up her hands in a calming gesture.

"It's okay, Olivia. We won't call your dad. Not yet."

"Liv," Sarah said, smiling with relief. Although the smile was fake, the relief was not.

"Excuse me?"

"You can call me Liv," Sarah said. "That's what my mom calls me."

"What about the police?" A voice chimed in from the back seat.

All eyes focused on Ben, who had turned his game off

and removed his headphones. "Won't your mom call them when you aren't at home?"

Sarah could have kissed the kid. He was as good as a plant in the audience. "No," Sarah replied, shaking her head. "I've run away three times in eighteen months. If the authorities find out I left again, child services will step in."

"Would that be such a bad thing?" Eric asked, keeping his eyes on the road.

Sarah shrugged. "I wouldn't mind living with my dad. Except that he's a recovering alcoholic, and it took him months to land the job in Grand Marais. Having to look after me might be too much for him right now. He works crazy hours, and his schedule isn't very consistent. I probably wouldn't see him much."

"Look, we're halfway to Grand Marais already. How about we figure this out once we get there?" Natalie offered. When Sarah nodded, she turned to Eric.

"Fine." Eric tightened his grip on the steering wheel.

Silence settled over the vehicle again until Chelsea's voice boomed from the backseat. "Are we there yet?"

CIRCLES OF LIGHT chased one another across the surface of a dirt road and were soon obfuscated by a cloud of snow, dirt, and rocks that rose in a swirl. Four blades, as thin and dainty as dragonfly wings, slowed their already lazy spin. A trio of massive tires touched down, bouncing as the tremendous bulk they supported accepted its place on unsettled earth.

The Black Hawk groaned and creaked like an old man easing into an armchair as it settled onto *terra firma*. Its engines' roar faded as the chop of its slowing blades lessened to a muted rumble. As Lieutenant Peterson had argued earlier, the helicopter's blades had limited clearance. Still, the aircraft fit between the banks of trees on either side of the road with room to spare.

The aft cabin door of the Black Hawk slid open, and Crew Chief Butters stepped out, followed by Lieutenant Peterson. Butters turned on his flashlight before approaching the tree cover. Peterson hurried after him, and the light from Butters's flashlight knifed through the darkness, bobbing up and down.

"This is bullshit," Peterson whined. Butters nodded but didn't comment. "I mean, where are the ground troops? They have Humvees equipped with M240s, and we're the ones hoofing it through the forest? What a clusterfuck."

"Speaking of which, where's *your* flashlight?" Butters asked.

"Left it in the chopper. But I remembered this." Peterson waggled his standard-issue Sig Sauer M18. "Figured it'd be more useful than—"

Butters held up one hand and pointed his flashlight toward a nearby clearing littered with downed trees and smoldering branches.

"There he is." Butters tiptoed into the clearing, his head and flashlight on a swivel. He avoided the cavity made by the Hydra missile's impact and picked his way through the debris. He stood over Jackson, who lay unmoving in the snow. "Shit, it's the DNR guy." He directed his flashlight along the length of Jackson's body.

"How do you know?" Peterson asked.

"Because we're looking for an unidentified eight-foot-tall hostile creature. I don't think 'Black guy in a red parka and Timberlands' fits the description."

"Maybe not in your neighborhood, but it does in mine."

Butters ignored Peterson's joke and checked Jackson for a pulse. "Jesus, this guy's alive."

"What about the other one?" Peterson looked around wildly. "The hostile?"

The crew chief aimed his flashlight into the darkness. "There's nothing else out here."

"Are you sure?"

Butters made another pass with the flashlight. "Well, I haven't taken a census..."

"That's very reassuring."

Butters scowled. "You're welcome to take a look with your flashlight. Oh. Wait. That's right, you left your flashlight on the chopper like a—"

Fred appeared in front of him.

Butters didn't register what was happening until the beam of his flashlight fell on the creature. He reached for his sidearm, but before he could draw, Fred swept the man with his arm, knocking him into a pile of downed conifers.

A gunshot rang out, and Fred roared. He batted at the sides of his head, whirling toward the source.

Peterson stared, his Sig Sauer shaking in his hand. Fred growled and rushed forward. The co-pilot ran, but Fred was on him in a few strides. He dipped his shoulder and slammed into Peterson with such force that the man was out cold before he hit the ground.

Fred stood over the unconscious lieutenant when a Carney's voice buzzed from Peterson's discarded helmet. "Peterson? Hey, are you guys all right? I thought I heard—"

Fred stomped Peterson's helmet into a pancake of plastic and circuitry, ending the inquiry.

～

CARNEY HUDDLED in the cockpit of the Black Hawk, staring into the dark forest. Considering he was at the controls of a multi-million-dollar military aircraft armed with a massive machine gun and a complement of lethal missiles, he should have felt safe. He didn't. Whatever lurked in the woods terrified him.

"Peterson, this is Carney. Come in. Are you guys okay?" Carney knew his crew members were not okay, but the sound of his own voice made him feel less alone. He prepared to make another inquiry when Kirk's voice crackled through his headset.

"Chopper 2, can you confirm the target has been neutralized?" Much of the commander's earlier brusqueness had left his voice.

Carney swallowed hard and took a moment. "Uh, sir? I think Peterson and Butters have been neutralized."

To his credit, Kirk's response was prompt yet sympathetic. "Tough break, son, but listen to me. I still need you to get out of that bird and confirm the kill."

The last thing the lieutenant wanted to do was exit the Black Hawk, but what choice did he have? The major had given a direct and unambiguous order.

Carney killed power to the chopper's engines. As they powered down, he unbuckled his flight harness and checked to make sure his sidearm was in its holster before rising from his seat. He glanced at the M240 stand. The machine gun would be a damn sight more useful than his 9mm, but he'd never trained on the weapon and wasn't even sure he could remove it from the tripod. With a sinking feeling, he turned from the M240 and opened the front port door.

"You still there, son?" Kirk's voice came through his

headset. Grateful for the brief reprieve, Carney responded quickly.

"Yes, sir. I'm here. Preparing to exit the chopper now."

"Excellent. Glad to hear it. Keep in constant communication, Captain. It's imperative we confirm the target's status. Do you understand?"

Carney nodded, even though he knew Kirk couldn't see him. He had to admit, the man's voice instilled confidence even as he was essentially asking Carney to commit suicide.

The captain stepped out of the chopper. His feet had scarcely touched the ground before something grabbed him by his flight jacket and hoisted him into the air. He found himself face to face with something more terrifying than anything his imagination could have conjured.

The creature looked like a cross between a crocodile and a monitor lizard. Its snout wasn't as long or pointed as that of a crocodile, but was slender and filled with dozens of razor-sharp teeth. It had large, forward-facing eyes, the eyes of a killer.

But this was no dumb animal. This was an intelligent being. Carney ignored the creature's rank breath and took a deep one of his own. This might be his last communication with the major, and he hoped he wouldn't sound as scared as Peterson had. "Negative, sir. The target is not neutralized. Repeat, the target is not neutralized."

WHEN TIM FREIDA CALLED HIM, Kirk had listened with a smirk as the man relayed Charlie Battice's concerns. Although Tim had said the woman was a world-renowned tracker based in Wisconsin, Kirk found her story suspect. That was until the folks from Washington called.

He didn't know at the time that the call originated in

Washington, D.C., as the screen on his satphone only indicated it came from an "UNKNOWN CALLER." Typically, Kirk wouldn't have answered, but only a handful of people had the number, and those few who did wouldn't have called after 9 pm, absent an emergency.

The man on the other end of the line identified himself as Agent Dodge of the UAPTF. He offered no rank or title and omitted the organization's full name, Unidentified Aerial Phenomena Task Force, as well as its stated purpose, leaving Kirk to look up that information after the call. That was probably for the best. Kirk Campbell had neither the patience nor the imagination to entertain the existence of UFOs, let alone an honest-to-goodness Federal agency tasked with documenting and cataloging reports of their terrestrial visits. Had Dodge not dropped both Tim Frieda and General Wirth's names in the first thirty seconds, Kirk would have politely bid the gentleman goodnight and placed the phone in a dresser drawer.

Kirk, however, listened intently as Dodge reiterated the scant information General Wirth had already provided. *Something* roaming Superior National Forest was responsible for injuries to at least one civilian, as well as livestock, and possibly several wild animals. Kirk's mission was to locate and apprehend the target, if human, and terminate with prejudice, if not. Kirk secretly wondered what the target might be if not human, but as an experienced and loyal guardsman, he required no additional information to undertake his mission. Nonetheless, it troubled him that the UAPTF had known he'd spoken with Tim Freida. He'd talked to the coffee shop proprietor on his private mobile phone and assumed Tim had called on a business line.

He'd questioned Dodge about the agency's authority to listen in on a private call, and, to his surprise, found the agent forthcoming. In what Kirk would, in hindsight, recognize as a veiled threat, the agent asked Kirk if he, Marnie, and the kids (he'd referenced Scottie and Sarah by name) had ever had a conversation in the privacy of their home about a specific product or service, only to have that same item show up in their internet feed or as an unsolicited email.

When Kirk admitted he had, Dodge assured him Big Tech wasn't listening in on his conversations, but the government was. In return for telecommunication providers allowing the FCC, FBI, and other agencies to peruse network and telephony traffic, the government forwarded transcripts of product-related conversations to the providers, who then sold the information to retailers. The Feds kept the juicy stuff for themselves.

Both satisfied with and disturbed by Dodge's explanation, Kirk quickly changed the subject and asked why the UAPTF didn't handle the mission on their own. Again, the man opted for candor and explained that if reports of a dangerous entity turned out to be nothing more than a somnambulant bear, a pack of wolves, or a rogue mountain lion, it was easier to blame the DNR or the National Guard than take the heat themselves. Familiar with the National Guard's reputation and operations, Kirk again accepted the agent's explanation without question.

As he breathed in the chilly night air, Kirk doubted the wisdom of so cavalierly accepting his assignment. He had been happy to provide his services when contacted by Commander Wirth, but between the downed Lakota and missing Black Hawk crew, things had turned into a shit show, possibly a career-ender. But he was no quitter. There had to be some way to salvage it.

"Cooper, fire up this Humvee. We've got a job to do."

Cooper could hardly contain his excitement. "Where to, sir?"

"Up the Mountain. We'll cut the son of a bitch off at the pass."

"The mountain, sir?"

"*The* Mountain, unless you know of another mountain nearby just called 'the Mountain.' "

Cooper squinted at his superior officer. "But it could be anywhere. Why there?"

Kirk wasn't sure which annoyed him more, the little twerp questioning his order or not ending the question with "sir." He decided he didn't care. The cold had seeped through his gear, and he was eager to get back home to Marnie and the kids.

"Because, Lieutenant. That's where I'd go. "

30

Captain Carney watched the creature go apeshit on the Black Hawk. It started with the M240, which it ripped off the tripod with its bare hands, and then used to destroy the pods containing the Hydra missiles. Carney was concerned that one of the Hydras might ignite as the creature hammered the pods into so much techno trash, but was thrilled the beast seemed to have forgotten about him.

Besides, if Gork, as he'd taken to calling the creature (unaware he'd incorrectly recalled the name of a character from a popular late sixties science fiction program), happened to blow up the helicopter and himself in the process, so be it. It would be a great story to tell his grandkids someday. Assuming no one from the government decided that his first-hand knowledge of what was clearly a creature of extraterrestrial origin presented an unacceptable threat to national security. Hell, they might lock him away in a padded room until the end of his days.

Gork lowered the M240 and turned toward Carney.

Crap, maybe the alien could read his thoughts.

Gork stomped over, toting the fifty-pound M240 like it weighed nothing, and tossed it at Carney's feet. The pilot looked up, confused but calm. If Gork had intended to kill him, he would have done so already. Although it made no sense that Gork would kill his team while sparing him, Carney rationalized his survival on the fact that he, unlike Peterson and Butters, had not shot at Gork.

His moment of self-reflection was interrupted by Gork yelling at him in guttural barks, hisses, and snorts. Carney looked at Gork during the entire undressing, knowing the worst he could do in such situations was look away. Having been on the receiving end of several tongue-lashings during his career, he took this one, situational oddity notwithstanding, in stride. That seemed to placate Gork, and after speaking his piece, the creature stomped away.

Carney sat motionless. While it appeared he was free to leave, he had no means of doing so. The Black Hawk was no longer flight-worthy, and Gork had knocked out the radio, rendering Carney's headset useless. Nonetheless, he headed for the inert helicopter. The cockpit was intact and would protect against the cold while he determined his next move.

JACKSON SAT against a large birch tree, one of the few in the vicinity left unscarred by the missile blast. Crew Chief Butters and First Lieutenant Peterson sat on either side. Both looked like absolute hell, but Peterson looked worse off than Butters. The bedraggled co-pilot watched Jackson through lidded eyes. The surreptitious scrutiny didn't escape Jackson's notice.

"You got something you want to say, Lieutenant?"

Peterson straightened as if gathering the courage to respond.

"I don't get it. Why would you help that thing? It tried to kill you."

"Only after I tried to kill him."

"But you were only doing your job."

Jackson shrugged. "And he was only trying to survive."

"Christ, you sound like one of those idiot tree-huggers." He spat out the words, making no attempt to hide his disgust.

"Context matters, Lieutenant."

"Not to me, it doesn't."

Jackson looked the lieutenant up and down. Although his flight suit was torn, tattered, and covered in mud, the man looked better suited for office work than combat.

"Yeah? And how many people have you killed?"

Peterson squirmed but didn't answer. Jackson turned his attention to Butters. The crew chief was probably less than ten years older than Peterson, but the worry lines around his eyes and mouth hinted at a far less coddled lifestyle.

"How about you, Butters?" Jackson asked. "What's your ledger look like?"

Butters' expression went from placid to defensive, prompting Jackson to clarify. "I'm not judging. Just asking." The crew chief relaxed but didn't look as if he felt exonerated.

"More than I care to think about."

Peterson pulled his jacket up to his neck as far as it would go. "Well, what about you, tough guy?" He directed his question toward Jackson. "You ever shot anyone?"

"More than I care to think about." He shared a knowing look with Butters.

"*How* many?"

Jackson ran through a list in his head. "I'd say, probably not as many as Butters, but I'm willing to bet more than you."

"Right. A game warden?" Peterson snickered. "Who'd you shoot? Some guy with an expired fishing license?" He looked at Butters. The crew chief didn't acknowledge him.

"My partner." Jackson didn't wait for Peterson to ask follow-up questions. "We were chasing some gang members through the Southside when—"

"Wait." Peterson interrupted. "You were a cop?"

Jackson nodded.

"Why didn't you say so?"

"Can you shut up and let the man tell his story?" Butters glared at Peterson.

"My partner and I got separated," Jackson continued. "He went radio silent, and I thought something had happened, so I went from house to house, thinking the worst. Finally, I found him in a tool shed with some kid. The kid's pants were around his ankles."

Peterson gasped, and Jackson waved his hand. "Nothing like that. He'd hooked jumper cables to a car battery and connected the other end to the kid's genitals. He was going to torture a confession out of the kid. Told me if I couldn't handle it, I could wait outside."

"You shot your partner over some piece of shit kid?"

Jackson's jaw tightened. "As if he had no responsibility for his actions...or mine."

"Explains why you're with the DNR," Butters said.

"It does?" Peterson looked confused.

"He got blackballed, you idiot," Butters growled. "No police force in the country is gonna touch him. No cop in the world is gonna ride with him." Butters shook his head in a show of sympathy. "That's gotta suck, man."

"For who?" Peterson was apoplectic. "He shot his partner." He glared at Jackson. "What did you think was going to happen?"

"Don't be a dick, Peterson."

"He's right." Jackson shook his head, eyes downcast in silent lament.

A twig snapped with the sharp report of a firecracker, and all three men whirled to see Fred watching them from a few feet away. Peterson and Butters scrambled to their feet.

Butters' eyes grew wide. "How can something that big move so quietly?"

Peterson grabbed for his sidearm. "Let's see him move with a hole in his chest."

"I wouldn't do that," Jackson warned. "I shot him twice at close range with a .460 slug." He omitted the part about the slugs bouncing off the moose skull. "Just pissed him off." He motioned for Peterson to lower the gun, but it wasn't until Butters did the same that the man complied.

"It's okay," Jackson said to Fred in a soothing voice. Fred grunted several times and kept his distance, but didn't stray more than a few feet away.

Butters gawked. "Is he...protecting you?"

"We had a sort of mouse and the lion moment. Maybe he thinks he's returning the favor." Jackson looked at Fred. "Right before the second missile hit, he threw his body over mine. He shielded me from the blast."

Peterson perked up. "How far away was the blast?"

Jackson shrugged. "I don't know, maybe forty meters."

"Told you I wasn't off target," Peterson declared triumphantly. "If it wasn't for that...lizard, it would have been a kill shot." When Butters responded with a look of disgust, Peterson turned to Jackson with a trite grin. "No offense."

Jackson looked at Fred. "You better get going, big guy. Kirk won't be happy you took out another chopper."

"You know Major Campbell?" Peterson's voice squeaked with incredulity.

"For almost thirty years.

Peterson scoffed. "If this is how he treats his friends, I'd hate to see what he does to people he doesn't like."

Fred let out a sudden bark that brought all three men to attention. They watched as Fred shrugged off the bear skin to reveal a statuesque frame of taut, muscular flesh. Fred was ripped. His torso was long and lean, his legs narrow except for the powerful thighs and calves. His coloration was like that of an alligator, dark on the tops of his lanky forearms, outer thighs, and shoulders and light on his inner thighs, chest, and belly. His pebbled skin consisted of thousands of smooth bumps, like the skin of a monitor lizard.

"Hey, he doesn't have any junk. He's like a Ken doll!" Peterson exclaimed.

"It might be recessed." Butters winked at his fellow guardsman. "Which means it's still bigger than yours."

Despite himself, Jackson glanced at Fred's midsection. The hulking creature wore a form-fitting garment that blended with its natural coloration. "It's underwear. He must have worn it under his suit."

"What suit?"

"His flight suit, dumb ass." Butters rubbed his face.

Peterson puzzled. "What would *he* need a flight suit for? He's an animal."

"He's wearing underwear and a bearskin poncho made of bear skin. He's obviously intelligent."

"Yeah, but where'd he *come* from?"

"Christ, Kyle. Where the hell do you think he came from? Space."

Peterson cut his eyes at Butters, then watched with a sullen expression as Fred circled in place, stomped his giant feet like a dog tamping down its favorite sleeping spot, then sank to the ground with a tired grunt, finally letting his gaze rest on Jackson.

"What's he doing?" Butters asked.

"Watching over him like a goddamned nanny," Peterson teased.

Fred let out a sharp hiss followed by a guttural growl that sent Peterson backpedaling.

"Sorry! Sorry!" Peterson cried out as he raised his hands in surrender.

Butters and Jackson shared a grin.

"That's one scary-ass nanny," Butters marveled.

31

Eric pulled into a space at a convenience store parking lot and turned around to face the three children in the back seat.

"Okay, Ben and Chelsea, you two know the drill. Potty, treats, drinks, meet at the front door, then back to the car together. Nothing over five dollars each, no T-shirts, maps, trinkets, or trash, so don't ask. Got it?" Ben and Chelsea unbuckled their seatbelts. Ben reached for the door and was about to fling it open.

"Ben..." Natalie issued a quiet but stern warning. Ben checked the parking spot next to the Highlander before opening the door. Chelsea slid out without a word and headed for the convenience store without waiting for her brother. Natalie watched them enter the store and sighed. "I wish she watched out for him a little more."

"Or at all." Eric smiled at Sarah. "Okay. You're here safe and sound. Call your father and let him know you're here. We'll drop you off at the restaurant."

Sarah nodded. "Can I use the bathroom first? I wanted

to go in Duluth, but I was afraid you guys might have called the cops already." Eric and Natalie exchanged a glance.

"I'll come with you. I could use a pit stop myself." Natalie opened her door and looked into the backseat, where Sarah was sliding toward the passenger-side door. "Hey," Natalie called, and Sarah froze, one hand on the door handle. "Same rules apply to you, young lady. Potty, treats, drinks, meet at the front door, then back to the car. Got it?"

Sarah blinked. These people are so nice, like sitcom nice. "That's very kind of you." Sarah looked at Eric, who, although smiling, looked wary. Sarah maintained her smile but added a gracious nod for good measure. "Thank you." Eric nodded in return. She slid one foot out the door and stopped. She turned back to Eric, her head tilted to one side. "Are you from Canada...originally?"

"St. Paul, Minnesota. Born and raised." He grinned. "I married Nat for the PR card." Eric saw Sarah's confusion. "It's like a green card for Canada." Sarah was still confused. "Never mind. That's not how it works, anyway."

SARAH STEPPED inside the store and surveyed her surroundings. An older man with a white beard and a red vest stood behind the counter. His name tag read "Blaine." Near the back of the store, a teen, also wearing a red vest, whose name tag Sarah couldn't read from a distance, mopped the floor. He hummed along to piped-in music as he performed his task.

At this time of night, customers outnumbered employees, but only by a slim margin. By Sarah's count, there were four: herself, Ben, Chelsea, and Natalie, compared to the two employees.

Sarah had been there before. Her family frequently visited Grand Marais during the summer, mostly to dine at the abundant restaurants and enjoy what her mom described as "the quaint and quirky charm" of the town's thriving arts and crafts community.

Of course, she hadn't been looking to ditch a family of four the last time she was here. But she recalled some pertinent details. The store had only one entrance, at least for customers, and strategically placed security cameras everywhere. This would make ditching the family difficult.

"Everything okay?" Sarah whirled to see Natalie standing next to her.

Sarah looked sheepish as she stepped toward the door. "I left my backpack in the car."

"Do you need it?" Natalie asked.

"My tampons are in my backpack."

Natalie gave Sarah a conspiratorial nod. "I'll grab your backpack. Wait here." Natalie dashed out of the store.

While waiting for Natalie to return, Sarah scanned the store for the kids. She spotted Chelsea in the magazine section, perusing the fashion publications. Sarah noted Chelsea clutched a bag of deep-fried onion snacks and a bottle of cherry vanilla soda in one hand while hugging a box of Trix cereal under her armpit. The girl was stocking up on American junk food.

Sarah turned her attention to the store's expansive candy aisle and wasn't surprised to find Ben staring at the Wonka-esque variety of sweets. The boy checked the prices under each display, apparently intent on purchasing as much sugary booty as possible.

She snickered and glanced into the parking lot. Natalie and Eric were engaged in a heated discussion. She would have found the argument concerning, except that Natalie clung to Sarah's backpack as she gestured angrily at Eric through the open passenger side door.

Sarah felt a twinge of guilt, certain she was the topic of their discussion, but her guilt quickly dissipated. This was a perfect opportunity.

Sarah hurried to the candy aisle and stood next to Ben. "Problem, little guy?" Consternation etched Ben's grubby face. "I don't have enough money." He gazed forlornly at the row of treats.

"How much are you short?" Sarah adopted a helpful tone.

"Three dollars." The unhappy kid's body slumped.

"That's a lot of money." Sarah tapped her foot and stroked her chin as if deep in thought. "Tell you what." She reached into her pocket and retrieved four dollars, the remnants of the twenty-dollar bill she'd used to pay for her pop, French fries, and tip at Shepard's. "This is all yours if you do me a favor."

Ben's eyes widened. "Okay."

"Don't you even want to know what it is?" Sarah laughed.

"Nope."

Sarah checked to ensure Chelsea remained occupied. "When I give the signal, I want you to grab a bottle of chocolate milk out of the refrigerator and accidentally drop it.

Ben frowned. "I like chocolate milk. Why would anyone wanna waste it?"

"Do you want the money or not?" Sarah questioned whether using the little boy as a diversion was a good idea, but she didn't have time to explain that the chocolate milk was one of the few drinks that still came in a glass bottle.

Ben held out his hand. "Half now, half after the job is done."

Sarah's jaw dropped. "Where did you learn to ask for half up front?"

"The internet. Duh."

"Well, today's your lucky day." Sarah held out her hand with the crumpled bills. Ben snatched the money and whirled toward the wall of candy.

"Your mother is going to come in with my backpack. When she does, I'll go into the bathroom. When I come out, that's your signal to drop the bottle. Got it?"

Ben nodded, unwilling or unable to take his eyes off the candy.

"Are you sure?" Sarah worried the six-year-old boy might get distracted by all the candy and not notice her leaving the bathroom.

Ben nodded and waved Sarah off.

Sarah saw Natalie stomping into the store. She hurried over and met the woman at the counter. "Sorry." Natalie sighed. "Eric isn't the most trusting person in the world. He thought you might grab your backpack and take off without calling your parents. He wanted to search your backpack, but I wouldn't let him."

"I'm not going anywhere until I hit the bathroom." The two women walked to the back of the store, where a grimy sign read Restrooms. Sarah stopped at the bathroom door, and Natalie handed over the backpack. Sarah pushed open the bathroom door and noticed Natalie following. "Do you mind?" Sarah said, offering an embarrassed grin. "I'm still getting used to this whole thing, and I'd kinda like to do it without a crowd."

Natalie's eyes bugged. "Omigod, I'm so sorry. I'll give you

some privacy." She turned her back on Sarah and stepped away from the door.

Sarah spun on her heel and headed into the bathroom.

The restroom was cramped, consisting of a sink and a single toilet shoved against the far wall. Sarah smirked at the ancient tampon dispenser on the wall as she locked the door. She threw off her coat and sweatshirt, leaving only a thin T-shirt. Then she untied her boots and unlaced them far enough to kick them off her feet.

Kneeling on the disgusting floor, she dug into her backpack and pulled out thermal underwear and a matching long-sleeved shirt. They weren't the old-fashioned waffle-weave pattern but the high-tech, lightweight kind that felt like you weren't wearing any thermals. Sarah pulled the thermal shirt over her head and slid her arms through the sleeves, then shimmied out of her jeans and into the thermal underwear, tucking the bottoms of the long johns into her socks to create a seal against cold air. She tucked the bottom of her T-shirt into the waistband of her thermal underwear to create another seal. As she reached for the backpack again, she was startled by a knock at the door.

"You alright in there?" Came Natalie's voice.

"Yeah. Had to read the instructions again, but it's all good." Sarah was amused and alarmed at how easily the lies flowed. She reached into the backpack and pulled out a pair of black, water-resistant snow pants lined with wool. She slipped into the snow pants and stuffed her feet into the boots, wobbling as she slid her feet in.

She knelt and tied her shoelaces, then pulled on her coat. She zipped the coat, then rifled through the backpack, digging into its many pockets before pulling out a mass of black material, which she stuffed into her coat pocket.

"Olivia?"

"Coming." Sarah zipped up her backpack and turned for the door. Stopping, she ran to the toilet and flushed, then hurried to the sink, where she ran the water, pressed the soap dispenser, and waved her hand under the paper towel dispenser before sprinting back to the door. She took a deep breath and walked out.

Natalie stood in the doorway, wearing a puzzled expression. "Did you change pants?"

Sarah blinked. "Uh, yeah. I made a mess of the other ones."

Natalie's expression went from puzzled to sympathetic. "Oh, sweetheart..." She lunged forward and hugged Sarah, who gasped in surprise. Sarah peered past Natalie to search the store for Ben when she heard the crack of shattering glass and a high-pitched wail.

Natalie released Sarah and bolted for the storefront.

Although amazed Natalie could discern that the unintelligible bawling was from her child, Sarah wasted no time and dashed for a set of grubby double doors marked "Employees Only." The distance was less than ten feet, but it seemed like a mile as she rushed past the restrooms, hoping against hope there wasn't a third employee taking inventory in the back of the store.

As she burst through the double doors and into the back room, she saw nothing but stacks of soft drink pallets, coats on a rack, and mountains of potato chips. Her heart beat in her throat. Her window of opportunity was small, and time was short.

"Olivia?"

Sarah nearly fainted when she heard Natalie's voice. Despite recognizing the woman's voice, it had taken her a second to register that *she* was Olivia. Sarah fought the urge to panic as her head swiveled in search of an exit. She made at least two scans of the rear wall before spotting the red Exit sign over a battered steel door with a horizontal push handle.

"Olivia?" Natalie's voice was closer.

Sarah sprinted to the door and shoved, praying she wouldn't trip an alarm. The heavy door swung open, granting Sarah her freedom and depositing her into the bitter cold night. She stepped away from the door as it slammed shut, then listened to make sure Natalie hadn't followed. Satisfied she was in the clear, she started down the narrow alley behind the station.

"Hi there."

Sarah yelped.

Eric stood a few feet away, hands thrust in his coat pockets and his hood over his head. "Where are you *really* headed?"

"To see my dad."

"Come on. We both know that isn't true."

"Yes, *it* is." She contemplated making a run for it, but the alley was short and narrow. Even if she were faster than Eric and in better shape, the most out-of-shape adult could run her down before she could put any appreciable distance between them.

"Where does your father work? Assuming he is actually here?" Eric sounded amused, impressed even. Perhaps he was more curious than anything.

Sarah took a chance. It would be easier to convince one of the two adults to let her go, even if he was the more suspicious of the two. "The National Guard."

Eric laughed. "Right."

"He was deployed to Afghanistan, and when he got back, he wasn't even home two days before they called him with another assignment. My mom said it's a short gig, but that's what they said last time. A month, maybe two. He was gone eighteen months." Tears formed at the corners of Sarah's eyes. She hadn't intended to cry, but saying aloud what she felt brought everything to the surface.

Eric crossed his arms and laughed. "You almost got me, kid. The tears drove it home."

Sarah glowered. "If you don't believe me, look him up. There's a story about him in the *Duluth News Tribune*. Major Kirk Campbell of Massasauga River, Minnesota."

Eric grinned. "So, your last name's Campbell? What's your first name? Because I'm betting it isn't Olivia."

Sarah huffed and turned toward the store. "Forget it. I'll call my mom to come get me." She yanked on the door to find it locked. The feelings that had welled up before returned in a torrent. She burst into tears and banged on the door, frustration fueling her tantrum.

"Olivia?" Came a voice from inside the store. "Are you out there?"

Sarah backed away from the door. Her adventure had come to an end.

"Go."

Sarah turned, mouth agape. "What?"

"Go! Now!" Eric hissed as he pointed to the end of the alley.

Sarah didn't wait for him to tell her a second time. She took off at a full sprint; her backpack banging against her shoulder as she scrambled down the alley.

"Be careful!" Eric called after her in a whisper. Once Sarah disappeared around a corner, he banged on the door. "Nat? It's me. Open up!"

The door opened, and Natalie peered out. Her expression went from one of confusion to suspicion. "What are you doing out here?"

"When I saw the commotion inside, I thought Olivia might try to sneak out the back door." Eric threw his hands up. "I think I just missed her."

Natalie looked past Eric into the night. "Poor thing. I hope she'll be alright."

"Yeah. Me too."

32

Jackson had no sooner closed his eyes for a moment's rest than the growl of a revving engine jarred him awake. Peterson scrambled to his feet. "About time."

Jackson stared at Fred, who stood primed and ready to face the approaching threat.

"There are too many of them. You have to go."

A pair of headlights appeared in the distance, tiny at first but growing larger as the roar of the vehicle's engine grew louder. Within seconds, the vehicle transformed into a boxy SUV.

"That's not one of ours," Butters said.

"Dammit." Peterson fumed as he sat back down. "Where's the freaking cavalry when you need them?"

Butters shot his fellow guardsman a look. "What do you need saving from? The worst that could happen now is a minor case of frostbite."

"I gotta take a dump."

"So, go. What's stopping you?"

Peterson looked into the woods. "I can't poop outside."

Jackson watched as the approaching Ford Explorer skidded to a stop. "Who is that?"

The driver's door opened, and Charlie leaped out.

"Jackson!" She dashed across the snow to Jackson and wrapped her arms around him, causing him to wince until she let go.

"I can't believe you're alive!"

"Hey!" Jackson protested, feigning offense. "I'm not *that* incompetent."

She shook her head, displaying both impatience and relief. "But the downed helicopter, and the explosions, and…"

"I got a little help from Crew Chief Butters." He nodded toward Butters. The man's face lit up in an "aw shucks" grin.

Charlie let go of Jackson and grabbed the startled crew chief in a bear hug. Butters peered helplessly at Jackson until Charlie suddenly released him, eyes narrowed.

"Wait. Are you the one who launched the missiles?"

"Uh, no. That would be him." Butters said, indicating Peterson with a tilt of his head.

"That's Peterson," Jackson said evenly. "He almost killed me."

Peterson looked like he wanted to crawl into a hole.

Fred made a noise like a dog throwing up, drawing everyone's attention. Jackson raised a hand in a calming gesture, forgetting it probably meant nothing to Fred. "It's okay. She's good people." The conservation officer smiled, and Fred seemed to relax. "See? Everybody's calm, everybody's—"

Fred let out an earsplitting roar, the suddenness and ferocity of which nearly made Jackson soil himself. Jackson gawked at Fred until he saw the TNW clenched in Charlie's hands.

"Get away from it," Charlie commanded.

"Charlie, what are you doing?"

"I know you want to help him, but he killed Mattie." Charlie raised the TNW to her shoulder. "He's dangerous…"

"He's also the reason I'm alive." Jackson glared at Peterson.

Charlie's face registered confusion.

"He was scared, in pain." Jackson reasoned. "If I were in his place, I would have done anything, killed anyone, to survive. But he didn't. He let me live. He let *you* live."

"But why not, Mattie?" She asked, eyes wet with tears. She tightened her grip on the TNW, but when Jackson gave her a pleading look, she relented and dropped the weapon. As Butters dived for the rifle, she stepped over him and made her way to Jackson. He stroked her back as she shook with the force of her heavy sobs.

"I'm sorry," Jackson said, but when he heard it out loud, he feared it came off as trite.

The woods behind them rustled.

Butters whirled, raising the TNW. "Who's there?" He fingered the rifle's trigger.

"National Guard," came a voice from the trees. "Don't shoot."

Butters and Jackson exchanged a look. Their confusion turned to relief as Carney emerged from the tree cover, hands in the air. Seeing Butters and Peterson, the pilot lowered his hands.

"Holy shit! You guys are alive?"

"Yes! And you'll never guess who's here!" Butters pointed to Fred.

Shock registered on the captain's face upon seeing the giant lizard standing passively. "No way! I was pretty sure he killed you guys!"

"I know, right?" Butters laughed. "Turns out Fred's kinda cool."

"You named it Fred?"

"No. They did." Butters pointed at Jackson and Charlie with a flourish as if introducing them at a cocktail party. "That's the DNR guy, and that's some lady who likes to give hugs."

Carney blinked in disbelief. "How the hell did you and Gork survive the missiles?"

"Gork?" Jackson looked to Butters for an explanation, but the crew chief only shrugged.

"You know, the lizard dude from…" Carney trailed off as the ground under their feet vibrated.

"What is that?" Charlie asked.

"Humvees."

The roar of powerful diesel engines filled the forest in corroboration of Crew Chief Butters' pronouncement.

"Hell yeah!" Peterson whooped. "It's the fucking cavalry!"

"Those guys won't think he's so cool. Major Campbell is on the warpath." Carney looked at Fred. "Better get him outta here."

Before anyone could respond, machine-gun fire erupted around them. Everyone, including Fred, dropped to the ground.

"Why are they shooting at *us*?" Charlie yelled as bullets continued to whiz overhead.

"They don't even know we're here. They're after Fred." Jackson scanned the clearing. "Butters, you still got that flashlight?"

"Yeah? Why?"

"Do you know Morse code?"

"Only since I was ten," Butters bragged, keeping his head low.

"Can you signal your buddies?"

Butters pulled his flashlight from its holster and aimed into the forest. He shone the light in bursts, three short, three long, then three short, repeating the signal until he heard a voice.

"Cease fire!" The first call was followed by a second, a third, and so on, until the machine gun fire petered out, then stopped altogether. "Stand up with your hands up," a nervous disembodied voice echoed out through speakers mounted on the Humvee.

"I can't," Butters shouted.

The speakers remained silent for several seconds. "Why not?"

"I need my hands to stand up...and to hold the flashlight."

"Yeah, could you maybe not shine the flashlight at us? Makes it kinda hard to see."

Butters looked to Jackson. It was the conservation officer's turn to shrug.

"Is this seriously happening?" Charlie muttered.

Butters drew his legs underneath him. "Okay, I'm gonna stand up now."

"Tell him no sudden moves," a hushed voice said over the speaker.

"Shut up, Kenny. I know what I'm doing."

Butters rocked back and forth and sprang to his feet, then promptly lost his footing as his feet shot out from underneath him. He hit the ground with an "oof".

"We said, 'no sudden moves!' " The disembodied voice was defensive now.

"I fell!" Butters said.

"Sorry."

Butters stood again. This time, he remained upright and walked to the Humvee, arms raised.

Jackson couldn't hear the crew chief's conversation but watched as Butters pleaded his case. When the crew chief lowered his hands and shot him a glance, Jackson turned to Charlie. "I need you to talk to Fred."

"What?"

"He won't leave unless you convince him."

"Why can't you convince him? He's your pet." She said in a harsh whisper.

Jackson pointed to his ribs.

"Fine." Charlie edged toward Fred, who was hiding behind a massive cottonwood tree.

"Ma'am? What are you doing?" came a guardsman's voice. "Stay where you are."

"Just stretching my legs." Charlie pretended to stretch, then dashed for the cottonwood. Searchlights lit up the clearing, heralding the premature release of half a dozen rounds.

"Hold your fire! It's a girl!"

Although the machine gun fire quickly ceased, Charlie kept running until she joined Fred behind the massive tree. Fred looked at her with wide eyes and issued a soft grunt.

"You have to go," Charlie said sternly.

Fred stared.

"Go away, shoo! You have to leave."

Fred let out a chirp and stamped his feet.

"Go on..." Charlie pleaded, pointing toward the woods. "Before I change my mind." She leaned against Fred and pushed. Fred didn't budge. Instead, he snuffled like a nervous show pony and peered at Jackson.

Jackson made the walking motion with his fingers.

Fred cocked his head to one side, and Jackson pointed toward the far side of the clearing and made the walking motion again, this time wiggling his fingers so fast they became a blur.

A piercing tone resonated through the forest, cutting their nonverbal conversation short. Emanating from everywhere yet nowhere, the tone had an alienness about it, as if borne of an instrument never intended to be played by human hands or heard by human ears.

"What now?" Peterson clasped his hands over his ears as the tone continued unabated.

"What the fuck was that?" came a confused and angry voice from behind the wall of headlights.

"Cell phone," Charlie yelled, obviously stalling for time.

"Well, are you going to answer it?"

"Uh…sure," Charlie peeked around the tree and gave Jackson a questioning look.

Jackson responded by mimicking her expression. He was at a loss. And then Fred's giant hands appeared. One at first. And then the other. They aligned horizontally, one above the other.

"What the…?"

Fred's hands curved, the top claws arching downward, and the bottom claws curving upward, forming two halves of a sphere like the hands of a child shaping a snowball.

Jackson's eyes widened. "Barf ball." He began a frantic search of his coat pockets. Finally, he reached into his inside coat pocket and retrieved the silver orb.

It flickered a faint orange.

Jackson looked up and saw Fred extending an open palm. He wanted the orb.

In his condition, there was no way Jackson could throw the orb to the cottonwood tree. There was certainly no way he was going to risk getting shot by overzealous guardsmen. He pondered for a second, then brightened. He grunted as he struggled to his knees, drew back, and tossed the orb underhand like a softball pitcher. The effort caused him to collapse. He watched from the ground as Fred tracked the orb like an outfielder and plucked it from the air.

FRED RETREATED behind the cottonwood and turned the orb over in his hand. Satisfied no harm had come to the shiny sphere, he looked at Charlie.

"Uh, hi. About that whole rifle thing."

Fred leaned down and placed his snout on the top of Charlie's head.

"Omigod, omigod, omigod...?" Charlie's exclamation came out as one long word.

"What's he doing?" Came Jackson's voice from across the clearing.

"I don't know. What are the guys with guns doing?"

"Who wants to know?" The anonymous guardsman snapped.

Fred uttered a soft hoot, like an owl.

"Are you okay?" Jackson asked.

"I think so."

"You don't sound very sure."

"Who am I, the lizard whisperer?"

Fred repeated the hoot, this time drawing it out like a melancholy whale's call. The sound was both eerie and beautiful.

"What was that noise? Who's that talking?"

"Shut up." Jackson snapped. "What's Fred doing?"

Charlie looked up at the giant creature. Realization

crossed her face as she watched the muscles in Fred's face shudder with micro-tremors.

"I think he's... crying?" Her response came as a whisper, heard only by Fred and herself.

Fred sank to his knees and bowed before Charlie. She stepped forward, wiping at the tears spilling down her cheek, and placed her chin on his head as he had done to her.

"I forgive you."

Whether he felt the vibrations from Charlie's weeping, heard the pain in her voice, or simply decided he had run out of time wasn't clear, but Fred rose to his full height and stood before her.

"Be safe." She barely got the words out before the unit leader's voice echoed through a megaphone.

"Times up. We're coming in!"

Charlie reached up and placed her hand under Fred's chin. "Go."

Fred bolted for the woods.

"There it is! Fire! Fire! Fire!"

Bullets ripped through the air, shredding foliage and kicking up snow in the departing creature's wake. The shots went wild, and Fred appeared to be in little danger until the unit leader screamed for his men to lead their target. They concentrated fire where the road met the forest, cutting off Fred's path into the woods. The M240s sprayed bullets in a torrent, the large caliber rounds tearing up the ground in a jagged line that made its way toward Fred. Seeing the inevitable intersection between himself and the machine gun fire, he dropped to the ground.

A round caught the creature in the arm, and it let out a fearsome roar that startled the gunner into stopping.

"Keep firing!" The unit leader screamed.

Suddenly, an explosion rocked the area. Every head in the vicinity swiveled to see the Explorer consumed by a fireball that sent waves of heat and smoke toward the nearby Humvee.

While the guardsmen gawked at the bright orange flames, Jackson yelled at Fred's curled-up form. "Go! Go! Go!" Fred raised his head. It took him only a moment to clamber to his feet and gallop for the forest, where he vanished into the arboreal wall.

With Fred gone, the machine-gun fire slowed to an occasional half-hearted pop.

Jackson stared after Fred, oblivious to Charlie's approach until she rested a hand on his shoulder. "Don't worry. The way these guys shoot, he'll be fine."

"Kirk won't stop. Not until Fred is dead."

"Yeah, I got that impression. Maybe Fred could use a little help."

Jackson faced Charlie. "Are you sure?"

FRED LUMBERED THROUGH THE FOREST. His initial escape had seen him hurry toward his goal, energized by the orb's indication that his ship had located him. But his energy had since faded.

His tired feet caught on roots and rocks, slipping and sliding on the slick incline of the mountain. Every step jarred his body, jolting the wounded arm and awakening the pain in his leg. He was tired, hurt, hungry, and cold. Even if he made it to the top of this rock, there was no guarantee they would be there. Yes, the tracking device had activated upon receiving a signal, but there was no guarantee the ship was still in the vicinity. What if they had simply passed over him on their way home?

Was it worth all of this? What was the point?

Fred's pace slowed with each invasive thought. His strides grew shorter, the arc of his arms smaller, and the volume of his breaths shallower. He knew now he wouldn't make it. Neither his body nor his mind possessed the resolve. Why not lie down and let the flat-faced creatures fall on him with their crude weapons and put an end to his suffering?

Fred skidded to a stop and bent at the waist, his lungs heaving, forked tongue lolling. This was it. He'd had enough. He lay down in a pile of tiny needle-shaped plants, pulling his legs against his body as he settled under the heavy pelt.

Here was as good a spot to die as any.

33

Sarah knew she'd made a mistake twenty minutes into her hike. Although she'd traveled the route frequently, it had always been late spring, summer, or fall. The road to the Mountain presented a unique challenge in winter.

Based on the road signs she'd encountered along Highway 7, The Mountain was almost twenty miles away, something she'd never considered, given that her parents had always driven. Like most kids her age, when riding in the car, she either had her nose in her tablet or book or stared out the window with no regard for the distance to their destination.

Sarah had been walking for almost two hours, including the fifteen minutes she'd spent walking away from The Mountain, hoping to throw Eric off her scent if Natalie cajoled him into looking for her or calling the local police. By the time she reached Devil Track Road, she'd lost all feeling in her toes, and her eyelashes had frozen together, making it difficult to see. She also found breathing difficult. Her moist, warm breath dampened the outside of the balaclava, causing a crust of ice to form over her nostrils. Adding to the misery was the fact that her fingers, which she'd balled into fists inside her gloves, felt like icicles against her palms. *She wished she had worn mittens.* The shared heat would have kept her fingers and palms warm. Right now, she would have gladly exchanged the dexterity afforded by gloves for extra warmth.

Sarah plodded toward the Mountain on autopilot, oblivious to the sound of her boots crunching in the snow. Her mind had disconnected from her body an hour ago as a matter of necessity. Had she thought about the cold, the darkness, or the fact she'd seen no evidence of another human soul in almost ninety minutes, she would have stopped and sat down in the snow. Only the ability to disconnect from her body had kept her moving.

Although successful in keeping Sarah's feet in motion, retreating into her mind brought no peace. Guilt wracked her brain. Guilt at how her mother would panic when she awoke to find Sarah gone. Guilt at how her decision to run away would shift her parents' focus away from Scottie's recovery. The extent of her selfishness slammed into her, and she let out a muffled sob.

Sarah stopped on the icy shoulder of a curved stretch of highway and reached into her coat pocket to retrieve Scottie's cracked phone. She'd placed the device there, hoping her body heat would keep it warm. She wouldn't know whether the phone worked until she turned it on. She hesitated, knowing that turning it on would allow her mother to pinpoint her location. She shuddered at the thought of being grounded until she turned thirty. But it beat freezing to death.

Sarah slid her hand out of her glove and turned on the phone. It took its time, but the black screen and four white squares eventually appeared. Sarah typed in Scottie's pass-code and waited for the app screen to come up. The screen brightened as the app screen appeared.

Again, she hesitated. Her mother's number was in Scottie's phone. Before she could talk herself out of it, she tapped the entry titled *Mom Cell*. Nothing happened. Sarah jabbed the entry again. The phone pulled up Marnie's cell number, and the familiar red and green phone icons appeared, then vanished from the screen, replaced by "CALL FAILED."

"What the...?" Sarah shook the phone and hit the call button again. The result was the same. She squeezed the disobedient phone in her now frozen hand and was about to slide it back into her coat pocket when she noticed "no signal" in the upper right-hand corner. She held the phone over her head and checked the screen. Still nothing.

After stuffing the phone into her pocket, she slid her hand into her glove. Sarah should have known better; she wasn't far from where Scottie usually lost cellular reception.

"Crap." Sarah looked around. Middle of freaking nowhere. Nothing for miles. No houses, no stores, no lights. And then there they were. Headlights. Moving at high speed. Sarah blinked the ice from her eyelashes and squinted. She could hear the vehicle. Loud. Aggressive. Sarah considered running into the brush. It could be some weirdo looking for trouble.

She scampered for the brush and melted into the lush pine needles where she could watch the vehicle approach. Now out of reach of the wind, Sarah's eyes stopped watering, and her eyelashes parted, allowing her to focus. She recog-nized the vehicle almost immediately. The boxy shape, the closely set round headlights sandwiched between orange turn/parking lights, the wide front end, and the telltale drone of giant all-terrain tires on pavement.

She smiled. The vehicle barreling toward her was a Humvee. Not a Hummer, but a Humvee utility vehicle. As the daughter of a National Guardsman, Sarah had been around enough of them to know one when she saw one.

She stepped out of the brush and waved her hands above her head. She would have yelled for good measure, but knew the men inside the Humvee could barely hear one another, let alone some kid on the side of the road. Her best bet was to get their attention through movement.

Sarah regretted having dressed all in black. The deliberate wardrobe choice had seemed clever while sneaking through the streets of Grand Marais, but now felt less so. Her mind flashed to online articles about joggers or cyclists who had worn dark clothes at night, rendering themselves invisible to drivers.

Despite the powerful beams of the Humvee's headlights, she needed to stay a safe distance from the road to avoid being clipped by the vehicle's bumper and flared fenders. But this stretch of highway was straight, and the track of the Humvee's headlights wouldn't stray far from the pavement. She needed a diversion.

Sarah searched for something she could use to flag down the truck. Unfortunately, she'd stumbled upon a litter-free section of the highway. There wasn't even an errant pop can or potato chip bag to use as a reflector.

As the Humvee continued toward her, she reached inside her coat and pulled out Scottie's phone again. Yanking off her glove and entering the passcode, she brought up the main screen. Her numb fingers fumbled with the phone as the Humvee barreled toward her.

Growing frantic, she accessed the flashlight utility and pointed the phone at the highway.

The Humvee flashed past. The gust of wind created by the three-ton vehicle's passing flung Sarah face-first into a snowbank. She raised her head in time to see the Humvee's brake lights glow red as the vehicle skidded to a stop; the tires howling as they dug into the pavement. Overjoyed, Sarah bounced to her feet and dashed for the idling vehicle.

As the rear driver's side door opened, a man in fatigues leaped onto the highway. Propelled by long legs and a determined stride, he quickly closed the distance between Sarah and the Humvee. He towered over Sarah, standing at least six-four. His breath rose in puffs from a broadish nose and full mouth. Even in the dark, the caramel hue of his skin was apparent, as were the soft curls of his close-cropped dark hair, indicating he was of mixed heritage.

"Are you okay? Are you hurt?" The man sounded more concerned than angry. Even had he been angry, Sarah probably wouldn't have noticed. She was too busy noticing how much he looked like the actor from that British TV show about London high society that her mother liked.

"I'm fine," Sarah stuttered, pulling the balaclava from her head.

"Good." A look of relief quickly replaced the guardsman's look of incredulity. "The way you hit the deck, I thought we clipped you."

"Nope. I'm fine. Just a little cold."

The handsome guardsman looked back at the waiting Humvee. "By the way, she's fine," he yelled. "Thanks for asking."

"She?" came a questioning voice. "Is she hot?"

"She's a kid, you perv," the guardsman yelled.

"Nice friends," Sarah teased. She glanced at the guardsman's coat and saw a patch showing his name was Murphy.

Murphy smirked. It wasn't the creepy smirk of some leering weirdo but the agitated look of someone exasperated.

"What are you doing out here? It's gotta be like three degrees out."

"I was hiking, but it was farther than I expected."

"Hiking to where?" Murphy drew his coat collar tight around his neck.

"The trailhead."

"Why the fuck—" He caught himself and smiled. "I mean, why would you do that at night?" He looked around at the dark woods.

"I'm looking for my dad." When she said the words aloud, Sarah realized how stupid they sounded. "He's on the mountain somewhere."

"The Mountain?"

"No, El Capitan."

Murphy's eyes narrowed. "Oh, you got jokes."

Sarah smirked. She was feeling pretty cocky until the sharp, bugle-like honk of the Humvee's horn startled her enough to make her gasp. Murphy pretended not to notice. He shoved his hands in his pockets and lowered his head against the cold.

"We're headed that way ourselves. You want a lift?"

Sarah searched Murphy's face. He didn't look dangerous, but she hadn't thought the busboy looked dangerous. She was cold, exhausted, and out of options. There was nowhere to retreat to.

"Sure. I guess so." She accepted the invitation nonchalantly, as if she had offers lined up.

The Humvee's engine revved, and the horn honked again, this time with several bleats in rapid succession. Murphy saw doubt linger on Sarah's face.

"Don't worry. They're obnoxious, but harmless." Murphy started toward the Humvee, then noticed Sarah wasn't following. "I know it's scary. You don't know them or me, but I'm the squad leader. If anybody so much as looks at you sideways, I'll put my foot in 'em, knee deep." He pointed to his name badge. "Second Lieutenant Sean Murphy. From Detroit Lakes. My parents are Garrett and Carla, my girlfriend's name is Whitley, and my best friend is a Belgian Malinois named Stella."

Sarah started toward the Humvee. If she was going to get into a truck with a stranger, it might as well be one who knew how to pronounce Belgian Malinois. She caught up with Murphy, and they walked together.

"Where are my manners? I never asked your name."

Sarah pondered whether her Olivia identity had outlived its usefulness. "Sarah."

"Nice to meet you, Sarah." Murphy stopped next to the Humvee. "You said your dad's in the Guard? What's his name?"

Sarah shot Murphy a look, and he laughed. "Relax, I'm just wondering if I know him."

"Major Campbell."

Murphy's eyes bulged like he'd just eaten a ghost pepper. "*Kirk* Campbell?"

"Do you know him?" Based on the guardsman's reaction, her question was a formality. She knew her father had a reputation as a hard-ass, a trait that, although valued by the brass, did nothing to endear him to those who served with or beneath him.

"He's our commanding officer," Murphy said, tilting his head toward the idling Humvee.

"Great. So, you'll give me a ride?"

"Guess I have to." He opened the rear passenger door and held it open for Sarah.

She peered into the vehicle. Inside were four more guardsmen, a stack of twelve packs, cigarettes, and assorted snacks, including chips, cookies, and several cans of sprayable cheese.

Murphy gestured toward his four comrades. "Sarah, these are the guys: Crawford, Tillerson, Dolezal, and Perozoso." Murphy gave each man a stern look. "Guys, this is Sarah. She's on her way to the Mountain to see her dad. Major Campbell."

Four pairs of eyes bugged. Tillerson, square-headed, granite-jawed, and steely-eyed, craned his neck from the driver's seat. "Are you nuts? If we take her with us, Campbell will know we went into town. He'll lose his shit."

"What do you want me to do? We can't leave her on the side of the road," Murphy said. "She'll freeze to death."

Crawford, a chubby African-American man with an easy smile and chocolate skin, and Tillerson, a hulking, ruddy-toned brunette with intense blue eyes, exchanged a glance.

Murphy rubbed his face, then looked at Sarah. Her face was still flushed from the cold. "You wouldn't rat us out, would you?"

"I can't lie to my dad." Sarah's voice was matter-of-fact. "But... I could forget to mention where I was when you picked me up..." The five men shared hopeful glances. "In exchange for some chips and a can of cheese." Sarah pointed to the two cans of sprayable cheese, trying not to laugh at five grown men terrified of being tattled on by a fourteen-year-old.

"That's extortion," Murphy offered with an amused grin.

"Yep." Sarah pointed to one can. "I'll take the Sharp Cheddar, please."

"Hey!" Crawford whined. "That's the best one!"

"Duh." Sarah beamed as Murphy handed her the chips and cheese. She broke open the bag of chips, dug out a handful, and sprayed cheese on each chip, one by one. Murphy nodded toward the front seat, where Tillerson, shaking his head, put the Humvee in gear.

Dolezal, blonde, blue-eyed, with prominent eyebrows, and Perozoso, slight of build, olive-skinned, with a slight curl to his dark hair, stared ahead. Sarah guessed they weren't as amused by her as Murphy and Crawford. Or maybe they were too worried about what awaited them on the Mountain to concern themselves with the girl and her mouth full of cheese and chips.

"Enjoying that cheese?" Crawford teased. Sarah nodded but didn't speak. Her mouth was too full. Crawford laughed and then frowned. "Wait. Isn't Major Campbell from Duluth?"

"Massasauga River." Sarah covered her mouth to avoid grossing him out with her half-chewed snack.

"How'd you get all the way up here?"

"Hitchhiked."

Murphy's face clouded. "You got into a car with a stranger?"

Sarah gulped down a mouthful of chips. "Strangers. Plural."

"You rode with a bunch of strangers for two hours?" Murphy stared at her in disbelief.

"I'm not an idiot." A piece of a potato chip shot out of her mouth and bounced off her hand. "It was a mom, a dad, and their two kids. A nice Canadian family."

"How do you know they were nice?" Murphy challenged.

Sarah stopped eating long enough to respond. "How do I know *you're* nice?"

Crawford laughed. "She got you there, Murph."

Murphy chuckled dutifully but looked concerned.

34

Fred's eyes fluttered open with a gasp as he sucked in a lungful of air. He found it cold and fresh, unlike the *Deras'* stale recycled atmosphere. He sat up and shook his head, clearing his mind as he took in his surroundings. To his dismay, the blanket of white still covered every visible surface; the towering plants still loomed over him. The white satellite still hovered above. He wasn't on the *Deras*, having been awakened from induced hibernation by a vivid nightmare.

This godforsaken planet was real. The *Deras* had been the dream. No, not a dream. The beeping sounds and flashing lights that assaulted his senses while guiding the dying ship into icy water at extraordinary speed had been real. But they might as well have been a dream.

Why did his mind torture him with memories of his failed mission? Yes, he'd failed to land the *Deras* on this hostile planet safely, but that wasn't his mission. His mission, the crew's mission, was to test the technology needed to find a new home for his people. That mission had failed the moment Adhara had pierced the veil between their universe and this one. And now he was stuck here alone, the rest of the crew dead, with no way back home. Except the orb had sung and glowed, announcing the presence of other Ahliwarins.

Despite how he felt, there was a chance.

Fred struggled to his feet. Needles of pain shot through his legs and back. His brief respite had allowed his muscles to cool and contract, and they'd become reluctant to function. He stretched and walked in place. As his muscles warmed, the pain subsided. He would still need to move slowly. Not as slowly as before, but slowly nonetheless.

The thought of maintaining a leisurely pace reminded him of his recent traveling companion, the flat-faced creature. It had moved slowly. Partly, Fred surmised, due to injury; partly due to its stubby legs and tiny feet. A pang of remorse knifed through him like the icy winds that blew on this planet. Already enveloped in sadness, Fred found himself sinking further into its depths. Sure, the noisy, smelly creature had injured him, but Fred had grown accustomed to its presence, eventually enjoying its company as much as he had Adhara's.

WHOOMP! Shock waves slammed into Fred, knocking him off his feet. Some kind of projectile had exploded close by. Suddenly, it seemed the entire mountain echoed with explosions. They had found him.

He looked up the incline toward the top of the rock. It was not far, but far enough away that he could no longer afford to move deliberately. Measures would have to be taken—drastic measures. Fred wavered. The process caused great pain, but he had no choice.

He must change or die.

Fred leaned forward, shifting his center of gravity beyond what his legs could balance. As he fell, his hands shot out as if to break his fall, but instead of bracing for impact, his arms *absorbed* the impact, allowing him to meet the ground gracefully. Once on all fours, his spine loosened, undulating freely to accommodate the movement of his long arms, which now worked with his legs to hold him off the ground. He bellowed. He'd thought the pain in his muscles intense, but this was far worse. The nerve that ran the length of his back burned as if a hot poker had been inserted into the hollow of his spine. Every branch of the nerve—the legs, arms, neck, toes, and fingers—shared the sensation. Even his eyes hurt, boiling like eggs inside his skull.

This was to be expected, he told himself. But he hadn't *resorted*, as Ahliwarins referred to the practice of walking on all fours, in a very long time, and he'd forgotten how much it felt like being incinerated from the inside out.

Of course, he had been on all fours when he'd attacked his traveling companion, but that had been different. That had been a mere change of posture, like when captive Merebunta scurried down from their perches and walked about on their hind legs, to the delight of younglings who rewarded them with bits of food. Ramming the flat-faced creature hadn't required the transformation of his spine, lungs, and metabolism that accompanied resorting. Resorting occurred at a cellular level and had consequences. At his age, resorting was bound to cause lasting damage. But he didn't care.

He bellowed again as his lungs expanded to twice their normal size, gorging on the planet's plentiful oxygen and dumping it into his blood, which his oversized heart pumped throughout his throbbing body, sending oxygen-rich cells to every extremity, every fiber. His vision sharpened, his sense of smell heightened, and he could hear the flat-faced creatures' hearts beating in their chests.

Fred took a few tentative steps. His steps were light and his muscles sinewy, reminiscent of his younger self. He felt no cold, no pain, no fatigue. Emboldened, he sprang forward, propelled by four powerful limbs, traction secured by four sets of razor-sharp claws digging into the ground. The feeling of power was indescribable.

He ran harder, gobbling real estate in chunks, each stride carrying him quadruple the distance he'd covered on two legs. He moved like never before, like he never would again, fast and strong, plowing through snowdrifts and over saplings, leaping crevasses several times his length, scaling rocks nearly twice his height. The forest, once an impediment, was no longer an obstacle. The cold, the elements, nothing would stop him from reaching the top.

The surrounding air still echoed with explosions and whistled with the passage of lethal projectiles. No matter. Fred dodged them with ease, bobbing and weaving at dizzying speed. If the flat faces had experienced difficulty targeting him before, they must be mad with frustration now. His head swiveled, and he saw them climbing over one another in their desire to destroy him, forgetting their training as they narrowly avoided shooting one another, drawing curses and angry screams from their brethren.

Fred rocketed up the incline, legs pumping and extending. As he scampered for the rock's summit, he grew less concerned with the flat faces and preoccupied with the idea of departure.

This preoccupation made him careless.

Fred crested the rock and stopped to rest. The flat top of the mountain was dark and quiet. The sounds of gunfire had ceased, and the roar of engines had faded into the natural sounds of the night. He had made it.

He shifted his weight backward, preparing to lower himself onto his haunches when white light seared his retina, blinding him. His arms reflexively resumed their normal function, covering his face against the unexpected luminosity. His pupils contracted, adapting to the light, and he lowered his arms to find himself face-to-face with one of the loud, boxy vehicles.

A pair of flat faces perched atop the vehicle, one the size and age of his former traveling companion, the other smaller and less mature. Between them was a weapon similar to the one his flat-faced ally had carried. Except this was larger and longer. With its band of sharp-tipped projectiles attached to its side and protruding legs for support, this weapon was doubtless more formidable.

And it was pointed directly at him.

KIRK STARED in disbelief at the creature. It looked like a computer-generated nightmare out of a sci-fi movie. But it was no nightmare and no special effect. It was very real. He could smell its rank odor from twenty yards away, an off-putting scent reminiscent of the garter snakes he used to catch on his grandparents' farm.

The creature breathed heavily, its eyes darting back and forth, tongue flicking out occasionally. The thing's size and shape came as a surprise. Radio chatter among the chopper crews had indicated it was tall, but what he saw before him squatted on all fours, like an alligator, although with its long limbs, it stood at least four feet high at the back, as tall as a pony. With the head posted atop the longish muscular neck, it was even taller. The mere sight of the creature would have petrified Kirk had it not been for the locked and loaded M240 at his side.

"Cooper?" Kirk said without taking his eyes off the creature.

"Sir?" Cooper's voice cracked.

"Engage the target."

"Yes, sir." Cooper moved his thumbs to the machine gun's trigger, but before he could fire, the creature dodged out of his sights and disappeared. Cooper yanked the M240 back and forth, trying feverishly to reacquire his target, but the creature moved too fast, and he lost sight of it in the near-black backdrop of trees. "Shit!"

By the time he trained his sights on the creature again, its enormous reptilian head loomed over him and, with one arm, thick as the trunk of a young aspen, wrenched the machine gun from its stand. Cooper screamed and backed away as the creature leaped from the ground to the Humvee's roof and, rising on two legs, drew back its fist. Cooper squeezed his eyes shut against the impending blow.

"Hey! Over here!" Kirk waved his arms to get the creature's attention. The coiled muscles of its neck rippled under green-gray skin as it whirled toward Kirk, teeth bared. Kirk drew his Sig Sauer M18 and fired two shots from the stubby pistol. Although mere feet separated him from his target, neither round found its mark.

The creature dipped its head like a boxer dodging a jab and, with unnatural speed, knocked the pistol from Kirk's hand. Kirk stood his ground. He pulled his survival knife and drove it into the creature's shoulder. The creature bellowed, yanked the knife from its shoulder, and hurled it across the clearing. It grabbed Kirk by the neck and lifted him into the air. Kirk's legs kicked and twitched like those of a captured bullfrog, but his squirming was of no use. He felt himself held fast in the creature's grasp, squeezed by a massive hand that constricted his windpipe and threatened to crush the vertebrae in his neck.

With his vision blurring, Kirk looked into the creature's face and marveled at the intelligence in its eyes. Jackson was right. This was no dumb animal. But then Kirk's thoughts turned to Marnie and the kids as the creature drew back one muscular arm.

"No!" A voice echoed from the treeline.

The creature's bicep bulged, prepared to strike, but after a moment, it lowered its punching arm, leaving Kirk to swing from the other.

"Put him down."

The beast grunted softly but released Kirk, who fell six feet to the ground.

Rubbing his neck, Kirk stood up and peered into the tree cover. He couldn't see anyone. Cooper's head moved on a swivel, too, as he tried to locate the mystery speaker.

"Sir?" Cooper's voice trembled.

"Easy. I think we got a friendly." He squinted, just making out Jackson propped against a tree at the forest's edge. He shook his head in disbelief. "What the hell are you doing, Jack?"

"Keeping you from making a mistake."

"Killing a monster isn't a mistake; it's my mission."

"He's not a monster." Jackson stepped from the shadows, wincing at the pain the movement caused his injured ribs. "He's an intelligent, sentient creature."

"I don't care how smart it is. It almost killed five of my people."

"Five people who attacked him without provocation."

Kirk seethed. "Well, it killed that kid. That makes it a monster in my book."

"Yeah? And how many people did you kill, Kirk?"

Kirk flinched. Jackson's question had landed like a Mike Tyson punch.

"Outside Kabul," Jackson pressed. "Hurt, scared, alone. Surrounded by enemies. What did you have to do to make it back to Marnie and the kids?"

The muscles in Kirk's jaw tightened. He hadn't questioned his actions in Kabul. Just as he didn't fault the C-17 crew for leaving him behind, he'd only omitted the grisly details because he feared Jackson would judge him.

"Yeah, well, you know the saying. 'Boys do what they want to do; men do what they have—'"

A crackle of static burst from the Humvee's radio. "Major, are you there?"

Kirk had momentarily forgotten about his squad. He scrambled into the Humvee and snatched the radio handset from its cradle. "Campbell here. Where the hell are you guys?"

Unseen engines roared in answer to Kirk's question as a quartet of Humvees burst into the clearing. Two took up positions alongside Kirk's Humvee, while the remaining two positioned themselves on the opposite side of the clearing, boxing in the creature.

Kirk thrilled at the boxy transports' arrival. "What the hell took you so long? And where's my other Humvee? Where's Murphy?"

The guardsman hesitated. "We thought he was with you, sir."

"What? Why didn't somebody get him on the horn?"

The guardsman opened his mouth but emitted only a

strangled gurgle. Kirk prepared to tear into the mute guardsman when Cooper tapped him on the shoulder.

"Now would be a good time to terminate the threat, sir. We have numbers."

Kirk regarded the beast, which stood motionless in the intersecting beams of the four Humvees' headlights, and gave Cooper a slight nod.

The lieutenant caught the attention of the four gunners. "Take it down!"

Bursts of machine gun fire ricocheted off the trees as the creature, yelping in pain and bellowing with anger, resumed his four-legged pose and disappeared into the woods under a hail of rounds, camouflaged by smoke, pinprick muzzle flashes, and the cover of night.

"Hold your fire!" Kirk's voice was barely audible over the chattering of gunfire, yet the command somehow reached the gunners' ears, and the barrage of gunfire died down, leaving only the whir of idling engines.

"Dammit." Kirk searched the woods for signs of the departed creature.

A guardsman hopped down from the nearest Humvee and moved to the forest's edge, where he took a knee and peered at the snow.

"He couldn't have gotten far, sir. There's an awful lot of blood leading into the woods."

Kirk reached into his Humvee and retrieved a pair of M4A1 assault rifles. "Guess we're gonna have to go after him."

Cooper climbed down from the Humvee, and Kirk handed him a rifle.

An electronic bleat echoed throughout the clearing. Sixteen pairs of eyes traced the source to the orb, which sat half-buried in the snow, blinking deep purple as it sang its shrill song.

"What is that?" Cooper tilted his head.

"Grenade!" Kirk hit the deck. All except Cooper took shelter wherever they could.

Cooper peered at the orb, brow furrowed. "Sir, I don't think that's a grenade."

Kirk peered from his crouched position behind a Humvee. "Since when do you know what an alien grenade looks like, Lieutenant?"

"It started blinking on its own," Cooper said with a shrug. "That doesn't seem like something a grenade would do."

Kirk climbed to his feet and brushed the snow from his uniform. "Then, what the hell is it?"

"I'm thinking maybe a homing beacon."

The guardsmen saw Jackson limping toward them. There was a clatter of metal and composite plastic as rifles pointed at Jackson.

"Stand down." Kirk motioned for the guardsmen to lower their weapons. "Beacon for who?"

Jackson looked at the sky. "I don't know. But I'm guessing we're about to find out."

NIGHT HAD NOT YET GIVEN way to morning when a thin line of light edged the horizon to the east, cleaving the sky into hemispheres of fading stars and shimmering water. Lights appeared beneath the water's surface, growing brighter and more defined by the second. Some moved on a fixed path while others danced like minnows on a jig. Differing in size, color, and intensity, there seemed to be no rhyme or reason. One thing, however, seemed evident.

The lights were rising toward the lake's surface.

None of the men gathered atop the Mountain possessed eyesight keen enough to see Lake Superior, fourteen miles away, in detail. Had they possessed such eyesight, they'd have seen a dark object ascend from the depths and crash through the Lake's ice-crusted surface from below. They'd have witnessed foam and pieces of ice skitter across the object's dusky outer shell and then plunge into the roiling water.

Instead, the men marveled at the distant lights like children watching fireflies on a summer night. It wasn't until the dark shape glided from Superior to The Mountain that they had an inkling of what was coming.

As the dagger-shaped vessel—equal parts stealth fighter and submarine—approached the Mountain, Lieutenant Cooper pulled his M18 from its holster, checked the chamber, and released the safety. He set his feet and aimed at the ship hovering two hundred feet above the clearing.

Kirk snickered. "What do you think that popgun of yours is gonna do?"

Cooper's shoulders slumped, and he slid his pistol back into its holster.

Kirk returned his gaze to the hovering craft, and a wave of uncertainty washed over him. He clenched his hands into fists as he weighed the consequences of taking action. He glanced at Jackson, who also stared at the sky.

"These are your friends, Jack. Are we talking *ET* or *Independence Day*?"

"I think they're here to retrieve their guy." Jackson never took his eyes off the alien craft. "If we give them Fred, they'll probably just take him and go."

"I disagree, sir," Cooper interjected. "That thing looks like a combat ship to me. I recommend we not wait for them to strike first."

Kirk scratched his chin. Although irritated by Cooper's impertinence, the little twit had a point. One creature had been a handful, and if the ship contained more of them, his squad could ill afford to be caught flat-footed. Still, the craft hadn't been aggressive and appeared devoid of any weapons. The last thing Kirk wanted was to mow down a bunch of unarmed ETs. Such a massive blunder would end what remained of his career with the National Guard.

"Light 'em up!" Cooper screamed, pointing at the hovering vessel.

Kirk stuck his fingers in his ears as the air erupted. M20s, M4s, and M203 grenade launchers unloaded round after round into the air in a salvo that went on for a full thirty seconds until Kirk waved his arms and shouted, "Cease fire! That's enough!" Once the last of the shots subsided, he spun toward Cooper. "What the fuck is wrong with you? Who told you to give the order?"

Cooper stared at the ship, his mouth wide open.

"I asked you a question, Lieutenant!"

When Cooper failed to answer, Kirk followed the guardsman's line of sight upward. His expression went from anger to disbelief as the haze of burned gunpowder cleared, revealing a ship that bore no signs of damage. Not a dent, scratch, or hint of a crack in the ship's ebony exterior or smoke-tinted canopy.

"What the hell?" Cooper whispered.

"At least they didn't fire back," Jackson said.

A low hum excited the air. It was as if an electric charge had passed right through them.

"Out of the Humvee!"

"But, sir—" Cooper began as Kirk bolted to the vehicle and grabbed him by the arm. Kirk shoved Cooper, but the First Lieutenant's foot caught on the M240's broken tripod, and he tumbled headfirst off the Humvee, taking Kirk with him. Although both men hit the ground hard, Kirk shook out the cobwebs and looked up at the ship.

Appendages underneath the ship glowed amber, then angled toward the clearing.

"Take cover!"

Kirk never saw whether his men heeded his warning as a brilliant flash of light lit up The Mountain, blinding the guardsmen and rendering them and their weapons inert. When Kirk's vision returned, he saw his abandoned vehicle shimmering and gawked in disbelief as the Humvee sank into the snow-covered earth.

He rubbed his eyes. The truck's rubber tires had melted away, lowering the vehicle by more than a foot. Only after a wall of heat singed the hair on his face did Kirk notice the Humvee's glass window inserts sliding out of their frames in a gloppy mess that looked like lava. The vehicle's aluminum exterior bubbled. The Humvee was melting.

"Cooper, we gotta move." Kirk sprang to his feet and stumbled away from the Humvee. A few steps away, he whirled to see the lieutenant lying motionless in the melting snow. "Cooper!" Kirk staggered back to the man and tugged his arm. When Cooper didn't regain consciousness, Kirk dropped to his knees and tried to lift the lieutenant to a sitting position.

"Cooper, come on. Get up!" Kirk tried again to lift him, but the lieutenant's limp body refused to cooperate, and he dragged Cooper away from the bubbling hunk of metal. Once clear, Kirk collapsed to the ground, grunting and puffing. He was still catching his breath when the roar of an internal combustion engine and a pair of headlights pierced the darkness. Too exhausted to scramble out of the vehicle's path, Kirk braced for impact.

The headlights veered, and the Humvee skidded to a stop, its rear end in the clearing and the front end partially embedded in the burning trunk of a towering white pine tree. Its doors burst open, and Murphy, followed by his squad of guardsmen, jumped out, M4s at the ready.

Murphy aimed for the hovering ship and opened fire. "Take it down!"

His squad followed suit. Although lacking the concussive boom of the M240s, the M4s made a considerable racket that rendered Kirk inaudible, forcing him to wave at Murphy.

"Cease fire! Cease fire! Cease fire, you fucking idiots!"

One by one, Murphy, Crawford, Tillerson, Perozoso, and Dolezal stopped firing, and the clearing went quiet.

Kirk's face was scarlet. "What the hell are you doing?"

Murphy puzzled. "We heard the M240s and thought you could use some help, sir."

Kirk jabbed a finger at the ship, which remained unharmed and intact. "Read the goddamned room, Murphy. Bullets don't work. You're not doing anything but wasting ammunition."

Murphy glanced at the unharmed ship. "Sorry, sir."

Kirk glared. "Where the hell have you been?"

Murphy and Crawford exchanged a look. "Say again, sir?" Murphy stuck his finger in his ear and wiggled it. "My ears are still ringing."

"I asked where you were."

Crawford stepped forward. "We got sidetracked, sir."

The guardsman's response only further infuriated Kirk. "Sidetracked by what?"

"We...uh, stopped to help a girl on the side of the road, sir." Tillerson, Dolezal, and Perozoso nodded in unison.

Kirk looked around. "What girl?"

Crawford looked to Murphy for help.

Murphy grinned. "Actually, sir, it's a funny—"

A deafening explosion rocked the clearing as the white pine, still sparking and smoldering, split at the Humvee's point of impact, sending the top half of the burning Goliath downward.

The tree crashed on top of Murphy's Humvee, and a frightened shriek resonated from within.

"Sarah!" Murphy bolted toward the burning vehicle.

"Sarah?" Kirk looked to Crawford. "My Sarah?"

Crawford nodded, and Kirk peered through the smoke and flames at the burning Humvee, eyes wild with fear. "Sarah!" His words were lost in a whoosh as the downed pine's boughs and needles, ignited by burning sap, sent a column of flames and thick black smoke into the sky.

"Don't worry, sir. Murphy's got her!" Crawford's assurances proved incorrect as the inferno forced Murphy's retreat despite Sarah's muted screams.

"No!" Kirk raced for the burning Humvee, but the wall of flame held him at bay. After several valiant but impotent attempts, he too was forced to concede defeat. He stared helplessly into the fire as all hope of Sarah's surviving dissipated.

"What the fuck is that?" Crawford pointed toward the far end of the clearing, where two figures emerged from the woods, mere outlines in the haze of smoke. Murphy joined

Crawford, and they drew their sidearms, anxiety etched on their soot-covered faces.

"Jesus…" Murphy whispered. He and Crawford gawked as an eight-foot-tall biped strode toward them, accompanied by a much shorter companion.

Murphy and Crawford raised their pistols.

"Put those guns away," Jackson growled. When both men hesitated, Jackson reiterated his command. "Do it now!"

Crawford gave Murphy a dubious look but holstered his pistol. Murphy hesitated, casting a fearful glance at Fred, but eventually did the same.

Fred looked at Jackson. He nodded. "Go."

Fred lurched past Murphy and Crawford, who yelped in surprise as the creature came within inches of them, then disappeared into the smoke and flames.

From inside the flames came a wrenching of metal and a bellow of pain, followed by a resounding thud as something heavy fell to the ground. After an eternity, Fred emerged from the inferno, carrying a silvery bundle in his massive arms. His skin was charred and split, and pus oozed from the cracks. His breath came in a labored wheeze, and each step he took was deliberate, as if he bore a tremendous weight.

He trudged past Murphy, Crawford, and Kirk, stopping only when he reached Jackson, to whom he held out his parcel. Jackson carefully unwrapped one end of the bundle, revealing Sarah in the Mylar thermal blanket.

Kirk's Adam's apple bobbed in his throat. Tears streamed down his cheeks, but he remained motionless, content to wait for the towering creature to surrender his daughter.

Jackson pointed to the ground, and Fred uttered a high-pitched squeak that seemed impossible for a creature of his size. With surprising gentleness, the creature lowered Sarah to the ground.

Kirk ran to Sarah and dropped to her side.

"Sarah?"

Sarah's eyes opened, and she acknowledged her father with a slight smile.

"Hi, Daddy." Her voice was hoarse from the smoke.

"Are you okay, sweetheart?"

"I think so. I got on a lot of insulation."

Kirk grinned, then suddenly scowled. "What the hell are you doing here?"

Sarah's brow knits as if the answer were obvious. "I came to see you."

Kirk laughed. "Does your mother know where you are?"

A groan prevented Sarah from answering, and they turned to see Cooper coming to. The lieutenant peered through squinted eyes that widened when they saw Kirk.

"Somebody check on Cooper," Kirk growled as he flagged down a pair of guardsmen. They hurried to Cooper's side, and Kirk returned his attention to Sarah. She looked up at him with a puzzled expression.

"Was that Uncle Jackson?"

Kirk nodded. He searched the clearing until he spotted Jackson. "I should check on him."

"Be nice," Sarah warned.

"I will." Kirk struggled to his feet.

"I mean it," Sarah yelled after him amidst a coughing fit.

Kirk started across the clearing. Even though the pain of walking made him wince, he kept moving until he reached Jackson, who was busy attending to Fred.

Kirk cleared his throat, and Jackson looked up.

"I need to talk to you."

Jackson looked right through Kirk.

"Look, I know I've been a jerk the last few days…"

"Shut up, Kirk."

Kirk took a deep breath, prepared to unload, when Jackson pointed skyward. Kirk craned his neck just as a shadow uncoupled from the underside of the dark ship and tumbled earthward.

"What the hell is that?" Jackson asked, tracking the dark object's trajectory. The two men watched as the shadow ended its tumble and righted itself. An orange glow lit up one end of the object, revealing a distinct shape that resembled an enormous bat.

"It's a dropship," Kirk muttered. "Small, maneuverable."

The drop-ship shot across the sky, then flipped onto its back and made a graceful outside loop before leveling off and hovering fifty yards above the clearing.

"Holy crap," Kirk gushed. "How do they know how to do an Immelmann?"

"They shot out of the lake, flew through the air, and melted a Humvee, and you don't think they've figured out how to do loop-to-loops?"

Kirk acknowledged Jackson's point with a shrug and looked to the sky again. A row of orange lights lit up the drop-ship's belly, forcing both men to shield their eyes from the glare. Kirk peered through his fingers, unwilling to miss a moment as the tiny craft spun on its vertical axis and descended until it set down amidst the Humvees.

"Major?" Murphy appeared at Kirk's elbow.

"Steady, boys," Kirk called to his unit in a calm, commanding voice. He knew they were scared, but it was clear the alien vessel outgunned them, and he couldn't afford a repeat of Cooper's overzealous response.

"Here we go."

The rear of the drop-ship opened, and four black-suited

figures, each taller than Fred and bulkier in build, exited down a ramp. Their featureless helmets swiveled on their long necks as they held instruments of advanced design and unknown purpose chest-high at the ready.

"Commandos," Kirk uttered reverently. He watched, enthralled, as the aliens rushed past the entire unit of stunned guardsmen to Fred. "They've come for their buddy."

Three aliens kneeled next to Fred while the fourth stood watch. They pelted Fred with various chirps while poking, prodding, and scanning his body with their instruments. Fred pushed them away, growling and sniping, but his rescuers continued their examination, tending to his charred skin and peering into his eyes until Fred relented with an indignant snort.

"Not commandos, MEDVAC," Jackson said with a smile. Using Kirk as a crutch, he climbed to his feet and pushed his way between the aliens to Fred, ignoring the aliens' snarls until one jabbed him in the ribs, causing him to yelp and raise his hands in surrender.

"Calm down, I'm just here to see Fred."

Fred opened his eyes, saw Jackson, and snuffed softly.

Jackson scowled at the alien. "See? I told you." The alien threatened another jab, but Fred warned him off with a wrathful hiss. The alien retreated, and Jackson knelt. He placed a hand on Fred's shoulder, the only place he could find that wasn't charred or covered with blood.

"How are you doing, Big Guy?" While he'd tried to sound upbeat, the sight of Fred's burned body proved too much, and the words came out in a husky rush. He cleared his throat and was about to turn away when he felt a weight on his hand. He looked down.

Fred's blistered hand rested on his.

"What's up, buddy?"

Fred opened his mouth, revealing broken teeth stained red with blood—a sound like a bird call issued from his mouth.

Jackson blinked, questioning for a moment whether he'd heard the sound.

Fred, despite obvious pain, clasped his arms together, grabbing himself close to the elbow as he'd done in the forest.

"*Tohmanziya.*"

Jackson shook his head. "I'm sorry. I don't understand."

"So, you were the one making all that noise in the cave."

Sarah appeared next to Jackson and peered curiously at Fred. Fred stared at the young woman as if he were a nonbeliever encountering an angel.

"He's making a hugging motion." She imitated the gesture. "That means he trusts you. He's telling you that you're friends."

Jackson pursed his lips and tried to replicate Fred's utterance, but only emitted flecks of spittle and a grunt that sounded like he'd received a punch in the stomach.

"Give it up."

"What? Why?"

Sarah pointed to her mouth. "He doesn't have lips. He probably doesn't even have vocal cords. That would be like him trying to say 'skateboard'."

Jackson considered for a moment, then clasped his arms together, grabbing his elbows.

Fred trilled. The sound, although weak and accompanied by gurgling from deep inside his throat, was heartfelt. The bruised, battered, and burned creature was fading fast.

Jackson wiped his eyes as tears welled. He had more to say and knew the moment deserved more; that Fred deserved more. An alien barked a cryptic order and waved its instrument in Jackson's direction. He felt an urge to snatch the alien's weapon and jab him with it when he felt Sarah's hand on his shoulder.

"Time to go."

With a reluctant nod, Jackson struggled to his feet. He found himself in danger of falling, but Sarah held him up. He turned to Fred and offered a mournful smile.

"Safe travels, my friend."

"Bye, Rocket Man. Thank you for keeping Uncle Jack safe." She tried to smile, but her lips trembled as she too fought against the onset of tears. "And for saving me."

Fred looked from Jackson to Sarah, then back to Jackson, then closed his eyes.

The aliens swooped in and surrounded Fred, forcing Jackson and Sarah out of the circle until a wall of long limbs in black uniforms hid the injured creature from sight.

Sarah ushered Jackson away from the landing party, and they walked in silence, content to observe the bustle of activity around them.

"Rocket man?"

"Yeah, like the song. He's from space, right?"

Jackson laughed, and the pain in his ribs, which seemed to have subsided while he knelt next to Fred, raced through him like an electric shock.

"What's so funny?"

"Some people think the song is actually about—"

"Drugs. Yeah, I know," Sarah said. "But I like to think it's about guys like my dad."

"Your dad?"

"Yeah. He goes on dangerous missions. Most of the time, he doesn't even know why." Sarah shrugged. "It's not about the loneliness of space; it's about the loneliness of sacrifice."

Jackson acknowledged the comment with a grunt. Sometimes that kid sounded like an eighty-year-old trapped inside a fourteen-year-old body.

"You and my dad are a lot alike."

He chuckled. "I don't know about that."

"Except, you don't have a family anymore."

Jackson whirled, stung by the girl's words, but when he looked at Sarah, he saw Kirk's affable grin and a faint crinkle at the corners of the teenager's eyes—Marnie's eyes.

"Not true. I have your dad, your mom, your brother, and you. You're my family."

35

The sun had reached its apex by the time the guardsmen convinced themselves the aliens weren't coming back. Nonetheless, they milled about like concertgoers at the end of a three-day outdoor festival, looking at each other with a mixture of shock and excitement, unable to believe what they'd witnessed. No one wanted to break the spell by leaving.

Kirk helped Jackson into one of the Humvees and got him settled in the passenger seat. He scanned his friend's face and saw a glazed expression. The man spent three days in the frigid forest, where he was chased by helicopters, blasted by a missile, and befriended by a creature from another planet, only to have it hunted and wounded by his best friend. It was no wonder he was out of it. The human mind can only take so much.

Kirk circled to the other side of the Humvee and let out a long sigh as he slid into the driver's seat. His last few days had been only slightly less eventful than Jackson's, and his body demanded that he close his eyes, if only for a moment. His heavy eyelids descended, and his head nodded. He was almost asleep when a sound disturbed the midday air, jarring him to attention. His eyes popped open, and he scanned his surroundings for signs of trouble.

Another dark shape moved across the sky.

"What now?" Jackson mumbled groggily.

Kirk tracked the shape as it sped toward them. "Helicopter."

"No thanks. I've had enough helicopters to last a lifetime."

The black chopper, which shared the lethal lines of an Apache AH-64 and the RaiderX's stacked dual rotors and submarine-like backward-facing tail rotor, approached at astonishing speed, moving faster than any rotary-wing aircraft Kirk had ever seen. Once overhead, just as the alien drop-ship had done, it stopped on a dime and descended, alighting with the grace of a Russian ballet dancer.

"That is some next-level shit," Kirk whispered.

The Humvee's rear passenger door opened, and Sarah peered in. "Who are those guys?"

"UAPTF."

Sarah's eyebrows knitted.

"Unidentified Aerial Phenomena Task Force. My guess is they want to talk to us."

The helicopter doors parted like those on an elevator, and four agents wearing dark sunglasses and black fatigues climbed out. The agents passed in front of the Humvee single file, one carrying a medium-sized briefcase and two carrying long canisters. The fourth agent, an older balding man, also held a canister, but it was thicker and longer.

"Honey, stay here with Uncle Jack." Kirk slid out of the driver's seat and held the door open as Sarah scrambled around the Humvee and climbed behind the wheel.

Kirk closed the door and strode across the clearing

toward the quartet. The fourth agent deviated from his path to intercept.

"Major Campbell, I presume?" The agent was stocky but not overweight, his physique likely the result of a lifetime of rudimentary but effective calisthenics. Kirk nodded, recognizing the man's voice as that of Agent Dodge, who had contacted him about locating the creature.

"Nice of you folks to show up after everyone's left the party."

"That's by design, Major. UAPTF's mission is to catalog and record, not intercept or interact." Dodge nodded in the Humvee's direction. "That Bennett?"

"It is."

"What's his story?"

"Tough day," Kirk replied.

"Civilians." Dodge's nose crinkled with disdain.

"According to my intel, Conservation Officer Bennett just spent three days evading capture by a superior force. That's pretty badass in my opinion."

"You mean *your* superior force?"

Despite a body racked with aches and pains, Kirk stood ramrod straight, his expression one of unabashed defiance. "I stand by my assessment."

Dodge turned to his colleagues. "Okay, let's line 'em up and lock 'em down." His subordinates popped their canisters, pulling out what looked like rifles but turned out to be traveling chairs. Dodge opened his canister, removed a portable table, and sat down, setting the briefcase in front of him.

"How about we start with you, Major?" He gestured to the open seat opposite him.

"I'd rather stand." Kirk cleared his throat. "And just so you know, I plan to plead the Fifth."

"Really?" Dodge chuckled. "Because, if it were me, I'd want a chance to explain why I authorized the use of large-caliber machine guns, helicopter-mounted rockets, and grenade launchers to pursue a civilian, or how that same civilian eluded not one but two choppers and several dozen armed National Guardsmen dispatched under my command."

Dodge leaned back in his chair. "But that's just me."

"Do you think nobody heard the Humvees, helicopters, and gunfire? Or saw the fire and lights? What are you going to do about that?"

"Do you think this is the first time we've had guests, Major? Because it isn't. It happens so often we have a protocol for them. And for *our* people."

Kirk seethed at the implied threat. "You can't keep this quiet. There are too many people involved." Kirk gestured toward the discombobulated contingent of scurrying guardsmen. "One of my guys is bound to talk. One of the families living at the base of the mountain is bound to post footage. Someone is going to do an interview on the local news. It's inevitable. *Human nature* is inevitable."

A smile spread across Dodge's face. "People have mortgages to pay, jobs to keep, secrets they prefer stay hidden. Everyone."

"You're talking about blackmail."

Dodge sighed. "You sure you don't want to have a seat, Major?"

Kirk collapsed into the chair, and Dodge seemed to relax, having quelled Kirk's half-hearted insubordination. "Listen up. I'm going to need everyone to relinquish any device on their person capable of transmitting, receiving, or replicating any form of communication, including photographs, videos, films, text, emails, or any other digital content. These items will not be returned. Is that clear?"

Although addressing the entire clearing, Dodge zeroed in on Kirk, who searched his pockets, located both the satphone and his personal cell phone, and set them on the table.

"Great." Dodge slid a paper and a pen in front of Kirk. "Non-disclosure agreement. By signing this document, you understand, acknowledge, and agree that you may speak only to the United States government about your experiences, subject to prosecution and imprisonment, for as long as deemed necessary to protect national security. I'll spare you the legal mumbo jumbo, but suffice to say, if you breathe a word of what you've seen without our express consent, I will see to it you spend the rest of your life, not in, or around, but *under* Leavenworth..."

36

F red blinked away the thin layer of mucus covering the corners of his eyes and identified his surroundings as a storage unit. He was strapped to a small cot, not because he was a prisoner, but to prevent him from floating off the bed in zero gravity. The crew must have turned the unit into a makeshift medical bay. His wounds were dressed with healing foam or wrapped with cellular bandages to speed the regeneration of skin and flesh.

"Selamat."

Fred jolted at the deep voice and scanned the room for its owner. He spied a thin, helmeted figure in black staring at him from just inside the hatch, arms folded over his chest. The figure, sensing Fred's apprehension, shook his head.

"You are awake. Excellent. Fear not, Dito."

Fred cast off the straps and struggled to a sitting position. His wounds were still fresh, and the slightest movement filled him with pain despite the drugs coursing through his flight suit. "Are you the commander of this vessel?"

The figure nodded, removing his helmet to reveal a face

even more weathered and scarred than Fred's, and sunken eyes showing an advanced age. "I am Captain Bijak."

"How is this possible?" Fred asked in a meek voice.

"How is what possible?"

"You. This ship. I assume this is the *Perkasa*?"

Captain Bijak nodded. "It is."

"But how could the *Perkasa* have been prepared for launch so quickly?"

Captain Bijak chuckled. "The Cadre are not fools. They knew of Adhara's plan."

"Plan?"

"The Fracture." Captain Bijak elaborated. "She never believed crossing the Vast would save our kind. She insisted that a door to another universe was the only way, but the Cadre wouldn't hear of it. As you know, Adhara rarely accepted limitations, so we readied the *Perkasa* as soon as the *Deras* departed."

"How did you arrive so quickly?"

Captain Bijak patted the bulkhead. "Telemetry relayed from the *Deras* to Karataj Base. Every movement, every deviation from its path. Using that information, we fine-tuned the *Perkasa's* performance."

"And entry? How did you reach the surface without crashing?"

Captain Bijak beamed. "We followed every detail of your entry. Even as we emerged from the Fracture, we ran scenario after scenario, trying to determine a route that wouldn't result in the *Perkasa's* destruction. Each attempt failed. Only after we took into account your actions was the AI able to determine a landing that wouldn't kill the entire crew."

"But I failed." Fred dropped his head in shame.

Captain Bijak waved him off. "We learned from your

crash. From your mistakes, mistakes made under duress. The AI created a scenario that allowed the *Perkasa* to enter the planet's atmosphere safely. It appears Adhara was right to rely on your experience."

Fred's mind raced. Hearing the captain acknowledge his heroics was almost enough to make him forget his injuries.

Captain Bijak's wrinkled lips receded to reveal broken teeth stained yellow with age. If it was a smile, it was a wry one. "I admired Adhara. Her determination and genius were beyond question, but the arrogance in thinking she alone could decide the fate of an entire race was nothing short of treasonous."

Fred bristled, but the chime of four tones over an intercom stymied any further response.

"We are approaching the Fracture and will enter it soon." Captain Bijak returned the helmet to his head and turned for the hatch. As the hatch hissed open, Fred glimpsed the blackness of the Vast and a sea of stars on the ship's central display. He had only a moment to admire the view before it gave way to a shimmering opaqueness. Fred squinted as translucent red, purple, and blue light with the viscous quality of liquid soap spread across the entire canopy. The undulating plasma might have been horrifying had it not been so beautiful.

Captain Bijak cocked his head at a curious angle. "You have not witnessed the Fracture?"

"I was in induced hibernation. When I woke, we were racing toward the planet. I had no time for sightseeing."

Captain Bijak offered a deep bow. "I meant no disrespect. You have done the people of Karataj a great service, Dito. In finding us a new home, you have saved us all."

Fred returned Bijak's gesture. "I pray the inhabitants are more welcoming upon our return."

Captain Bijak flicked his gloved hand dismissively. "Invasion and colonization of the planet will be swift and easy. We are superior in every way." Captain Bijak approached the hatch, and it hissed open. "Enjoy the view from the rear portal. When you next see the planet, it will be Ahliwarin." He floated out of the room, and the hatch door hissed closed behind him.

Fred floated to the aft portion of the storage room. He hadn't noticed the portal when he woke. He'd been more concerned with where he was and who might float through the storage room door. Now, he peered through the portal and into the Vast.

The planet glistened, suspended in the vacuum amidst the velvety black backdrop and twinkling celestial bodies. As it had when he'd first seen the planet, its many and diverse colors captivated him, except now, no longer under duress, he had time to study the orb, taking in the varied hues of the seas and the Great Masses. The spectacle took his breath away. Adhara had been right. Despite the cold and uninviting environment he'd experienced, the planet seemed to radiate hope. It brimmed with the essence of life, rather than the stench of decay that permeated his dying world.

He returned to his cot and pondered all he'd encountered on the cold and uninviting world, specifically those he'd met there. The one who'd injured him and later become his friend, the ones he'd spared after they'd hunted him, and how they'd later helped him escape. The one he'd decapitated out of anger, and the one he'd bitten out of fear. He also thought of the youngling he'd plucked from the flames.

What would their future become when the Ahliwarins returned? Would they and the Ahliwarins live in harmony, sharing the resources of their world? Probably not. The flat-faced creatures possessed weapons. Peaceful creatures did not need weapons. There would be conflict.

His fellow Ahliwarins had already demonstrated their willingness to consume resources until they were exhausted. They wouldn't share the new world with the flat-faced creatures. Perhaps at first, but as resources inevitably grew scarce, the Ahliwarins would take what they needed by force. With their advanced technology and voracious appetites, the Ahliwarins would displace or enslave the flat-faced creatures, or even use them as a source of food.

The prospect infuriated him. The Ahliwarins had had their time. They had ignored the consequences of their unchecked consumption and, when faced with the option to change or become extinct, elected not to change. Fred didn't judge his fellow Ahliwarins. He was as guilty as any of taking from Karataj while offering nothing in return, but he could not condone the inevitable slaughter that would follow the migration of Ahliwarins from his world to this one.

Fred looked at the storage room door. Captain Bijak's crew would be preoccupied with their return through the Fracture, at least long enough for what Fred needed to do. He closed his eyes and concentrated. After a moment, his chest heaved, and his throat undulated. As he had done in the cold of the strange planet, he gagged over and over until he regurgitated flesh, bones, and fur...along with the orb.

Although he'd been attended to upon arrival, the *Perkasa's* onboard medic had focused on his most obvious wounds. No one had taken the time to scan his digestive system. He picked the orb from the half-digested meat and stared at it. He returned his gaze to the portal. The shining world was already gone, lost among the Vast's multitudinous points of light. No matter. He'd already made up his mind. The new world was not the Ahliwarins' to spoil.

Fred grasped the slippery orb with both claws and gave the top half a sharp turn to the left. Twenty red lights bisecting the orb in equatorial fashion blinked in unison, keeping time with an alarm that sounded like a buzzer on a game show. After four flashes, they held steady for four beats before blinking again. This time, the lights skipped every other bleat of the alarm, as one light went dark with every second pulse of the alarm—a countdown.

Fred closed his eyes and pulled the orb against his chest.

37

The patio at Frieda's Coffee and Whatnot sat on a hill overlooking Lake Superior. In early June, before the mosquitoes laid siege to the blood of all living things and before the sun's rays beat down on the city of Two Harbors, the patio was the ultimate spot to watch colorful sailboats, giant freighters, and the occasional yacht, head to or from the Lift Bridge in Duluth.

Freida's was a particular treat in Two Harbors, given much of the property overlooking this part of the lake had long since been turned into resorts or family homes for the wealthy. Few spots remained where the average person could enjoy the view, but because Tim inherited the shop from his mother, he was grandfathered into the location. No amount of money offered by land developers or pressure applied by local politicians could convince him to sell.

Tim sat in the chair closest to the door, keeping an ear out for the chime of the bell above the shop's front door. Jackson sat next to him, the only one wearing a jacket on the cool afternoon. Next to Jackson, at the round table, was Jasper, clean-shaven except for a tidy mustache and sporting a White Sox cap with wisps of short hair peeking out. Lexy sat only inches away, looking lovely in a floral-patterned sundress.

To Jackson's amusement (and annoyance, occasionally), Lexy had been all smiles since she and Jasper had become an item during Lexy and Jackson's three-month paid suspension from the DNR. While Jackson had suffered acute boredom during the suspension, the time off had given Lexy and Jasper plenty of time to "hang out" in Lexy's tiny apartment.

Next to Lexy was Harlan, mostly healed after being impaled by the branch. He still felt stiffness and pain in his shoulder from time to time, but that was to be expected, given his steadfast refusal to adhere to his physician's prescribed physical therapy regimen.

Across from Jackson was Charlie. She sat with her back to Superior, her seat affording her a perfect view of Jackson, with whom she had been sharing surreptitious glances all afternoon.

"What are you so worried about? You're not fooling anyone." Lexy giggled as Charlie sipped her Arnie Palmer, pretending not to hear. "Why would that Dodge guy care about a couple of old farts shacking up on the weekends?"

"Hey! I'm not old." Charlie pointed at Jackson. "*He's* old."

"She has a point," Jackson said, ignoring the slight as he looked across the table at Charlie. "Of the six of us, only you and I actually saw Fred."

"Sure, rub it in." Harlan shook his head wistfully.

"All I'm saying is there's no reason for *any* of us to sneak around."

"What about Tim?" Charlie asked. "Should we even be talking about this around him?"

"Please," Tim said with an indignant sneer. "I was a gay

man in the Navy during 'Don't Ask, Don't Tell.' The government *knows* I can keep a secret."

The table burst into laughter, and Jackson reached across the table and took Charlie's hand.

"Things *would* be easier if we lived closer. We could get a place close to the Blatnik Bridge. It's less than an hour commute from there to Two Harbors, and you could zip across the river to Wisconsin whenever you wanted."

Charlie calmly sipped her drink until the straw slurped. "Or you could move to Wisconsin."

Confusion creased Jackson's forehead. "Why would I do that?"

An impish smile spread across Charlie's face.

"Better beer, better cheese, lower taxes… and no aliens."

THE END

ABOUT THE AUTHOR

Alan W. Porter has called California, Iowa, Maryland, Kentucky, and North Carolina home, but now lives in Minnesota, where frequent family trips to the North Shore of Lake Superior inspired this novel. A lifelong storyteller, Alan has loved movies, writing, and reading for as long as he can remember. (He even wrote, produced, and directed an unauthorized sequel to *Star Wars* back in fifth grade.)

He earned his undergraduate degree in English from the University of Iowa and his Juris Doctorate from the Iowa College of Law, and in 2009 was awarded a McKnight Fellowship in Media Arts for his screenplay *The Saint of Denmark Falls*. When not writing, Alan enjoys films (good and bad), music of all genres (good and bad), the occasional unnecessarily graphic video game, and the company of his beloved wife, son, and cat.